For JRH
without whom I might never have known Cambridge
'O my America! my new-found-land.'

Contents

1	Poisonous Port	1
2	Sheepshanks	10
3	The Chapel	18
4	At the Woolsack	29
5	A Reinforcement Arrives	36
6	So Rudely Forced	52
7	The Pryevian Library	58
8	Inquiries	72
9	In the Combination Room	81
10	Cupid and Psyche	86
11	Bottom Disappears	91
12	Reappearance of a Rapist	96
13	Mrs Moffat	100
14	Jenkins Again	110
15	Found Out!	113
16	Figgins Co-operates	117
17	At the Bumps	120
18	Smythson's Narrow Escape	123
19	Tête-à-Tête	132
20	Mutton's Lamb	137
21	Police at Work	142
22	The May Ball	151
23	A Bout in the Bushes	159
24	Dead as Mutton	162
25	A Talk with the Master	167
26	Mrs Garmoyle	176
27	Is It Austrey?	182
28	Wolf in Sheep's Clothing	190
29	Investigation	200
30	Bunce Makes an Arrest	205
31	Fenchurch's Hypothesis	212
32	Positively the Rapist's Last Appearance	223
33	The Hunt is Up	226
34	Tying Up Loose Ends	233

Academic Murder

Author's Apology

If some things in this book are not as some Cantabrigians know or remember them, I claim literary licence; and I hope that any liberties I may have taken with the oeconomy of the University will be forgiven. Like the real Cambridge, my evocation is part fact, part fiction; half myth, half memory. Though the presentation of degrees no longer falls on a Tuesday, over the centuries this ceremony undoubtedly has proved a movable feast. A certain amount of telescoping has occurred in places to accelerate the pace of the story – it is unlikely a May Ball would be held the day the Bumps end – but this is, after all, only a fairy-tale set in Academe.

1 Poisonous Port

'. . . And that he calls for drink, I'll
have prepared him
A chalice for the nonce.'
Hamlet, Act IV, Sc. 7.

The decanter of port passed along the polished surface of High Table. Fenchurch watched as the tall candles in their branching silver candelabra illuminated its depths, transmuting the wine in its crystal envelope into a globe of crimson fire. Among the murky shadows of the Great Hall it glowed brightly, resembling, he reflected, a roc's-egg-sized ruby from the *Arabian Nights* or perhaps, to descend to a less fanciful metaphor, an alchemic potion: but of which kind? The sort to kindle desire, or to extinguish life? The colour, he mused, representing as it does both sides of the coin — life-breeding passion and violent death — would be equally suited to love-philtre or to poison, though if one must choose between the two, a love-potion seems an unlikely elixir to be served to the Fellows of a Cambridge College.

Fenchurch allowed himself to speculate pleasurably upon the improbable image of his peers, inflamed *en masse* by the substitution of an aphrodisiac for their post-prandial port and madeira; the ensuing scene would, he decided, more closely resemble a warlocks' Sabbath by Goya than a Rubens bacchanal. He had a momentary vision of Garmoyle, the stiff, sour Pryevian Librarian, goatishly cavorting in the Great Court clad only in his academic gown which streamed out behind his scarecrow form like a sable banner — it was to be hoped the night was a clement one — of the monumental Dr Shebbeare, Master of Sheepshanks, in ponderous pursuit of a fugitive nymph, the earth shuddering beneath him as he steadily lost ground. . . . Regretfully, Fenchurch let these vignettes slip away, to be replaced by a panoramic view depicting a concerted attack upon the precincts of Newnham, one of the women's Colleges, by elderly devotees of Priapus. Shrieking female undergraduates in wrappers and curling-papers (for Fenchurch's knowledge of feminine trappings was rather dated) were slung over stooping academic shoulders and carried off in a Cantabrigian version of the Rape of the Sabine Women. Yet another picture rose unbidden in his mind's eye, this time of a phalanx of Furies armed with hockey-sticks advancing upon the foe to defend their weaker sisters from the invaders. There was no doubt who would come off the worse in that encounter. . . .

'Garmoyle's drunk again,' muttered a voice in his right ear. It was Professor Tempeste, holder of the Bacon-Bungay Chair of Chemistry. Fenchurch noticed that the port decanter was no longer making its measured peregrination clockwise in company with the madeira, but had halted in front of Garmoyle who, when not filling his glass from it, held on to the bottle with a proprietary hand as if he were afraid someone would snatch it away from him.

'Disgraceful,' hissed Tempeste indignantly. 'Damned poor show he's putting on for Lord Cavesson – he might at least keep a grip on himself until *that's* over.' Dr Shebbeare, the Master of Sheepshanks, was staring with measured disapproval at Garmoyle, whose dour face had assumed a tell-tale flush. His shirt too, Fenchurch was startled to observe, was suffused with the colour of blood. A glance upward made it clear that this phenomenon was caused by the reflection of the stained glass opposite; the late evening sun of the northern latitudes was streaming through the floridly hideous heraldic windows with which Sir Oliver Sheepshanks had seen fit to adorn the otherwise chaste sixteenth-century Great Hall of the College. Garmoyle was seated opposite a representation of the Sheepshanks arms (gules, a chevron or between three sheep rampant, argent) which accounted for the sanguinary appearance of his shirt-front. It was an accident of the light and seating: if he had been placed a few inches more to the left, he would instead have been tinctured with the emerald-green quarterings (vert, a lamb trippant or) of d'Ewes. As the sun sank lower, Garmoyle's shirt became white once more, but the bibulous flush on his face remained.

Contrary to the habit of most Cambridge Colleges, the Fellows of Sheepshanks take their port in Hall instead of repairing to the Combination Room – a gloomy but not unimpressive custom. The Hall is one of the oldest parts of Sheepshanks: its massive dark panelling covered with portraits of past Masters and benefactors, headed by an ill-tempered rendition of Henry VIII, and its heavily carved and painted ceiling of scarlet and gold (the Tudor Rose much in evidence, since Henry was responsible for building the Hall), make it an imposing place.

High Table sits on a dais at the far end of the Hall. It is situated conveniently near the enormous fireplace, once the only heating for the great chamber. Even now there are few who scorn the fire's grateful glow on evenings in winter and early spring when the river-chill creeps across the lawns and permeates the ancient stones. Sheepshanks's Great Hall is a place both dignified and stately: its atmosphere of slightly pompous but impressive antiquity, intensified by the candlelight which is still the only form of illumination, is not dispelled even by the absurd central window of stained glass directly above High Table which portrays Sir Oliver Sheepshanks, the 'Poppadum Nabob' and chief benefactor of the College, seated upon his favourite elephant. At least once a year an undergraduate wit remarks that it is possible to tell which is Noll by the wig. Though the jest is nearly as old as the window, it must be confessed that it has a certain aptness; for in addition to a formidable nose, there is a distinctly pachydermous quality about Sir Oliver.

'Good God!' The outraged voice of Tempeste sounded in Fenchurch's ear once more. 'I'm damned if I'm going to sit and watch the man drink himself into a stupor. Why doesn't the Master take Lord Cavesson away? Garmoyle can sit here by himself all night if he likes, but I don't see why we must.'

'It isn't very long since we finished dinner, actually,' said Fenchurch mildly. 'It's just that Garmoyle has been drinking more single-mindedly than the rest of us.' He glanced over at the Master, who was looking as annoyed as his bland countenance ever permitted him, but who so far showed no signs of adjourning elsewhere as he was engaged in conversation with his right-hand neighbour. Dr Shebbeare was Johnsonian in bulk and appearance; he only wanted a full-bottomed wig to make his resemblance to the Great Lexicographer complete. There the likeness ended, however, for he lacked both his prototype's conviviality and his sudden lapses into melancholia. Dr Shebbeare was possessed, in fact, of a temperament almost irritatingly withdrawn and imperturbable. He was unfailingly civil, but his disposition was phlegmatic and monotonously plane like a Dutch landscape or the fen country which stretches beyond Cambridge; not for him the Alpine extremes of crag and valley indulged in by Dr Johnson. It was murmured by his less charitable colleagues that the reason he had been appointed to the Mastership of Sheepshanks was that as he was the sole candidate with no dissenting opinions at all, there was nothing controversial about him. In general, only a determined man could find a subject upon which to disagree with Dr Shebbeare; rather than dispate a point, he would withdraw like a great Galapagos turtle into his carapace. As controversy is the lifeblood of scholarly communities this was a frailty not lightly passed over by his peers.

At the Master's right sat Henry Huntingfield, fifteenth Earl of Cavesson, a man of middle age with the patrician features of a well-bred greyhound – a long, narrow nose and dark, lustrous eyes in a head whose bones lay close to the surface combined with a lean and finely-sinewed body to produce the likeness. It was as though centuries of careful breeding had honed the Cavesson stock down to the essentials, eliminating from the strain any extraneous physical characteristics. Even his colouring was neutral, like a sort of class-camouflage. He must once have been fair; now his hair was a pale grey and his complexion bore no trace of ruddiness, yet the effect was not unpleasant. He was the only man present not wearing a gown, for he was not a member of either University: like his father and grandfather before him, he had gone to Sandhurst and thence into a Guards regiment. Despite his lack of an academic background Lord Cavesson gave an impression of quiet competence and a discreet intelligence; the aura of one born to command surrounded him.

Indeed, thought Fenchurch, his errand at Sheepshanks called for those qualities in addition to the wisdom of a Solomon. The library of one of Lord Cavesson's predecessors had been deposited on permanent loan in the Abbot's Library at Sheepshanks. This had been done early in the last century, and there the books had remained undisturbed until Ernest Garmoyle, in search of material for his edition of Paul Prye's diaries, went through some of the early manuscript material. He was looking for the text of a sermon mentioned disparagingly by Prye, a fulmination by the Rev. Dr Jeremiah Bedworthy against fornication which had been delivered at St Paul's in March 1678 and which Garmoyle hoped to turn up in a cache of Bedworthy's papers included in the Cavesson collection, for the clergyman's wife was a distant connexion of the Huntingfields. Unexpectedly bound in with some of Dr Bedworthy's writings – most unexpectedly, considering that the bulk of his sermons were diatribes against the sins of the flesh – was a highly lubricious narrative poem written in the hand and style of a century earlier. In fact, to use a contemporary idiom, the poem was hot stuff. It was elegant in language, supple in metre, and distinctly steamy in atmosphere.

Although the first Elizabeth's reign was not his period and literature was not his field, Garmoyle only needed to read the quarto sheets through once to have a very good idea of what it was he had stumbled across. At first he had been sceptical. The manuscript, it is true, attributed the poem of *Cupid and Psyche* to Shakespeare, but Garmoyle was too downy a bird to be caught with that lime – he was well aware that the copiers and compilers of early poetic anthologies had an insouciant habit of affixing a known name to any anonymous scrap that came their way, as was doubtless the case here. But a short incursion into the body of the poem soon brought him to a different opinion. It was obviously very early Shakespeare: boyishly exuberant, not yet liberated from the more restrictive poetic conventions of his predecessors, a trifle gauche perhaps – but Shakespeare beyond the shadow of a doubt. Unless – he checked the binding. The cord with which the quires were sewn to form the spine of the book was clearly contemporary with the late seventeenth-century binding, and was so rotten that there was no possibility of the volume's having been tampered with. If the manuscript was a forgery, it must have been done nearly three hundred years ago and forgotten. And it didn't have the smell or the feel or the texture of a forgery. . .

Garmoyle's instinct was accurate. He showed the poem to Austrey, who was not only Sheepshanks's resident lecturer on

Elizabethan literature, but a Shakespearian scholar of international reputation. Austrey approached the find with judicious caution: he applied all the tests of paper and palaeography, of spelling and style, of word-form and imagery, of metre and rhyme, and came at last to the same conclusion that Garmoyle had reached – Sheepshanks had in its possession a unique manuscript copy of what was probably the earliest poem extant written by Shakespeare.

Now Lord Cavesson had arrived at the invitation of the Master to see what was to be done about it. It seemed that the ground-rules for the permanent loan of a collection to an institution were imprecise, and the members of Lord Cavesson's family who held an interest in the collection deposited at Sheepshanks might well, when they learned of the discovery, demand a sale. Since the final decision would rest with Lord Cavesson, as the head of his family, he was visiting Cambridge in order to discuss the matter with Dr Shebbeare before coming to a decision. Fenchurch noticed that the two men, with simultaneous tact, were refraining from any mention of the subject at dinner; no matter how important the outcome to Sheepshanks, it was not at present a matter to be aired in public, even so private a public as the Senior Common Room.

Garmoyle raised his head from the contemplation of his now empty wine-glass and glared at an inoffensive young man in clericals seated across the table who was discussing one of Bach's fugues with Grubb, another of the younger Fellows. 'Still fiddling with that blasted organ, Crippen?' he asked unpleasantly. 'You're a big boy now. Don't you think it's time you found some grown-up games to play?'

Crippen turned scarlet. He was the Chaplain, newly appointed, and a gentle soul. The delight of his life was the extremely fine sixteenth-century organ which had been given to the Chapel by Catherine of Aragon. Fenchurch glanced at the Master, whose broad rubicund face remained bland; it was his theory that one had to learn to defend oneself in the occasional rough-and-tumble of the Combination Room. Generally, of course, the attacks were more polished, and consequently more difficult to ward off.

Grubb looked smug. Just let the old bastard try that on *me*, he was thinking, and I'll show him a thing or two. Grubb, a recently elected Fellow, was a grammar-school product, and as an undergraduate had been something of an anomaly at Sheepshanks, which has the reputation of being one of the most expensive and socially exclusive of the Cambridge Colleges. The young men of Sheepshanks drive small fast Italian sports cars, lead the way on the hunting field — like Magdalene with its Trinity Foot Beagles, the College still maintains its own pack of fox-hounds — and has names which are frequently seen in newspaper accounts of the races at Ascot but rarely on the list of firsts posted in front of the Senate House. An unsympathetic government, however, had seen fit to place, by means of scholarships, some cuckoos in this aristocratic nest, and Grubb was one. He was undeniably brilliant in his field of economics and as the Master, though disliking him personally, did homage to excellence when he found it, in due course he saw that Grubb was offered a Fellowship, trusting to time and the civilizing influence of the Senior Common Room to smooth away the rough edges. Unfortunately he was not as astute a judge of character as he liked to think himself and failed to recognize the broad streak of intellectual arrogance and resentment in Grubb, who relished railing at the privileged classes even as he enjoyed being a member of them (for to be a Fellow of some Cambridge Colleges is to be highly privileged).

Grubb, in fact, was suffering from a form of moral schizophrenia: he detested this bastion of class prerogative but was unable to resist gorging upon its fruits. He was honest enough to realize what was happening to him, and the consequent conflict made his personality even more abrasive than usual. To appear at High Table was upsetting to his *alter ego*; he attempted to quiet its promptings by persuading himself that he only dined there because it cost nothing, but it was really because the cook was one of the best in Cambridge. Tonight, for example, they had been served fresh salmon with a superb *sauce mousseline* and asparagus from the College kitchen garden. Despising himself, Grubb had watched covertly to see how the others dealt with the long stalks, and then in last-minute revulsion had defiantly cut them up with his knife instead of dipping them in the melted butter with his fingers like the rest. If those were their nasty upper-class ways, they could keep them. His family might call dinner tea and eat it in the kitchen at six, but at least they didn't eat like savages the way 'gentlemen' did. Look at Garmoyle too — revolting pig. Grubb might not be a gentleman, but neither did he drink so much at dinner that he couldn't keep his head off the table.

Austrey was beginning to look concerned. He was a man of a kindly disposition in early middle age, tending to plumpness, with hair that — to his great chagrin — curled vigorously. He possessed a great deal of charm as well as a first-rate brain, and his desire to be comfortable extended to his fellow-creatures. It distressed him to see anyone upset. He turned to Alan Smythson, the Librarian of Sheepshanks's Abbot's Library seated at his left, a tall man who would have been startlingly handsome except for his sharklike smile.

'Garmoyle's overdoing it a bit tonight, don't you think?' he said in a low voice. 'He's nearly finished off the port single-handed. And as far as I could see, he drank his way through dinner — I don't think he touched a morsel of food.'

Smythson shrugged his shoulders indifferently. 'He generally does overdo it nowadays,' he replied.

Now Garmoyle was signalling to the butler, who stood discreetly by a door behind High Table which led into the Combination Room. Bottom (for that was his unlikely name) came forward and bent over him in a stately fashion. 'More port,' said Garmoyle, pointing to the empty decanter in front of him. Bottom was seen to hesitate. 'Get me more port, man. I tell you, this one's finished. Damn it, are you deaf?' Bottom looked for direction to the Master, who shook his head slightly and appeared to send a message to some far distant machine constructed to raise his great bulk from the chair. A sort of shuddering motion presaged movement, but it was movement infinitely prolonged and ponderous, like the King of Elephants rising to salute his subjects.

The Master's refusal appeared to infuriate Garmoyle, who with the low cunning of the inebriate had caught his exchange with the butler. He lurched to his feet and over to the sideboard within which spare decanters of port and madeira stood ready. Seizing the port, he returned to his place and poured himself another glass. The Master by this time was upon his feet, his gown billowing about him like a great black sail as he prepared to pronounce grace before he led the procession from the dinner table, but Garmoyle ignored the implication of his rising. 'I won't offer any of you more port,' said Garmoyle to the table at large while he sprawled in his chair, 'as I daresay you've all had quite enough already.' He leered at them drunkenly and raised his glass.

There was a shocked silence which was broken again by Garmoyle, who had swallowed his wine in one gulp and was now making a face of displeasure. 'Bloody awful stuff – where'd ye get this from?' he asked Bottom rudely. '– Aha! I'm onto your little game,' pointing an unsteady finger at the unfortunate butler. 'Thievish sh-steward, that's what you are.' He recovered the mastery of his tongue with difficulty. 'Sh-selling the College port, are you, and giving us pig-swill in its place so you can pocket the difference? Didn't think we'd notice, eh? This is vile stuff, I tell you – absolute poison – worst I ever tasted.' And as Bottom, the Master, and the Fellows of Sheepshanks stood appalled at this tirade, he muttered 'Poison' once more to himself, and collapsed onto the table with a crash of breaking glass.

The others, who an instant earlier had been in a state of horrified paralysis, were galvanized into action. Several pairs of hands lifted him from the ruins and carried him into the Combination Room, where he was laid on a leather Chesterfield sofa. By common consent those in front parted to let Tempeste through; he was a scientist, not a physician, but they felt he was the best qualified among them to cope with the situation. He leaned over the unconscious form on the sofa for a moment, then turned to face them. 'The man's dead,' he said abruptly.

2 Sheepshanks

'Die, and endow a College, or a Cat.'
Pope, *Moral Essays*

There are, alas! few places in the world like Cambridge. She is fortunate in having escaped the heavy industry her sister Oxford suffers, but the difference between the two does not lie solely there. Cambridge is a country market-town still, endowed with a delightful intimacy. Her city limits were altered scarcely at all between the thirteenth and nineteenth centuries; and even now, despite the acres of new housing which are gobbling up fields and pastures, she is not greatly changed. Oxford is monumental, larger than life-size. The Broad, one of Oxford's chief streets, lives up to its name; it is wide and grandiose, while the primary streets of Cambridge — Trinity, King's Parade, St Andrew's, Regent and Trumpington — wind and twist like the narrow medieval pathways of which they are the direct descendants, altering their names every half-mile or so in a devious attempt to mislead the unwary, and the main entrance to the centre of the town over Magdalene Bridge is a triumphant bottleneck. One holds one's breath as huge lorries and buses squeeze their way between the crazily leaning houses of Bridge Street in a seeming attempt to pass camels through a needle's eye.

The Oxford Colleges are vast and imposing, their windows so high that the passer-by cannot (supposing he were so inclined) peer into them; and the College quadrangles, though well-kept and tended, are austere in design and sparingly planted with flowers. The Colleges of Cambridge, on the other hand, are enticingly approachable. Several are tucked away where one would least expect to find them, like prizes in a treasure-hunt. They are built to a more human scale than those of Oxford, and the head gardener of each seems to vie with his fellows in the production of the most vivid and profuse blossoms. In the appropriate seasons every court and Fellows' garden is a riot of geraniums, roses, phlox, tulips and narcissi, the eminently suitable bachelor's button, pinks, Michaelmas daisies — every flowering plant that will grow in that climate. Purple clematis clings to the Gothic Revival screen-wall of King's; baskets of fuchsia hang in the cloister at Jesus; the first sign of spring is the appearance of crocuses by the river along The Backs, soon followed by a field of daffodils in The Wilderness behind St John's.

Cambridge is a mosaic of improbables — a fleet of ducklings carefully shepherded by their mother through the hazards of the Cam as she teaches them to avoid the ubiquitous punt-poles, the Wren Library of Trinity where one studies in a bay surrounded by silence and old leather bindings and Grinling Gibbons woodwork. She is cream cakes at Fitzbillie's, the pastry-shop nonpareil up the street from the Fitzwilliam Museum, where for a modest sum one may purchase a prosaic round loaf or Cornish pasty, or a Sybaritic Devon split oozing fresh cream and strawberry jam. She is the Fitzwilliam, where one may gaze at Egyptian faience or Chelsea shepherdesses and buy, as one leaves, the postcard of an indecent painting by Hogarth which surely no one would have the temerity to send by Her Majesty's mail. She is The Backs, the fields behind the river Colleges, dappled with sunlight and sheep. She is the crooked passage which leads to the Market Place by Peas Hill, perhaps the smallest hill on record. She is the Market Place with its awninged stands crowding one another off the pavement, where one may buy yard-long cucumbers or sheepskin mittens or clotted cream and farm butter displayed on straw mats or Indian jewellery or anemones or second-hand books or fresh fish or cracked china, and where the citizens of Cambridge have been shopping for at least a millennium. She is a lunch of bread and cheese on the College lawns along the banks of the Cam while the punts float past, she is glorious spring days when it seems as though the sun must always shine there, she is wet black umbrellas and raw mist and a drizzle that permeates every layer of clothing, she is bicycles ridden by madmen. She is all of these; but she is more, far more than the sum of her parts, and long may she flourish!

Sheepshanks College is often overlooked by tourists and visitors to Cambridge. It is tucked in at the very end of The Backs between St John's and the newer courts of Magdalene. Visitors who begin their tours at Peterhouse and Pembroke, then visit Magdalene and the other Colleges on the east side of the city, frequently find their endurance flagging by the time they have got through the courts of Trinity and John's, and omit Sheepshanks as a consequence. Not as large as Trinity or John's, not as spectacular as King's, not as appealing as Clare, which always seems bathed in a golden light, or as Queens' with its ancient passageways and wooden Mathematical Bridge designed in the form of a giant puzzle, Sheepshanks is nonetheless worth seeing. It is not one of the oldest Cambridge Colleges, but its antecedents are respectably antique, for it was founded in the fifteenth century as Agnus Dei College on the site of a suppressed monastery. The wealthy merchant who endowed the College for the education of clergy hoped by this means to smooth his path to heaven, and in the statutes he provided for daily masses for his soul to be said by the clerks. His family, however, succeeded in blocking some part of the moneys set aside in his Will for that purpose, so the new College was very poor and ramshackle, and by the end of the century had become virtually moribund. In 1514 Henry VIII re-endowed Agnus Dei as a monastic order to celebrate the marriage of his sister Mary to the King of France. The priorship was in the gift of the French king, who used it as a heaven-sent opportunity to rid himself of the presence of one of his less desirable cousins.

As one can imagine, the Abbé Dieudonné with his entourage was not enthusiastically welcomed by the English monks whose spiritual welfare he had been sent to supervise. He, on his part, was indifferent to his churlish reception. The English were a race of pigs, the countryside was of a flatness and hideousness unsurpassable, but *n'importe* — when the old king died he would return from banishment to the glittering court of which he was so fond. In the meantime, *on peut s'amuser* — one had one's lute, one's lapdogs and one's pretty acolytes with which to divert oneself. In addition, he was possessed of an artistic bent and decided to occupy a part of his leisure by tearing down the old chapel — a shabby affair, in any case — and building a new one in its place. His aesthetic sense was challenged by the dreary seat of exile in which he found himself (the only decent building was the Hall, which Henry had had erected), and the abbé, once comfortable quarters for himself had been arranged, set about constructing a chapel *à la mode*. It was conceived as a *tour de force*, a hybrid triumph of the Mannerist style produced by the French artisans whom he had brought over with him in tandem with local craftsmen. When Louis died and Francis I ascended the throne of France, the abbé thankfully returned to his native country with his train of cooks and catamites, leaving the chapel, a number of books (most of which were wholly unsuited to one who had embraced the religious life), and a great deal of scandalized gossip as the sole legacies of his stay in Cambridge.

From that time until the eighteenth century the history of Agnus Dei is a lugubrious one. The New Learning coupled with the outrageous stories left in the wake of the French prior resulted in the ousting of the monks, and Henry appointed a Master for the governance of the College. But both College and Master fell out of favour over the question of divorce; for the Master was a devout churchman and a loyal adherent to Queen Catherine, who had made many gifts to Agnus Dei, the splendid chapel organ in particular. The stubborn Master was soon removed and martyred, but the taint of his disgrace lingered about his College. Subsequent Masters possessed, it appears, an equal ineptness in the art of expediency. The Master at the commencement of Mary Tudor's reign was a supporter of the Lady Jane Grey; his successor when Elizabeth I came to the throne was an ardent Roman Catholic; while the record of the Master in the 1630s and 1640s is the most deplorable of all, for he was a confirmed Low Churchman until the eve of the Long Parliament, when he became a convert to Laudianism with all the fervour of which a religious turncoat is capable. To complete this unedifying history of collegiate decline, it must be reported that at least one of the Masters in the eighteenth century was a rabid Jacobite. Over the centuries Agnus Dei had become very poor and unimportant indeed: when the fickle sun of Henry VIII's favour disappeared, a twilight of poverty and neglect fell upon the hapless foundation. Various rulers, displeased by its intransigence in matters spiritual and temporal, had gradually shorn it of its lands and endowments, and by the latter part of the eighteenth century Agnus Dei was virtually a nonentity.

At this juncture an unexpected saviour made his appearance. Sir Oliver Sheepshanks, known the length and breadth of England as the 'Poppadum Nabob', had been an official of the East India Company. Like other men in that time and place he had amassed an enormous fortune. It was whispered that his methods of making money were not altogether scrupulous; in fact, his nickname was the result of a *coup* which, though undoubtedly ingenious, was not perhaps altogether palatable to those with finicking ideas of honour. He had conceived the idea of requiring a licence from each household for the making of poppadums and chupatties, those flat breads which are a staple diet in India. By controlling the supply of grain from which poppadums are made and the wheat for chupatties, he was able to force the merchants into demanding proof of licence from anyone who bought from them. It has been surmised that his tax was partly responsible for the Indian ferocity in the affair of the Black Hole of Calcutta, which occurred shortly after the imposition of Sir Oliver's levy.

By this and other equally dubious means Sheepshanks became immensely rich and upon his return to England he was created a baronet by a grateful monarch, after which he sought to perpetuate his newly dignified name by becoming a benefactor to his old College. He had, it appears, grown enormously fat on curry during his stay in India: at least, if we take Horace Walpole's rather uncharitable word for it. 'A prodigious Man-Mountain (as disproportionate to our eyes as was Gulliver to the Lilliputians) late returned from the Indies seeks entrance to the world of Fashion,' writes Horry to one of his numerous correspondents. 'He is one of your Count Roupees, raised to a title upon a pinnacle of Bengali gold. The *on-dits* declare his wealth so vast that I wonder he has not purchased an Earldom at the least, but he builds a monument to posterity at Cambridge which may yet exhaust his Midas' purse. Rumour says his new College is a None-such of Eastern splendour.'

Walpole underestimated the extent of the Sheepshanks fortune, but even so, it was a near thing: between building and endowment in the effort to satisfy his intellectual pretensions, Sir Oliver came close to scraping the bottom of his financial barrel, and it was just as well for the future of Sheepshanks

College that he had not set his sights higher than a baronetcy after all. The building fever is one of the most genteel (and most certain) ways for a gentleman to impoverish himself: both England and Europe are strewn with monuments to an injudicious passion for architecture. In an age, however, which suffers from the gigantism of office buildings spawned by huge faceless corporations, when architects vie with one another to produce façades of an unspeakable blandness, when New York has become a forest of monoliths without character or individuality — a modern Stonehenge run riot — and London and Paris are rapidly following suit, for a man to bankrupt himself by extravagant self-expression in stone seems a laudable folly.

Sir Oliver Sheepshanks engaged an architect to design his new College in the style of an Indian temple or palace. This in itself would not have been unusual on a small scale: the gardens of the gentry were filled at that time with gazebos, tea-houses, and summer pavilions contrived in the Indian or Chinese taste. But these were small and used for frivolous purposes; it was unheard-of to build a University College in the Eastern mode. The architect, a man named Dovedown, proved a pliant medium for Sir Oliver's designs and meekly put his patron's plans into execution without imposing any touches of his own. Thus the nabob's College reproduced every foible of Eastern architecture — the minarets of a mosque, an abundance of domes, ogee arches and lavish ornamentation carved in the stone, decorated tiles with Persian motifs; and in the centre of the Great Court he placed a fountain, the source of which was a trumpeting stone elephant with water flowing from his upflung trunk. Fortunately the Master and Fellows were able to dissuade Sir Oliver from carrying out his original plan of replacing the Great Hall, the Chapel, and the building which housed the Pryevian Library; he grumbled a bit, but finally conceded that their antiquity was worth preserving. In fact, his funds were running rather low at that point, and he secretly contemplated doing something about the disputed buildings later when the state of his fortune had improved and the Master (who headed the opposition, and was getting on in years) had retired or died.

As it happened, however, Sir Oliver died first in consequence of a brain fever brought on, it was thought, by his excitement over the completion of Sheepshanks' Great Court: the day the last stone was set into place he fell into a fit from which he never recovered. So the Master won in the end, and the older parts of the College still remain. In the nineteenth century there was a brief flurry of agitation to tear down the Chapel and put up one by Sir Gilbert Scott, but luckily a temporary period of straitened circumstances prevented the Fellows from acting on this plan, and the Chapel still stands in all its pristine glory. Attached to it in the metaphysical sense is a choir school which supplies the justly famed choir of boys' voices, less renowned than those of King's and St John's, but equal to both in quality. It is still known as the Agnus Dei Choir School, having been founded by the Abbé Dieudonné for motives into which we shall not inquire, but which were undoubtedly not entirely musical.

Sheepshanks has not been without its scholars. Among the students who have matriculated there are the Rev. Sylvestrer Swan (1502–1555), who composed sacred poetry in a distinctly erotic vein (he is now considered a literary ancestor of Donne), was unfrocked and ended his days in a madhouse; Paul Prye (c. 1633–1679), contemporary historian and founder of the Pryevian Library; John Wamersley (1721–1787), poet, whose best-known work is his 'Ode to Mr Saml Sutton upon his Discovery of a means for Preventing the Scurvy'; Henry Wildgoose (1748–1800), the writer of a twelve-volume work in which he attempted to confute Gibbon's theory of Rome's decline; Erasmus Bendlowe (1745–1838), who cited Scripture in an effort to prove his contention that Christ and the Apostles were really Freemasons; and the Rev. Ambrose Nethersole, F.R.S. (1813–1899), the noted lepidopterist, who bequeathed his extensive (if unwelcome) collection of butterflies to Sheepshanks.

The Edwardian era ushered in a preponderance of human butterflies among the undergraduates of the College; and frivolity rather than scholarship is still the most notable characteristic of the students there. The Master regards this trend with a lenient eye, for, as he has remarked, the world contains far more pebbles than diamonds and it is the duty of the universities to polish both. Since preferment in the world outside Cambridge (a world sometimes totally disregarded in the calculations of Cantabrigians) still depends largely on who, not what, one is, it is as well that a man who is to govern, whether in politics, law or business, should first be exposed to the broadening influence of the University. After all, Dr Shebbeare adds, expanding on one of his favourite theories, young men in general are very silly, and it is just as well for 'em to get it out of their systems early on. While many would dispute his thesis, it is true that the bookworm who immerses himself in his studies to the exclusion of all else has missed what is the essence of Cambridge: that cross-pollination resulting from the many varied experiences and ideas — some serious, some trivial — which may produce an unexpected flowering.

3 The Chapel

'The Gothic cathedral is a blossoming in stone. . . . The mountain of granite blooms into an eternal flower.'
Ralph Waldo Emerson, *Essays*.

Although he had been born and raised in Cambridge, Inspector Bunce was unfamiliar with the ways of dons, since neither his birth nor his calling had brought him into much contact with them. Bunce's father and grandfather had kept a butcher's shop in Silver Street, and his elder brother was now continuing the business. Bunce's Best Beef was a byword in Cambridge: they gave you value for your money, and there was no nonsense about holding down the scales when you weren't looking. The younger Bunce had been not a clever, but an observant boy. His mind was not quick, but it was accurate in its calculations, and he worked to solve a problem with a bulldog tenacity, worrying at it constantly until it was finally unravelled. When he joined the local police force it had seemed an inevitable step, and his talents served him well there. This stolid young man was not lacking in shrewdness, and his simple exterior had often misled malefactors into underestimating his abilities. Now he was nearing retirement age, but he had yet to investigate a crime in a College. The Colleges in general police themselves, possibly a hangover from the days when benefit of clergy brought immunity from capital punishment. In any event the worst crime likely to occur in College these days was a bit of petty pilfering, though he had heard some nasty stories about certain goings-on at times, particularly at King's and St Jude's. Still, that was not the business of the police, but of the Fellows, though from what he'd heard some of *those* were as bad as any.

But the reason Bunce now had the job of interviewing the members of Sheepshanks's Combination Room was neither petty nor a matter of sexual irregularity: it was for the purpose of investigating the murder of Ernest Albert Radcliffe Garmoyle, M.A. Cantab., Prye Librarian, who had been felled, not (as was at first commonly supposed) by the decayed state of his much-abused liver, but by an outsize dose of arsenic. Although well-versed in the shoals of ordinary human nature, Bunce was ignorant of the deeps of the academic mind; had he been more cognizant of the undercurrents inherent in scholarly life he might perhaps have been less surprised by murder than by the fact that the character-assassination so prevalent in academic circles does not more often slip into the realm of the material.

Murder connected with the University had thrown Bunce off-balance. Not only was it an unheard-of occurrence, but murder in Cambridge itself was rare, though the latter had become rather less unusual since the local hotels and restaurants had taken to hiring so much foreign help. Some of the kitchen staff would as soon stick a knife between your ribs as look at you — only last week the police had been called to the kitchen of the Woolsack Inn in Bridge Street when the cook threw his cleaver at one of the waiters for letting a Baked Alaska melt before it was served. But murder in one of the Colleges — that was another matter; it had never happened during Bunce's years on the Force. And if all the Fellows were going to be as difficult to interview as Mr Fenchurch, it would be a wonder if he ever got to the bottom of it. It wasn't that Mr Fenchurch wasn't trying to cooperate; no, it wasn't that at all. It was just that the way his mind worked was alien to the pragmatic Bunce. And it must be confessed that this afternoon Fenchurch was being physically elusive as well: for a smallish man he certainly covered the ground.

When Inspector Bunce arrived for the interview, Fenchurch was about to meet his class on medieval architecture. The programme for the afternoon was a walk about the town, as Fenchurch was a firm believer in empiricism, particularly when the evidence was all about one. The culmination of his peripatetic lecture was a visit to Sheepshanks Chapel, where the view of Cambridge and the surrounding country from its roof was equalled only by the prospect from the top of King's Chapel and the tower of Great St Mary's, the University Church. The radio report that morning had described the weather, with the usual hedging of English forecasts, as 'cloudy with sunny intervals' (occasionally it is varied by inversion and becomes 'sunny with cloudy intervals'), the word cloudy as employed by the BBC being a euphemism for rain: moderate rain, heavy rain, rain so light it is a mere mist, or a downpour so strong that rivulets stream down the ribs of one's umbrella into the back of one's neck and one's feet and trousers are drenched.

By afternoon the cloudiness had settled into a steady drizzle, but this of course had no effect on Fenchurch's plans, for if one waits in Cambridge for fine weather in order to do something, it is very likely that it will never be done. So armed with a large and rather battered black umbrella and wearing his walking-costume of tweed golfing plus-fours, a sweater and sandals, he set off, bearing Bunce with him, to meet his students at the Great Gate of Sheepshanks. When the Inspector protested that he had planned to interview Mr Fenchurch in his rooms, Mr Fenchurch replied reasonably that it was just as easy to talk while walking. 'I don't lecture constantly to my students, you see—if I did, they wouldn't look at anything properly—so you can ask me your questions in the intervals. Besides, it's healthier: exercise brings the blood to the brain. If we sat in an overheated room indoors while you asked your questions, your mind wouldn't work nearly as well. I daresay you'll find our walk will make your brain far clearer and more alert.'

If the pace of the walk had anything to do with Mr Fenchurch's theory, then he ought to be able to solve the case in no time, the Inspector reflected glumly as Fenchurch trotted briskly to the appointed rendezvous with Bunce in tow. The days of walking a beat were far behind Bunce (in any event his figure did not willingly lend itself to strenuous exercise) and now he preferred a motor-car to shanks' pony as a means of conveyance for any distance. Once they had collected Fenchurch's students, however (the usual lot of long-haired undergraduates, thought Bunce disapprovingly: the girls in dingy ankle-length calico skirts bedraggled by the rain or scruffy jeans; a few of the boys in what he thought of as proper kit of tweed jacket and college tie, others in brightly striped wide trousers and vivid shirts), they settled into a more comfortable way of going and Bunce was able, in sporadic bursts, to obtain answers to the questions he had come to ask.

'When did you first suspect something was wrong, sir?' he

asked Fenchurch as they walked along Trinity Street, crossing from Gonville and Caius College. They were on their way to St Michael's Church, where the cadavers dissected by the eminent anatomist John Caius had been interred, accompanied by the full-blown ritual of the Church and a procession of the Master and Fellows of his College.

'What precisely do you mean by "wrong"?' inquired Fenchurch. 'If you wish to know when I first realized Mr Garmoyle was poisoned, I'm afraid my answer will not enlighten you, for I expect you knew about it before I did. In brief, Inspector — I can speak only for myself, but I suppose my colleagues will give you the same answer — I thought the man had suffered some sort of fit from his excessive drinking, and I assure you that we were horrified and incredulous when Professor Tempeste indicated that he might have been poisoned. I did not take his remark seriously until the police informed the Master that it was indeed the case.'

'Well, then, sir, did anything strike you —,' began Bunce, but they had stopped outside the church, and Fenchurch had already turned to his students to explain its historical and architectural importance.

After the inspection of the church's interior (damn' cold, but at least it kept the rain off your head, reflected Bunce gloomily) they walked along King's Parade to the main gate of King's College. As the lecture had temporarily ceased, he tried again. 'Did you notice anything odd at dinner?' he asked Fenchurch.

'Oh, indeed, very odd; yes, yes, decidedly so,' replied Fenchurch. Bunce listened hopefully. 'Bottom — the College butler, you know — brought up a claret for dinner.'

The Inspector looked blank. 'That wasn't quite what I had in mind,' he said.

'But don't you see,' said Fenchurch, 'he must have been very perturbed, very perturbed indeed — one might go so far as to say *distrait* — yes, I think that would be the proper word — to do such a thing. We were served fish for dinner, you know. It must have been the first time in his life he had made a mistake of that sort. Poor chap — he was absolutely appalled. He kept shaking his head and saying, "I don't know wot things are coming to, sir, nor 'ow I could 'ave done such a thing. I must 'ave been woolgathering, Mr Fenchurch, sir." '

Fenchurch's imitation of Bottom was perfect and unconscious, the result of an association which had stretched over forty years. 'It was something to do with the port,' he added to close the subject; it was not one which held a great deal of interest for him. His mind, released, leapt to the problem of the motif carved under one of the windows on the Gospel side of the Sheepshanks Chapel chancel. Might it reinforce his theory of Druidical influence upon the stonework. . . .? But the Inspector would not leave him alone.

'Something to do with the port? That could be very important.' This baffling man maddened him. None of the Fellows so far had been easy to interview — the Master had been positively daunting, and so had Professor Tempeste, who had virtually sneered at the use of so mundane a poison as arsenic. 'A hackneyed choice,' he had remarked with a scarcely disguised curl of his lip, as though the murderer's lack of imagination were to be attributed to Bunce; 'one of the common or garden variety of poisons and hardly worth bothering about.' (If the eminent Professor's turn of phrase was equally hackneyed, no doubt it is unrealistic to expect that a noted scientist should be as original in his speech as in his research.) Grubb had been sullenly defensive, Peascod abstracted, Mutton woolly; and, as for Lord Cavesson, Bunce was quite frankly in awe of him. The Inspector had small acquaintance with the peerage (aside from the youthful perpetrators of undergraduate pranks); moreover, Lord Cavesson was the Lord Lieutenant of his county. Only Austrey with his innate tact and charm had been at all easy to handle. It was not that Fenchurch lacked charm, or meant to be difficult, but he disconcerted the policeman.

'The arsenic was in the port,' said the Inspector desperately. He was beginning to feel as though he must be speaking through some sort of distorting substance which turned his words into gibberish by the time they reached the ears they were intended for.

'Oh,' Fenchurch said. 'Then surely you have talked to Bottom.'

'I haven't been able to reach him since the report from the lab came in. It's his day off and they said at the College that he was visiting his sister in one of the neighbouring villages. They none of them seem to know which one.'

'Rather sly is old Bottom — he claims she's his sister but she may be a lady-friend, or why would he be so coy about where she lives? Still, he'll be back like clockwork tomorrow, so you'll be able to question him then. Look here, I'm nearing the end of my lecture — it's in two parts, and I gave the first last week. There's only the Grand Finale to go now, if you can wait, and then I shall have time to tell you about Bottom and the claret.'

Inspector Bunce agreed, as he didn't really know what else to do, and they proceeded to Sheepshanks Chapel with a crocodile of undergraduates bringing up the rear. Fenchurch had already shown them the other points of interest at the College and given a short talk on the eighteenth-century architecture which, while undoubtedly striking to the eye of the beholder, was not of great complexity to that of the architectural historian.

The fountain in the Great Court had been turned off, but the rain took its place, splashing dismally on the upflung trunk and broad back of the trumpeting elephant. Lucky bugger, thought Bunce crossly, at least he's used to getting wet. They entered the porch of the Chapel and with an effort Fenchurch pushed open one of the great iron-bound oak doors, black with age and candle-smoke. Inside, a cool green luminosity filtered through the windows and the stone floor was dappled with sequins of light from clear sections in the stained glass, like the floor of a forest glade. Bunce looked closely at the great columns soaring up to the roof far above and saw that they were carved to resemble giant tree trunks, the branches reaching up to interlace in an intricately plotted tangle which formed the fan-vaulting of the ceiling. The craftsmen who had worked the stone had given individual characteristics to the columns: Bunce recognized oaks, ashes, beeches, elms, among them.

The word *chapel* as applied to Sheepshanks is misleading, for to most people it bears a connotation of smallness. Dieudonné's chapel, though not so large as King's (whose size would suffice for a cathedral), is still much greater in extent than most College chapels, and the impact of the thrusting stone trunks with their spreading boughs pleached far above the head of the beholder is awesome. This sylvan motif is carried out in the great windows which take up most of the wall-space of the Chapel, so that the walls are formed of screens of coloured light. Each window portrays a scene in the life of the Virgin; the stone tracery, like the fan-vaulting, is worked in the shape of boughs and twigs so that the leaves painted on the window-glass seem to grow from lapideous branches.

The predominating colour of the windows is green — every variation, every imaginable shade of green. This verdure nearly overwhelms the small figures in the windows, giving the effect of a world in which Nature is the ruling force and man of no more consequence than a grasshopper. The Annunciation takes place in a garden where pale green willows bend over the figures of Mary and the angel, set off by the richer greens of grapevines and fig-trees in the background. In another window an angel appears before a few insignificant shepherds whose improbably fluffy sheep huddle in a great meadow like a vast green sea, and a third shows the Nativity set in a grotto sheltered by a wood in which the foliage again dominates the scene. The little procession representing the Flight into Egypt winds through a wilderness of vegetation where vine tendrils seem to wrap themselves about the hooves of the small tired donkey in an attempt to impede his progress, and huge tree-limbs laden with leaves as large as dinner-plates bar the narrow path.

The Chapel, as Fenchurch has pointed out in his lectures, is predominantly secular in ornamentation: that would doubtless account for the fact that very little damage was done to it during the periods of religious upheaval in the country. Even the rood-screen and organ-case given by the notably pious Queen Catherine are decorated with the arms of England and Aragon and carved with love-knots which encircle the intertwined initials of Henry VIII and his queen, for they were a present to the Chapel upon the birth of a daughter. Instead of saints upon the walls below the windows, the niches there contain painted heraldic devices and silvered unicorns (the chaste and somewhat inappropriate badge of the Abbé Dieudonné) coupled with the royal lilies of France. The pose of each unicorn is slightly different from that of its neighbour; each argent lily is in a different stage of flowering, and the stems and leaves form varying patterns on the creamy stone.

The string course flows along the walls of the Chapel, a band of intricately cut foliage. The bosses of the lierne-vaulting in the small chapels which open off the nave are carved in the shape of woodwoses — wild forest men with leaves and acorns in their hair — and other faces, half-man, half-beast, have horns peeping through tangled locks that are like the crisped curls along the necks of bulls; strange Pan-like creatures also appear in the wood-carving of the choir. Above the High Altar a statue of the Virgin stands upon its pedestal; it is the only obviously sacred ornament (aside from the windows) which has been incorporated into the edifice, for the carvings on the choir-stalls and those tucked into the stony foliage of the walls are of mythical beasts — basilisks, demons, fauns and gryphons — and small woodland animals — hares, squirrels, badgers and moles. It must be confessed, however, that at first glance the Virgin might be mistaken for a statuary version of *la dame et la licorne*, for her arms are childless and by her side, her hand resting upon its gleaming horn, is a unicorn, the symbol of purity: a leafy window above embowers them. Curiously enough though the figures are painted the Virgin does not wear the blue robe which usually distinguishes her, but she is garbed instead in a flowing green gown picked out with golden flowers and she holds a lily in her hand. The effect is oddly pagan, as though a statue of Persephone had been set up in a saint's niche.

Inspector Bunce trailed behind Fenchurch and his charges, listening with half an ear and looking with half-disapproving eyes. He had never been in the Chapel before; as a matter of fact, he wasn't one for churches aside from his parish church which he attended without fail each Sunday and which was as different from this one as chalk from cheese, being small, late Victorian and so Low in churchmanship as barely to stay within the Anglican fold. Sheepshanks Chapel was, he had to admit, beautiful in a queer sort of way, but it made him feel uncomfortable, as though strange creatures who resented his intrusion were lurking just out of sight behind the bark-carved stalks of the columns. It was with relief that he turned to follow Fenchurch, who beckoned them to a small door at the back of the nave, producing as he did so a large iron key from his pocket. He fitted it into the lock and opened the door, disclosing a narrow corkscrew staircase which spiralled upwards in a dizzying fashion. It has been mentioned that the Inspector was not athletically inclined. His emotions must have shown clearly on his face, for Fenchurch smiled gently at him and said, 'You may stay down here if you wish, though it would be a pity to miss the view.' He turned toward the staircase, and with uncommon agility bounded up the steps like a small terrier. Bunce was tempted to make use of his dispensation, but the sight of Fenchurch taking the stairs with such unconcern stung him into making the attempt. 'Damn it, he's half my size,' he thought to himself, 'and older too, I shouldn't be surprised.' Puffing and blowing and groaning with the effort, Bunce hauled himself painfully after the students. It was the usual sort of English ecclesiastical staircase, which is to say that it was brutally hard to climb. Radiating from a central post, each wedge-shaped step was just narrow enough to make Bunce's heels hang dangerously off the edge, and the stone had been worn over the centuries into a deep declivity at the centre, making the footing of the climber even more precarious. Bunce could see that some of the steps had been patched in places in an attempt to mend them, but even the newer stone had worn down so as to make the going difficult and it was barely possible to grasp the central shaft from which they fanned out in order to pull oneself from one level to the next. To make matters worse, the Inspector was the last of those ascending the staircase so that a spiralling gulf curled below with nothing between him and it. He shut his eyes and clung feverishly to the meagre hand-hold. The twisting stair seemed to have no end; vertigo, hitherto unknown to Bunce, seemed about to overtake him, scrabbling at his shoulders like one of the small leering demons he had noticed carved in the dark oak of the choir. Once it managed to scramble up to his head it would smother him, and in his efforts to beat it off he would have to let go the hand-hold which was his only safety and down he would tumble, with nothing to stop his fall down those tortuous corkscrew stairs. . . .

With relief he saw that they had reached a stopping-point; a door stood open in a stone archway above him, and Fenchurch's students were in the act of filing through it. Bunce's feelings were much like those of a shipwrecked sailor upon catching sight of a landfall. With renewed strength he climbed the last uneven steps, followed a brick passage, and clambered up several steps and a sort of stone mound to find himself in a stranger place than he had yet seen. It was obviously man-made, but the hugeness and queerness of it gave it the appearance of a landscape in another world. Terraces of stone sloped upward in widening concentric half-circles to a central spine, like the reverse of the patterns made by hardening lava when it pours down the cone of an erupting volcano. Great rough-hewn oak beams supported the roof of the loft which stretched, it seemed in the half-light, astonishingly far.

As they picked their way gingerly along the highest point (it felt rather like walking along the backbone of a sleeping Leviathan) Fenchurch explained the engineering of the vaulted ceiling below them. 'It is only safe to walk on the centre section,' he said, pointing to it with his furled umbrella. 'The stone is thick enough here; but a foot or so away, it may be as thin as three-quarters of an inch, and if you stepped there you would break through as though it were an eggshell and plunge to the marble floor eighty feet below, incidentally,' his voice took on a disapproving tone, 'ruining one of the finest examples of fan-vaulting in the country, so do step carefully.' One of the girls with them gave a gasp of delighted terror and Fenchurch twinkled: he enjoyed giving pretty young ladies a pleasurable fright. At intervals along the stone ridge, holes had been bored through the great blocks which locked the vaulting into place. A man kneeling beside one of them could peer through the aperture and see the verger with a group of sightseers looking like ants on the chequered marble below. These openings, Fenchurch explained, had probably had pulley-ropes threaded through them to haul up a sort of boatswain's chair so that the vaulting might be cleaned when necessary; if one came up here while a service was being held, he added, one could hear the music better than in the choir eighty feet beneath.

They filed back along the central spine of the ceiling and Bunce allowed himself a small grunt of relief: now they would get down to ground level and brass tacks. But the tour was not quite over. As they approached the door by which they had entered the loft, Fenchurch turned aside, fished another imposing key from his pocket, and unlocked a smaller door opening onto the roof which Bunce had not noticed earlier. Stepping cautiously out onto the leads in the wake of the others, the Inspector was pleasantly surprised to find that the stone parapet, which looked so low from the ground, was in fact sufficiently high to keep him from experiencing any sense of danger. A narrow walkway led between it and the steeply rising roof, up which some of the more daring undergraduates were already clambering, like mountain-goats suddenly metamorphosed into humans; one in particular, with a scraggy beard which he was vainly endeavouring to cultivate, lent himself to that fantasy. The Inspector declined to follow their example. He remained on the flat, leaning on an epicene and especially hideous gargoyle carved in the shape of a cockatrice with a human face and a forked tongue issuing from its mouth (thought by some scholars to be intended as a representation of the French prior, who was notoriously lax in paying his workmen). Bunce was unexpectedly rewarded for his dogged perseverance in the line of duty, for the sullen rain-clouds which had lowered all day over Cambridge chose that moment to part, revealing a luminously blue sky. Sunlight gilded the wet leads and picked out the deep green velvet of the mosses growing undisturbed in the crevices of the weather-pocked stone. Entranced, Bunce gazed below him, where the town was spread out like those maps of cities in early books which depict each house and shed and garden and pathway. There was the river gleaming like poured silver along the verdure of The Backs. The inclement weather had left it almost deserted, though Bunce noticed several punts being launched to take advantage of the break in the rain. There was King's Chapel, looking like Loggan's engraving of it; there the sprawl of courts that forms St John's where the Cam is spanned by the Bridge of Sighs, reproduced by the whim of some nineteenth-century Italophile. The random pattern made by the narrow passages leading off Trinity Street was revealed, and the wedge formed by the two primary streets of the town: one could still see the shape of the medieval town as Fenchurch had described it in his lecture, when Trumpington Gate was the outer limit to the south. The Inspector was not a sentimental or an imaginative man, but as he gazed down on the confines of his bailiwick, he felt an indefinable satisfaction with his lot.

4 At the Woolsack

Bunce took another draught of his pint and sighed contentedly. The contrast between the cosy, nearly deserted, saloon bar of the Woolsack with its gas fire and pleasant fug and the chilly grey afternoon outside (for the sun's appearance had been brief), was pleasing to one who had attained the shelter of the former. His emotions might be compared to those of a soul who, having slogged his way through purgatory for the required duration, has finally been admitted to the outer limits of Heaven. Now that his most pressing thirst was quenched, he looked at Fenchurch expectantly and said, 'Well, sir?'

Fenchurch emptied his glass unhurriedly. 'Since it was the port which was poisoned, Bottom's distress over the missing decanter may have some relevance,' he said reflectively, shaking back his mane of white hair. He was beginning to get into his stride as lecturer, a rôle he always enjoyed. 'I was the first in the Combination Room before dinner that evening —'

'What time would you make it, Mr Fenchurch?' asked the Inspector.

'About seven, I should think. Yes, that's right — it was Monday, and as I walked across Great Court I heard the bells begin.'

'The bells?'

'Great St Mary's bells. They ring the changes on Monday evenings, and the ringers begin punctually on the dot of seven — one can set one's watch by them.'

'I see,' said Bunce.

'When I arrived at the Combination Room, Bottom, as I told you, was extremely upset. He is a creature of habit; he has been at the College for many years, and he takes his duties most seriously. I asked what the matter was, and he replied that he could not find the spare decanter of port.'

'Ah?' said Bunce inquiringly.

'You see, Inspector, Bottom has evolved a system to ensure that there is no possibility of running out of port or madeira: he fills two decanters of each, and keeps the spares in the sideboard. In this way he is able to produce them immediately should the supply in the first decanters run out.'

'But surely that is a commonplace precaution to take?' said Bunce.

'So I should imagine,' replied Fenchurch, rather annoyed at the interruption. 'It is the sort of thing I should expect any butler to do. But it is almost a mania with Bottom. Once when he was a young man and had just been appointed butler, he neglected to do it. There were guests at dinner and one decanter of port was not sufficient. It was a frightful embarrassment to him (I understand that the Master at the time was quite cutting) and he has gone to great pains ever since to ensure that it will not occur again.'

'And so— let me see,' said Bunce, scribbling away busily in the notebook which he had set upon his knee, 'there were two extra decanters, were there— one for port and one for madeira?'

'Yes,' replied Fenchurch. 'Bottom always keeps the two which he plans to use that night on a silver tray on the sideboard. The two extra are kept in the sideboard, on the right-hand side, I believe.'

'So if he needs them, they're right to hand, so to speak?'

'Exactly.'

'But what happened the night Mr Garmoyle was poisoned? Did the decanter disappear completely?'

'No, no, no; if you wouldn't interrupt you'd understand,' said Fenchurch, looking at him severely. There is nothing more off-putting for one accustomed to the expectant silence of the lecture hall than to have another voice break into his peroration. He gazed reflectively at the gas fire, marshalling his thoughts. 'Bottom told me that he had arrived in Hall— he generally does so at 6.30 —' he added hastily to forestall the glint he saw forming in the Inspector's eye, 'to see that the table was properly set and that everything was in readiness for serving sherry in the

Combination Room. To his consternation he found only one decanter inside the sideboard, the one containing madeira. He immediately went, he told me, to the kitchens, where he found the waiter who is responsible for setting High Table and asked him if he had removed it for any reason. The boy replied in the negative; Bottom searched the kitchens in case someone else might have taken it there, but he could not find it. He then proceeded to the wine cellars where, as I have told you, he made the shocking mistake of bringing up a claret to be served with the salmon we were to have that evening. Upon returning with the wine, Bottom found that the missing decanter had reappeared.'

'And when would that be?' inquired the Inspector, his pen poised over the notebook.

'I do not know; you will have to ask him,' answered Fenchurch with asperity, the flow of his rhetoric checked. 'At the time I considered it a trifling domestic upset, notable only for its effect on Bottom (and on our dinner, for he had uncorked several bottles before he realized his mistake, and as a result the hock we had did not have time to settle after its journey from the cellars). If I thought anything of it then, it was simply that he must be beginning to lose his grip and had missed seeing the decanter, which had been there all the time. In the light of what happened to Garmoyle, however, I am inclined to think now that the disappearance of the port decanter bears a sinister significance.' He finished his pint and Bunce rose from the table, picking up the two thick glass mugs as he did so. 'This round is on me,' he said, ringing the bell to summon the barmaid from the busier public bar next door. After a moment's delay she arrived, plump and comely, to refill them, exchanging a few jocular words with the Inspector meanwhile; they had become acquainted during the affair of the homicidal cook. Fenchurch raised his mug courteously in a gesture of thanks, drank, and asked, 'Does the poison give you some indication of who the killer might be?'

Bunce reflected briefly on the scathing remarks made by Professor Tempeste on the murderer's choice of poison and said, 'Not really. We've searched the Fellows' rooms, of course, and come up with nothing there, as we expected. But arsenic isn't all that difficult to get hold of, and we think we know where this lot came from. If we're right, anyone might have done it.' He had almost said 'any one of you', but stopped himself in time.

'Do you mean that there was a cache of the substance in College?' Fenchurch sounded incredulous.

'There's a lot of old-fashioned fly-paper in one of the storerooms near the kitchens,' replied Bunce grimly. 'All anyone would need to do with that is soak it in water until the arsenic coating dissolved. Arsenic kills most quickly in liquid form.'

'I know little about poisons, unlike Tempeste; they are not in my field of competence, my dear sir. I thought, however, that arsenic was generally longer in taking effect. Could Garmoyle possibly have been poisoned with something else?'

'No, it was arsenic all right, we're certain of that; though you're not wrong about the time — often arsenic is a lot slower. But the length of time depends on several things: how much is used, whether the stuff is liquid or solid, whether the victim's stomach is full or empty. That's what had us puzzled at first — the way it worked so fast when the subject had just had a meal. But I understand he didn't eat anything to speak of — that would explain it.'

'Oh, dear me, yes,' said Fenchurch gently. 'Garmoyle had got to the stage where he drank his dinner. I'm quite certain that all he consumed last night was wine.'

'Well, you see, generally it takes some time to work — the poison, I mean — say a half-hour to an hour,' Bunce said, warming to his task of explanation. 'But if the victim takes it on an empty stomach, it works much faster. And another thing. Arsenic usually causes vomiting followed by purging — it's not a pretty sight. But sometimes, as apparently happened in this case, the poison attacks the nerve centres, and gastro-intestinal symptoms will be almost or even completely absent. In such cases acute collapse occurs in company with anaesthesia of the limbs, and is soon followed by a coma, terminating in death.' He paused, beaming, and leaned back in his chair. He was rather pleased by his mastery of this textbook quote, and it was a pleasant sensation to be preaching to the preacher for a change.

Fenchurch was looking shocked. 'It sounds a singularly unpleasant way to die,' he said.

'Generally it is,' replied the Inspector. 'Your Mr Garmoyle

was lucky, if you can call it that — he might have been a great deal more uncomfortable before he died.'

'And you say that you think the arsenic came from fly-paper. I cannot imagine one of my colleagues taking such a coldly premeditated action.'

'Of course it's possible that someone who wasn't at dinner poisoned the wine,' said Bunce helpfully, 'now that we know the decanter disappeared for a bit.'

'That makes little difference,' Fenchurch answered. 'Surely you don't seriously entertain suspicions of the kitchen staff.' Bunce shook his head. 'Nor of the undergraduates in the College.'

'Well, it's always possible one of them had a grudge against him,' said Bunce dubiously.

'You mean to suggest that one of his students resented a caustic remark written on a paper turned in for tutorial and poisoned him in revenge? I think not. Unless I am greatly mistaken, and I assure you, my dear Inspector, I wish with all my heart that I were, it must be one of us.' His distress was evident. 'Such a cruel way to die — why would anyone choose that method?'

'It *could* have been a lot nastier for him,' reiterated Bunce.

'But don't you see, that is not the point: the killer could not have known in advance which effect the poison would have on Garmoyle, even though he had a tendency not to eat anything at dinner. There are other poisons available with less drastic symptoms, are there not? I am woefully ignorant of such matters.' He gazed inquiringly at Bunce.

'Prussic acid — that's cyanide — causes instantaneous death and isn't too hard to get hold of.'

'Then you take my meaning. The murderer could not have known that death would be swift for Garmoyle — he deliberately chose a poison which he knew might well be an intensely painful and lingering means of killing him. I find it absolutely incomprehensible that any of the men I know would do such a thing.'

Bunce looked quizzical.

'I see you think I am being *naif*. Not really. I know that they all have failings — who has not? I am not vain enough to think that I myself am entirely free of them. But although I may not take all my colleagues blindly at their own valuation — although perhaps I do not even like all of them — it is still quite a different thing to feel that any of them would be capable of murder. And to use a means which might be agonizing as well as fatal — no, it is difficult to believe of anyone I know. It makes me angry,' he said half to himself, 'it makes me very angry. You will have heard it said that Garmoyle was a drunkard. I daresay he was, and it was growing worse. Yet that does not obscure the fact that he was a very competent scholar in his field; and his drinking, no matter how great a social problem it was becoming, had not yet, by all accounts, begun to interfere with his work. Poor fellow! he was very conscientious in his way. One evening he told me, while he was in his cups, that he was always careful not to begin drinking until he had finished his work for the day. *And* I believed him. "I swear it's the truth," he kept saying. He was afraid it would be assumed that his work had been improperly carried out because of his drinking. He showed me some of his recent research on Prye's diaries the other day and there is no question that it was good, though the Master was inclined to disagree. And look at the result of one of his tangential studies. If he had not followed up a very minor lead in the diaries, the Shakespeare poem might not have reappeared for another few hundred years, if ever. Its discovery, serendipitous though it might be, was a direct result of his conscientiousness and thoroughness. It is a disservice to scholarship to kill a man like that.'

Inspector Bunce looked a trifle taken aback. Fenchurch added, 'You must not think I am a callous or an unprincipled man. Murder is always wicked and wasteful. But there are not so many men of Garmoyle's calibre that we can afford to take his death lightly.'

'Yes, but I gather the same can't be said for him as a person,' said Bunce cautiously.

'It is true he was not a pleasant man. He was very clever, and so he was able to be very unkind when he chose.'

'Who was he unkind to?' asked Bunce.

'That would scarcely be a motive for murder,' Fenchurch said quickly. 'You must understand that barbed speech is an accepted outlet for the academic who wishes to — "let off steam", I believe it is called. Not that everyone avails himself of the privilege, by any means; and those who do are not necessarily liked, but they are tolerated.'

'I take your point, sir; who was it that Mr Garmoyle insulted?' reiterated Bunce.

'I shouldn't be surprised if he had insulted everyone at one time or another. It was his speciality, and no one took it seriously: you must realize that, Inspector. He was an unhappy man; not agreeable, even at the best of times, but I think his drinking combined with something he could not resist to goad him into unpleasantness. I was sorry for him,' finished Fenchurch.

'I see. Now, Mr Fenchurch, can you think of anyone at Sheepshanks who might have a motive for the murder?' Fenchurch was silent. Bunce went on, 'I'm not asking you to betray your friends, but if you think of anything which might be helpful, I should be very grateful if you would ring me up at headquarters. Remember, sir, that a murderer is dangerous, and if you shield someone out of a mistaken sense of loyalty you may be indirectly responsible for another murder — perhaps even your own.'

Fenchurch looked at him for a moment. Then he said, 'Yes, I shall do all that is in my power to assist you. I am appalled, both at Garmoyle's death and the means which were used to effect it. I cannot undertake to expose all the privacies of my colleagues' lives to you, for one becomes almost indecently knowledgeable about these matters in the close quarters of College, but if I think of anything that may be useful, I shall report it at once. Perhaps I can aid you in finding the murderer — my own work in its way is a sort of exercise in detection, you know.'

'Very kind of you, sir,' Bunce said politely. He was thinking: if they all take this attitude about telling me anything — and they will, they will! — I shall be lucky if I ever get to the bottom of it. There's one that might crack, but I can't be certain — I bet they've put the fear of God into him. It will be tricky work handling him in any event. It's a real bitch of a case; I shall be glad of some help from Scotland Yard.

5 A Reinforcement Arrives

The help from Scotland Yard stepped off the 11.45 train from Liverpool Street Station; it was neatly, not to say nattily, packaged in a well-tailored dark blue worsted suit, a cream silk shirt, and a cream-and-navy striped tie. The Detective-Inspector (for that was his rank) was on the short side, a fact of which he was unpleasantly aware, though otherwise he was exceedingly pleased with his attributes, both physical and mental. He had a sharp nose, light-blue eyes which were on the small side, and a well-barbered chin. The Detective-Inspector was known as a perfectionist, particularly in the important matters of his choice of tie and the daily burnishing of his Lobb shoes. It was proverbial at the Yard that Pocklington knew all the right people; if in fact he did not know quite every one, he was at any rate acquainted with a sufficient number to account for the self-satisfied expression which he habitually wore.

Inspector Bunce, who had driven to the Cambridge railway station to meet the back-up force from London, was somewhat disconcerted: his occasional encounters with the myrmidons of Scotland Yard had not prepared him for this. The Yard policemen he had worked with before had been large and solid, and though they wore plain clothes their garments had carried a faint aura of regulation issue — anything further from this exquisite could not be imagined.

They walked past the guard at the ticket barrier and on to the front entrance of the station where Bunce's car, parked at the taxi-rank with several cab-drivers eyeing it resentfully, awaited them.

'You will understand, hem — Inspector Bunce,' said Inspector Pocklington, pronouncing the title in a slightly incredulous tone as though some error must have been committed in the bestowal upon Bunce of a rank equal to his, and perching gingerly on the edge of the Mini seat (it was Bunce's own car) as though he did not wish to be contaminated by it, 'that this is an extremely delicate affair. The presence of Lord Cavesson would make it so in any event; moreover, the Master of Sheepshanks — still Dr Shebbeare, I believe — is not without a good deal of influence in certain quarters as well.' His manner made it clear that if it were not an important case it would not have been necessary to send him. Bunce nodded dumbly; more than his worst fears were being realized. He had, as one who was well aware of his own limitations, been anxious for help; at the same time he had been worried about the unknown quantity which was about to descend upon him. But none of his forebodings had been dark enough to include anything like Pocklington.

'Fortunately,' Pocklington continued, 'I had just finished a case, and so I was able to come. As it happens, I am a Sheepshankian.' His hand touched his tie, which bore the College colours, as he spoke. 'Now,' he said briskly, taking a thin morocco notebook and a gold fountain-pen from his breast pocket, 'exactly what have you discovered so far?' There was an unspoken implication that before long Inspector Pocklington would uncover much more.

As Bunce threaded the little car through the maze of streets which forms the centre of the city of Cambridge, he described the murder and the events surrounding it. 'Anyone could have found out that Mr Garmoyle would be at dinner that night — if it was Mr Garmoyle the poison was intended for,' he said. 'The butler, Bottom, keeps a book in the Combination Room and the Fellows who are planning to come to dinner sign the book in the morning, adding the names of any guests they plan to bring, so the kitchen staff will know how many to cook for — High Table has a different menu from that given to the undergraduates, you see.'

'Yes, yes, yes,' cried Pocklington, with a little wave of his hand which indicated that any details of a domestic nature at Sheepshanks were an open book to him.

'There were no guests that night except Lord Cavesson. As he had come to discuss the disposal of the Shakespeare manuscript belonging to his family, the Master had requested that no one but members of the College be present,' continued Bunce doggedly. 'He thought there might be talk if someone outside Sheepshanks found out that Lord Cavesson was there.'

'Were all the Fellows at dinner that evening?' inquired Pocklington.

'No,' replied Bunce, 'two were absent. Mr Peascod — he works with old handwriting, I understand — had a dinner invitation of long standing at King's, and Mr Mutton was ill. One of the waiters took a tray up to his room. But it doesn't narrow down the field, so to speak, because if Mr Fenchurch is right about when the decanter of port was poisoned, any of them could have done it.'

'What, old Fenchurch? Is he still about?' said Pocklington. He sounded astonished, Bunce thought wryly, as though the gentleman in question must be a centenarian at the least. He ought to have seen him hopping up those Chapel stairs, said Bunce to himself; that'd change his tune. 'He was my tutor,' Pocklington added by way of explanation.

'As I see it, there are two problems: was Mr Garmoyle meant to be the victim, and if so, why?' Bunce said. 'We can't be certain that the person intended to be killed was killed. My feeling, though, is that the murderer meant to get Garmoyle. He knew Garmoyle would probably drink his way through dinner and wouldn't stop afterwards, he knew that the others would likely have quit long before the second decanter was put into play so there was little risk of poisoning anyone else. Moreover, several of the gentlemen were not drinking that night, so there was no chance at all of their being poisoned.' He ticked them off with the aid of one hand and the rim of the steering-wheel. 'It seems that everyone knows Dr Shebbeare drinks only madeira — he never touches port. Professor Tempeste doesn't drink at all. I am told he was once an alcoholic and now feels strongly about liquor of any kind. Mr Fenchurch is in training for one of those sponsored walks in aid of Dr Barnardo's Homes — the participants walk thirty miles or so, and every mile means more money for the orphans as the backers undertake to pay so much per mile — so he won't drink anything but beer for the time being; he subscribes to the theory that beer is strengthening. The others at dinner were Mr Smythson, the

Abbot's Librarian; Mr Austrey, who authenticated the Shakespeare manuscript; Lord Cavesson; Mr Crippen, the Chaplain; and Mr Grubb, who is a Fellow in Socio-Economics or something of the kind.'

'Grubb?' said Pocklington, looking disdainful. It was obvious there had been no Grubbs among the Fellows when he was at Sheepshanks.

'He's the one I have hopes of,' Bunce answered. 'He clearly hates the lot of 'em, and it's possible I may get him to talk. They're a closed community — quite a tight-knit little group, and it's impossible to get anything out of them aside from the fact that Garmoyle drank and had a nasty tongue, which I should have found out from other sources anyway. But of anything more than that — not a peep. The only one I can see breaking his self-imposed silence is Grubb — he's not one of them, not a "gentleman", I mean, and I think he resents being told to keep his mouth shut for the good of the College. Unless I'm mistaken, nothing would please him more than to see them all in hot water. He was in a sullen mood when I talked to him yesterday, as though he'd just been given a talking-to. I didn't get much out of him then, but I thought I'd try him again when his resentment had had time to ferment.' He stopped the Mini in front of the Woolsack and said, 'We thought you would be comfortable here, and it's convenient for Sheepshanks. I'll park the car by the Great Gate and meet you there in ten minutes if that will suit.'

He waited until Pocklington, managing to look as though he were slumming, entered the Woolsack before he pulled into Agnus Dei Passage, the narrow lane known locally as Aggie's Passage which leads to the main entrance of Sheepshanks. In front of the Great Gate, a huge oaken gateway into which for convenience's sake a smaller wicket-gate has been let, is a cobbled courtyard where authorized persons — the Fellows and their guests — may park their cars; the police had been extended this courtesy for the duration of the investigation. Bunce looked in at the Porter's Lodge to explain that he was the car's owner and to enquire if Mr Grubb was in his rooms.

'As far as I know he is, sir,' said the porter on duty. 'Would you like me to send up and make certain for you?'

'No, thank you,' replied Bunce. 'I'm waiting for a gentleman. You may know him: Inspector Pocklington of the C.I.D. He was an undergraduate here some years ago, I understand. Will you tell him I've gone into the Great Court?'

'By all means, sir,' said the porter with a noticeable lack of enthusiasm. He remembered Pocklington well, as the nastiest piece of work in his three years at Sheepshanks. 'Lovely morning, isn't it — not like yesterday. 'Orrible weather, that was.'

Bunce agreed to the obvious and walked out of the Lodge into Sheepshanks's Great Court. The sky was clean-washed with scarcely a cloud in sight, and the Oriental domes and pinnacles of the College stood out against its dazzling cerulean blue. A cloister formed by ogee arches ran about three sides of the court, off which staircases leading to the students' and Fellows' rooms opened. Over the surface of the stone sketchily-clad figures in exotic costume leapt, crawled, twisted, writhed in *basso-rilievo*. Sir Oliver had brought back drawings of temple friezes which portrayed the Indians in every aspect of daily life and had demanded that his stonemasons reproduce the sketches faithfully in order to impart an authentically Eastern flavour to the façade of his new College. Inspector Bunce peered up at some figures over the doorway leading to Professor Tempeste's rooms, and then walked on hastily: it appeared that Sir Oliver's drawings had omitted no detail, however indelicate to European eyes, of mankind's preoccupations as depicted by the native sculptors.

The fountain in the centre of the Court had been turned on. Glittering arcs of water hung suspended for an instant in air before they cascaded down the elephant's back into the waiting basin. Crystalline drops from the spray clung to the velvety lawn at the edge of the fountain and glistened like spangles on the blades of grass; bright flower-beds outlined the limits of the court. The great bulk of the Chapel loomed to Bunce's right, its façade uncompromisingly Christian among the pagan minarets: so might the Pope look surrounded by a bevy of Balinese dancing-girls.

Bunce smoked a cigarette while he waited for Pocklington to walk over from the Woolsack. As he was carefully stubbing it out on the stones of the path, Pocklington made his appearance and together they walked to Grubb's rooms. He was a bachelor Fellow and so lived in College, but as he was the most junior of the Fellows, his rooms were not to be found in either Great Court or Paul's Court, which provides a glimpse of the river, but in a small block of rooms behind the kitchens. It was a section of Sheepshanks which must once have been noisome, though now it was perfectly salubrious, if less than picturesque. Bunce inspected the doorways until he found one with a clutch of painted signs which informed the viewer than H. Plunkett, N. Trewbody, and A. Grubb had rooms opening off this staircase. They climbed up a flight of splintery stairs to the first floor and Bunce knocked on the door at the head of the steps. A surly voice called, 'What is it? Oh, it's you again,' said Grubb ungraciously as he opened it. Pocklington stepped in and looked about him with a scarcely concealed sneer; clearly these rooms were not the sort he had occupied in Sheepshanks. They were, it must be admitted, unprepossessing rooms to begin with, for Grubb as Junior Fellow had obviously been given last choice, but his ideas of interior decoration had not improved matters. There was a worn brown rug on the floor with a tweed fleck of red and bright blue; a badly made copy of a Swedish armchair covered in grubby orange cloth with antimacassars of multi-coloured crochet was placed next to an unprepossessing table which had a matching crocheted doyley in its centre. A desk covered with books and papers and used ashtrays stood by the window with a folding chair before it, several pop-art and rock-group posters hung on the walls, and from the inner side of the partly opened door to the bedroom a pneumatic blonde, whose perfunctory clothing left nothing to the imagination, leered coyly — clearly she had been extracted from the centre of a men's magazine and tacked to the wood. Grubb caught the direction of Bunce's eye and moved to shut the door, flushing darkly as he did so. 'I thought I'd seen the last of you,' he said disagreeably. 'I told you everything you wanted to know yesterday.' His look dwelt with disfavour upon Inspector Pocklington, whose air of nattiness and smug self-approval obviously irritated him.

'This is Inspector Pocklington of Scotland Yard,' said Bunce. 'Mr Grubb.'

They nodded coldly to each other. 'I don't see why you brought him along,' said Grubb to Bunce. 'I can't tell him any more than I've told you.' His manner was that of a man who has been goaded nearly to breaking-point.

'I think, you know,' Bunce replied, 'that there is quite a lot more you could tell, if you chose.'

'Oh?' sneered Grubb, who was beginning to show signs of losing both his self-possession and his temper.

'Yes — I think you could tell me who at Sheepshanks might conceivably have wished Mr Garmoyle dead. Murder isn't a game, you know, Mr Grubb. It is deadly serious, and if we don't find out pretty quickly who did this one, we may find ourselves with another on our hands.'

' "Murder isn't a game?" ' Grubb burst out furiously. 'You're wrong — that's exactly what it is around here. Anyone can see you're not upper class, any more than me —' he shot a venomous sidelong look at Pocklington. 'If you were, you'd be treating murder like a cricket-match. That's what old Bugbear,' he reverted to the undergraduate nickname for the Master, 'did when he came up to give me a little pep-talk this morning. Oh, it was very delicately done, I'll give him that, he didn't summon me, he did me the honour of waiting on me in quarters to show how magnanimous and humble he could be. "One must play the game, Mr Grubb," he said to me. "It is not — ah — cricket (I believe that is the correct idiom) to disclose the private affairs of one's colleagues, even if one feels one is acting in the public interest. To do so might well muddy more waters than it clears." ' He mimicked the weighty delivery of the Master with vicious precision. 'Do you know why I hate him? You can bet I was the only one he felt he had to point it out to. "We must all keep up the side, Mr Grubb; I feel certain you understand." Sure I understand — they'd shove the whole thing onto me if they could — I'm the misfit, the charity-child.' He gave the phrase an oddly bitter twist. 'Why the hell should I risk my neck perjuring myself for a lot of bastards who spend all their time looking down their patrician noses at me? Not on your life, mate.' Scowling, he flung himself into the orange chair.

'I assure you, Mr Grubb, *we* do not treat murder lightly,' said Bunce.

'Or, for that matter, any attempt to cover up evidence,' chimed in Pocklington, apparently deciding that it was time his presence was felt.

'If you have information which you think would assist the

police, I urge you to tell us,' Bunce added. 'It may be actionable if you do not, and by giving it you could prevent another murder. I ask you again: is there anyone at Sheepshanks who, to your knowledge, might have a motive for the murder of Ernest Garmoyle?'

'Why don't you ask me if there was anyone who *didn't* have a motive?' replied Grubb. 'It would make your question a lot easier to answer. Why do you think they're so anxious for everyone to keep his mouth shut? I suppose you know he was an alcoholic.'

'We have heard that he was known on occasion to drink too much,' answered Pocklington.

' "Known on occasion to drink too much—" That's a laugh. He fell into the sauce every evening like clockwork and lapped it up until he was stiff. Tempeste despised him: he's AA himself and he used to give lectures in the Combination Room about how disgusting it is to watch a man degrade himself. Hypocritical old swine — I bet he's done it often enough in his day.'

'So Professor Tempeste and the murdered man were not on good terms?' Bunce asked.

'You've got ears, haven't you?' answered Grubb rudely. 'What d'you think I've just been telling you? Tempeste said Garmoyle was a disgrace to the College and he carried on about it like a Temperance reformer. He and the Master were trying to get rid of Garmoyle — at least that was the rumour I heard. Of course they wouldn't confide their little plots to a Junior Fellow.'

'Indeed — who told you about it then?' Pocklington asked.

Grubb coloured. 'I can't — don't remember,' he replied with an attempt at nonchalance that failed noticeably.

Bunce cast up his eyes and muttered a silent prayer. It was obvious that this young misfit, for all his scorn of his *milieu*, had a penchant for listening at keyholes to the machinations of his betters so as to keep a finger on the pulse of Sheepshanks. This all-too-human failing made him an invaluable witness — indeed the only witness in the case at all likely to utter. Here he was, seething with discontent, a plum ripe for the picking, and Pocklington was about to put his foot in it by suggesting that his methods of gleaning information were not those of a gentleman! Bunce could see the visible signs of moral disapproval gather on his colleague's brow and his mouth open in preparation for speech. How had the man ever become a policeman? Even after making allowances for family influence, it seemed incredible. Hastily Bunce cast him a quelling glance, tinged, he hoped, with the proper amount of conscious inferiority and said, 'Before the drinking got bad, did Mr Garmoyle and Professor Tempeste get along in the normal way?'

'I wouldn't know. Garmoyle has been a boozer ever since I've been a member of the Senior Common Room,' Grubb replied sullenly; he seemed uncertain whether to be relieved or disgruntled by his escape from exposure as a latter-day Paul Prye.

Bunce thought a moment before speaking again. This young man was going to take some handling, though it wouldn't be nearly so bad if Pocklington would just keep his mouth shut. Suddenly Bunce's dilemma was solved quite literally by the bell — the bell of the clock in Great Court which is affectionately known in the College as Old Noll. The clock-face is affixed to the belly of an elephant rampant which adorns the arch over the main gate; perhaps in revenge for this indignity, it has never been known to tell the time correctly. To compound the confusion entailed by this dyspeptic timepiece, the chime which announces the hour to the inhabitants of Sheepshanks and its purlieus pursues its own erratic contrapuntal course, being frequently in error and seldom in concert with its partner. It was a blessing for Bunce that it choose this moment to ring the hour of three, though it was a good twenty minutes fast, for it enabled him to glance at his watch (ignoring the correct time indicated on its face) and say, 'There! if I hadn't nearly forgot! The Master asked me specially to tell you that he will be driving over to Oxford for dinner and would you be so kind as to see him before he leaves at 3.30. Of course, if you'd rather talk to him tomorrow —' he paused with cunning deference.

Secretly Pocklington, despite his air of unconquerable self-esteem, was flattered by the desire of his old preceptor to speak with him. There is a subtle exhilaration in returning to a place where one was once (despite one's undeniable merit) as disregarded as a grain of sand in the desert, to find oneself consulted and one's words attentively, nay anxiously, awaited by those who formerly were as gods. This was mead to the thirsty and Pocklington was not about to miss his bumper. 'No, no,' he said fussily. 'I expect it would be better to talk to him now while you finish here,' and with a glance of barely-veiled disdain at his squalid surroundings, he departed. Bunce breathed a sigh of relief, and even Grubb looked a shade less defiant.

'Now,' said the Inspector, leaning back in his chair and feeling for his pipe, a blackened and charred relic which Mrs Bunce frequently but fruitlessly endeavoured to dispose of. 'I don't have to tell you, Mr Grubb, that we need your help.' As he spoke he allowed a stronger East Anglian flavour to creep into his speech. 'You see, lad, they're all sticking together, and we can't have that, can we? If I can't get any information from them, I shan't be able to find the killer. If one of them's the murderer, you don't want to shield him, do you?' He paused.

'Shield him? God, no. I'd like to see the lot of them swing,' Grubb said vindictively. 'All right, I'll tell you what I can, but you won't let them know where you got it from, will you?'

How did I ever get into this business? thought Bunce with sudden distaste; I should have stuck with butchering hogs. Aloud he said, 'We always protect our sources. You needn't worry about that. If there's a piece of information we have to use, we'll say it came from outside Sheepshanks.'

'After all, I'm only doing my civic duty,' said Grubb virtuously, his small close-set eyes glittering with malice. 'One must cooperate with the police in any way one can on a serious matter like this.'

The Inspector had finished stuffing his disreputable pipe and was now engaged in lighting it. This was a signal to those who knew him that he was about to get down to work. 'What I should like,' he said, 'is your opinion of each of the Fellows — a quick-study of their characters, so to speak. It would be most helpful to us.' Because you are so observant and perceptive, was the message his benign countryman's demeanour conveyed. Grubb expanded perceptibly under this pediplanate flattery and began to grow almost chatty.

'As a matter of fact I've been analysing them all for some time,' he said. 'My subject is socio-economics; I'm preparing a study of the effect a class-system has upon the economy of a country — how the effeteness of the upper classes seeps through and rots the whole structure of a nation. Of course a place like this, which is rooted in class-consciousness and privilege, shows the entire process in microcosm. Take the Master, for instance: he wanted to replace Garmoyle as editor of the Prye diaries because he was too much of a boozer to do a decent job on them. Shebbeare tried to keep it all on the q.t., of course, but you couldn't help knowing about it. Anyway, one afternoon they had a fearful row — it started in the Pryevian Library, but when Dr Shebbeare left Garmoyle was roaring curses at him out of one of the windows so I couldn't help hearing what was going on — I just happened to be crossing Paul's Court at the time,' he added belatedly.

I bet, thought Bunce. Aloud he said, 'Mr Fenchurch told me that in spite of the drinking, Mr Garmoyle's work hadn't begun to suffer.'

'That wasn't what the Master thought,' replied Grubb. 'He was in a proper sweat trying to get someone else for the diaries. The story was that he wanted a co-editor to work with Garmoyle, but that was just an excuse. What he really wanted was somebody to take over — he was scared to death Garmoyle would make a muck of the diaries and show up scholarship at Sheepshanks. The Master's always going on about the decline of scholarship and keeping up standards — he had an article about it published in *The Times Literary Supplement*. It would be one in the eye for him if the critics had one of Sheepshank's own to tear apart. And Prye's diaries have a close connexion with the College, which would make it worse. Garmoyle must have known once he let in a co-editor it would be the beginning of the end, and he wouldn't hear of having anyone else around. Between them it was a rare old catfight.'

This was proving even more profitable than Bunce had anticipated, but he could not resist a question, at the risk of halting Grubb's spate of words. 'What has that to do with your socio-economic theory?' he asked.

'The whole system is corrupt,' answered Grubb. 'In a classless society Garmoyle would have been out on his ear in no time and someone competent to do his job would have replaced him. There would be no Masters or officials in the Colleges — all the intellectuals would strive together as equals for the betterment of the common people.'

However desirable the classless society might be, reflected Bunce, it seemed unlikely to be achieved by imperfect mankind; moreover, if it ever came into being he doubted that Grubb would recognize in it the Utopia he sought. 'Were Mr Austrey and Mr Garmoyle friends?' he inquired. 'I understand they had worked rather closely together on the Shakespeare manuscript.'

'Friends?' said Grubb. He gave a single rusty hoot of laughter, like an owl that has been startled from sleep. 'You must be kidding. I've seen Garmoyle, when he'd been drinking, look at Austrey as if he'd like to throttle him. Friends — not bloody likely.'

'Why? Was there some reason for professional jealousy between them?'

'There was jealousy, all right, but not the professional kind. Austrey was indulging in a bit of slap-and-tickle with Garmoyle's wife and the poor bastard didn't like it.'

'Are you certain of this?' asked Bunce.

'It was a rumour floating about College, and whether it was true or not, I'd be willing to take my oath Garmoyle believed it. I can't say I blame Mrs G. — she's American, not bad-looking — and Garmoyle must have been pretty rough to come home to when he was drunk. I don't think much of her taste, though.' He made a slight unconscious preening movement, as though to indicate a better choice available to her. 'What's more, the Master and Garmoyle did agree on one thing — trying to persuade Lord Cavesson to leave *Cupid and Psyche* at Sheepshanks — typical of their upper-class bigotry, trying to keep culture away from the people— but Austrey thought it might be a good idea for the manuscript to end up at the British Museum or one of the other big libraries where it would be more accessible and have proper protection.'

'Ah, yes, the manuscript,' said Bunce half to himself, 'but that's no motive for murder, surely. Did Mr Smythson, as the Librarian of the library in which the manuscript was found, have any opinions about the disposal of the Shakespeare work?'

'He agreed with Shebbeare and Garmoyle that it should be kept here— I think he wants to have it to show off— but he was furious at Garmoyle for going over his head to give it to Austrey. It was sitting unrecognized, bound in with some old sermons in the Abbot's Library, when Garmoyle came across it. Smythson thought that etiquette demanded it be returned to him, but instead Garmoyle took it to Austrey to authenticate and then left it in the Pryevian Library for safekeeping without a word of his discovery to Smythson. There wasn't half a row when Smythson found out — they had a slanging-match in the Combination Room — at least Smythson and Garmoyle had, Austrey wouldn't say much. Smythson was going on about professional ethics, and Garmoyle had been drinking so he told him to shut up, that he wouldn't know a Shakespeare manuscript if it came up and bit him so why was he complaining because Garmoyle had taken it to a Shakespeare authority? Then Smythson screamed that it was the last time Garmoyle would ever set foot in the Abbot's Library, and Austrey too,' continued Grubb, obviously savouring the memory of the combat.

'What of the other Fellows?' asked Inspector Bunce, determined to mine this vein to its bottom while he had the opportunity. 'Were any of them on bad terms with Mr Garmoyle? What of Mr Fenchurch, for instance?'

'Oh, they had a bit of a quarrel over the Chapel history Fenchurch is writing — he's always going on about it,' said Grubb. 'Nothing serious.'

'What sort of quarrel?' Bunce asked.

'Nothing much,' Grubb replied evasively. 'Just the kind of dispute the Fellows around here are always having.'

'You mean Mr Fenchurch had one theory about something and Mr Garmoyle had another?'

'That's it — pretty childish really, arguing over the architecture of a building five hundred years old when the masses are waiting to be fed.'

'What exactly was the quarrel about?'

'How should I remember? I wasn't paying attention; it wasn't worth listening to,' replied Grubb airily.

Who d'ye think you're fooling, feller me lad, thought the Inspector, there's been no other bit of gossip too petty for you to put your ear to the keyhole for — a proper Peter Peep you are — but he let the subject drop. 'Did Mr Garmoyle argue with any of the others?' he asked.

'He was always ragging Mutton about his book,' answered Grubb readily, evidently eager to change the subject. 'Poor old sod — I don't know why Garmoyle couldn't leave him alone.'

'What book?' asked Bunce.

'Haven't you heard about Mutton's book? It's the College

joke. He wrote a study of the reign of Catherine the Great — of Russia —,' his manner implying 'in case you didn't know,' 'and the publishers brought it out as a paperback bestseller, the kind with a bosomy wench on the cover. Of course he hasn't been taken seriously since. No one ever mentioned it to him except Garmoyle — he used to kid Mutton about it when he was in his cups.'

'It must have been a very bad book,' said Bunce.

'I wouldn't know whether it was or not,' Grubb replied carelessly, 'but he hasn't written anything since. It's all past history anyway — it must have happened twenty years ago. They say it made him rich and you'd think with all that brass he'd be able to cock a snook at the lot of them, but I hear that only made it worse. Money doesn't seem to matter much in Cambridge.' Puzzled, he shook his head and continued, 'Garmoyle would get at Mutton when he'd been drinking — it was after dinner mostly — and tell him he was an academic failure. He'd really rub it in — Garmoyle had a tongue like a rasp.' He gave a slight shiver, as if an unpleasant memory had just recurred. 'Crippen knows all about that; you ask him what Garmoyle used to say to him about his organ-playing. There were times he nearly had the poor bugger in tears — he always knew Crippen was good for a rise.'

Bunce caught the faint but unmistakable smell of a red herring being dragged across his path, but he did not interrupt.

'You'd think that organ was Crippen's baby,' Grubb continued contemptuously, 'the way he carries on about it, but there was no call for Garmoyle to go on at him the way he did. And he used to make fun of Crippen's name too; he'd ask him if he'd committed any interesting murders lately — that sort of thing. It sounds silly, but Crippen hated it; he's embarrassed about his moniker.'

'What about Mr Peascod?' asked Bunce; the Chaplain seemed an unlikely prospect for a murderer. 'Was Mr Garmoyle rude to him when he was in his cups?'

'Rude to Peascod?' Grubb gave his disconcerting hoot of laughter. 'I'm not saying he didn't try, but have you met Peascod?'

In his brief interview with Mr Peascod, Inspector Bunce had found himself utterly baffled: it was as if the man were surrounded by a wall of fog or cotton-wool. No doubt he was a great scholar, but he seemed totally oblivious of the world around him. Bunce was still not certain that Peascod had absorbed the import of the questions he had been asked, but the effort of repeating them had been a task for which he was unable to summon the energy; he felt as exhausted as if he had been shouting across a very great distance. 'So Mr Peascod didn't react to any of Mr Garmoyle's taunts?' he said.

'Garmoyle would make remarks about the uselessness of monographs on the Carolingian minuscule till he was blue in the face, but he might as well have been talking to that blinking elephant in the middle of Great Court for all the notice Peascod paid him. Peascod is as cut off from the rest of us as if he were living back in the Dark Ages with his blasted bits of handwriting. The only way to get his attention is to shove a piece of mouldy old parchment under his nose. Personally, I think he's dotty. They should have hauled him off to the local looney-bin years ago.'

Much as the Inspector disliked this bumptious young man, he was inclined to agree with his analysis of Mr Peascod. The man was an anachronism — surely he would be unable to exist outside the walls of a college or a monastery. Deciding that he had quite enough to mull over for the time being, Bunce took an amiable leave of Grubb, who was feeling as pleasantly purged of his venom as if he had spent the afternoon on a psychiatrist's couch; more so, in fact, since a psychiatrist is bound by oath to keep secret any revelations made to him. By baring his soul to the police instead of a physician it was odds on that he had brought the shadow of Nemesis close to one of the people he hated, a satisfying thought.

As Bunce crossed Great Court on his way to the Master's Lodge he saw Mr Peascod with Mr Mutton, who appeared to have recovered from his recent indisposition. They were strolling on the close-clipped grass, a prerogative allotted only to Fellows and their guests. Mutton nodded politely to the Inspector; Peascod, apparently engaged in rapt contemplation of a palaeographical problem, did not see him. The two formed a contrast as they walked together. Peascod, a splendid-looking old man with a magnificent head, only lacked a beard to pass for Michelangelo's Moses, and it was rumoured that in his far-off youth he had been a rugger Blue. His nickname among the undergraduates was inevitably Old Codpiece; it is doubtful whether he noticed this disrespectful epithet or whether, noticing, he had any idea to what it referred, for that virile article of apparel is some centuries younger than the Carolingian minuscule. Mutton was shorter than his companion and combined a resemblance to the species of his namesake with a wraithlike quality. Fleecy white hair, a bleating note in his voice, and a tendency to self-effacement gave him the aspect of an ovine ghost. His feet were unusually small, and he walked with an awkward skipping movement like an elderly sheep that is trying to recollect how to gambol. In addition, he was the possessor of a Roman nose in a long and lugubrious face reminiscent of the shop-keeping ewe encountered by Alice in *Through the Looking Glass*. As this ill-assorted pair approached, Inspector Bunce quickened his steps. After his prolonged session with Grubb he had not the fortitude for another conversation, however fleeting, with Mr Peascod.

6 So Rudely Forced

'The poor thing,' said Mrs Bunce. 'Ooh, it's ever so shocking.' She had a soft plaintive voice, like the cooing of a mourning-dove. Inspector Bunce looked up from his eggs and sausage. He had grown accustomed over the years to ignoring his wife's frequent and inconsequent remarks, but he was in an expansive mood: his eggs had been perfectly cooked, the toast was hot, and there was local honey from Coton down the road with which to anoint it.

'What's shocking?' he inquired.

'This awful rape. Did you know about it, Alf? You didn't say anything to me,' she added reproachfully. This was unsurprising, for it was not Bunce's habit to share his work with her. Early in his marriage he had learned that his wife's understanding was not equal to his, and he conducted himself accordingly. There was no harm in her, but she was a little foolish and rather dull, and if Bunce had waited to wed instead of falling in love at twenty-two with the prettiest girl in his village he might have done a great deal better for himself. Her pansy eyes had faded to a blank and shallow blue, dark lovelocks had metamorphosed into a rigid grey perm — an unbecoming fashion *de rigueur* among a certain age and class of Englishwoman — and a buxom but neat figure had spread until its owner *en profil* resembled a pouter pigeon. Bunce would not have objected to these outward manifestations if her mind, like her figure, had undergone some form of expansion, but it continued as resolutely fixed over the years as her unyielding coiffure, which seemed sculpted of some metallic substance. In short, nothing remained of those bucolic and fleeting charms which sometimes give their possessor a semblance of wit by deafening her admirers to the sense (or nonsense) of her words; and Kathleen Bunce stood revealed as a very silly woman. Still, it was not her fault, and though as a companion she left much to be desired, she had a sort of simple good nature which made her acceptable as a live-in housekeeper, so Bunce had made the best of his bargain.

As it happened, he had heard nothing of a rape and supposed that it must have taken place after he had gone off duty the day before. He reached across the table for the front page of the Cambridge *Argus*, which his wife held out to him. The newspaper had used its largest and blackest type in setting the headline which announced this relatively unusual event — 'UNDERGRADUETTE RAPED IN COLLEGE!' it screamed. In calmer typeface below he read: 'Thursday, June 10. Last night an outrage was perpetrated upon one of the women students of Newnham College. At approximately 8.45 as she was reading in her room, Miss X heard a noise at her open ground-floor window. She looked up to see a strange and frightening figure climb over the sill — a man wrapped in an academic gown, below which the bottoms of his trousers were visible. His hands were muffled in the sleeves of the gown and he carried a string shopping bag. His face was concealed, or rather distorted, by what appeared to be a woman's sheer flesh-coloured stocking drawn over it and a dark knitted cap hid his hair. Before his victim had time to make an outcry the intruder seized her and covered her mouth with his hand. She struggled but he overpowered her and carried her to her bed. Miss X states that he then said to her in a hoarse whisper, "If you make a noise I will kill you." Taking a pair of women's bedroom slippers from the string bag, he removed his own shoes and put them on — Miss X described them as high-heeled cerise velvet mules with a pouf of ostrich feathers — and proceeded to rape her. Afterward, she told the police, "When he had finished he told me that if I did not stay where I was until he had gone he would kill me. Then he replaced the mules in the shopping-bag and put on his own shoes before climbing out of the window. A moment later I heard the sound of a motorcycle starting just outside. I looked out and could just distinguish a figure riding off along Sidgwick Avenue."

'Question: Did you see what he looked like without his mask?

'No, I could not tell what his features were like because the stocking material flattened them, and he kept his mask on whilst he was in my room.

'Question: Were you able to determine the colour or make of the motorcycle upon which he made his escape?

'The moon was not out, and it was too dark to see anything but its outline.

'It is to be hoped that the Cambridge police will soon discover the perpetrator of this foul crime. Inspector P. Jenkins, who is in charge of the case, assures us that no effort will be spared. He requests that any member of the University who is missing an M.A. gown will inform him immediately, as it is possible that the rapist is using a stolen gown as his disguise. Student associations are being formed for the protection of young women, and many of the male undergraduates have volunteered their services for patrol at the women's Colleges.'

Bunce folded the paper and put it on the table. 'I'd better be getting to work,' he said heavily, rising from his chair. 'We seem to be having a regular crime wave.'

At the police station he encountered Inspector Jenkins, a plump, garrulous man who had been buttonholing all his colleagues on the morning shift to tell them the details of the case. He was about to go home when Bunce made his appearance, but though Jenkins had had a long night of it he postponed his departure in order to tell the tale once more, for he respected Bunce and wanted his opinion of the affair.

'The girl's name is Philomela Partridge,' he said, 'though she looks more like a wren than anything else — one of those studious girls, I should think, with her nose always in a book. She was more scared than hurt, but there's no question that it was rape. She was hysterical by the time she got out to raise the alarm, poor kid; she said he stood over her like a ruddy great bat flapping its wings — he had his arms in the sleeves of an academic gown — and she nearly passed out from fright. Lucky for her in a way; it seems she was only half-conscious when he raped her.'

'I wonder if the gown will help to catch him,' mused Bunce.

'I thought of that, but it's not likely — in this town those gowns are thick as crows in a cornfield. It's true that he was wearing an M.A. gown and that they're different from the ones worn by the undergraduates — they're longer, with long flat hanging sleeves instead of the choirboy kind, but there are plenty of those about, too. I was given quite a lesson on the different kinds of gowns by one of the Fellows at Newnham last night — quite a surprise she was, young and pretty.' He winked. 'She told me that sometimes you can tell the College an undergraduate gown is from — at Trinity they're dark blue instead of black, for instance — or there may be facings or chevrons on it. But the M.A. gowns are all identical because they're University, not College, gowns.'

'All that is assuming the rapist is connected with the University,' said Bunce, 'but anyone can go in and buy a gown from one of the outfitters.'

'Or steal one, for that matter,' Jenkins answered, sighing. 'We're checking the shops to see what has been bought lately. June isn't the season for purchasing academic gowns, so if the rapist got one recently there's a chance someone might remember him, but between you and me, I don't expect it will do much good. If the man is connected with the University, he would already have one. If he isn't, it would be easy enough to nip into one of the Colleges and pinch one. The only M.A. gowns at Newnham are owned by the Fellows and research students and are relatively difficult to get hold of, but the people there told me that just down the road at Darwin College there are two cloakrooms full of the things. It's a graduate College so there are a lot of M.A. gowns — you have to be over twenty-five to be a Master of Arts — and most of the students leave them in the cloakrooms during the day to wear at dinner. There's a porter nominally on duty but often he's called away from his office, and anyway he wouldn't be likely to question a man carrying a gown — most of the members of Darwin live out, so there's bound to be a few he wouldn't know by sight. I was told that half the time the students don't even look to see whose gown they're putting on for dinner — they use any that comes to hand. To complicate the situation further, there are stray gowns in the cloakrooms left by students who have completed their research and left Cambridge, so although we're asking anyone with a missing gown to notify us, there's a good chance the rapist could have stolen one and nobody would know it. And other Colleges are probably just as easy to steal from —

the rapist could be anyone in Cambridge, not just a member of the University.'

Both men looked glum at this conclusion. Jenkins added, 'It couldn't have happened at a worse time, either, with May Week coming up. If the man is set on raping again, he'll have a field-day among all the goings-on.'

May Week is an institution typical of Cambridge, for it is actually held in June and is nearly a fortnight long. After Full Term is ended and the Bumps (the College rowing competitions on the River) take place, May Week begins. It is a time of plays and concerts, but above all of the May Balls. Nearly every College has its Ball. May Week is a season of gaiety and release after examinations: the Colleges vie with one another in the lavishness of their dances; and although the older members of the University may complain that things are not what they once were, and rock music in many cases has replaced waltzes in the elegant tents set up for dancing in the College courts, fresh salmon at supper is still traditional, followed by sugared strawberries with champagne to dip them in. Those students with stamina hire a punt in which to convey their girls to breakfast afterward at Grantchester, a village in the High-Picturesque style situated on the Granta River (which is only the Cam with another name — Cambridge's river, like her streets, changes its appellation every so often as an antidote to *ennui*).

Bunce nodded in agreement with his colleague's statement. The revelry associated with May Week would make it difficult to police the town. At that time there is always a sufficient number of girls who are willingly dragged into bushes or the odd potting-shed to confuse the issue and provide a series of potential embarrassments for the constabulary as well as unparalleled opportunities for the rapist, should he decide to repeat his crime. 'What about the motorcycle — was it his or might he have stolen it?' he asked. 'Any leads there? I assume you checked it out along with the gown.'

'Any leads?' Jenkins gave a bitter laugh. 'Since the information on the rape appeared in the papers, there have been no less than nine — *nine*, mind you — reports of stolen motorcycles, all gone missing within the past day or so. The owners were mostly undergraduates, with some local youths, a shop assistant from the stationers' in Sidney Street — even one of the trendier

Fellows of Pembroke: chap with red hair in a pigtail and a beard like a Cossack's.' He looked shocked. 'Honest to Gawd, sometimes I wonder what the University is coming to.'

'Have you eliminated any of them as suspects?'

'We're checking their alibis as a matter of course, naturally; it's barely possible the rapist is among them and is using this method to deflect suspicion from himself, though he'd be a damn' fool if he has — it 'ud be a lot more likely to attract it. Still, we have to chase up every lead, no matter how idiotic. Most of the motorbikes will probably turn up soon. Several of the blokes admitted to getting tight and forgetting exactly what pub they left 'em at, and the rest may have been temporarily borrowed for a joy ride. Wherever they've gone, it's been no use to us to have them reported, I can tell you — it just means a lot of work for nothing. And the ladies' slippers were more of the same — nothing of the kind reported to have been in stock within memory in any of the local shops — from the sound of those we've got one of those nasty fetishists on our hands.' Jenkins rubbed his hand over his eyes and gave a yawn. As he got to his feet he said, 'Time to go home, I reckon. You'll let me know if you get any bright ideas, Alf? We've got to nab him quick or there *will* be a dust-up — the newspapers are sharpening their knives for us already.'

'I thought the *Argus* was rather decent this morning for a change,' said Bunce.

'Yes, but that won't last long. The reporter who interviewed me — it was that bugger Figgins — made it clear that as soon as there is a respectable time-lapse he's going to start in with the "incompetent police" routine — they've got the wind up with a murder and a rape in the same week. And that's just the local rag — wait till the London papers jump on the bandwagon.' He gave a grimace. 'To think that only yesterday I was grousing because we'd a couple of burglaries and a greyhound-doping to clear up. Ah, well, off to bed and breakfast.' He waved a pudgy hand and disappeared down the corridor.

7 The Pryevian Library

Fenchurch had arisen early that morning to take a short but bracing walk of six miles or so before breakfast in the country surrounding Cambridge. Upon his return he cut through King's in order to drop off a note for a cousin at the Porter's Lodge: Cambridge is still a nineteenth-century town in many ways and the telephone is considered something of an innovation. The leisurely pace of life induced by a system which employs the letter as the most common means of communication is counteracted by the paradoxical bustle of activity incurred by this antiquated method. Letters deposited by hand at the College Lodges or sent (during Full Term) by the inter-College post herald invitations to lunch, tea, dinner; to lectures on Georgian silver, the Wars of the Roses, brass-rubbings; to meetings of the Bibliographical Society, the Heraldic and Genealogical Society, the St George's Day Observance Society (whose sole apparent reason for existence is to provide an excuse for extravagant dinners). Things are constantly happening in Cambridge, particularly during Full Term; and a pocket diary is an absolute necessity for keeping one's social, as well as academic, commitments straight.

Fenchurch handed in his letter to the Porter and walked up King's Parade past the Senate House and the Old Schools to Trinity and Bridge Streets on his way back to Sheepshanks. As he passed the Woolsack the barmaid was engaged in sweeping the steps which lead to the public bar. Fenchurch raised his cap to her and she waved a cheerful greeting in return. He entered Sheepshanks by the Great Gate, and was meditating with pleasurable anticipation upon his approaching breakfast when he encountered Dr Shebbeare, flanked by Austrey and Lord Cavesson.

'Ah, Fenchurch,' said the Master. 'Will you join us? We were just on our way to the Pryevian Library to have a look at the Shakespeare manuscript. Lord Cavesson has not yet seen it. Poor Garmoyle's death and the ensuing interviews with the police threw us rather off-stride yesterday, and as I had a dinner engagement with the Master of Balliol and Lord Cavesson was invited to dine with Sir Roger Oakington, we decided to wait until the morning. Mr Austrey, as our resident authority on Shakespeare, has kindly consented to accompany us; perhaps you also will honour us with your society.' Having delivered himself of this stately peroration, he scarcely waited for Fenchurch's assent before shepherding his charges across the lawn to Paul's Court and the Pryevian Library.

The entry for Paul Prye in Venn's *Alumni Cantabrigienses* is succinct and uninformative:

Prye, Paul, s. of Peter, of Pepyng Priory, Pepyng Magna, Wilts, gent. *Agnus Dei Coll*, matric. 13 Nov., 1648, aged 15; d. 1679.

Aubrey is almost equally abrupt: 'Obscurely born, he was little both of mind and body,' he writes dismissively, in his *Brief Lives*. 'Banisht the Court for his tricks. Dr Swadling, who was physitian at his death-bed, saies he dyed of chagrin.'

There is no mention in either source of Prye's expulsion from College for spying upon one of the Fellows in an unbuttoned moment with the chambermaid and his subsequent attempt to blackmail the indiscreet don. After being sent down in disgrace for this misdeed, Prye went to London, where he supported himself by composing indecent ballads and writing scurrilous squibs and political pamphlets for both Royalists and Parliamentarians. His attitude toward these parties was wholly impartial, for his political affiliation was dictated by the amount of pay involved. Toward the end of the Commonwealth, however, it was only the Outs who bothered with such tactics — the Ins were more concerned with suppressing all opposition — and thus by sheer accident Prye built up a record which might be construed as one of loyalty to the Stuarts. After the Restoration he turned to acting in the newly opened theatres for a time, until a distant cousin, one Fenella Willing, became one of the King's incidental mistresses and employed Prye in her attempts to jockey for position at Court and in the Royal bed. He proved a superb gleaner of information and set up a highly efficient spy network to relay the backstairs gossip quickly and accurately to her ears. At the same time Prye augmented his income with odd jobs, generally unsavoury, done for anyone with cash in hand, and a profitable sideline in pimping; his talents were well-suited to the Court of Charles II.

Eventually, though, he began to overreach himself, having in the course of his researches turned up a marketable item or two on the fair Fenella. By this time she had lost the attentions of the King but had found favour, thanks to her cousin's proficiency at procuring, with one of Charles's ministers, and she was able to persuade her lover to have Prye jailed on a trumped-up charge. A taste of prison made him amenable to the notion of retirement at Pepyng Priory (his father having died in the meantime) and Fenella's minister arranged for a pension to be paid him on condition that he stay there. During his years in London Prye had filled a series of notebooks with remarks in a private shorthand on the activities, official and unofficial, at Court; there was little in bed or out that had escaped his notice. A typical entry from Prye's diary should serve to establish the tone and bent of his mind.

> Rose betimes. Head in sad case, for I was well fox'd the night before. Waited upon my Lord D — [habitual caution is not easy to discard, even when writing in shorthand]. His hatt a vastly unbecoming shade of Peuce. Upon leaving the place, did see Mrs H—, Lady D—'s waiting woman, privily admit a gallant to her chamber, and did watch their Frolicks through my spy-glass. [One of Prye's associates at Agnus Dei was an inventor of parts and had devised a sort of keyhole periscope. It had been employed in the incident which resulted in Prye's expulsion from Cambridge, and was of great use to him in his later career.] Upon his departure went boldly in and threatened to tell her Mistress all that I had witnessed. She wept, to no avail, then thought to offer me her *chose* if I kept Mum . . . and so to bed.

From this excerpt it may be gathered that Paul Prye is not one of the more attractive figures of Charles II's reign: he stands revealed in his diary through his own words as a bully, a coward and a sneak. But he made ample amends for his conduct in the eyes of historians by leaving an unrivalled record of the Restoration period; and by his amassing of a small but choice library which contains, among other treasures, a surprising quantity of particularly fine books with the marks of ownership of the Royal library and a number of valuable government documents which had mysteriously vanished from the official archives. Prye's library is also notable for its comprehensive collection of bawdy literature; some of the most scabrous of the anonymous broadsides in its holdings were in fact written by him at the request of Mistress Willing in an attempt to blacken the reputations of her rivals.

After his banishment from Court Prye was an embittered and disappointed man — at Pepyng Priory, a damp and gloomy habitation, he sought an outlet for his energies by adding to and cataloguing his library, but his chief occupation was refining, editing and annotating his diary. Thwarted ambition increased the vindictiveness of a disposition already naturally malevolent, and the notebooks are laced with venomous comments about his contemporaries. Upon Prye's death, the result of a fit caused by hearing that the politician responsible for his exile had been granted an earldom, his library was left to Agnus Dei on condition that the notebooks containing the diary be kept in perpetuity by the College. In order to implement his wishes another Cambridge College, St Jude's, was named in Prye's will as having visitation rights: if ever it should be found that any of the shorthand volumes have been removed from the Pryevian Library, all Prye's books will revert at once to St Jude's.

The building in which the Prye Library is housed is one of the happier examples of architecture at Sheepshanks. Its ground floor consists of a small arcade formed by a concatenation of rounded arches; above, the windows of the Library rhythmically pierce the façade of golden Cotswold stone imported for its construction. It stands at the far end of Paul's Court and is first viewed across a vista of lawn; through wrought-iron grilles which mask the windows on the river side, one catches glimpses of water and the occasional punt. The total effect is of a diminutive version of Sir Christopher Wren's library at Trinity.

Dr Shebbeare and his entourage mounted the staircase leading to the first floor and the massive door which guards the entrance to the Library. The Master produced a key for the modern lock that had been fitted to the door and opened it, waiting for the others to file through before entering himself. Despite Fenchurch's longing for the porridge which, but for the Master's interference he would even now have been consuming in his rooms he was struck, as he was each time he entered it, with the beauty and tranquillity of the place. The Pryevian Library consists of one long chamber, handsomely panelled in the style of the late seventeenth century. Ranged at intervals along the walls are twelve ornately carved book-presses which once belonged to Paul Prye. At one end are placed exhibition cases and a desk for the Librarian, and at the other several large work-tables are provided for the use of scholars. Wide floorboards have been polished by use and the passage of years to the colour and lustre of tortoise-shell; over them are thrown a couple of large and handsome Persian carpets whose great size is dwarfed by the size of the room. All in all, it is the beau-ideal of a gentleman's library.

The room was a trifle stuffy — no one had used it since Garmoyle's death — so Dr Shebbeare flung open one of the casement windows to let in air. The douce and gentle sun-warmed breezes of early summer flowed through the opening he had made and toyed with the green damask curtains which hung there. The Master crossed to the Librarian's desk and began opening drawers.

'Austrey tells me that Garmoyle kept the Shakespeare manuscript in that press.' He pointed to one which stood next to the open window and continued to rummage in the desk drawer. 'Ah, here it is — this key opens all the book-presses,' he explained to Lord Cavesson, 'except the one containing Prye's diaries. He had it fitted with a secret mechanism: so no one could snoop, I suppose.'

The others drew near as Dr Shebbeare unlocked the lower portion of the book-press with the small key he had just found. The shelves of the upper three-quarters of the presses were covered by glass so that one could see what was within, but the bottom section of each was protected by solid carved doors. Lord Cavesson craned forward as the left-hand side swung open, disclosing a row of smallish volumes in leather bindings.

'Would you mind just having a look, Austrey? I expect you'll recognize it at once as you're so familiar with it,' said Dr Shebbeare. Austrey ran a practised eye over the spines and picked out one rather fat quarto volume which was bound in plain brown calf. He opened it.

'No, that's not it,' he said in a vexed voice, replacing it on the shelf, 'but it's very like — I say, here it is.' He pounced on a similar binding. 'No, blast it, that's Wycherley's *Comedies*.' Austrey worked his way through the likely-looking books on the shelf, becoming more annoyed as he did so. At last he rocked back on his heels and looked up at the Master. 'It's not here,' he said.

'Nonsense, my dear Austrey, I expect you've mistaken the book-press,' replied Dr Shebbeare.

'No, I haven't,' Austrey said definitely, 'but it's possible Garmoyle may have moved it for some reason. Let's try the upper shelves.'

Some hours later (it was nearly lunchtime, and Fenchurch had long ago renounced any hope of breakfast) the quartet sat in the midst of chaotic piles of books in various colours and sizes. They had methodically emptied each bookcase in turn in order to make a thorough check and to ascertain if the volume containing the Shakespeare manuscript had been accidentally pushed back out of sight, but it was nowhere to be found. Every cranny of the Prye Library had been searched, and the book was simply not there. The Master, despite his phlegmatic temperament, was visibly embarrassed and, in the customary fashion of those who are upset, rounded on Austrey. 'Why didn't Garmoyle keep the manuscript in the book-press with the secret compartment?' he demanded. 'That would have provided *some* additional security.'

Austrey flushed. 'I'm afraid that was my doing,' he said. 'Garmoyle suggested it but I never could get the hang of the latch, and as I sometimes took the key from the Porter's Lodge and came up to work on the manuscript when he wasn't here, he very kindly consented to keep it in one of the other bookcases. But in any event no unauthorised person would be able to get a key to enter the Library.'

'Yet the book is missing,' the Master said grimly. Suddenly he brightened. 'It is possible that Garmoyle took it to his rooms for some reason. Careless of him, but he may have done so; we had better look there.' He turned to Lord Cavesson. 'I cannot tell you how horrified I am that this should have occurred, and I do assure you —'

Lord Cavesson waved an urbane hand in dismissal. 'Not at all — think nothing of it. These things happen. I feel certain that it has simply been mislaid and will turn up shortly. You have done all you could in the circumstances to protect it.'

They set to work replacing the last of the books. When all the volumes had been returned to the shelves, the Master locked the presses and put the key back in the drawer of Garmoyle's desk. Upon leaving the Library the four men walked to the Porter's Lodge in order to obtain the key to Garmoyle's rooms. These were in the Great Court of Sheepshanks; as he had been a married Fellow, they were not living quarters, but instead he had been provided with office space in College. Garmoyle had in fact spent most of his time at the Prye Library, so the two cramped rooms served him more as a storage-place for reference books than an office. It did not take long to go through the bare rooms which primarily contained books piled on shelves, tables, desk; most of the volumes were indisputably modern, so they were able to make quick work of the search.

When they had completed the unfruitful task Dr Shebbeare said gravely, 'Gentlemen, I need scarcely tell you that this is a very serious matter. My lord,' turning to Lord Cavesson, 'I should like, with your permission, to consult the police. I feel that it would be unwise to keep the disappearance of the *Cupid and Psyche* to ourselves any longer.' Lord Cavesson nodded agreement. 'But I think, until we have discussed the matter with Inspector Bunce,' continued the Master, 'that it would be the wiser course not to mention the loss to anyone else outside our circle, even the other Fellows. I trust you all agree.' There was a murmur of assent.

'It is certainly imperative that we call in the police,' said Fenchurch. 'There may, after all, be some connexion between the missing manuscript and poor Garmoyle's murder.'

This possibility clearly had not occurred to the others: although all of them were reasonably humane men, they had temporarily forgotten about Garmoyle's death — the precious manuscript was uppermost in their minds. It was a disquieted and discouraged group that trudged back to the Porter's Lodge. Responsibility for the safety of the Shakespeare manuscript weighed heavily on the Master. Austrey, as the person who had handled it most recently, also felt responsible, but he experienced as well a far more personal emotion at the thought of its loss — it was as though an adored mistress or a beloved child had been snatched from him. Fenchurch too felt a great, if more general, concern at its disappearance; and if Lord Cavesson was not in the usual way much interested either in manuscripts or in Shakespeare, still, as the head of his family and the possessor of what amounted to a National Treasure, he was shocked and disturbed, though generations of good breeding enabled him to conceal the fact out of consideration for his host.

By common consent they adjourned to the Master's Lodge where Dr Shebbeare made a telephone call to the Cambridge police station. Inspector Bunce was out to lunch but was expected back shortly, and a message was left for him. This information reminded the company that they themselves had not yet lunched, and the Master ordered sandwiches and whisky to be served. Under the circumstances Fenchurch felt justified in departing from his strengthening regimen of beer. Although it was growing late the sandwiches were hardly touched, but the level of the whisky decanter descended rapidly. After they had consumed several stiff drinks the front doorbell was heard and Dr Shebbeare's butler appeared at the library door to inform them that Inspectors Bunce and Pocklington were waiting in the hall.

Inspector Bunce was experiencing a certain elation. The disappearance of the *Cupid and Psyche* manuscript made him feel that there must be a connexion of some sort with Garmoyle's murder and that therefore his store of leads to the killer had increased. Pocklington, on the other hand, was in a state of some annoyance, the result of being ruthlessly dragged by Bunce from a late and lengthy meal at the Garden House. He had been forced to rush through his *gâteau* and had had barely a swallow of coffee.

'I can understand your worry over the loss of the manuscript,' Bunce said to Dr Shebbeare, 'but I consider it very significant indeed to the course of the murder investigation.'

'Then you think whoever killed Garmoyle may also have stolen the manuscript?' asked the Master.

Bunce pulled at his ear reflectively. 'I shouldn't be surprised,' he said. 'It's a bit of a coincidence, having two crimes at once in the same place. Though to make certain it was stolen and not just mislaid, we shall have to search Mr Garmoyle's house and likely places in College, and recheck his office and the Prye Library as well. I suppose there's no chance of your having taken it home with you by mistake, is there, Mr Austrey?' he asked jocularly, but his eyes were shrewd. I shouldn't be surprised if one of 'em had got absentminded and torn out a couple of the pages to use the backs for lecture notes, he thought. What a prize lot they are — they treat a priceless object as though it were a novel from the public library. That lock on the Prye Library door, for instance — I had a look at it yesterday when I went through Mr Garmoyle's effects. It's new all right, but it wouldn't keep a serious-minded burglar out for more than a couple of minutes. And they leave that book — which the Master tells me is worth hundreds of thousands of pounds at the very least — there for safekeeping without a qualm.

Austrey replied firmly that he was quite certain he had not, during a fit of abstraction, put the *Cupid and Psyche* in his pocket and walked off with it. Inspector Pocklington was evincing signs of muted petulance at being disregarded for so long and said officiously, 'It's time we went to have a look at the Library.'

'We might as well,' Bunce agreed, 'we're just about finished here. Mr Austrey, perhaps you would be so kind as to come with us and show us how to open the cabinet with the secret latch.' A thought struck him and he went on: 'Mr Austrey, can you tell me whether the manuscript was still there right after Mr Garmoyle's murder?'

'It was in its usual place on Monday — I know because I worked on it that afternoon — but that is as much as I can tell you. On Tuesday there was a meeting of the Degree Committee on English, so I did no work on the *Cupid* that day; and since then, as you know, things have been rather at sixes and sevens.'

'That's no use then — I wondered, you see, if Mr Garmoyle's murder mightn't have been a cover-up for the theft; but unless someone else saw the manuscript or noted its absence in the meantime, there's no way to tell.'

'No one else would have been authorised to go to the Prye Library without Mr Garmoyle,' said Austrey. 'But he may have shown it to someone on Tuesday.'

'That's an idea — I shall look into it. Though as for the murder,' said Bunce heavily, 'I should have expected a knock on the head rather than poison if theft was involved.'

'Unless it was premeditated because the thief was hoping by means of the murder to cover up the theft for a few days, until he could dispose of the manuscript,' put in Fenchurch.

'Do you mean he might have killed Garmoyle so everyone would be too upset to think of the manuscript? So that Mr Austrey, for instance, would be too preoccupied to work on it, and no one else would think to check that it was still there? It's possible,' Bunce said thoughtfully.

'If it was an outside job, the killer might not even know that Mr Austrey was working on it,' offered Pocklington.

The members of Sheepshanks sat stunned. *If* it was an outside job . . . the horrid probability was rapidly brought home to them that it was not — both murder and theft bore all the earmarks of the home-grown article.

'But surely,' said Lord Cavesson, 'you can't mean Mr Garmoyle was murdered simply to facilitate theft — that would be quite appalling.' His nostrils quivered in fastidious distaste.

'I've heard of worse motives,' Bunce replied. 'While it's a fact nobody liked the gentleman, that's not necessarily going to get him killed. The manuscript, though, that's another matter. People have been known to kill for a couple of bob, and the Shakespeare poem is worth a great deal more than that.'

'It is true that the *Cupid and Psyche* is very valuable, but I don't see what good it would do a thief,' Fenchurch said thoughtfully. 'Too many people know about it — no one who stole it could hope to dispose of it.'

'That's so,' said Austrey. 'Unless he knew of a collector who was willing to purchase stolen goods.'

'The man would have to be thoroughly unscrupulous to wink at murder.'

'I've no doubt there are such men,' Dr Shebbeare broke in, 'but I should think they are not always easy to find when one wishes to sell to them.'

'There is another alternative,' Austrey said. 'We could be dealing with a madman — someone who simply wants it for himself. In that case,' he shrugged ruefully, 'I suppose I should be a prime suspect.'

'No one is being accused, Mr Austrey,' said Bunce. 'As I see it, the situation is this way: either Mr Garmoyle was murdered for reasons unknown and the disappearance of the manuscript has nothing to do with it, or he was killed to cover up the loss of the poem. Perhaps it will still turn up — even now it's not impossible that it has simply been mislaid — but I would say, after your search, that it seems unlikely in the highest degree.'

'I expect the manuscript was stolen for an American,' Pocklington said. 'Most of their collectors don't care about the origins of a piece so long as it's what they want. We had a case of fraud at the Yard only the other day. A gullible Chicago financier who was staying at Claridge's thought he was buying Henry VII's chapel from Westminster Abbey. The confidence man who "sold" it to him told him the chapel would be removed stone by stone under the pretext of having renovations done. We only found out about the swindle because the con man was resentful at being jewed down on his price and posted a letter to the police before taking off with his profits to the Continent.'

This long-winded anecdote had little point and less interest for his hearers, but they listened politely enough. As soon as he had wound it up Bunce announced that they had better waste no more time before examining all the possible places where the manuscript might be concealed, and he went off with Pocklington to perform this task, assisted by Austrey and a couple of constables. Fenchurch was preparing to take his departure when the door-bell rang again. The butler appeared shortly afterward to inform Dr Shebbeare that a Mr Grimes of Scunthorpe's, the well-known auctioneers in Piccadilly, wished to speak to Lord Cavesson.

'That fellow! Certainly not,' exclaimed Lord Cavesson. 'He showed up at Tantivy Hall the other day and I refused to see him. I can't think how he found out I was here.'

But it was too late to rid themselves of Mr Grimes, for unknown to the butler, he had followed at his heels and now stood in the doorway. It will be easiest to describe Mr Grimes by his attributes, for the man himself was curiously nebulous. His suit, diction and manner were impeccable, as befitted the standards of Scunthorpe's (the oldest auction house still in existence), but at close range these seemed characteristics to be assumed at will, like the colours of a chameleon. His face had a mobile quality, and one felt that with a change of clothing he might appear to be someone quite different. In fact, there was a faintly un-English flavour about Mr Grimes, a hint of something exotic; one felt that his name might as easily be Zlinsky or Rabinovitch as Grimes.

'I hope I do not intrude,' said this gentleman in a soft accentless voice, though it must have been obvious to him that he was doing precisely that. 'I have a message for your lordship from Lord Merlin.'

Lord Cavesson's eyes were chill as rime. 'I thought I had made it clear to Lord Merlin —' he began.

'Indeed you did, my lord,' said the man deferentially, 'but he had a thought on the subject which he felt might be helpful to you and he asked me to convey it, as it was necessary for him to be in Munich this week.'

'We shall be happy to withdraw, Lord Cavesson,' the Master said, 'so that you may have your conversation in privacy.'

'I thank you, Dr Shebbeare, but there is no need,' replied Lord Cavesson. 'I do not wish to speak to this man.'

Mr Grimes's feelings did not appear to be wounded in the least by this uncompromising speech; perhaps he had none. 'I shall take only a moment of your time,' he said persuasively. 'Lord Merlin felt it was most important for you to know all the facts before coming to a decision.'

Lord Cavesson considered this. 'Very well,' he said grudgingly, 'but there should be nothing which you cannot tell me in front of these gentlemen.'

'Lord Merlin particularly requested,' replied Mr Grimes suavely, 'that I deliver his message in private.'

Lord Cavesson made an exasperated movement as if to say, anything to rid myself of this man! and the Master and Fenchurch left them. As soon as they were alone, Lord Cavesson said sharply, 'Well? I told Merlin when he spoke to me at my club that I thought it damned cheek, and my sentiments have not altered. This is a family matter which at present is not the concern of any outsider.'

'As a Director of Scunthorpe's, Lord Merlin is naturally concerned about a piece so indisputably precious as an unpublished work by Shakespeare written in his own hand,' murmured Mr Grimes in tones meant to soothe. 'As a not inconsiderable portion of Britain's glorious literary legacy it should be cherished with a proper regard to its worth. Lord Merlin feels an interest in seeing that a home be found for the manuscript which is suited to its significance, and he is offering the resources available to Scunthorpe's as a means to that end.'

Lord Cavesson said abruptly, 'And what is your rôle in all this? Are you perhaps an expert on Shakespeare? Or on Elizabethan handwriting?'

Mr Grimes was unabashed. 'No, my field is objects of virtu; in this matter I am serving solely as Lord Merlin's humble messenger.'

'I see,' said Lord Cavesson. 'Well, you had better give me the message, then. What is it?'

His brusqueness did not disconcert Mr Grimes, who said with apparent inconsequence, 'I so much admired your beautiful Tantivy Hall when I was there — what a superb example of the English country seat. A pity these old mansions are so costly to keep up in these sad times. The exquisite plasterwork in the hall, for instance — I know of a craftsman who could repair it perfectly, but of course it would be expensive. It is such a tragedy to see these evidences of past glory crumble.'

Lord Cavesson was by nature and breeding a courteous man, but his patience had worn to the breaking-point. 'I fail to see what my house has to do with this conversation,' he said coldly. 'You are the one who initiated it, over my protests. I have no wish to hear what you have to say, but I should be grateful if you would say it and get it over with so I may return to my own affairs.'

Instead of being hurt by this blunt speech, Mr Grimes appeared positively delighted. 'Ah, you wish me to get down to brass tacks — that too is my wish. It is sensible to say what is important and to leave the rest to others. Very well, then. Lord Merlin sympathizes with your predicament — such a responsibility to have to make so momentous a decision — and wishes to smooth your path in any way possible. He feels an altruistic interest in the disposition of the manuscript; surely it would be a pity for such a treasure to be buried away, even in so charming a setting as this. And of course, security would be very difficult here,' he added practically.

'Yes, yes,' said Lord Cavesson impatiently. 'Merlin has already told me all this. If you have anything to add, do so; otherwise . . .' he glanced pointedly at his watch.

'As a man of discernment,' Mr Grimes continued, unruffled, 'it is obvious to you that it would be to the advantage of Scunthorpe's to have so valuable an article to sell. However, it is not only the fee we should obtain by handling the sale, but the prestige of being the auctioneers of what may be conservatively described as the most important literary find of the century. Therefore Lord Merlin has instructed me to say that the Directors are prepared to offer a very generous commission if the selling of the Shakespeare poem is put into our hands.'

Lord Cavesson's features hardened into a stony mask. He did not raise his voice but its timbre made it peculiarly distinct. 'Get out,' he said.

'Please understand, my lord,' said Mr Grimes, himself misunderstanding, 'this information is not meant to influence your decision in any way; but in the event that you decide to have Scunthorpe's handle the sale you personally will receive a third of our commission. It is our way of showing that we are more concerned with Art than money.' He looked pious.

'Get out,' repeated Lord Cavesson from between his teeth.

Mr Grimes stood his ground, certain of a cordial reception once his offer was wholly comprehended. 'Naturally, your family would not be advised of our agreement; the transaction would be entirely private, as between gentlemen,' he said.

' "Gentlemen!" ' repeated Lord Cavesson contemptuously. 'How dare you bandy that word about? You may inform Lord Merlin that if the manuscript does go up for sale, it will most certainly not be sold by Scunthorpe's. Good day.' And he opened the door to the hall with such finality that the imperturbable Mr Grimes, much to his own surprise, shortly found himself on the doorstep, facing Great Court.

8 *Inquiries*

It had been decided by the two inspectors that it would be best to search Mr Garmoyle's house first, as they had ascertained from Dr Shebbeare that the search in College during the morning had been a thorough one; therefore they elected to run a fresh scent. The house itself was unexceptional, a moderate-sized bungalow on Cranmer Road. Mrs Garmoyle, however, was distinctly the opposite: she was slender, of medium height and ash-blond. Her attraction was definite but muted, as though grief or some other emotion (fear, perhaps?) had cast a veil over her features. Inspector Bunce unabashedly watched her and Austrey together to see if he could obtain corroboration of the gossip retailed to him by Grubb, but beyond a certain grave courtesy on Austrey's part, an attitude which might be expected toward a recently bereaved widow, he could discern nothing.

With Mrs Garmoyle's permission they explored the house from top to bottom, but nothing remotely resembling the Shakespeare manuscript emerged as a result of their efforts. The search did not take long — most of Garmoyle's working books were in College and the house, except for some feminine gear in Mrs Garmoyle's bedroom, was as neat and as bare as an hotel suite — it did not seem to have been a home in the classic sense for either of them.

When the police had finished, they thanked Mrs Garmoyle and repaired to the Prye Library to see if a second cast might not turn up the manuscript there. But after several hours of concentrated examination of the bookcases, Bunce was forced to admit that the search conducted earlier by Dr Shebbeare and his followers had indeed been thorough. Pocklington rapidly wearied of these mundane pursuits and wandered off to ring up the Yard, as a means of indicating his importance to the world at large. This was a relief to Bunce, who found his presence somewhat inhibiting. Pocklington maintained a constant air of disapproval over the provincial methods of the Cambridge police, but though Bunce at this point was anxious for help of any sort, Pocklington seemed unable to furnish constructive suggestions. He sneered discreetly at Bunce's attempts to solve both murder and theft, but that was as far as he was inclined to go. He seemed to regard himself as an overseer licensed only to criticize; and to consider that his other duties consisted primarily of engaging Lord Cavesson, Dr Shebbeare and any other persons of consequence in conversations designed to impress them with his own superiority.

The search of Garmoyle's rooms in College produced the same discouraging lack of results. At the end of it Bunce asked, 'Is there no other place where the manuscript might possibly be, Mr Austrey?'

'No legitimate place,' Austrey replied emphatically.

'Then I suppose we must assume that it has been stolen,' said Bunce. 'Would it be difficult for a thief to get hold of a key to the Prye Library?'

'I should ask the Porter,' Austrey answered. 'There are to my knowledge only two keys: the one held by Garmoyle as Librarian —'

'That was still on his keychain; in fact it's the one I'm using now,' Bunce interposed.

'— and the one kept in the Porter's Lodge; I used that at the times when Garmoyle was not in the Library and I wished to work on the Shakespeare poem.'

'Hasn't the Master keys to the buildings at Sheepshanks?'

'I believe he has — in fact, I've seen them. They're a set of master keys — a great bunch of them on an iron ring. I understand that he keeps them locked up and only uses them in emergencies when another key isn't available. He used the Porter's key this morning.'

'Isn't the Porter's Lodge rather an insecure place to keep keys?' asked Bunce.

'Not really; it may seem that way, but there is always a Porter on duty, and he would not dream of giving a key to an unauthorised person,' Austrey replied.

'I see — so unless someone was able temporarily to borrow and copy Dr Shebbeare's or Mr Garmoyle's key, which seems improbable, the only way to get into the Prye Library without jemmying the lock or climbing in the window (which they didn't — we checked for that) would be to take the Porter's key.'

'That's right; but if anyone actually did so, he must have returned it, since it was there this morning,' said Austrey, 'and he would have had to take the key without the Porter's knowledge.'

'I suppose,' Bunce said, 'the thief might have borrowed the key to the Prye Library by breaking into the Porter's Lodge at night. Or he may have access to one of the keys that open the Lodge — do you know who holds those?'

'That would be impossible,' replied Austrey. 'There is a Porter on duty all night. The College gates are locked at midnight, you see, so that anyone wishing entry after twelve except the Fellows, who have their own keys, must call the Porter to let him in. Undergraduates are supposed to be in College by midnight unless they have special permission to stay out later, so any who may be illegally at large after that hour often resort to less orthodox means of regaining their rooms; if the Porter sees them climbing over the wall he is to report it.'

'So there is always someone in the Porter's Lodge,' said Bunce. 'Well, that's one possibility gone.'

'Yes, though the man on duty then generally catnaps through the night. But I should think he would waken quickly enough if he heard anyone enter.'

'I think,' Bunce said, 'that I had better speak to the Porter and check the Lodge for signs of illegal entry, just to be on the safe side.'

They walked across Great Court with two large constables trailing somewhat disconsolately behind, like bloodhounds who have lost the trail, to the Porter's Lodge just inside the Great Gate of Sheepshanks. There Bunce dismissed his assistants to check the windows and door for indications of having been forced while he proceeded, with Austrey for company, to question the Porter on duty. Hobbs was highly indignant at the suggestion that it might be possible for someone to have borrowed the key to the Prye Library without his knowledge.

'Anybody wot oughtn't to, get hold of one of them keys? I should think not,' he said virtuously. 'Why, as you can plainly see, sir, they are 'anging right there at the back of the Lodge so that any individual wishful to abstract one would have Me to deal with before doing so,' and his manner implied that any person so lost to all moral sense would find him ready to defend to the death the key in question.

'I don't necessarily mean someone you don't know. Are there no occasions when one of the members of the College mightn't enter the Porter's Lodge?' Bunce asked.

'You have undoubtedly noticed that there are no telephones in the Fellows' rooms; when we are in College we generally use the one in the Combination Room, but if one of us is on his way out of the main gate it's easiest to use this one. Mr Hobbs very kindly allows the Fellows to do so when they are in a hurry,' interposed Austrey.

'Natcherly I didn't think you was referring to one of the Gentlemen,' said Mr Hobbs with dignity. 'I would expect *them* to be Above Reproach, *even* to the police,' and he fixed poor Bunce with a fishy stare that clearly indicated his opinion of a man who would make that sort of mistake.

'It is my Duty to explore all possibilities,' replied Bunce, thinking, Good lord! now he's got me talking in upper-case, too. 'No one is accusing any of the Fellows simply because they had access to the key. What about the undergraduates?'

This assurance slightly mollified Mr Hobbs, who answered scornfully, 'Them young scallawags! Think I'd let 'em come clambering around here like a parcel of monkeys? Not that they don't try. It's always, "Mr 'Obbs, I 'ave to ring up 'ome; Mr 'Obbs, I got to call my Mum and I'll reverse the charges." Mum in a pig's eye! More likely it's a girl in London and if I turn my back for a second the next thing you know I've a call with extra charges on the bill and no one owning up to it. Make no mistake, Inspector, if one of them limbs had been in 'ere I'd of knowed it.'

'What about the man who comes on duty in the evenings?' Bunce asked.

'Joe and I take turns at night duty — he feels the same as me about the little weasels. You can check with 'im, but if he's let any of 'em in I shall be very much surprised.'

'Does he sleep soundly, do you know?' asked Bunce. 'If someone were to enter during the night, would he be likely to hear him?'

'Well, I must confess he does fancy his drop of an evening, which sometimes makes him a bit owrkard to rouse, but 'ow could anyone get in for him to 'ear when 'e locks 'isself in so as not to be disturbed?' replied the practical Mr Hobbs. 'There's only one Lodge key — barring the Master's — and I gives it to Joe when he comes and 'e gives it to the morning man when he leaves, so as to make it possible for 'im to lock up in case of an emergency.'

As if to hammer home the unwelcome fact, the constables reappeared to report that they could detect no signs of breaking and entering. Frustrated, Bunce went outside to double-check their investigation, but was as unsuccessful as they in finding anything of significance. Before he left he took down the names and addresses of Joe and the morning porter in order to check whether they had admitted anyone to the Porter's Lodge, but he doubted it would produce results.

At this juncture Fenchurch was to be seen walking briskly across the grass towards the Porter's Lodge. 'Ah, there you are,' he said, tossing back his thatch of snowy hair, 'I thought I should still find you here. Inspector, Lord Cavesson has had a rather odd visitor, and as I was on my way to my rooms I volunteered to see if you had left.' He told them of the appearance of Mr Grimes. 'Directly the man had gone, Lord Cavesson consulted the Master and myself,' Fenchurch concluded, 'and we advised him to let you know at once. We cannot imagine that the man has had anything to do with the disappearance of the manuscript — if he had, he would scarcely have called on Lord Cavesson — but it is decidedly queer that he should have turned up at just this moment.' He tilted his head to look quizzically at Bunce.

'If Scunthorpe's have found out about the Shakespeare manuscript, it could be an indication that others are on the trail as well,' said Austrey. 'We have all done our best to keep the matter quiet, but it is obvious that the news has leaked somehow.'

'Yes,' agreed Fenchurch. He said to Bunce, 'We had hoped not to announce the discovery until after the decision as to the manuscript's disposal had been made — I cannot imagine how word could have got out. The Master felt that it would be far better if Lord Cavesson were able to come to a decision without the pressures of publicity. Lord Cavesson has told no one at all; nor, I feel certain, have any of the Fellows. But even if a dealer less scrupulous than Scunthorpe's has got wind of the manuscript somehow, what use would it be to him to steal it?'

'Some time ago Mr Austrey mentioned collectors who are willing to buy stolen property — if one of them bought it from the thief, would you be able to swear it was the manuscript that was here?' asked Bunce.

'Of course,' Austrey answered positively. 'Any of us could identify it, and I know most of it backwards and forwards. There's no question but that it would be recognized — it is, after all, unique.'

'Have any photographs been taken of it since it was found?'

'No,' said Austrey.

'So proof of ownership would depend on your word and that of your colleagues — a handful of men in all. It might be impossible to sell it in Europe or the States, but a not too particular private collector in, say, South America or the Near East might be willing to take a chance that the Cavesson family and Sheepshanks wouldn't be able to prove ownership to the satisfaction of his country's police — that is, providing they found out he had it in the first place.'

'In that case, Japan might well be a possibility,' Austrey mused. 'The Japanese are strangely fond of Shakespeare and Chaucer; each term we have a couple of their scholars in residence here to study Middle English and Elizabethan literature — a curious taste on their part, I've always felt. I suppose the thief might find a market for the manuscript there at the rate Japanese industrialists have been buying up our Renoirs and racehorses recently.'

'Even Japan, despite her ties with the West, might be reluctant to repatriate the manuscript if the buyer was very highly placed and claimed he had bought it in good faith,' Bunce agreed. 'You see, you've all kept the matter in the family, so to speak, so far, and a purchaser could claim that he had had no idea the poem was stolen when he bought it.'

'But assuming the thief is a dealer in literary curiosities who had got wind of a prize for the taking,' said Fenchurch, 'where did this hypothetical dealer (and, for that matter, the unhypothetical Mr Grimes and his mentor, Lord Merlin) get his information? No one knew about the *Cupid and Psyche* but Lord Cavesson, the Master and Fellows of Sheepshanks, and the Director and the Keeper of Manuscripts of the British Museum, whom I feel certain you will agree are above suspicion in this matter. It seems then that it must have been one of us who revealed the information to an outsider — that is what Lord Cavesson thought when he was first approached by Lord Merlin. At that time, however, he saw no point in upsetting the Master by mentioning it to him.'

'Unless,' said Bunce, 'one of the College servants . . .'

'Impossible!' Fenchurch snapped. 'The only one who might conceivably have overheard us discuss the matter is Bottom, and I should trust him implicitly — it would be more likely that one of us was indiscreet in mentioning it than that he would betray the College by selling information. As for the possibility of *his* being indiscreet — well, he would not have lasted as butler for forty-odd years if there were any likelihood of that.'

Austrey agreed. 'Well, then,' said the Inspector, 'couldn't one of you gentlemen (present company excepted, of course) have let drop an injudicious word or so? Mr Garmoyle, for instance — he was known to take a drop too many at times, and he was married. Could Mrs Garmoyle —' He was stopped short by the look on Austrey's face.

'Helen — Mrs Garmoyle — would never do such a thing,' said Austrey indignantly. 'And Garmoyle was much too professional, even in his cups, to tell her anything about it,' he added hastily.

So I *have* got your number, my boy, thought Bunce, well-satisfied by the results of his little foray. And it's Helen, is it? There's no denying she has something, though her face may not be up to launching a thousand ships (the Inspector rather fancied a spot of poetry in his evenings at home) — at any rate Austrey's got it pretty bad.

'I fear the situation may be even graver than we think,' Fenchurch said. 'If it were only a matter of disclosing information, it might have been done inadvertently, in all innocence, by one of the Fellows. But have you thought that if the Shakespeare manuscript is stolen, as it appears to be, it must almost certainly have been taken with felonious intent by one of us, if the Porter's testimony is to be believed?'

There was a stunned silence. Even Bunce had not yet taken this premise to its logical conclusion; up to this moment the sinister Mr Grimes had exclusively occupied his thoughts.

'I cannot believe,' Austrey said, 'that any of our number would be capable of such an action.'

'Yet the facts undeniably point in that direction,' replied Fenchurch.

'I cannot,' said the Master, 'believe that one of the Fellows of Sheepshanks would be capable of so reprehensible a deed.' He paused. 'Unless — yes, it might be . . . have you questioned Mr Grubb?'

'Oh, surely not,' Austrey protested. 'There's no denying that he's a rude, raw boy — I must confess I don't much care for him — but I'm certain he would not do such an ungrateful and dishonest thing.'

'In any case, I am not certain he possesses the nerve for it,' said Fenchurch. 'He has the malice, perhaps, but I think he would be too frightened to carry out the theft. He propounds his Socialist theories to anyone who will listen, but in fact, if you have noticed, he is surprisingly cautious in everything but speech. I think he is a little afraid of us.'

'It could not be any of the other Fellows,' declared Dr Shebbeare. 'Loyalty to Sheepshanks, if nothing else, would prevent them. But I do not see any other way a key could have been procured; I have checked my set, which is safely locked up in my desk where I left it, and I always carry the desk key in my pocket.' His usually bland physiognomy showed signs of great stress. Lord Cavesson answered soothingly, 'There can be no question of one of the Fellows doing such a thing, Master. Perhaps the Porter's Lodge was broken into late at night while the Porter was asleep and the key borrowed then.'

Dr Shebbeare brightened visibly. 'Of course, of course; a brilliant idea. How foolish of none of us to think of that before. I expect that's exactly what happened, eh, Inspector?'

'I'm very sorry to have to say so, sir,' Bunce replied, 'but I had thought of that, and I checked the Lodge for signs of illegal entry. There are none that I can see, and it shuts up tight as a drum, so unless one of the Porters. . .' he paused delicately.

The Master was outraged. 'That,' he said with finality, 'is impossible. All three have been employed by the College for nearly thirty years, and I would vouch for their honesty as I would my own.'

'Is there no way the lock of the Prye Library might have been opened without one of the College keys?' Fenchurch asked. 'With a skeleton key, perhaps, since we seem to be dealing with international thieves of resource, or by picking the lock?'

Bunce shook his head. 'You can't use a skeleton key with that sort of lock, and if it had been picked there would be scratches on the wards. No, I'm afraid that if you refuse to consider any of the Porters as possible suspects, the field is pretty well narrowed down to the Fellows.'

'In that case,' Dr Shebbeare said, 'I have no recourse but to apprise them of the situation.'

9 *In the Combination Room*

After dinner that evening the Fellows of Sheepshanks were convened for an extraordinary meeting in the Combination Room. Lord Cavesson, although intimately concerned, had with his usual tact elected to absent himself; but all the Fellows were there. Mutton, gazing about him with his customary vagueness, was ensconced in a corner. Professor Tempeste was engaged in declaiming upon a new chemical discovery to Peascod, who appeared not to be listening. Grubb and Crippen, as the youngest of the dons, had been left to themselves and were attempting to make the best of it. Fenchurch and Austrey, the only two present besides the Master with knowledge of the reason for the meeting, had unconsciously withdrawn a little from the others, despite Smythson's efforts to draw Fenchurch into conversation. He was delivering a monologue on librarianship, a dull enough subject at any time and all the more so now, as the atmosphere of the room was crackling with repressed curiosity. It was not surprising that most of those present expected to hear news of Garmoyle's murder; and there was a slight lessening of tension in the expectation that Dr Shebbeare was about to announce the discovery and arrest of the murderer by the police.

After several moments the Master entered the room and they all fell silent. 'I have,' he said heavily, 'a deeply shocking circumstance to relate to you. The Shakespeare manuscript of *Cupid and Psyche* has disappeared from its place in the Prye Library. We— Mr Austrey, Mr Fenchurch and I— have made a thorough search, as have the police, and it is not to be found. If any of you can inform me of its whereabouts, I beg you to do so at once; I need not emphasize the gravity of the situation. Aside from the great value of the document, it was lent to Sheepshanks in trust by the Cavesson family and we are responsible for its safety. As an almost priceless object, its loss is disastrous; as a scholarly resource, its loss is incalculable. Although Mr Austrey has been editing the manuscript, he has not yet completely transcribed it.

'The circumstance which weighs most upon my mind, however, is one which you will all feel with me.' And he went on, with obvious distress, to tell them of the series of conclusions which had led the police to decide that one of the Fellows must be involved in the theft of the manuscript.

There was a low horrified buzz in the Combination Room. Though academics are not infrequently accused of plagiarism, the question of a more corporal sort of theft rarely arises among them. Reaction varied from disbelief to indignation. Professor Tempeste was one of those who responded in the latter mode; he snorted and sputtered in such an alarming fashion that several of the Fellows half expected him to have a seizure upon the spot. When the first wave of reaction had passed, Dr Shebbeare raised his hand for silence. 'I need hardly tell you that I have as perfect confidence in the integrity of all of you as I have in my own.' There was a muffled snort from Grubb, and the Master stared at him with distaste. 'I do not for one moment believe that any of you would so far have forgotten honour as to be connected in any way with a plot to purloin the Shakespeare manuscript, but I felt that I must acquaint you with the suspicions of the police. If you have seen anything of a dubious nature in the environs of Sheepshanks during the past few weeks, I ask you to inform me of it, for it may prove a means of apprehending the real criminal.'

The Fellows left the room in small knots, talking animatedly as they went. Two remained behind, Mutton and Smythson. For one so insubstantial, Mutton could be surprisingly quick when he wished, for he deftly shot out of his corner and cut in front of Smythson just as his colleague was in the act of opening his mouth to utter.

'Master, may I speak with you for a moment?' Mutton inquired. 'In private,' he added with a pointed glance at Smythson, who had perforce to withdraw, though with an ill grace.

When they were alone Mutton said to Dr Shebbeare, 'I- i- it distresses me to have to speak to you, but I feel that I must, in order to clarify matters. Perhaps you did not know that I am a distant relation of Lord Cavesson.'

'I must confess I did not,' replied Dr Shebbeare, surprised.

'The tenth earl of Cavesson married one of the Moutons (the French branch of the family, you know, who came over at the invitation of their cousins, the d'Ewes of Little Shearing, at the time of the unfortunate Revolution); and the great-great-aunt of the present Lord Cavesson was the wife of the Reverend Septimus Wooll, who later took his mother's maiden surname and became Mutton-Wooll: he was my grandfather, so there is a double relationship. My father later dropped the hyphenation,' Mutton explained simply.

'I see,' said Dr Shebbeare, who did not see at all. The realm of higher mathematics, in which he dealt academically, was clarity itself to him; even Bottom's accounts for the wine-cellar, which might have perplexed a Newton, were not beyond his powers; but he found the ramifications of Mutton's genealogy distinctly confusing.

'Lord Cavesson and I were not acquainted before he came here; indeed, I do not believe he realizes that we are related, as it is a very distant connexion, and I did not like to put myself forward when we met by reminding him of it. But you see that the relationship puts me in an equivocal position, for I should be one of those who would benefit from the sale of the Shakespeare manuscript. I have been awaiting a suitable opportunity to inform you and Lord Cavesson that I have a conflict of interest in the matter and therefore feel that I must withdraw from the decision-making. I wish to make it clear to you that I told n-no one of its discovery, n-n-nor did I remove it in order to sh- show it to a dealer.' He was growing more agitated as he spoke, and his head shook slightly. 'But it did occur to me that if the police should learn of the relationship they might think that I had temporarily — er — "borrowed" the poem for a day or so with the intention of showing it to someone versed in the art of selling such things.'

'My dear fellow,' protested Dr Shebbeare, 'it is inconceivable that you would be suspected of such conduct.'

'Of course I did not touch the manuscript, but I could not

blame the police for putting such a construction on the facts when they discover them, and so I thought it best to make a clean breast to you at once. I understand that if the manuscript were sold it would be a matter of a great deal of money.'

'But my dear Mutton — forgive my mention of a painful subject, but surely it would be obvious to the police that the income you derive from that book of yours would in any case make you immune to temptation of that sort.'

'The income from my biography of Catherine the Great,' replied Mutton with a shudder of repugnance, 'is sent each year by my solicitor to a deserving charity: this year it is the Fund for Distressed and Homeless Donkeys. I felt I had no right to touch tainted money; and living in College, my wants are few.'

'Quite right, quite right,' Dr Shebbeare answered heartily, 'and all the more reason why you would have nothing to do with the purloining of the Shakespeare manuscript.'

'But I am not at all certain the police would view matters as we do, so I should be grateful, Master, if you would notify them directly of my connexion with the manuscript; or perhaps you feel that I should ring up Inspector Bunce myself?'

'I do not think that is necessary. I shall be happy to mention it to him, and I am certain you need have no fears on that account.'

They left the Combination Room together and parted company in the Court. Dr Shebbeare was returning to the Master's Lodge when a figure darted out from the cloister edging Great Court. It was Smythson.

'I say, Master, might I just have a word with you?' he said with an air of studied nonchalance.

'I do not feel, Mr Smythson, that this is a suitable moment to discuss your academic aspirations,' Dr Shebbeare said with some asperity. 'The Governing Body will consider all qualified candidates for the post of Prye Librarian at the proper time.'

'But Prye's will stipulates —'

'We have gone over this ground before, I think,' interrupted the Master impatiently. 'The Governing Body will take Prye's wishes under advisement, but I have consulted the College solicitor and he informs me that they are not binding in law.'

'Not binding in law,' repeated Smythson. His jaw dropped, but he recovered himself and said, 'In any event, Master, that is not why I wish to speak to you. The fact is that I had no idea you were under the impression that the *Cupid and Psyche* was missing.'

' "Under the impression!" ' Dr Shebbeare exclaimed. 'You don't mean you know where it is!'

An expression of unlovely self-righteousness spread across Smythson's features. 'Of course I do,' he said. 'It is in the Abbot's Library, where it belongs.'

The Master stared at him, utterly flabbergasted. Relief, incredulity, and fury warred simultaneously within him; relief won for the moment. 'If you are not perpetrating a singularly ill-timed joke, let us go at once to fetch it,' was all he said. They walked in a smouldering silence to the entrance of the Abbot's Library, which opens off the cloister of Great Court. Dr Shebbeare was digesting this new development; he had many questions to ask as well as a piece of his mind to deliver, but he felt an almost superstitious need to get the precious object within his grasp first. Smythson wore a look of defiant bravado; it was clear that he intended to brazen out what promised to be a very sticky situation.

Neither spoke a word until they were in the Abbot's Library, a long room which Sir Oliver Sheepshanks had incongruously (considering the exterior architecture of the place) chosen to furnish in Strawberry Hill Gothic. The setting sun threw shafts of light at intervals through leaded windows across the bays, picking out here a row of books, there a crocketed and pointed arch carved in the panelling. Smythson approached one of the bookcases (which had glazed doors but no locks) and removed a small, unprepossessing volume from a shelf. It was quarto-sized and bound in rather scuffed brown calf; there was no ornament to speak of on the covers, but on the back was unevenly stamped in peeling gilt 'SERMONS'. To the untutored eye it exactly resembled at least five others on the same shelf. With hands that trembled the Master took it and opened the cover. On the inner side was a bookplate with the arms of Huntingfield: vert, a hare passant gules, scutted or. He turned the leaves carefully until, at the centre, he came to a page written in what was plainly an Elizabethan hand. It was the Shakespeare manuscript.

10 *Cupid and Psyche*

'So this is what all the fuss was about,' said Bunce in a wondering tone. He was holding in his large red hand the volume which contained *Cupid and Psyche*. It had been returned to the Prye Library for safekeeping (all the keys were now in the possession of the Master) and Bunce had expressed a wish to see it.

'That's it,' Austrey said. 'I expect it doesn't look like much to you, but it is the most astonishing thing I have ever seen.' His hands were reverent as he took the book from Bunce and opened it. 'There is little question that this is in Shakespeare's holograph; if so, it is unique. There are no other existing manuscripts known to be in his hand.' He turned a few pages at random. 'It is a poem no one knew existed, and almost certainly pre-dates *Venus and Adonis*, which was written in 1592-3. Shakespeare probably arrived in London in 1586 or 1588 — no one is certain of the exact year. It has always seemed odd to scholars that he produced nothing that was published in the five or six years before 1592. This poem helps to fill the gap — it must have been written after April 1590, for it was then that Queen Elizabeth's favourite, Robert Devereux, Earl of Essex, married Frances Walsingham, who was the widow of Sir Philip Sidney. Elizabeth of course was enraged, and the poem is a clear allusion to this incident — she is the implacable Venus of the myth. Shakespeare used the story of Psyche as an allegory for the scandal which erupted at court when the Queen found out about Essex's marriage. It is a highly indiscreet work politically, and bawdy as well, with incestuous allusions to the Venus–Cupid relationship. I should guess that he wrote it expressly for Essex, who may have circulated it privately among his friends. At any rate, it is obvious why the poem was never printed and why Shakespeare described *Venus and Adonis* as the "first heir of my invention" — he was hoping the other poem would be conveniently forgot. Actually, I suspect that the two are companion-pieces — I shouldn't be at all surprised if *Venus and Adonis* wasn't a rather naughty dig at the Queen's unrequited infatuation for Essex.

'But while all this conjecture is very entertaining,' continued Austrey, 'what makes the piece really valuable to scholars, aside from the fact that it is a previously unknown work, is that the manuscript is clearly a working copy — Shakespeare has scribbled all over it, crossing out a word here and adding a phrase in the margin there. Its worth to students of English literature is inestimable.'

Some of Austrey's enthusiasm communicated itself to Bunce, though he was slightly bewildered by all the information he had just been given. The book, which only a moment ago he had privately considered quite a scruffy little thing, he now regarded with new eyes. He took it from Austrey and gazed in perplexity at the crabbed handwriting on the open page.

'I can't make any of it out,' he said in surprise. 'What does this mean?' and he pointed to a stanza in the middle of the leaf. Austrey obediently took the book and glanced at the verse Bunce had indicated.

'Psyche has just lighted the lamp and seen her lover for the first time,' he explained, and began to read at the place designated by Bunce.

> 'Glew'd to her lampe, shee saw nor scales nor sting.
> In stead, a forme of liuing Iuorie,
> The louely boy lapped in doue plumag'd wings,
> Loue snar'd by loue, from loue no more will flee.
> His corrall pappes mockd rose buddes, those gilt lockes
> That tumbled down his necke shamed *Venus* flockes.
>
> Loues scepter that late throbbed with passions sap,
> Now meeke as a doue, nested 'twixt snowy thighs,
> Twin globes beside. . .'

'That's enough,' said the Inspector hastily, turning the colour of beetroot: the meaning of what he had just heard was not altogether clear to him, but he knew instinctively that it wasn't Nice. Austrey had not noticed the content of what he was reading: he possessed the scholar's indifference to the lubricious and was more interested in the peculiarities of the manuscript than in the indecency of the text.

'You see,' he explained, pointing at what appeared to Bunce to be the tracks of an inebriated hen, 'this was not one of the fair copies Shakespeare may have made for the Earl of Essex and his friends, but very likely the original rough draft of the poem. That, aside from the fact that the poem itself is unique, is what holds such particular interest for scholars. Do you see where he has marked through the word "dove"? Perhaps he suddenly noticed he had used it in the preceding stanza. And the metre is a bit uneven in places; I expect he smoothed that out in a later draft — assuming that he ever did finish the poem, of course.'

The Inspector was far more interested in Smythson's behaviour than in literary research. 'Dr Shebbeare told me why Mr Smythson claims he hid the book, but it doesn't make sense.'

'I think it does,' replied Austrey. 'The man is all compact of vanity, and I'm afraid none of us took his feelings sufficiently into consideration in the temporary disposal of the manuscript; or in the permanent one, for that matter. Garmoyle, as you know, came across the Shakespeare poem in the Abbot's Library whilst engaged in research there, and I daresay he was not very diplomatic in his handling of the situation. You see, of the two libraries at Sheepshanks the Pryevian Library is by far the more important. The post of Prye Librarian is traditionally filled by a scholar of international reputation, whereas the Abbot's Library is a much more local affair. Smythson has always been a trifle touchy about the difference between the two, and about his background before coming to Sheepshanks as a Fellow — for years he was with the BBC as a writer and announcer, you know, and before that he dabbled unsuccessfully in acting. It would have been more tactful of Garmoyle to consult him when he made the discovery.'

'Do you mean to say Mr Smythson didn't even know at first that the Shakespeare manuscript had been discovered?' demanded Bunce.

'Oh, dear me, no; that was the really shocking thing, don't you see, and one cannot help but sympathize a little with Smythson's grievance, bloody man though he is. Apparently Garmoyle simply gathered the volume up with his papers without a word to Smythson and walked off with it to the Prye Library, where he locked it up in one of the book-presses. Then he showed it to me in order to get my advice on its authenticity, and we took it to the Master. I did remonstrate with him over his high-handed conduct. I thought it would be kinder to bring Smythson into the affair, but Garmoyle absolutely refused.'

'Why didn't Dr Shebbeare insist on it?'

'His attitude was the same as Garmoyle's — he was not anxious to include Smythson in the matter. I think the Master may feel he made a bit of a mistake in appointing him Abbot's Librarian — he is not really an academic success.' Now that the manuscript inquiry was solved and had proved to be unconnected with murder, Austrey was permitting himself to be mildly indiscreet about some of his colleagues. I wish he'd be this frank about the things that might help, thought Bunce sourly; the flap over the Shakespeare manuscript, though an interesting sidelight on life at Sheepshanks, was, after all, immaterial to the matter at hand now that the poem had been recovered.

'I must say, however,' continued Austrey, 'no matter how much provocation he had from Garmoyle and the Master, it seems distinctly childish to hide the book in a fit of pique. As you suspected, Smythson entered the Porter's Lodge under the pretext of making a telephone call and took the key when the Porter wasn't looking, returning it in the same way. It seems he had the playful notion of embarrassing the Master and myself when we went to show it to Lord Cavesson and found it wasn't there — a joke in very poor taste due, I fear, to television influence — so vulgarizing. I suspect there may have been several other minor motives for his little jape as well: Smythson has been vociferous against a sale — he feels possession of the poem confers a certain prestige on the Abbot's Library, don't you know — and he has been quite sharp about my editing the manuscript. I suspect he may have had an idea of doing it himself, though frankly he has little background in the period.'

Austrey was too kind-hearted to say that Smythson was not in the remotest degree equipped to edit *Cupid and Psyche*. 'It was very foolish of him to hide the manuscript, and could not possibly have done him any good in the long view. But Smythson is rather apt to rush his fences, particularly when he feels he has been slighted, and I suppose he did not think of the consequences.' He was speaking now more to himself than to Bunce.

'Now that the poem has been found, it's really none of my affair, officially speaking,' said the Inspector, 'but do you think Lord Cavesson will decide to sell the manuscript?'

'I expect it will depend to some extent on the wishes of his family, but I am under the impression that if it is not sold it will be given to a larger library. Both Dr Shebbeare and I would agree with a decision of that sort. Although originally the Master would have preferred to see it kept at Sheepshanks, he has taken the larger view — the manuscript is really too valuable to keep here. The publicity once we release the news will be too great, and the responsibility both of protection and of making the poem available to scholars is beyond the limitations of the College. Then there is the legal point, to be settled with the Fellows, of what exactly constitutes a permanent loan — it would appear to be a contradiction in terms — but it would really be very short-sighted for any of us to wish to retain the manuscript.'

'I'm pleased for your sakes that the book has been found,' said Bunce, 'but I admit it's knocked all my theories into a cocked hat, I had hoped the theft would give me a lead to Mr Garmoyle's murderer.'

Austrey gave a start; in the excitement of the manuscript's recovery he had completely forgotten what many would consider the more serious crime.

'Bless my soul — of course! Poor Garmoyle,' he exclaimed, rather ashamed that he had so quickly obliterated his colleague's murder from his mind.

11 Bottom Disappears

Inspector Bunce returned to the police station on Parker's Piece no wiser about Garmoyle's murder than he had been several days earlier. As he passed through the glass doors at the entrance, he encountered Inspector Jenkins on his way out.

'Morning, Peter,' Bunce greeted him. 'Any breaks yet?'

'No such luck — it's a proper stinker, it is,' Jenkins said, making a face. 'Take my advice, lad, and don't get yourself mixed up in a sex case. There you are, sitting pretty with a nice quiet refined little murder. *You* haven't got the London dailies all breathing down your neck — oh, no,' and he shook his grizzled head like a bull tormented by flies.

'I've enough problems without the papers coming down on me. Anyway, I reckon they will soon enough when the news at Sheepshanks gets about,' said Bunce glumly, and proceeded to describe the developments in the case. He did not tell Inspector Jenkins outright about the Shakespeare manuscript, for there was no longer a possibility that it was directly linked to Garmoyle's murder, and he felt it was not his secret to tell. He alluded to it, however, in vague terms as a discovery which would bring Sheepshanks very much into the public eye when it was divulged.

'So here I am, back at square one,' he finished.

'Perhaps your killer is my rapist,' said Jenkins hopefully. 'Not that that'ud do much good, without a lead for either of us. Where's your bright boy from London? Can't he pull a rabbit out of the hat for you?' He tipped Bunce a wink; he had not taken to the precise and immaculate Pocklington.

'I haven't a clue where he is, and anyway, he's as much help as my grandmother,' Bunce replied bitterly. 'The last I saw of his lordship was yesterday afternoon when he went off to ring up the Yard— "to consult his superiors," he said, though from the way he acts you'd think his only superior was God Almighty.'

Taking his leave of Jenkins, Bunce trudged up to his office and began, for lack of anything better, to draw up a list of suspects with possible motives for Garmoyle's murder. After three-quarters of an hour he looked at his handiwork:

1. Dr Shebbeare.
   Could have killed Garmoyle for the sake of the College — has what Fenchurch describes as a 'passionate regard for the scholarly reputation of Sheepshanks.' Had argued with G. over editing of Prye diaries. Opportunity: he could have kept them all at the dinner-table intentionally in the hope that G. would start on the second port decanter.

2. Mr Austrey.
   Undoubtedly in love with Helen Garmoyle — may have chosen murder as means of obtaining her. Question: did G. mistreat his wife when drinking? Possible incitement to murder.

3. Mr Smythson.
   Could resentment as a result of being ignored in the affair of the Shakespeare ms. be a motive? Flimsy, even taking academic vanity into account.

4. Mr Crippen.
   Wounded feelings over G.'s insults? Very unlikely.

5. Mr Mutton.
   Possibly fed up with G.'s gibes about his book — again unlikely. But what if G. were against selling ms.? Mutton told the Master he did not want money from sale, but he could be lying. No one has mentioned Garmoyle's position (if any) on sale — try to find out.

6. Mr Fenchurch and

7. Mr Peascod. (After much cogitation and pencil-licking the Inspector put down:)
   No known motive.

8. Professor Tempeste.
Only possible motive seems to be hatred of alcoholics — it's a bit far-fetched to think he poisoned G. out of disapproval of his drinking, though by all accounts he's slightly dotty on that one subject.

9. Mr Grubb.
Probably wouldn't mind sticking a knife into any of them, but why would he single out G.? Unless G.'s viper tongue drove him too far — seems far-fetched. Though there was something in my conversation with him . . . see if there is anything in it.

Bunce contemplated this list with dissatisfaction. Suspects with no motive, suspects with slight motive — no one with a good solid reason for killing Garmoyle except possibly Austrey. As the Inspector quite liked Austrey, this aspect of the case made him feel depressed. On the other hand, he reflected, brightening, they're an exceedingly odd lot, so perhaps what seems a weak motive to me wouldn't be to them. Professor Tempeste, for instance — could he be so obsessed by the subject of drink that he would be willing to commit murder in order to remove this blot on the escutcheon of Sheepshanks? Or the Master — could his concern for scholarly reputation have got so out of hand that he would kill to preserve it? He seems to have spent a longer time than usual at table that night, though it could simply have been because Lord Cavesson was there. I can't imagine anyone sane killing someone for either reason, but it's possible none of 'em are altogether sane on certain subjects. Even Mr Fenchurch and Mr Austrey, who seem to have good sense about most things, get an odd look in their eyes when they start talking about things like architecture and mildewed old manuscripts.

This line was leading Bunce nowhere, so he decided to approach the problem from another direction. What about the College servants? he thought to himself. No, that's no good — I've gone over it all before. There is really no suggestion that any of them could be involved, aside from the availability of the port decanter. The only thing in that direction that might provide a fresh lead would be to interview Bottom — Wednesday is his day off and he left Sheepshanks Tuesday night after dinner, before it was realized that Garmoyle had been poisoned. Bottom must have returned to College yesterday morning; in the excitement over the loss of the manuscript I forgot to speak to him — I'll do it now.

Upon concluding this interior monologue, Bunce rose decisively from his desk — here at last was something he could do. At that moment the telephone rang and he answered it. 'Good morning, Inspector,' the orotund tones of Dr Shebbeare sounded in his ear. 'I am most alarmed; our butler, Bottom, has not returned from his day's leave. I was not cognizant of the fact until last night at dinner, and I hesitated to disturb you at that hour, but it is most unlike him; he is entirely dependable and has been so for forty years. I hope he has not met with foul play.'

'Do you know where he customarily spends his free time?' asked Bunce.

'I have inquired of the College servants and none of them has any idea, except that it is in a village on the outskirts of Cambridge.'

'That's a great help,' Bunce said sourly; still, he felt slightly more cheerful as he rang off. He had thought himself out; now he wanted action. If necessary he would knock on the door of every cottage in every village surrounding Cambridge until he unearthed the elusive Bottom. His attention had been deflected from the College butler by the abortive clue of the manuscript, but he now saw that it was imperative to speak with the man. As Bunce left his office Pocklington rounded the corner, nearly bumping into him.

'Ah! there you are. I have acquired information which has a great bearing on the case,' he said importantly, and launched at once into a description of his movements after he had left Bunce the day before. It seemed that he had spent most of his time during the previous twenty-four hours making and receiving London calls. 'The results of these are conclusive, I believe,' he said smugly, without giving Bunce an opportunity to speak. 'All the major auction houses and book-dealers were checked for a contact with anyone connected with the Shakespeare manuscript. Maule's admit they had a man over in Suffolk on the Tuesday and Wednesday who supposedly was appraising the contents of a country house near Saffron Walden. Now I reckon it would have been quite simple for him to nip over to Cambridge on one of those days — he had a car — and make contact with an accomplice at Sheepshanks. It's certain the manuscript has left Cambridge, and equally certain one of the Fellows must be in on the theft and very likely Garmoyle's murder as well. Personally I'd put my money on Fenchurch; he has admitted going up to London lately — to visit the British Museum Reading Room, he *claims*. But it could have been any one of them; I'll wager most of the Fellows have been in town recently.'

During this speech Bunce had been opening and shutting his mouth in a fruitless attempt to speak, like the Frog Footman in *Alice*. At last Pocklington, looking supremely pleased with himself, temporarily subsided and he was able to get in a word.

'That's no good,' he said, 'the book's been found.'

'What?' said Pocklington, infuriated. His face reddened and swelled dangerously at the prospect of his ethereal edifice tumbling to the ground. 'I don't believe it.'

'It's true,' answered Bunce. 'It was all a mistake — the manuscript was at Sheepshanks all the time. I tried to reach you at your hotel to let you know but you weren't in. Didn't they give you my message?'

'I dined and spent the night with friends in Huntingdon,' Pocklington said. He was so crestfallen at the demise of his beautiful theory that he had slightly deflated, like a balloon out of which some of the air has been let; even his clothes seemed a little larger than usual. Bunce took advantage of his unusually speechless condition to relate the history of the missing manuscript. 'So we're back to investigating just the murder again,' he finished. 'I've drawn up a list of the chief suspects — why don't you have a look at it while I try to find the butler?'

Pocklington was still so taken aback by the proofs of his fallibility that he allowed himself to be steered into Bunce's office without a murmur as Bunce put the list into his colleague's hands and gratefully made his escape.

12 Reappearance of a Rapist

'... There the shadowed waters fresh
Lean up to embrace the naked flesh.'
Rupert Brooke, *The Old Vicarage, Grantchester*

The willows rustled companionably against one another in the light summer breeze; where they drooped down to meet the river small circular ripples appeared on the smooth surface of the water. Larger ripples were evident in the centre of the pool where Dame Hermione Playfair was disporting herself, though *disporting* may be perhaps too frivolous a word for the sort of aquatic exercise in which she was engaged. Her imposing figure in its regulation black tank suit bore a certain resemblance to one of the smaller species of whale, an impression reinforced by her agility in the native cetacean element.

Dame Hermione Playfair, M.A., PhD, Cantab.; D.B.E.; Mistress of Lady Margaret Hall, was a lady of heroic proportions. The possessor of a formidable intellect, she advocated cultivation of the body as well as the mind: her favourite axiom was '*Mens sana in corpore sano.*' Lady Margaret customarily led the women's Colleges in sporting activities, and those girls seeking entry to its halls who were not athletically as well as academically inclined were gently steered to Girton or Newnham. As an undergraduate Dame Hermione's prowess on the distaff playing-fields of Cambridge had been legendary, as noted in its way as were her scholarly laurels.

It was her invariable custom, weather notwithstanding, to take her exercise in a small pool formed by a backwater of the Granta. Here in the warmer days of summer young women from the Colleges sometimes came to cool themselves off with a swim after sunning on its banks. But Dame Hermione was made of sterner stuff — rain or shine, snow or hail, she plunged daily into the river for her morning laps. Cold snaps did not deter her;

when the temperature sank below the freezing point she merely took the precaution of carrying a small axe with which to break any ice that might have formed during the night on the water's surface.

Though the morning was warm and grass-scented, Dame Hermione had the pool to herself. She did not linger over her bathing, for she intended to look in later on the Bumps, the annual Cambridge rowing competition which was taking place that week, and she had much to deal with in the matter of College business before indulging in further relaxation. She ended her exertions, as was her habit, with a strong backstroke and climbed up the bank where a towel and her clothing awaited her. Swathed in the towel as she briskly dried herself, Dame Hermione presented an indeterminate figure, like Shakespeare's mobled queen; and so it was that the equally muffled shape creeping unnoticed through the bushes did not pause to take counsel with himself. Had his eyes been able to pierce her enveloping veil (supplied by the linen-closet of Lady Margaret Hall) to the ominously well-muscled frame which it concealed, he might have reconsidered his projected attempt. Impressive though the lady's physical dimensions were in many ways, they were less calculated to inspire lust than a healthy respect; *Junoesque* as applied to Dame Hermione was something of an understatement. But as every exotic dancer worth her salt knows, it is the unknown which inflames; and so the masked form, wrapped in a black gown and with a pair of ladies' open-toed gilt bedroom slippers slung about his neck on a cord, inched closer to his unwitting prey.

Dame Hermione, with her back to the intruder, was engrossed in thoughts of College affairs and did not hear the cracking of twigs until the last second. She turned at the sound just as the man leapt at her; thus instead of being brought down with her face to the ground, she encountered him *vis-à-vis*. It is possible that her assailant was startled to find himself confronted with the face, not of another Philomela Partridge but of the sterner sort of Roman matron, though the stocking which flattened his face into the nightmarish semblance of a frog obliterated all signs of his reaction. The lady was not so hampered. An expression of distaste spread over her decisively modelled features — the brain famous for its lightning calculations in algebraic function scarcely needed so crude an indication of the apparition's intentions as the concealing mask he wore to fathom his purpose. Swiftly she disengaged herself from the recumbent would-be rapist, who lay sprawled as if stunned by exposure to her face; as she rose she gathered her towel about her with a regal gesture, like an outraged goddess.

'My good man,' said Dame Hermione with the icy disdain that had sent hapless undergraduates reeling from tutorial, 'I want no part of you.' Seeing her attacker still *hors de combat*, she advanced upon him, adding sternly, 'You, sir, are a disgrace to the University. I have read of your exploits in the newspapers, and a more dishonourable, ungentlemanly, un-English course of conduct would be difficult to imagine.' The rapist by this time had risen to his feet and was nervously retreating before the brawny forearm which she brandished to emphasize her point. 'A regimen of exercise and cold baths is what you want — running, rowing, field sports — healthy occupation that will exhaust your body and take your mind off unworthy thoughts,' she declared with enthusiasm as she moved her hobbyhorse into its stride. 'Hot baths are highly pernicious; they encourage laxness and are detrimental to proper thinking.' Her eyes fell upon the gown he was wearing and, incensed, she seized it. 'Take off that gown at once! It is an insult to the University for it to be worn in such pursuits. And an M.A. gown! You, sir, are old enough to know better. Take it off, I say!'

The rapist, shaking off his horrified lethargy, pulled away from her and began to run in an attempt to escape from this unexpected victim-turned-Fury. Too late he saw that he was on the brink of the pool. There was a moment of suspense while he tottered on the edge of the bank; then a splash indicated that suspense was over.

At that instant the bushes parted, revealing an elderly Pan in plus-fours, sandals and an antiquated sweater. 'My dear lady,' said Fenchurch, who had been taking his morning walk when he heard sounds of strife in the distance, 'is anything the matter?'

'Mr Fenchurch! I am delighted to see you,' replied Dame Hermione with aplomb. 'You are just in time to assist me to apprehend this man and escort him to the police station. This is most fortunate. My stockings, I think, will do duty as fetters.' And indeed those garments, being made of uncompromisingly sensible lisle, seemed fully sturdy enough to bind the prisoner. But while she greeted Fenchurch the rapist had taken this opportunity to ease himself quietly out of the pool. Fenchurch, looking in the direction indicated, caught only a glimpse of sodden black and a pale flash, as the fleeing figure glanced over its shoulder; apparently the wet stocking had proved suffocating, for he had pulled it off as he ran and it was dangling from his hand.

'The fellow's escaping!' exclaimed Fenchurch, and took off after him. 'Hi! stop!' he cried. But he was too late; the rapist had too long a head start for a pursuer to catch him up. Thus balked of his object, Fenchurch returned to the lady. 'My dear Dame Hermione,' he said solicitously, 'I trust you are unharmed.'

'You need not worry on my account — a weedy creature,' she replied with contempt. 'I told him he wanted building-up. If that is the sort of student the men's Colleges are admitting nowadays, they will come to regret it. At any rate, it is a burden off my mind,' added the redoubtable Dame. 'The defensive squadron I have organized will have no trouble in coping with *him* should he attempt to breach the walls of Lady Margaret. My girls are all in splendid shape; constant callisthenics are the answer — daily exercise the only way. I understand that you too are an exponent of *mens sana in corpore sano*,' she added, a shade of approval entering her voice.

'Ὑγίεια καί νοῦς ἐσθλὰ τῷ βίῳ δύο,* in the words of Menander,' answered Fenchurch gravely as Dame Hermione wrapped herself once more in the towelling, and they began to walk back to Cambridge together.

---

*'Health and intellect are the two blessing of life.' *Monostikhoi*, No. 15; the translation is supplied for those who, like the author, have been deprived of the benefits of a classical education.

13 Mrs Moffat

A very dusty police car pulled into the car-park of the Rope and Bucket, the solitary public-house in Cramwell. Bunce, who had already investigated fourteen villages that afternoon as possible hiding-places for Bottom, regarded the fifteenth with disfavour. Cramwell, a village situated between Cambridge and Huntingdon, is scarcely a contender for the Best-Kept Village award; in fact, compared to most of its neighbours it might with precision be termed squalid. The Rope and Bucket has an unkempt air, as have the dingy grey stone shops and houses on the High Street. Their woodwork is weatherbeaten and peeling, the roses straggling in postage-stamp front gardens have a neglected look as though it were hardly worth their while to bloom, the curtains flapping in slovenly fashion at the grimy windows are a dusty yellowish-grey. The appearance of the inhabitants of Cramwell is not much better than their dwellings. Lacklustre housewives shuffle up the street to the shop-cum-post office at the corner; the very hair-curlers which coyly peer from underneath cotton kerchiefs are a particularly repellent shade of pink.

But despite its unlovely aspect, Cramwell does have one attraction of sorts. Set in the centre of the High Street across from the parish church is a well: not a picturesque well, nor a well of any great depth or architectural interest, nor even a working well — just a well indistinguishable from many encountered in rural farmyards, except that it has gone dry. But this unprepossessing object is reputed to have one virtue: it is said that if one anxious to excel at his examinations throws silver into its depths, he will achieve his wish. It is proof of the continuing hold of superstition in this supposedly rational age that each spring brings hordes of Cambridge undergraduates (ostensibly come to Cramwell to view the church, a mediocre example of Gothic Revival which replaced a Norman oratory), and at this time showers of silver coins surreptitiously descend into the opening. The moneys thus collected are periodically fished out by the sexton and used for the church's upkeep, though it has been rumoured that several villagers are not above doing a little dredging on their own account on a dark night.

The chief appeal of Cramwell for academics lies in its interest for etymologists, as the puzzle of its name has yet to be solved. Some scholars declare that it is a contraction of Cranmer's Well and attempt to substantiate this theory by pointing to the local legend that Archbishop Cranmer, while a Fellow of Jesus, had the well dug in order to supply his College with uncontaminated water during an outbreak of the plague, since it was thought the wells in Cambridge were infected with the contagion. Other scholars of equal eminence, however, claim that until the Restoration the name of the village was Cromwell, at which time it was hastily altered to something more acceptable.

As they emerged from the car Bunce and the constable serving as his driver gazed with mutual distaste upon the scene before them. A mangy cat, engaged in a perfunctory and haphazard cleansing in the doorway of the pub, grudgingly moved aside to permit them to enter. Within, a slatternly barmaid was half-heartedly wiping the bar with a grimy cloth. Despite the unwelcoming look of the interior the constable looked wistfully at the beer mugs ranged on the shelves while Bunce questioned her, for it had been a long and strenuous day. The Inspector received only adenoidal breathing and a vacant stare in answer to his queries, but to his relief, just as his temper began to slip, the owner of the pub entered the room. If not brilliant in conversation, he at least was able to comprehend their errand.

'Bottom, eh?' he revolved the name slowly as he considered.

'An elderly man,' said Bunce. 'Tall, with white hair. He would only be in once every week or so at most, when he visits his sister.'

'Ah!' A light, dim as though viewed through sooty glass, faintly illuminated the publican's doughy features. 'Perhaps you mean him wot stays at Widow Moffat's— he says it's for his health. Claims his lungs is bad and Cramwell air helps to clear 'em, though he's the first 'as said so. He ain't her brother, but they do be thick as thieves.' A leer spread over his face as he pondered a moment. 'Now I think on it, Bottom be his name, right enough.' Doubt in the veracity of the ostensible reason for Bottom's visits to the Widow Moffat blended subtly in his speech with a native if misplaced pride that the climate of Cramwell should be thought salubrious; from his brief exposure to the atmosphere of the village, Inspector Bunce felt it would be more likely to cause than cure catarrh.

'Have you seen him lately?' Bunce asked. This was the man; there must have been a mistake made at Sheepshanks about his relationship to the lady.

'Not since last week, it were,' answered the pubkeeper after some cogitation, 'but most Wednesdays he turns up at six without fail. T'doctor's been to see Mrs Moffat,' he added inconsequentially, taking the cloth from the barmaid and using it to polish a cloudy glass with indifferent success.

'Has he?' said the Inspector. 'Do you know if it was Mrs Moffat he attended?'

'Not I; but Mrs Simms next door saw her hanging out a man's shirt to dry in back.' He turned away casually, though underneath he was seething with suppressed impatience for Bunce to be gone so that he might relay to his gossips the information that the police were looking for Mrs Moffat's mysterious lodger; moreover, the sooner they left and tracked down Bottom, who was undoubtedly lying low (perhaps suffering from a bullet wound) at Mrs Moffat's cottage, the sooner the next act of this absorbing drama would take place to enthrall the villagers. For Cramwell, on the surface stagnant and dull, had, like Walter Mitty, a thrilling secret life: its inhabitants shared an unholy passion for scandal. Indeed, the very name of the place had become a byword among its neighbours for unbridled curiosity. Cramwellians' days were largely spent in the assembling of bits of information and misinformation, their nights in arranging these fragments of fact and fancy into darkling mosaics of their own devising, fitting and refitting the pieces like sections of a vast narrative tapestry that has been cut into disconnected parts. No conjecture was too bizarre or too extreme to be entertained, and the picture thus formed by their concerted efforts varied from day to day, but generally displayed duplicity vying with depravity for the upper hand. Cramwell was like an anthill, a deceptively placid exterior masking the teeming within.

Bunce, who was ignorant of the intense eagerness with which the pub-keeper awaited his departure, inquired the way to Mrs Moffat's with a maddening insistence on accuracy. He received by degrees the information that you turned right at the church, went through the lych-gate and down the tiddly little path on t'other side past Vicar's garden, bore left onto Mowers Lane, and it was the cottage with a blue door; and departed at last with his constable, thus freeing his informant to shape and embellish a tale which would find an avid audience upon the arrival of the pub's first customers.

Following the publican's directions, they found themselves at the entrance to the lane. Mowers Lane might best be described as a cow-path — its head was in the village and its tail trailed off into the surrounding countryside. Except for two or three cottages, the lane was a mere track which ended in the hayfield beyond. After his view of the centre of Cramwell, the Inspector found Mrs Moffat's cottage an unexpectedly pleasant surprise. Unlike the drab and ill-kept houses along the High Street, Meadowlark Cottage was distinctly spruce. It had a cosy appearance with its neatly painted door the colour of cornflowers, thatched roof and carefully edged flower-beds which bordered a trim path. Bunce noted the last with approval (he was a great gardener) as he pulled the shining doorbell handle, his constable a respectful step behind him.

The woman who opened the door to his ring was as cosy as her cottage: small, round as a dumpling and as appetising, with a cheerful face and bright blue eyes that matched the paint on her front door. Her flowered apron was starched and crisp and a scent of cherry pie wafted through the open doorway; it all seemed slightly unreal, like a highly coloured picture in a children's book.

'Good afternoon, madam,' Bunce said politely. 'Have you by any chance a Mr Bottom staying with you?'

'Indeed I 'ave — are you Dr Mackay's partner? I do 'ate to disturb 'im — he's sleeping ever so sound. I'm sure he's better; he took a cup of broth just an hour ago — oh!' She gave a start of surprise; she had just noticed the constable, who had stepped to one side of the doorway. 'What do you want with my Fred? 'E's done nothing — 'e's been lying sick in bed for days — 'e 'asn't done nothing wrong.'

'Now, now, Mrs Moffat,' said Bunce in the emollient tone which he knew how to assume when necessary, 'we've no quarrel with Mr Bottom, none at all; but I must ask him some questions about a matter concerning Sheepshanks College.' Her words, he thought, had suggested more intimacy than was customary between landlady and boarder; perhaps the hints made by Fenchurch and the landlord of the Rope and Bucket had some substance.

'You don't mean to say they called in the police over *that*?' she said in a quavering voice.

'What do you mean?' asked Bunce sharply.

'That business about the claret — it's been preying on 'is mind ever since 'e took ill. 'E's down with a fever, and when 'e's not 'imself, he talks about it in a kind of wandering-like. It's not fair,' she said fiercely, ' 'e's worked there man and boy this forty year, and now they're 'ounding 'im because of the claret!'

'Compose yourself, Mrs Moffat,' Bunce said soothingly, 'what we have come about has nothing to do with the Sheepshanks claret. I must ask him a few questions about an incident which I feel certain does not concern him personally.'

'That's all right, then,' she answered, placated, 'though it's a pity to wake the poor man,' and beckoned them in. The cottage, as is customary, was constructed on a miniature scale so both the Inspector and his constable had to stoop to enter. She led them up a winding pair of stairs to a little room at their head where the invalid lay. Bottom was still flushed with fever, but his breathing was regular and he was resting quietly. Mrs Moffat shook him awake gently. 'Come on, old boy,' she said, 'there's someone here to talk to you.'

Bottom awoke gradually; at first he did not realize that there were strangers in the room. 'Wot time is it?' he asked, becoming agitated. 'I oughter be getting back to College.' His eye fell upon the window. 'It's getting late— I shall miss 'All, and young William, 'e don't know 'ow to serve a proper dinner yet.' He struggled feebly with the bedclothes.

Mrs Moffat knelt by the side of the bed, holding him down.

'You can't get up yet, Fred; you're ill. I knew we shouldn't have waked 'im,' she said in an indignant aside to Bunce, who moved to the foot of the bed so Bottom could see him.

'I am very sorry to disturb you, Mr Bottom,' he said in his mellow countryman's voice, 'but I've come to ask you about the occurrence at Sheepshanks on Tuesday evening.'

'The claret!' moaned Bottom. 'I brought up claret instead of hock to serve with the salmon. It's a thing I've never done before, I swear I 'aven't.' He huddled under the blankets, his arms embracing his knees, and gave a keening wail. Mrs Moffat, wiping her tears with the hem of her apron, was overcome in a corner, but she recovered herself sufficiently to leap at them like a tabby-cat turned tigress. 'You stop bullying 'im!' she declared angrily. "E's a pore sick man — 'e 'asn't done nothing wrong; you said 'e 'adn't!'

The constable, unnerved by these unseemly displays of emotion, had already bolted for the stairs but Bunce, a more seasoned veteran, stood his ground. He waited until Bottom's ululations had ceased and then said patiently, 'Mr Bottom, the incident I mentioned has nothing to do with your mistake about the claret — or if it has, it is only in the most incidental way. I am investigating the death of Mr Garmoyle; after you left the College to take your day off it was discovered that he had been poisoned.'

'There must 'ave been some mistake,' answered Bottom weakly but with a firmness surprising in one so ill. 'That isn't the sort of thing that 'appens at Sheepshanks.'

Mrs Moffat's only remark was a wondering 'Coo,' as the apron which she had thrown over her face after her outburst was slowly lowered.

'Nevertheless, I'm afraid it has,' Bunce replied, 'and I must ask you some questions which may assist us in finding the murderer. I understand that before dinner on Tuesday evening you were unable to find one of the decanters of port which are normally kept in the sideboard beside High Table.'

'That's right,' said Bottom mistily; he was clearly not yet entirely free of his fever.

'What time was it when you found the decanter was missing?'

'It must 'ave been 'alf past six,' said Bottom, trying to concentrate on the question, 'because that's when I always check to see High Table is set proper. Leastways, I *thought* the decanter was missing, but. . .' He paused uncertainly.

'But what?' prompted the Inspector.

'Well, when I come back, 'aving fetched the wine from the cellar,' a look of pain passed over his face as his *faux pas* was thus recalled to him, 'and another decanter — we've a full set of them, you see, enough to use for College Feasts — the second port decanter was in the sideboard where it belonged. Now I think back on it, my fever was coming on. I felt a bit off that night during dinner; I reckon I must 'ave 'ad an 'alloocination.'

'Perhaps,' said Bunce doubtfully. 'What time was it when you came back from the cellars with the wine?'

'It must 'ave been — let me see — about a quarter to seven. Yes, that's about what it was. I remember glancing at my watch to see 'ow much time was left before dinner.'

'I understand Mr Fenchurch was the first of the Fellows to arrive that evening.'

'That's right; 'e come in at the stroke of seven. Old Noll were just sounding the quarter past — it were running fifteen minutes fast on Tuesday, I remember — when 'e walked into the Combination Room. I was putting out the sherry at the time, being late, you see, on account of the mistake about the wine.' He closed his eyes to shut out the unwelcome memory.

'And you told him then of the port incident?'

'That I did; I was that bothered, and 'e's a kindly gentleman. 'E said to me, "Let's look again to make certain it has disappeared," and when we opened the door to the sideboard, there it was, sure enough.'

The uncomfortable thought crossed Bunce's mind that if there had been a switch of some sort with the port decanter, Fenchurch had been on the spot. 'Is the sideboard kept locked?' he asked.

'It useter be,' replied Bottom, 'till the key went missing; but as the undergraduates all think it's locked, there's no 'arm done.'

'But the Fellows know there is no longer a key?'

'Oh, yes, sir; they'd all know.'

'How long has this state of affairs been in existence?' As Bottom looked blank (his poor head was still reverberating with the throbbing of his fever), Bunce amended the question: 'How long has the key to the sideboard been lost?'

Bottom cogitated for a moment. "Appen it's been gone five or ten years or so,' he said vaguely. 'But I must 'ave been seeing things when I thought the decanter 'ad disappeared. It were there when Mr Fenchurch looked— I seen it with me own eyes. And afterwards I come all over queer in the Cramwell bus, so it must 'ave been the fever.'

Bunce refused to give up his only clue so easily. 'Have you had any other hallucinations since you became ill?'

Bottom pondered the question. 'Can't say as I 'ave,' he said at last, 'but my uncle Tom what served in India and 'ad chronic malaria, 'e said as fever 'ull do it every time. 'E used to see blue camels and an occasional ring-tailed baboon — that was the worst, 'e told me: it 'ud grin and chatter at 'im so 'orrible, 'e'd 'ave to take a glass or so of gin to blot the sight out— teeth yeller as old pianner keys,' he said, and shivered; whether from the thought of his uncle's demon monkey, or from fever, the Inspector was not certain.

Bunce reflected for a moment; suddenly he thought he glimpsed a way out of his difficulty. 'But your uncle saw things that weren't there— he didn't *not* see something that *was* there,' he pointed out triumphantly if rather incoherently, delighted with this flaw in Bottom's reasoning. It had considerably unnerved the Inspector to think that his only lead as to when the poison might have been added to the port was imaginary.

But Bottom was no longer attending to his interlocutor. 'Oh, my 'ead,' he moaned, unheeding, and burrowed deeper into his pillow. Bunce, realizing that he would not get anything more out of his witness in his present state, followed Mrs Moffat down the narrow stairs into her small front parlour with its sprigged chintz curtains and china spaniels demurely perched on the diminutive mantelpiece. 'Mrs Moffat,' he said as he prepared to join his constable, who was standing guard rather shamefacedly outside the front door, 'I understand Mr Bottom suffers from lung trouble. As he is a potentially valuable witness in this case, I think I had better arrange to have him transferred to a Cambridge hospital.'

'But Dr Mackay says he's better,' she protested.

'Nevertheless, it would be less trouble for you, and if there is any question of complications, I should prefer him in Addenbrooke's.'

'Oh,' wailed Mrs Moffat. Her face crumpled as the Inspector gazed at her in consternation. 'Don't take 'im away from me,' she wept. 'I should worry all the time. I know them nurses — always primping and flirting with the orderlies when they think no one's looking. They wouldn't take proper care of 'im, not the way I would.'

Bunce listened in astonishment: surely this was not the conventional attitude of a landlady toward her occasional lodger. He remembered Fenchurch's jesting words on the subject — was this why Bottom had been so cagey about his forwarding address on his days off? He said more gently, 'My dear Mrs Moffat, it will be far better for him, considering the state of his lungs. I shall speak to his doctor —'

'His lungs is perfectly sound,' she interrupted, swallowing a sob. 'That's just a tale we put about so as to explain why he come here every week. I knew him when I was a girl, you see. Dr Mackay said there was nothing to worry about from the fever so long as I was able to bring it down.'

'But why did you need an excuse for the village? Surely there is nothing wrong in his visiting an old friend.'

'You don't know what this village is like,' she replied bitterly as she gave her face a final dab. 'A more gossiping, nasty, spying lot of Peeping Toms I never did see, and what they don't nose out they make up among them. I did think about moving away when George died, but I'd got fond of the cottage and it was such a lot of trouble to pack and it was convenient for Fred to come 'ere on 'is days off, so I ended by staying.' She sighed. 'But everyone in Cramwell knew I 'adn't a brother, so we 'ad to make up something else.' And she told him her whole story — it seemed a relief to her after hiding it for so long. She and Bottom had been childhood sweethearts, but when he obtained a place at Sheepshanks it became rapidly obvious that she came second to the College in his affections. Bottom had put off the wedding several times on one excuse or another, and at last he confessed to her that he did not wish to marry, for he felt the connubial state inappropriate to one who served in College. She had married Mr Moffat but had always retained a soft spot for her Fred, and upon her husband's demise some twenty-five years ago she and Bottom had been reunited, though without benefit of clergy. She explained this omission: Bottom felt that if he married he would not have adequate time to devote to Sheepshanks. It seemed he had decided that by giving lip-service to the University's ancient tradition of celibacy he was in some fashion upholding its standards. Moreover, he was continuing a family tradition, for neither his father nor his grandfather had ever married. Apparently this state of affairs was sufficiently agreeable to Mrs Moffat for her to acquiesce in it. Perhaps her years of marriage to Mr Moffat had made her value a certain amount of privacy — at any rate this occasional *ménage* appeared satisfactory to both parties.

After this confession (Bunce could assume an almost clerically comforting manner when he chose) and the Inspector's assurance that her Fred would not be torn from her — since his ailing lungs were fictional he might convalesce in her care — Mrs Moffat grew quite cheerful, and waved a smiling good-bye to them as the car drove away. The Inspector was less sanguine. At best Bottom's testimony left matters no clearer than they had been; at worst it took away his one chance of pinning down the time the decanter had been poisoned. Moreover, he was beginning to wonder about Mr Fenchurch. Bunce felt an admiration for him that bordered on affection, and he was upset at the possibility of bringing Garmoyle's murder home to him. For the Inspector had one failing detrimental, if not fatal, to a policeman: a soft heart.

14 Jenkins Again

'So he's at it again,' concluded Inspector Jenkins, who was describing the latest event in his pursuit of the M.A. Rapist to his friend and colleague. 'Though this time he was scared off by a don from one of the Colleges — funny old boy named Fenchurch who has a habit of taking long walks.'

'Fenchurch?' echoed Bunce. 'That's queer; one of my murder suspects is named Fenchurch. Yours isn't from Sheepshanks, by any chance?'

'I believe he is — damn' stupid of me not to connect them,' replied Jenkins. He glanced through the folder he was carrying. 'Yes, that's his College, all right. Quite a coincidence.'

'Lucky for the lady he was there,' Bunce observed.

'Actually, I'm not certain it made much difference,' Jenkins answered. 'From the looks of her I'd say Dame Hermione could have coped singlehanded and had room to spare for a mugger or so. She's what the French call *formidable*.' The Jenkinses had once spent a fortnight's holiday in Paris, and Jenkins was not above occasionally reminding his associates of the fact.

'And neither of them saw any more of him to describe than the Partridge girl did?'

'No, although the man had taken off his stocking-mask when Mr Fenchurch saw him — I suppose it got in the way of his breathing due to being wet. But Mr Fenchurch said he couldn't make out the chap's features at that distance, so it's no help to us.'

'I wonder if you mightn't make it one,' said Bunce thoughtfully.

'I don't see how; if he didn't see the man's face, there's no way he could describe it.'

'No, but suppose you threw a bit of a scare into the rapist — something that'd make him think the police had a lead — wouldn't that help?'

'I don't see how,' said the obtuse Jenkins.

'For one thing it might make him lie low for a while, and if we could keep him from trying his tricks for the rest of May Week, we'd be a lot better off. It will be much easier to keep an eye on things once most of the students have gone; for one thing, there'll be fewer girls in Cambridge to try to protect.'

'But the rapist may go off for the Long Vac too, and then how will we catch him?' Jenkins pointed out.

'Maybe, but I'm betting he's a local — using a gown for disguise is a bit too obvious and might prove to be an attempt at laying a false trail. Any leads from the outfitters in town?'

'The only thing I was able to find out from them is that anyone can buy an M.A. gown here and count on not being traced. You still haven't told me your idea; not that it sounds like much,' said Jenkins ungratefully.

'I thought that you might get hold of that journalist from the *Argus* — Figgins, isn't it, the one who's been giving you a hard time over the case — and feed him a story. He's bound to use it — he'll be only too pleased to have an edge over the London papers. You could tell him that the man who interrupted the rape attempt noticed something distinctive about Dame Hermione's attacker; you needn't mention Mr Fenchurch by name,' he said, holding up his hand to keep Jenkins from interrupting, 'so he will be perfectly safe from reprisals, as the criminal won't know who he is. It's a long chance, I admit, but it might just throw the fellow sufficiently off his stride to leave a clue of some sort — he might change his method to something that will give you more of a lead — and I don't see how it can hurt.'

'You may have a point,' said Jenkins slowly. He added, 'But what if the rapist is one of Fenchurch's students and recognized him at the river?'

'That's a possibility, but a remote one,' replied Bunce, 'and don't forget, by the time he really had a look at Fenchurch, he was too far away to see his face. If you try the plan, it might at least give you a breather during the May Week festivities; and since the rapist was thwarted in his latest attempt, he may well try again soon unless he is discouraged.'

'It might not be a bad idea,' Jenkins said, revolving it in his mind. 'This next week will give him unparalleled opportunities for another rape. Perhaps it would be just as well to frighten him in hopes of putting him off for a bit. Come, lad, I'll stand you a pint while we make up a story for Figgins.'

15 Found Out!

The next morning Bunce knocked reluctantly on the door to Fenchurch's rooms. He had spent a disturbed night, for in addition to the fact that Fenchurch was the one person who was proved to have been nearby when the decanter of port was presumably poisoned, Bunce had remembered his careful disclaimer of any knowledge of poisons when they were discussing the effects of arsenic. It was no doubt a perfectly innocent statement, but so convenient that it left a small shadow in the Inspector's mind which he was unable to dispel.

He waited, listening, but could hear no sound. The Porter had assured him that though it was not yet nine, Mr Fenchurch would have returned from his matutinal walk. 'Reg'lar as clockwork, Mr Fenchurch is,' he had said. 'Off at seven, back at a quarter to nine, breakfast at nine sharp.' A moment ensued, then there was a patter of slippered feet and the door was opened by Fenchurch, arrayed in an aged but still respectable dark blue flannel dressing-gown and carrying a battered kettle. 'Do come in,' he said. 'I am just changing from my walking-clothes.' He ushered Bunce into an enormous and chilly sitting-room which, aside from a leather-covered sofa, a desk, a heavy mahogany dining-room table and several matching side-chairs — all of late Victorian vintage — was furnished exclusively with books. There were books in bookshelves, books in china cabinets, books on the chairs and table and floor; indeed, there was scarcely room on the table for the breakfast tray which the gyp had already brought up. Before disappearing into a room beyond, presumably a bedroom, to complete his toilet, Fenchurch cleared a spot on the sofa so that his guest might sit down if he were so inclined. While Bunce waited he amused himself by looking at a bookshelf beside the doorway of this room. Most of its contents were what might be expected: large and ponderous works on various phases of English history from the coming of the Romans to the late middle ages interspersed with slender volumes of poetry by Rupert Brooke, John Donne and the Elizabethans and the novels of Thackeray, Austen, Fielding and Trollope. One shelf, however, which was tucked into a corner, held a number of books with the sort of binding that is generally found on railway station booksellers' stalls; these volumes had an incongruously raffish air among their neighbours, like a couple of racing touts at a meeting of academics. Bunce, leaning over curiously to read their titles, saw that all of them were detective novels — surely an odd literary taste for a don. He picked up one at random: it was *The Stonehenge Murders*, written by Geoffrey Saltmarsh. Bunce replaced it on the shelf and examined *Dead for a Ducat*, *Blood Will Tell*, *Who Killed the Archbishop?* and *Bloodstains in the Bodleian* in turn, to find that Geoffrey Saltmarsh was the author of them all. Fenchurch reappeared while the Inspector was glancing through *Death Walks in Grantchester*.

'I've never gone in much for detective stories,' said Bunce conversationally. 'Somehow they don't seem restful to a man in my line of work, not the way Tennyson is, or Browning. *The Lady of Shalott*, now — that's poetry for you.' He rolled the sonorous first lines lovingly upon his tongue. ' ". . . That clothe the wold and meet the sky," ' he finished. 'That bit always makes me think of the country around here, except for the wold, of course; that's all wrong for Cambridgeshire. Speaking of Cambridgeshire, this book —' he displayed *Death Walks in Grantchester* in his large fist, '— surely the author must be a Cambridge man?'

To his astonishment Fenchurch flushed; an unmistakable dark crimson tide surged from throat to forehead. 'I believe he is,' he replied.

Though Bunce's question had been asked in all innocence, it was clear that he had stumbled upon something. ' "I believe he is"! That's a cool one,' he thought, wise to the ways of suspicious behaviour under questioning. 'If that's not a sign of guilty knowledge, I'd like to know what it is. Been writing whodunits on the sly, have you? That's a pretty fair way to find out about poisons and how to give 'em.' He thought again of his conversation with Fenchurch when the don had remarked that he knew little of poisons. Suspicion flared up in Bunce: who had ever heard of a detective-story writer who was ignorant of poisons? The Inspector might not be a mystery addict but even he knew that poison was the mainstay of the industry, particularly in books meant for the genteel trade, whose readers grew squeamish at the sound of bones cracking and the smell of blood. If Fenchurch was Geoffrey Saltmarsh, it was a dead cert he knew enough about arsenic and cyanide to write a monograph on the subject, not to mention the little-known arrow poisons used by the aboriginal tribes of South America. With genuine regret and a sense of personal injury, for he had come both to like and to trust the man, he said, 'Now, Mr Fenchurch, it won't do any good in the long run to hide it: isn't it true that you write mysteries under the name of Geoffrey Saltmarsh?'

Fenchurch's complexion underwent a change from dull fuchsia to a pallor that was alarming by contrast. 'I do not know how you have acquired the information,' he said. 'It is indeed true, but I do beg that you will not acquaint any of my colleagues of the fact. It is a secret I have managed to keep from them for many years, and I should not care to have it made public.'

'Then if I were you, I should keep Geoffrey Saltmarsh's books in a more private place,' said Inspector Bunce.

'I generally store them in a closed cupboard by my bed,' Fenchurch replied, 'but as the woodwork is being painted I moved them here temporarily. I see now that it was a mistake. I daresay it was a mistake to retain copies at all, but such, my dear Inspector, is the nature of vanity. They are poor things, to be sure, but mine own; and when it came to the point I found I could not bear to part with them.'

'It may well have been more of a mistake than you know,' answered Bunce grimly. 'Now, Mr Fenchurch, is it or is it not true that you told me you were ignorant of the way poisons work? I should be very sorry to think you lied, sir, for I have trusted you to some extent — more perhaps than it is wise for a police officer to trust anyone involved in a case he is investigating — but it is obvious that no one who has written a shelf of detective novels can possibly be without a working knowledge of poisons.' He paused significantly.

'So you think by that token I may be poor Garmoyle's murderer?' said Fenchurch. 'I cannot blame you for suspecting me, Inspector, but upon my word, you have no grounds for doing so on that account. If you will have the kindness to examine my *oeuvre* (if I may so style it without seeming unduly pretentious) you will see that not once have I dispatched a victim by means of the method popularized by the Borgias. In my books I have made use of many forms of weapon — several bronze paperweights, a Malayan *kris*, Italian *stiletti* (in *Dead for a Ducat*), and a pair of matched Napoleonic duelling-pistols, among others. The murderer of *Who Killed the Archbishop?* employed a garden rake, a bust of Socrates and a Crown Derby teapot in committing his crimes. You will find in my works other weapons of homely or exotic origin, but never poison — I have an aversion to the stuff. In my opinion it is a sneaking, cowardly weapon — one a gentleman would be ashamed to use. I do assure you, Inspector, that my ignorance of poisons is genuine and not feigned.'

Bunce was delighted to take his word for it; he made, however, a mental note to glance through all the novels attributed to Geoffrey Saltmarsh to make certain. Though willing to be convinced of his innocence, he was still not quite comfortable about Mr Fenchurch — a clever man determined to do murder might nerve himself to use a weapon he ordinarily detested in order to disarm suspicion, and Bunce gave Fenchurch full marks for cleverness and determination. It was clear that he could not yet be struck off the list of suspects for Garmoyle's murder. The Inspector, refusing Fenchurch's hospitable offer of breakfast, returned to his office a little wiser, but also a great deal more puzzled, than before.

16 Figgins Co-operates

Figgins had done Jenkins proud. At first he had been somewhat leery of the titbit proffered him — he had built his reputation at the *Argus* as a constabulary gadfly, and this rôle had of necessity somewhat impaired his relations with the police. He was, therefore, suspicious of Jenkins's sudden friendliness, and even more suspicious of his generosity. The bait, however, was too tempting for even a seasoned newspaperman to refuse: an exclusive slant on a story that was being covered by the London papers — the only fresh lead to the rapist who was terrorizing the women of Cambridge. Figgins was not a fool; he knew there was an element of fishiness about it — why, for instance, was he singled out for the prize? Why not give it to all the papers simultaneously? A small sly voice whispered that perhaps there was something wrong with the story — something which a London reporter would have noticed at once — but he stifled its murmurings, preferring to listen to Jenkins's explanation.

'We feel that the *Argus* is the best vehicle for this information,' Jenkins had said to him over a pint of beer in the courtyard of the Eagle.

'That's all very well, and don't think I'm not grateful,' Figgins answered cautiously, 'but why just the *Argus*? Not that I'm not pleased to have the exclusive, mind, but frankly I can't figure out why I've got it.'

'We want our point emphasized in the hope that the rapist will see your story and be frightened by it into giving something away,' replied Inspector Jenkins smoothly. 'The London papers might take the story, but there's a good chance they'd bury it or drop it for another item. By giving you the exclusive I am guaranteeing that you will give it prominence. Also, the rapist is almost certain to read your sheet, while it's by no means as certain that he sees the London rags. If they want it they can pick it up from the *Argus* later— you're a stringer for a couple of them, aren't you?'

'Yes,' replied Figgins, 'and this might get me into hot water with my contacts. They won't be pleased if they think I've held out on them.'

'Well, pass it on to them if you like,' said the Inspector magnanimously. 'As long as your editor doesn't mind, we don't. We just want to be certain it gets front-page coverage here so the bugger can't miss it.'

Jenkins and Bunce had agreed that the best way to ensure their item first-class treatment at the *Argus* was to grant an exclusive; that, they hoped, would blind the hundred eyes of that worthy newspaper to the fact that the bone it was being offered had very little meat on it. The story was a vague one: simply that during the attack on Dame Hermione the man who had come to her assistance had noticed something about her assailant which made the man readily identifiable should he encounter him again. Fenchurch had agreed to the deception. There was no risk for him as his name would not appear in the newspaper account and he had not yet discussed the incident with anyone; nor had Dame Hermione, at the request of the police. In fact there was very little in this news item which one could sink one's teeth into, but Figgins's editor, sensing that good relations with the police and a direct pipeline to later and possibly more startling revelations about the rapist might prove more beneficial to circulation than the paper's previous tactics, had aided the reporter in going all out for effect. 'RAPIST IDENTIFIED!' screamed a banner headline arrestingly if inaccurately on the front page of the Saturday morning edition. In the article itself the writer was reluctantly forced to admit that only one feature of the rapist (though that a distinctive one) had been identified, or rather taken note of, before the rapist bolted. Still, the information was sufficiently titillating to ensure a sell-out of the *Argus*, and sufficiently convincing to ensure that most of the male population of Cambridge would be intently stared at by someone at least once before the day was over in the expectation of finding a hitherto unnoticed wart or scar.

Inspector Jenkins grunted approvingly as he read the article, well pleased with their handiwork. For once he was glad that an occupational characteristic of newspapermen is their readiness to exaggerate any news with an element of the sensational. He took in the paper to show to Bunce and read it again over his shoulder. As he did so, a sudden thought came to him rather late in the game. 'Suppose the chap hasn't got any distinguishing marks?' he demanded of Bunce. 'Then we shall look a proper pair of fools.'

'So what?' replied Bunce. 'We haven't been specific about it — it could be anything, from the shape of his nose to a gesture he makes to the way he runs. The point is, he thinks there *is* something and he doesn't know what it is, and it's bound to rattle him. Everybody can find something queer about himself if he looks long enough. I'd be willing to bet the rapist found at least half a dozen odd marks on his mug — moles, a scar, a chipped tooth — before he finished shaving this morning. We know Mr Fenchurch was too far away to see him distinctly, but he can't be sure of that. Wouldn't you be nervous if you were him?'

Jenkins gave a chuckle and relaxed. 'I reckon you're right — if I were in his shoes, likely I'd have come up with a couple of features of my own by now!' He fingered his own less than classic beak. 'If I were our boy, I'd probably be asking around for the name of a good plastic surgeon this minute.' He laughed again and went back to his office.

17 At the Bumps

It was Saturday, the last day of the May Races. A sun-filled morning had become a cloudless afternoon and the populace of Cambridge, both town and gown, was employed in taking advantage of this unusual circumstance. Upon the river down by Stourbridge Common and Ditton Meadows the Bumps were in progress, and a holiday crowd lined the banks to watch them. Undergraduates in droves reclined upon the grass, the females of the species in brief halters, the males shirtless, anointing one another in an attempt to *sauté* themselves into a semblance of summer while the unwonted sun lasted; from a distance the rows of pale bodies looked like a troupe of albino seals dressed for a circus act. Their elders were more decorous in dress; so decorous, in fact, that they were distinctly uncomfortable in the uncommon heat. Elderly dons had assumed their summer-weight trousers early in honour of the weather (generally it was not necessary to get them out until July), but even these garments, constructed as they were of sturdy British wool, were somewhat warm for the occasion. None the less, although the Englishman's constitution is more inured to excessive cold than to heat, he is a stoic in the purest sense and can bear either extreme without flinching — witness countless tours of duty in India and equatorial Africa. It was, therefore, with the characteristic fortitude of their race that the academics of Cambridge submitted to the unaccustomed embraces of Apollo.

Upon the river the College crews were manfully striving to catch up with one another. The form of the May Races, in which boats from each College participate, is a curious one. Because the Cam is too narrow to allow two boats to race abreast, the contenders must begin each race strung apart at set distances along the stretch of the river. Each boat must endeavour to bump the one in front of it while avoiding being bumped by its pursuer. When one of the crews succeeds in a bump, the two boats involved draw to the side and the next day the victorious bumper starts in front of the vanquished bumpee. On Saturday, the last day of the races, the triumphant boat at the front of the procession has earned the proud title of Head of the River.

It was a colourful scene, fraught with the tension of suspense. From the banks of the river old Kingsmen, Trinitarians, Sheepshankians, Johnians urged on their boats in measured accents; the young displayed less restraint, uttering raucous cries of encouragement. As the throng watched the efforts of the straining crews, the calls of the coxes floated plaintively over the water and snatches of conversation eddied through the crowd. 'Corpus hasn't a chance;' spoken in gloomy tones by a local physician. 'Our best oar came down with a nasty case of appendicitis six weeks ago — damn' near died of it, the silly ass, but we managed to pull him through. The specialist I called in insisted the boy simply was not well enough in time to go into training — obviously not a rowing man himself. I said, "Moxon, why the *devil* couldn't you have waited until the Long Vac to make a mess of yourself. . ."'

From farther up the river came a rhythmic and startling chant of 'Jesus; Christ's' — neither blasphemy nor supplication, as it might seem, but merely the supporters of those Colleges cheering on their respective crews.

'. . . I bought *the* most fabulous dress for the Clare May Ball — absolutely smashing. . . .'

'. . . my tutor said to me, "You haven't a brain, not a brain: if there are any more like you about, God help us all," and then, do you know, my dear, he actually wept!'

'— Too shattering.'

'. . . have another sandwich.'

'Thanks, I will.'

'Egg or cucumber? . . .'

From a cluster of Sheepshanks Fellows stationed near the finish the gentle voice of Mutton was heard in converse: 'Austrey; yes, yes, John, it must indubitably be Austrey, you know. . .'

Then the final effort of the Sheepshanks boat to bump Trinity, the winner of the previous year, silenced the chatterers, and the crowd surged forward in one movement to obtain a glimpse of the outcome. Those in front were heard to shout, 'Hoy, stop shoving, can't you?'; 'I say, let a chap alone;' 'You're treading on my foot;' and remarks of a similar nature. As the two leading boats swept past the Sheepshanks contingent, there was a splash accompanied by a crack, and the Trinity boat faltered for an instant; for an instant only, but long enough to enable the Sheepshanks crew, with a last mustering of sinews strained to the uttermost, to bump her. Cheers resounded from the throats of the Sheepshankians present — all eyes were glued to the progress of the two boats as they shot past. A fervent 'Well rowed, oh, well rowed, Sheepshanks!' burst forth spontaneously from Fenchurch. He was the first to drop his eyes from the contenders to the stretch of river directly in front of him, and saw something that resembled a bundle of old clothes floating not far from the bank. Glancing about him at his companions, 'Good heavens,' he exclaimed. 'Smythson has fallen in!'

18 Smythson's Narrow Escape

Luckily Smythson, unconscious as the result of a clip over the ear by a Trinity oar, was floating on his back, so the inattention of his companions did not result, as it might have done, in a drowning. He was enthusiastically and unceremoniously fished out of the river by a couple of strapping undergraduates who were delighted to perform as heroes in front of their girls. In fact, the incident was enjoyed as an interesting diversion by all present except the main participant and the adherents of Trinity, who claimed a foul on the grounds of interference. Had it not been for the collision of Smythson's head with one of the Trinity blades which put the oarsman concerned off his stroke, they argued, Trin. must inevitably have been Head of the River once more. This premise was hotly disputed by all the Sheepshankians present, and acrimony flew thick and fast; at one juncture it looked as though Professor Tempeste and the corpulent Bursar of Trinity were about to come to blows. It was some time before Smythson was revived, as the attention of his companions had been diverted by this important point, but at last a doctor was ushered through the crowd and the injured man was led tottering to his rooms at Sheepshanks by Fenchurch and Austrey. Though the blow on his head had caused no permanent damage it was some time before he was able to utter anything more coherent than a series of pitiable groans. When at last he could speak, he croaked, 'Someone pushed me!'

'Yes, indeed, Smythson,' said Austrey sympathetically, pouring him out a glass of brandy (the doctor had certified him as basically sound but had suggested a mild stimulant). 'Drink this: it will make you feel better. Dr Lloyd said there was no concussion, luckily, but I expect you'll have rather a headache for a bit.'

'It was a frightful crowd,' Fenchurch remarked. 'I was nearly pushed in myself— I became concerned at standing close to the river bank when the press was so great — as you know, I do not swim. As a matter of fact, I had just stepped back from the edge when you fell in.'

'I wasn't pushed by accident,' said Smythson hoarsely. 'Someone shoved me in on purpose — I felt him do it.'

'Come, come,' Austrey replied in a tone meant to be soothing. 'Of course you felt it, but it was only someone who was in turn being pushed by the weight of the crowd behind him — certainly it was not intentional.'

'That's how much you know,' snarled Smythson; the brandy had restored him to his usual humour and he considered Austrey's tone offensive. 'You needn't speak to me as if I were half-witted. I distinctly felt someone put both his hands on the small of my back and push me in. Try and tell me *that's* an accident. It's obvious there is a homicidal maniac wandering about loose. First Garmoyle and then me — nearly,' he amended.

'But why should anyone wish to kill you?' asked Fenchurch. 'Have you an idea?'

'Why did someone kill Garmoyle?' retorted Smythson. 'For all I know, my replacing the Shakespeare manuscript in the Abbot's Library *where it belonged*,' he glared at Austrey, 'may have prevented an attempted theft of it from the Prye Library, and the thief may have tried to kill me in revenge for thwarting him, or possibly in order to obtain access to it if he thinks it is still there.'

'That sounds most improbable,' said Fenchurch, 'nor do I take much stock in your other theory of a maniac bent on eliminating the Sheepshanks Combination Room. But if you were attacked intentionally, the attempt would almost certainly appear to be connected with Garmoyle's murder. We must ring up Inspector Bunce at once and inform him of this development.'

When the telephone rang in Bunce's office, he and a temporarily chastened Inspector Pocklington were busy consulting a pile of books from the Public Library in the Guildhall. These represented the complete works of Geoffrey Saltmarsh, and between them the two policemen had skimmed through *Blood Will Tell*, *Dead for a Ducat*, *Death Walks in Grantchester*, and *Miching Mallecho* without finding a single trace of poison. However, there still remained *Bloodstains in the Bodleian*, *The Stonehenge Murders* and *Who Killed the Archbishop?* as well as several others to peruse before they were finished with their research. It was a double penance for Pocklington, who in the normal course of events disdained detective novels as a particularly vulgar form of entertainment; it was his custom to boast that he had never sufficiently lowered his standards as to open one. Moreover, he had rather fancied an afternoon spent on the river watching the Bumps. Bunce had let him off the lead just long enough to eat a ploughman's lunch at the nearest pub, but they were back at it in less than three-quarters of an hour.

Bunce put down *A Coffin for the Curate* in order to answer the telephone. Pocklington looked up from his volume with glazed eyes, grateful for any respite, even a momentary one. He had encountered a larger number of violent deaths in one afternoon than in nearly twenty years at Scotland Yard and as a result of his literary surfeit was beginning to feel slightly ill. Thanks to the influential contacts which had aided his career it had been arranged for most of Pocklington's work to be performed in an administrative capacity, as the sight of blood was apt to upset him. Indeed, he found even painted blood disturbing, such as the cover of *Come Away, Death,* upon which a nubile and scantily clad female with a ribbon of bright blood trickling from the corner of her mouth beckoned to a ghastly figure with a scythe in its bony hand.

'Bunce,' said the Inspector into the telephone receiver. The earpiece quacked several times. 'What?' he said explosively. 'Attempted murder? Are you certain? Who was it. . .? And he swears the push was intentional. . . Oh, you think it may have been an accident? We'll be over directly.' It would, Bunce reflected as he replaced the receiver, be preferable to leave Pocklington to his Saltmarshian labours and go alone, but despite the London Inspector's new-found and unwonted humility, he was the superior officer on the case and Bunce doubted he would agree to such a proposal. It would be wiser to avoid any possibility of a flare-up as long as they had to work together; and in addition Bunce, though a countryman, was not unaware that Pocklington was the possessor of important friends. The Cambridge Superintendent had given Bunce a hint along those lines, but he would have known in any case. Pocklington must be, else how could he have achieved his present position? For Scotland Yard is a hard school and it is not often that fools become inspectors there. Bunce was shrewd enough not to wish to attract the adverse attention of people in high places: Cambridge is not far from London, and Government officials possess a long reach.

'It's Mr Smythson,' he said in explanation to Pocklington. 'He was down by the river watching the Races and fell in — got his head bashed about by an oar, but no real harm was done. He claims someone pushed him in on purpose but Mr Fenchurch, who telephoned, is not so sure — there was a large crowd and he thinks it might have been accidental.'

The two men drove to Sheepshanks in silence. Pocklington was still feeling humiliated by his mistaken solution of the missing manuscript, and in any case he saw no profit in making himself pleasant to this bumpkin. Bunce, for his part, was relieved that the flood of Yard reminiscences in which Pocklington invariably served as hero and the thinly veiled criticisms of provincial police procedure to which he had been subjected for the past several days had ceased for the time being.

When they arrived at Smythson's rooms, they found Austrey and Fenchurch still there and Smythson in an irascible humour. An unexpected ducking is never likely to improve anyone's temper and Smythson's, at best, was uncertain. Moreover, the polite but ill-disguised scepticism of his companions concerning the mode of his entry into the river had not sweetened his disposition. Fenchurch and Austrey would willingly have left him to be interviewed alone by the police, but they felt their testimony might be useful in unravelling Smythson's garbled and self-important account.

Pocklington's sense of his own consequence, never long in abeyance, was rapidly returning now that he was away from his penitential reading; and he proceeded to question Smythson without waiting for Bunce to begin, as professional courtesy demanded. After he had spent some moments commiserating with the victim upon his unintentional immersion they were settling down to a discussion of who Smythson's attacker might have been when Inspector Bunce found it necessary to step in. 'Are you quite certain that you were pushed into the Cam on purpose?' he asked. Smythson turned a glowering face in his direction; he had obviously preferred the tactics of his first questioner.

'Absolutely; there's no doubt about it,' he replied angrily. 'Fenchurch and Austrey seem to think I am imagining things, but I assure you they're quite mistaken. It was no accident.' He darted a furious look at his colleagues. 'They're both so set upon it that I'm beginning to wonder if one of them didn't push me into the river — I shouldn't be at all surprised,' he declared vindictively, glaring in their direction.

'Come, come, Mr Smythson,' remonstrated Bunce, shocked by his accusation. 'You've no call to say such a thing.'

'I don't see why not; they were both very near to me at the time. It seems decidedly odd that they are so eager to persuade me I wasn't pushed in on purpose.'

'Who else was near you when you fell in?' Bunce asked. Smythson appeared so certain of the attempt to kill him that it was best for the moment to treat the incident as an effort at murder. It would secure Smythson's co-operation during the interview; and indeed, with one murder already committed, the Abbot's Librarian's theory was not as far-fetched as it sounded.

'A group of the Fellows,' answered Smythson sulkily; he considered that this attempt on his life was being taken very casually, and was inclined to be displeased. If it had happened to Fenchurch or to Austrey, they wouldn't be so damned offhand about it.

'A number of us had walked over from College to watch the Races,' Fenchurch interposed, 'and I believe we were all standing together during the last race.'

'You believe? Aren't you sure?' Bunce asked.

'As it was rather an exciting finish, I cannot be certain of the exact composition of our party at the time Smythson fell in —'

'— was *pushed* in —' hissed Smythson in a venomous undertone.

'— but certainly when the race began, and,' he thought a moment, '— yes, just after it ended, our party was still complete, to the best of my recollection. Wouldn't you say so, Austrey?'

Austrey too paused to think back. 'Yes, I think so. I don't remember that anyone had left,' he said finally.

'Which of the Fellows had gone to the Races with you?' demanded Pocklington, who was determined that Bunce should not have the investigation to himself.

'We all went,' said Austrey. 'Everyone was present at lunch, and someone — the Master, I think — suggested we go down to the river afterward. Sheepshanks has a strong eight this year,' he added, 'and we were all anxious to witness the outcome.'

'Yes, indeed,' chimed in Fenchurch eagerly, 'though we were not so sanguine as to be certain that we would prevail in our efforts to bump Trinity, who have been Head of the River for some years now.'

'There I disagreed with you, John,' replied Austrey, now firmly astride one of his hobby-horses; 'you will recollect my saying at the Lent Races that Sheepshanks was coming along remarkably well. I thought then we would very likely be victorious in June.'

'True, I do remember your prognostication,' replied Fenchurch judiciously, 'but you may recall my remark at the time that Jowkes's stroke was a trifle weak, which might have affected the outcome. I was happy to see today it has improved considerably.'

'But I feel that even so the other members of the eight would have counterbalanced any deficiency shown by Jowkes,' began Austrey, 'and Scott's superior performance last term —'

'Gentlemen, gentlemen,' Bunce interposed, 'I am investigating what may be attempted murder, and we seem to have got off the subject.' Fenchurch and Austrey looked sheepish. 'Do you remember who was standing closest to Mr Smythson just before he went in the river? Can you remember, Mr Smythson?' He turned to the Abbot's Librarian.

'Mutton and Fenchurch were standing next to me, I believe,' replied Smythson. 'I recall seeing Grubb to the rear at my left, and Austrey —'

'No, no, Smythson,' interrupted Fenchurch. 'Mutton and I were in front of you — I remember distinctly.'

'But then you stepped back, you said, because of the pressure of the crowd,' Austrey reminded him.

'Yes, that's what I meant to say,' answered Smythson. 'It was just before I was pushed that we were standing beside each other. But of course I couldn't have been behind you then, or it would not have been possible for the killer to push me into the river.'

'We are still not certain that it was the killer,' Bunce said. 'Though,' he added hastily, seeing a scowl develop on Smythson's face, 'it is a possibility.'

'A possibility?' demanded Smythson furiously. 'A possibility? I have just told you that I was purposely shoved into the river — do you doubt my word? *And* at a time when the boats were passing and I was almost certain to be struck by one of the oars — if that's not attempted murder I don't know what is. Your taking it lightly might be understandable if another murder had not just been committed, and upon another member of the Sheepshanks Senior Common Room at that! In the circumstances I consider it exceedingly remiss of you to be so offhand about the incident.'

'There is no doubt in your mind, then, keeping in mind the crowd on the river-bank, that your fall was not accidental?'

'None whatever.' Smythson's accustomed pomposity had fallen away and he spoke earnestly, without affectation. It gave his words a convincing emphasis. 'Inspector, I *felt* his hands on my back — I do assure you of that. And I am frightened for my life — if he has tried once and failed, no doubt he will try again.'

'As you are certain the push was intentional, it seems extremely likely there is some connexion between the murder and this occurrence,' said Pocklington briskly; he felt it was time to inject some Scotland Yard efficiency into this affair. It was always a mistake, in his opinion, to let the locals in on anything important. Bunce had only been put on the investigation because Pocklington's superior at the Yard, when assigning him to the case, had indicated it was to be handled in this fashion. The Chief Constable had requested it through his own influential channels, as Bunce had proved most helpful and discreet some years earlier in a theft in his own household — a matter of disappearing silver and a vanishing servant.

'If Inspector Pocklington is right,' said Bunce, 'it would appear that the person who has made an attempt on your life is almost certainly one of your colleagues. You say you were surrounded by Sheepshanks Fellows at the river-bank. Is there a chance that someone else might have edged unnoticed through the crowd to stand behind you — an undergraduate, for instance, intent upon a prank?'

'I doubt it, Inspector,' said Austrey. 'I was standing farther back from the river, and anyone attempting to do so would have found it necessary to push past most of the Fellows — surely he would have been seen by some of them.'

'I'm not certain of that,' Fenchurch remarked thoughtfully. 'Just before Smythson's accident we were all concentrating on the river, you know, and it is quite possible no one would have noticed either an interloper or a shift in our own composition.'

'Then we cannot entirely omit the possibility of an outsider, nor can we definitely eliminate any of the Fellows from suspicion,' said Bunce. He turned to Smythson. 'But it would certainly appear that your assailant is the same person who killed Mr Garmoyle, if only as an extension of the law of probabilities. I find it difficult to believe that there are two murderers running loose in Cambridge simultaneously, particularly two bent upon doing away with members of the same College. You realize, Mr Smythson, we cannot be absolutely sure that the attack on you was made with murderous intent; but I am inclined, in the light of recent events, to take it seriously. Don't you agree, Inspector Pocklington?'

'Indeed I do, as I believe I made clear earlier,' replied Pocklington pontifically. 'In fact, there is no doubt at all in my mind that this is the work of the same man, and I shall not hesitate to pursue inquiries to that effect.' He drew himself up and inflated his chest; just like these silly provincials to be hopelessly slow at making an obvious connexion. It was clear that Fenchurch and Austrey disliked Smythson and were trying to make it seem that he was exaggerating. Though Pocklington had not met Austrey before the murder investigation, as his tutor Fenchurch had possessed an infallible talent for taking the wind out of the young Pocklington's sails, and in consequence had been roundly disliked by him. But there was more to Pocklington's defence of Smythson. He felt an attraction to the man — Smythson was pukka, not like the usual greybeards who inhabited the University cloisters. He had an urban sophistication — the result, no doubt, of his years with the theatre and the BBC in London — that was lacking in most dons and that appealed to Pocklington. Moreover, the man had decidedly fine eyes and a body which had not gone to seed as those of so many academics do who lead what is, after all, essentially a sedentary life. Pocklington had not known him in his undergraduate days — Smythson had been several years ahead of him and had gone down from Cambridge before Pocklington's arrival — but he remembered the name (though when he first came up it had been plain Smith). Smythson had been known as a rowing man, he recalled, not in the first rank, but not to be despised — that, no doubt, would account for his fit condition. Pocklington recollected something else he had heard about Smythson which had interested him at the time.

Inspector Bunce was wishing for the twentieth time either that Scotland Yard had taken over the murder case entirely or had sent him a less insufferable confederate, but he merely said, 'I quite agree. If the assault on you was premeditated, the odds are greatly in favour of the perpetrator being Mr Garmoyle's murderer. I am sorry, Mr Smythson, that you have undergone such an unpleasant experience, but it may in the long run prove beneficial, as it may provide another lead to the killer.' Privately he thought he would have a talk with Austrey and Fenchurch about the likelihood of the incident being accidental after all. They seemed dubious, and it appeared that Smythson had a tendency to dramatize himself. But Bunce would have to be careful in his estimate of what they said on the subject since both Fenchurch and Austrey were on his list of suspects. It is true that his instinct was to trust them, and his instinct was better than most; but that was all the more reason why, if it went awry, the results might be disastrous.

19 Tête-à-Tête

'Inspector,' said Smythson, 'I feel that the moment has come when it would be wise for me to be completely frank.'

'I do agree with you,' Pocklington replied. 'An attempt has been made upon your life; now is the time to speak up and to tell me anything that may assist us in apprehending the would-be killer.'

'I came to you rather than to Inspector Bunce partly because I felt it would be easier to discuss these matters with one of my own — class, but also because I felt that *you* were much more congenial.'

Their eyes met and held. 'I shall be delighted to do anything I can to help,' purred Pocklington; matters were moving even faster than he had hoped when Smythson first rang him up. 'May one mention, by the way, that one has heard of your erstwhile prowess on the river? I was never fortunate enough to see you in action, but you were a legend in my time.'

'Surely not. You are too kind; you exaggerate,' said Smythson modestly, but he was obviously pleased. 'To clarify matters for you: up to the present we of the Senior Common Room have had, as *you* would understand, a tacit agreement not to discuss the private affairs of others in a way which might perhaps bring any little disagreements they may have had with Garmoyle under the unwelcome scrutiny of the police. While I have observed this taboo as long as I was able in conscience to do so, now I feel that things have gone too far, that justice is being obstructed. One must do all one can to help— that is why I have asked you to come to see me.'

'I do assure you that I appreciate your co-operation, Mr

Smythson.' Might one risk a touch of the hand, Pocklington wondered? The signs all pointed in that direction, but it was a bit risky so early in the game. He decided to play it safe.

'Do call me Alan,' said Smythson with an ingratiating smile. 'I feel as though we had known one another for years; and after all, we were nearly at Sheepshanks together.'

'A pity we were not— what a happy juxtaposition that would have been. Then you must call me Denis.' They beamed at each other.

'Will you take some sherry?' asked Smythson, suddenly recalling his duties as host.

'No, none, thank you,' Pocklington answered. He felt that his present exhilaration was quite sufficient, and he knew from experience that when he combined excitement of that sort with even a little alcohol, his behaviour was apt to become indiscreet. Moreover, delightful though this interlude was proving to be, Pocklington felt he had better get down to business, and there was the promise of other meetings to soften his regret. 'You mentioned something on the telephone that had to do with Mr Austrey?'

'Yes. I do not know whether the police have any idea that he and Mrs Garmoyle have been carrying on an affair, but I happen to know that it has been going on for at least six months— quite disgusting!'

'That sort of thing so often is,' agreed Pocklington; their eyes met again.

'Yes, isn't it? I was married once, but it was not long before it ended,' Smythson confided. 'I found it a most distasteful experience — I feel certain you understand. But to revert to Austrey's affair with Helen Garmoyle: that, it would seem to me, is sufficient cause for murder. Garmoyle frequently said— he spoke in general terms, but I felt it was meant for Austrey's ears — that he would never get a divorce, no matter what the provocation. He was a Roman Catholic and utterly against divorce in principle. Mrs Garmoyle is Anglican — what I believe they call in America *Episcopalian* — and of course has no such prejudices. I do feel, you see, that it is possible either Austrey or Fenchurch, both having been so near me at the river, may have had something to do with my mishap. Perhaps Austrey had designs on the Shakespeare manuscript in order to finance an elopement with Mrs Garmoyle and attacked me because I had inadvertently blocked his scheme when I replaced the manuscript in the Abbot's Library.'

'Had Mr Fenchurch any reason for wishing to dispose of Mr Garmoyle, to your knowledge?' inquired Pocklington. His dislike for his old tutor made him hope that Smythson would be able to furnish a strong reason for suspecting him, particularly as Bunce appeared to have a positive partiality for the man — it would be doubly pleasant to show up Bunce.

'He and Garmoyle had a running argument over Fenchurch's pet project, the building of Sheepshanks Chapel,' said Smythson with a titter. 'In fact, they had a set-to only a few weeks ago. Garmoyle told Fenchurch that he wasn't interpreting one of the documents correctly and claimed that it knocked Fenchurch's theory of attribution into a cocked hat. Fenchurch did not reply, but one could see he was furious. Grubb had been siding with Garmoyle during the discussion — as a matter of fact he said some rather rude things to Fenchurch in the process — but Garmoyle suddenly turned on Grubb. One suspects he had been drinking, as usual. He called Grubb a charity-child and said he would have been better off at a red-brick university. That's the place, said Garmoyle, for second-rate intellects. Not a complimentary thing to say at best, and a particularly unfortunate choice of words under the circumstances because, as it happens, Grubb *was* a charity-child. He was adopted and I understand he is extremely sensitive about it.'

'So Grubb, as well as Austrey and Fenchurch, may have had a motive for killing Garmoyle. But I wonder what reason Grubb or Fenchurch might have for wanting to kill you.' Pocklington pondered the problem. 'Could the killer be afraid that you might have seen him in an incriminating action — poisoning the decanter, for instance?'

Smythson paused for a moment. 'That had not occurred to me earlier, but now that you mention it. . .'

'Yes?' prompted Pocklington encouragingly.

'I was in and out of the Combination Room that afternoon,' Smythson said slowly. 'I had left some notes there at lunch on the history of the Abbot's Library (the present work could use some updating, I feel), and I went back at about five o'clock to fetch them. Then a little later — at six o'clock or so, I don't remember precisely — I was working from my notes and discovered that I needed to check a quotation from a book which I do not myself possess but of which there is a copy in the Combination Room. I seem to recall that when I went down, the door into the Hall was open. I did not look in that direction on either occasion, but I suppose it's possible the murderer was doctoring the port decanter at one of those times, saw me, and may on reflection have thought I had noticed him. Good God, suppose I *had* looked — it might have prevented poor Garmoyle's death!'

'I doubt it would have stopped his murder; at most it would merely have postponed it. Or, alternatively, the killer might have attempted to kill you if you had caught him at it.'

Smythson looked disconcerted; obviously he had not considered that possibility.

'Did you see anyone else in the vicinity on either occasion?' Pocklington queried.

'The second time I went down Mutton was in the Combination Room.'

'He was, was he? But wasn't he supposed to be ill? I understand he had dinner sent up to his rooms that evening. When you saw him, did he seem to be doing anything that might be construed as suspicious?'

'N-no, not that I can think of.'

'But he might have just finished poisoning the decanter in the other room, and if so, he might have thought you could have seen something?'

'Yes, I suppose he *might*. But I didn't actually see him do anything, you know, and he told me he had come down to take his name out of the dinner-book — you will remember that a book listing the Fellows and their guests who will be at dinner is kept in the Combination Room — and to leave a note asking Bottom to see that dinner was served to him in his rooms. None of the Fellows' sets have telephones, so he had to walk down. In any case, I understand the decanter could have been poisoned at any time that afternoon.'

'We have always thought the most probable time was late in the afternoon, and now that an attempt has been made on your life I should say it must almost certainly have been then. The killer must have noticed you there and feared you had seen him. And if I may say so with regard to Inspector Bunce's deductions

— *you* will understand these things — he is not quite — not *quite*. . . .'

'I entirely comprehend,' answered Smythson. 'So you think Mutton may be the killer — I hope you are mistaken. I should not like to believe him capable of such a deed, and I cannot conceive it to be so. He is the mildest of the Fellows; to my mind Austrey conforms more to the pattern of a murderer, and then there is the matter of his motive. I have greatly enjoyed our talk in other respects, however; I should not have expected that what is commonly known as a "grilling" — is it not? — by the police could be so *sympathique*. I understand that you will be dining in College this evening before the May Ball. I hope, my dear sir, that you will do me the honour of returning to these rooms for a drink beforehand — just the two of us.'

' "My dear Denis," ' corrected Pocklington archly.

'Of course: my dear Denis. I do hope you will be able to come.'

'I should be delighted, my dear Alan.'

20 Mutton's Lamb

Pocklington walked back briskly to the police station, well pleased with the results of his interview. (He had not requested a car for his excursion as he had not wished Bunce to know where he was going.) As he passed by the Chapel the androgynous quaver of a counter-tenor floated and hung in the air, causing him unconsciously to quicken his steps. As an undergraduate he had held a theory concerning the sexual ambiguity of counter-tenors which had been rather uncomfortably disproved when one of the senior choristers of the Chapel had vigorously and corporally resented his personal researches on the subject.

He bustled in to Bunce's office, where he found him studying a sheet of paper. 'I have vital information,' Pocklington announced importantly.

'Have you now? So have I,' returned Bunce with unaccustomed sarcasm; it was long past his dinner-hour and his nerves were beginning to shriek at the sight of this West End halfwit who had been foisted upon him. Bunce fervently wished he were not on the case at all — he wished Scotland Yard were handling it completely — but if he had to investigate a murder, why must he be saddled with this fop, this ninny, this ginger?* For his instinct told him there was something wrong with the man besides his folly and conceit. He sighed and held up a paper in his hand to show Pocklington. 'The afternoon post — late as usual; why the rates keep going up while the service gets worse, I can't think — has brought an anonymous letter accusing Mr Mutton of Garmoyle's murder — something about a sister of his

---

* *ginger-beer*: *queer* — Cockney Rhyming Slang.

Garmoyle jilted.' He handed the letter to Pocklington. Let him do some work for a change and maybe he'd stop making up absurd theories, Bunce reflected. The letter was on cheap paper procurable at any stationer's and was printed, as was the direction on the envelope, in plain block letters. Its message was brief and to the point: 'ASK MUTTON WHY HIS SISTER KILLED HERSELF WHEN GARMOYLE REFUSED TO HONOR THEIR ENGAGEMENT.'

'But this simply confirms my information,' Pocklington said excitedly when he had read the letter. 'I was conferring with Alan — Mr Smythson — and he mentioned Mutton as a distinct possibility for the murderer.' He gave Bunce the gist of his conversation with Smythson. The local Inspector found his conduct in stealing off on his own to interrogate a witness connected with the case highly unprofessional and said so roundly.

'I didn't,' replied Pocklington with indignation. 'He telephoned to consult me because he found me *sympathique* — that means sympathetic,' he explained graciously. 'I daresay he would not have answered questions as openly with someone else.'

'I see,' said Bunce from between his teeth. He was frankly enraged, but he saw no point in starting a fight when some provocative new material remained to be dealt with. Normally he would have felt that Mutton was one of the least probable prospects for the killer, but the letter which had just arrived, by giving him a compelling motive, put a different light on the matter. Hold on a moment though, thought Bunce — Smythson, by Pocklington's account, had not emphasized Mutton in any way while he was providing possible motives for some of the Fellows, but might he have sent the letter and reinforced its information by saying he had seen Mutton in the Combination Room? But there was no reason Bunce could imagine for him to do such a thing. Even if Smythson were Garmoyle's murderer, what good would he do himself by throwing suspicion onto Mutton? And that was leaving out the attempt on Smythson at the Bumps. With two separate signposts pointing in Mutton's direction the information was worth checking, though Bunce was suspicious of anything that that bungler Pocklington came up with. Mutton first, then, and afterward Grubb and — Austrey and Fenchurch. It worried him that the last two names kept cropping up. Austrey in particular had a very strong motive, and even Fenchurch's quarrel with Garmoyle was not altogether to be sneezed at in a community where the trivial, as the world measures importance, is magnified to what many might consider an exaggerated degree. Some of the academic controversies reminded Bunce of a story he had heard in his history class at school about two Russian religious sects that used to kill each other because one lot crossed itself with two fingers, while the other lot did it with three. Fine goings-on — and they called themselves Christians! There was no accounting for the vagaries of human nature, or what humanity might consider important enough to kill a neighbour over. Still, he'd be willing to wager good money on Mr Fenchurch's essential sanity.

Before they left the office Bunce telephoned the Sheepshanks porter to ascertain if Mutton was in College. He was, so they drove there to interrogate him. Pocklington was bursting with self-importance over his timely discovery. He made a disagreeable companion for Bunce, who found himself almost hoping Mutton would be found innocent simply to balk Pocklington of the satisfaction of being right. Mutton's rooms in College were very like Fenchurch's — large, lofty-ceilinged and sparsely furnished — except the furniture, which was Georgian and quite beautiful but which badly wanted the attentions of an upholsterer; and his books, which predictably were on Russian history. Mutton was just sitting down to tea when they arrived and hospitably asked them to join him. They both accepted, though Bunce felt guilty as he did so, and he trotted off to fetch more hot water from the bathroom, a chamber the size of most drawing-rooms but containing only a large zinc bath with a mahogany surround, a porcelain basin, and a hot-plate for his kettle.

When they were settled with cups of milky tea and a plate of digestive biscuits Bunce, feeling curiously like a traitor, brought up their reason for coming to see him. Forturately Pocklington, who was inclined to be greedy, had elected to eat his biscuit before instigating inquiries, and since his mouth was full Bunce momentarily had a clear field. 'Mr Mutton,' he said diffidently, 'I have a very delicate question to ask you, and I am sorry that circumstances require my doing so. I hope the answer will not cause you too much pain.'

Mutton seemed rather taken aback; he said, 'I assume you refer to my book and to its unfortunate method of publication.'

'No,' replied the Inspector, 'I do not.'

Mutton looked surprised. 'Then you had better ask your question,' he said imperturbably, 'though I warn you I cannot imagine what it could be.' He took a sip of his tea.

Bunce was so disconcerted by Mutton's reply that he scarcely knew how to begin. Pocklington too seemed startled by his insouciance.

'It is about your sister,' Bunce said after a moment.

'My sister? I have no sister.'

'But you did have, surely,' said Pocklington. 'We understood. . . .'

'Oh, yes, I had once.' A light seemed to play over Mutton's grey features, softening them. 'Yes I had almost forgot her. Such a pretty girl.' He seemed to muse briefly, then came back to the present. 'What do you want to know about her? She's dead now.'

'We have been told,' said Bunce, 'that there was some question at one time of — of an understanding,' he paused discreetly, 'between your sister and Mr Garmoyle.'

'There was. They were to have been married.' Mutton spoke in a wondering tone, as though once having remembered her, he was surprised that he could ever have forgotten. 'She was pretty, you know, so pretty — not at all like me.' He gave a low deprecating laugh. 'I often wondered how we could be brother and sister. Of course she was my half-sister, and much younger than I. She was like an elf or a sunbeam, dainty and small and always dancing — when she walked, it was like dancing. And she was so gentle; she could not bear anything to be hurt. She had fair hair and amber-coloured eyes. And she became even prettier after Garmoyle asked her to marry him, until — I never could understand what she saw in Garmoyle,' he said with finality.

'But why did he break it off?' prompted Pocklington.

'He found out there was no money. Our parents were dead, so I suppose he had expected there was some, on account of the Cavesson connexion, you know. But there wasn't.'

'And then?' asked Bunce gently. 'Forgive me for asking you,

Mr Mutton, but I must know.'

'She fell out of a punt and drowned whilst alone in one of the backwaters of the Cam — some people said she fell. I never believed it — she was so very unhappy, you see. I do not think she fell. She said to me once, "All I can see ahead of me is black, Richard; there's nothing left but the dark." So I did not think it was an accident. I did what I could for her, but it was so very little. What could an old bachelor who knew only life in College do?' he cried out bitterly. There was a silence. 'I wish you had not reminded me of her,' said Mutton, half to himself. 'I had nearly forgotten.'

It was evident they would get nothing more out of Mutton that afternoon. When they left, he was staring at the wall of bookshelves with an empty teacup in his hand. As Bunce shut the door quietly behind him he thought he heard the ghost of an utterance whispered in the room beyond, '— so pretty.'

21 Police at Work

It was too late to see anyone else that evening. As they left Sheepshanks Bunce managed — very cleverly, he thought — to detach himself from Pocklington, of whose company he had had a surfeit for the present. He found the task surprisingly easy, for unknown to him Pocklington was anxious to have sufficient time to change before drinks in Smythson's rooms and the May Ball — he wished to look his best. When Bunce returned alone to the police station he found that Mrs Bunce had telephoned several times while he was out to ascertain when he would be home for his supper. Just as he arrived in his office she rang again. She was in an acrimonious mood, one unusual to her for she was generally a placid creature. But she had planned to go to her sister's that evening and did not wish to stay at home until her husband's late return.

Bunce did not like his wife's sister, a socially ambitious and disagreeable woman who was adept at stirring up her more lethargic sibling. She for her part did not care for Bunce, whom she had always considered rather a *mésalliance* for her sister — their father had been a solicitor in a small way, while Bunce's father, though more successful financially, was only a butcher. Her attitude had always rankled with Bunce; he felt that she gave herself airs and was an unfortunate influence on his wife. The situation had worsened when he joined the police, for she thought a policeman was, if possible, more socially unacceptable than a butcher. Thanks to Bunce's rise to eminence in the local Force, Mrs Bunce was surrounded by more creature comforts than Mrs Ratchett, but she had been educated to believe that in marrying Bunce she had married beneath her and it served as a small but constant irritant between them. Bunce was hungry when he spoke to her on the telephone and his temper suffered as a result. Their conversation had terminated with his wife's announcement that Bunce could warm up his own supper when he came home — she had better things to do with her time than to sit around Balmoral Cottage waiting for him and was going off to the Ratchetts' to do them.

After she had rung off Bunce sat undecided for a moment; then, reckoning he might as well stay and work on the case as go home to a dark house and a cold supper, he stumped sourly off to the canteen in the basement for a slice of soggy pork pie and a cup of weak tea. Inspector Jenkins, who was on night duty, was finishing off a cup of coffee at one of the tables and Bunce joined him, setting his tray down and surveying it with a disapproving stare. He said crossly, 'Every year the food gets worse. And I didn't have lunch today, either.'

'At least the coffee's not bad,' replied Jenkins comfortably. He peered into Bunce's teacup. 'You should have taken that instead. Their tea is ghastly — never touch the stuff here myself.'

'Coffee disagrees with me,' Bunce retorted grumpily. 'If I drink it in the evening, I can't sleep.'

'You're in a rotten mood, aren't you, my boy? The College Killer getting you down? I hear that he had another try today at lowering the population of Sheepshanks's Senior Common Room.'

'It would seem that way.' And Bunce told him of the events at the Bumps.

'Well,' said Jenkins when he had finished, 'it does sound as though Garmoyle's killer has had another go at it. And you think Mutton may be the one?'

'I don't know what to think,' Bunce replied. 'Certainly everything at the moment points in that direction. God knows he's not the only one with a motive, but it looks as though he and Austrey have the strongest grounds — along with Mrs Garmoyle. But I don't see how she could have got into College to do the poisoning without being noticed, women still being enough of a rarity at Sheepshanks to attract attention. It would be much too risky for her to attempt. As for Austrey, murder would seem an excessively drastic solution for his problem, with divorce at hand whether Garmoyle approved of it or not — I daresay Mrs G. could have got an American divorce; they're not nearly so particular over there. Austrey has been such an obvious suspect from the start that I feel he is almost too good to be true.'

'Have you figured out yet how and when the poisoning took place?'

'I had assumed that it must have been done around 6.30, when Bottom discovered the decanter was missing. It would seem that the killer must have had possession of the port then, though he could have taken it at any time during the afternoon as long as he returned it to the sideboard between the time the butler missed it and the time it reappeared. The tables are all set after lunch, so the only risk anyone would run of being seen in Hall during the afternoon would be by Bottom toward dinner-time — the lads who set the tables are long finished. The murderer must have taken the decanter away to doctor it in private.'

'But why would the killer bother to carry it off? Why didn't he just get on with the poisoning where he was? Surely it must have been more risky for him to take the decanter away with him.'

Bunce clutched his head in his hands. 'How would I know? Maybe he forgot to bring the poison with him and carried the decanter to his rooms or wherever he kept the stuff. For all I know, the missing decanter had nothing to do with the poisoning — the port could have been poisoned hours earlier — we don't *know* that the disappearing decanter was the one with the arsenic in it. Perhaps Mutton is a secret drinker and sneaked off with some of the port to fortify himself before dinner.'

Jenkins looked thoughtful. 'That's an idea. But if it's true, then you're more in the dark than ever, as far as when the poisoning might have occurred. Does Mutton act like a boozer?'

'He acts like someone who's round the bend,' said Bunce in exasperation. 'Can you imagine forgetting you had a sister who killed herself? And he almost had me believing him for a moment — maybe I'm going off the rails too.'

'Take it easy,' advised Jenkins. 'They're a queer bunch, from what you've told me; and from what I've seen of that Mr Fenchurch, you're right. I like him but he's an odd duck, and as for Dame Hermione Playfair — whew! The way I see it, you'd better try to stick to the facts for the time being, such as they are, and worry about motive later. Now the facts you've told me are that the decanter could have been poisoned any time that afternoon — why not in the morning, by the way?'

'Because the port decanter in use was nearly emptied by the Fellows at dinner the night before and the butler had left it that way, according to the boy who helped him clear the table. I gather Bottom wasn't feeling any too well even then, so he didn't refill it until after lunch the next day — I say "refill" for convenience's sake, but actually it was a different decanter he filled with port. The boy told me that Bottom rotates the decanters; when one is empty he replaces it with a clean one and takes the used decanter to the kitchens to wash and put away. He always does it himself because he won't trust anyone else — he's afraid one might get broken. There are a dozen and a half decanters in the same pattern. Apparently they use that many for College Feasts and that sort of thing.

'I gather Sheepshanks acquired them sometime in the eighteenth century; there were two dozen originally and six have been broken since then. I checked the number myself in case some kind of a switch had been made — none are missing, so the decanter which was taken from the sideboard must have been returned. I am assuming that even if the disappearance of one of the decanters held no sinister significance, the killer did not poison the port until after Bottom had refilled the second decanter, otherwise there would have been no absolute way of knowing which held the poison and he would have risked slaughtering half the Senior Common Room of Sheepshanks. Once both decanters were filled and in place the killer could pretty well count on the butler beginning with the first one in the sideboard; Bottom keeps one of port and one of madeira toward the front. The two spares are well to the rear, since they are so rarely required. But he is apt, when refilling one, to shift them about so that the spare decanters don't sit unused for too long.'

'Perhaps the murderer marked one of the bottles so he would know which was which.'

'No,' stated Bunce positively. 'I went over both bottles carefully. Unless, of course, he removed the mark while Garmoyle was actually dying. Professor Tempeste very properly took the decanter into custody, leaving it in sight of them all so no one might tamper with it, as soon as he suspected poison might be involved, but there was a short period before he did so. Though everyone at High Table seems to have stayed in the Combination Room with Garmoyle after he was taken ill, and it would look highly suspicious in retrospect if anyone had been seen returning to the Hall then.'

'So it all boils down to the following,' Jenkins summarized. 'The arsenic must have been administered to the port some time after dinner the night before but most probably after lunch that day, since the killer would have had to juggle the decanters about on the day to avoid killing off some of the others if he poisoned it before Bottom did the refilling. That makes it possible for Mutton or Peascod, though they were not at dinner that night, to be the poisoner, doesn't it?'

'Oh, yes. It wouldn't be feasible for the poison to have been added to the port after dinner – someone would surely have noticed if the killer had poured the stuff in while the decanter was being passed round, so it must have been done earlier. Therefore Mr Mutton or Mr Peascod might easily have done it. There is one circumstance which points toward Mr Mutton, in fact. While it's true he had an excuse for going down to the Combination Room — he wanted to leave a note for the butler — still if he was feeling as ill as he claims, why bother to have dinner sent up?'

'Look here,' said Jenkins suddenly, 'suppose there is a comparatively innocent explanation for the disappearance of the decanter — maybe your idea about Mutton tippling isn't so far off the mark. One of the Fellows or the College servants, or even one of the undergraduates may have been in the mood for an afternoon snort — though he'd have to be hard up — revolting stuff, port. Everyone undoubtedly knew where to find it, *and* must have known as well that the sideboard wasn't kept locked. But if that's what happened, why was the decanter returned full?'

'Provided the thief didn't drink too much, he could have watered the port — it's possible the difference in strength wouldn't have been noticed. At any rate, there's no way of proving it wasn't done, as he would have had to take the decanter which was finished at dinner,' Bunce said glumly, 'otherwise we'd have two corpses on our hands instead of one. Fine kettle of fish, isn't it? *And* none of the Fellows has an alibi for the entire afternoon, so as far as we know any one of 'em could have popped in at any time and tossed the stuff in. It's true we know that Smythson, Mutton, and Fenchurch were all in the vicinity that afternoon and if the port was poisoned while the decanter was missing, as still seems most likely, all three men were in the Combination Room near the crucial period. Still, that's not solid proof. The fact is that any of the Fellows could have gone to the Hall long enough to add the poison without being seen by anyone.'

'What about means of obtaining the poison?' asked Jenkins. 'Does that eliminate any of your suspects?'

'The flypaper the arsenic was soaked off was kept in a storeroom in one of the passages off the kitchens. All the Fellows could have gone there without being noticed. There is a key to the storeroom which hangs in the Combination Room — among other supplies nuts are stored there, and it seems Dr Shebbeare is very partial to walnuts. It has not been unknown, apparently, for him to consume a large bowl of them in an evening and it upsets him very much if there are none obtainable. As a safeguard a key is left in the Combination Room, so the butler at the Master's Lodge may replenish the supply should it run out after Bottom and the kitchen staff have left for the night. There is,' concluded Bunce on a note of despair, 'no means of narrowing the field at that end; and as for opportunity to poison, you know already that no one can be definitely eliminated there.'

'Never mind, we've got all that sorted out as best we can,' said Jenkins encouragingly. 'Now we can get down to motive.'

'Motive — there you have the most miserable mares'-nest I've ever run across. Mr Mutton has the strongest one at the moment, I should judge, but Mr Austrey runs him a close second, and they've all got a motive of some kind, every single one of them, except the Chaplain and Peascod — and I shouldn't be surprised, the way things have been going, if motives turned up for the pair of them shortly.' He ticked them off on his fingers. 'Dr Shebbeare wanted to protect the reputation of Sheepshanks. Mutton considered the deceased responsible for the death of his sister. Fenchurch, by Smythson's account to

Pocklington, had a whacking great fight with Garmoyle over his precious Chapel history and Grubb stuck his nasty little nose into it and got bitten for his pains. (I thought that boy was keeping back something when I talked to him.) According to Smythson, Garmoyle hit Grubb where it hurt, and I should be surprised from his reputation for that sort of thing if he hadn't followed it up on other occasions. If so, it's possible that Grubb hated Garmoyle enough to murder him. Then there's Austrey, who everyone says is in love with Mrs Garmoyle; and Smythson, who was furious at what he considered Garmoyle's high-handed interference in the matter of the manuscript — though now someone's had a try at doing *him* in — and Professor Tempeste, who considers all alcoholics a blot on the landscape. Those scientific chaps are apt to be a bit casual about a couple of million lives or so when it interferes with their scheme of things — I wonder how they feel about one or two? They scare me. I ask you, what am I to make of 'em all? I'm out of my depth.' He shrugged in a wide gesture of disgust.

Jenkins scratched his nose reflectively. 'Have you thought,' he inquired, 'that the manuscript you were telling me about, the one that is so valuable, might have something to do with the murder even though it wasn't stolen after all?'

Bunce stared at him. 'How?' he demanded.

'You told me at the time that some of the Fellows disagreed about whether it was to go or stay at Sheepshanks. I wonder if one of them could have got sufficiently upset over the matter to kill Garmoyle — perhaps Garmoyle wanted it to go when the murderer wanted it to stay, or the other way around. There's no question, I take it, that Garmoyle was meant to be the victim?'

'That has been established to my satisfaction,' replied Bunce. 'He was the only man present who was likely to start on the second decanter of port in an evening. I don't know how the killer figured he would that night — perhaps it was just luck. Bottom tells me that there hadn't been an occasion to use the back-up port decanter for some time. But Garmoyle had been drinking a great deal more lately by all accounts, and despite the fact that he was married he had been dining in College almost regularly. The odds were that sooner or later he would start drinking the spare decanter.'

'Then Garmoyle must be the key to the murder, and he was

involved with this discovery at Sheepshanks which you've been so mysterious about. You told me that Smythson was angry because Garmoyle pinched the thing from under his nose — in fact, you've listed it as a possible motive for Smythson...'

'Not very seriously,' interrupted Bunce.

'Still, it must be pretty important, this manuscript, if feelings are running so high over it, and who's to say someone didn't feel murderous about keeping the thing at Sheepshanks? It would help if you'd tell me what it is, by the way.'

Bunce told him the story of the *Cupid and Psyche* manuscript. When he had finished, Jenkins whistled through his teeth. 'Good lord,' he said. 'No wonder they want to keep it quiet until they decide what to do with it. That's a story that would shove my rapist to the back page of the London dailies if it got out. But surely there's still a chance the Shakespeare manuscript is mixed up in Garmoyle's killing and the attempted murder of Smythson. Who, for instance, told Lord Merlin of its existence? You still don't know, and by your account it could only have been Lord Cavesson, the Director or the Keeper of Manuscripts at the British Museum, or one of the Fellows.'

Bunce looked ashamed. 'You're right; I oughtn't to have cut the manuscript out of the running so soon,' he confessed. 'We were all so relieved when it turned up again that it didn't occur to me there might be any motive besides theft which could involve it in Garmoyle's murder. Mr Fenchurch did mention that the Master had been opposed at first to having the manuscript leave Sheepshanks but that he had changed his mind. I wonder now whether all the Fellows agreed with him as to its disposition or if there may have been differences of opinion. I expect I'd better check it out. I feel a prize fool, Peter, to have overlooked that, but working with Pocklington has addled my wits. The man is enough to try a saint. He goes off half-cocked at every opportunity, and I've been so busy trying to keep track of him and his notions that half the time I don't know where I am.'

'Don't I know it,' said his friend sympathetically. 'That one 'ud have me turning my hand to murder in no time — talk about high-and-mighty bastards. And I don't much care for the cut of his jib — a bit off, if you get me. If that's one of their fancy London policemen, I'll take a country constable any time. The way I read him, he'd be as likely to get caught in a vice-raid as to conduct one,' he finished in disgust.

Bunce stirred his tea absent-mindedly. 'All the same,' he said, 'I think it's Mutton. I'll have to check the business about the manuscript, and I can't prove anything yet, but I'm nigh on certain it's Mutton. Poor old bloke, I hate to think I'm right and I hate like fury for one of Pocklington's idiotic guesses to hit the mark, but it's mighty convenient for Mutton that he had a reason for being near the Hall at the time we think the decanter was fiddled. And there's the letter. I'd like to know who sent that letter, but the information in it is certainly accurate and it gives Mutton a better reason than anyone else for wishing Garmoyle dead — better even than Austrey. After all, divorces can be arranged even when one party disagrees. And I can't help but think Mutton was coming it a bit strong when he made out he had forgotten all about his sister. It just isn't on for a man to forget something like that. No, put them all together, motive and proven opportunity *and* a logical reason for the attempt to kill Smythson — and the odds are it's Mutton.' He sighed. 'That's the trouble with police work. Nine times out of ten it's the ones that look as if butter wouldn't melt in their mouths that are the real bad 'uns — he seems a nice unworldly old codger. But I've got to get proof, Peter, I've got to get proof.'

After Jenkins left, Bunce sat disconsolately chewing his cold pork pie. It was difficult to believe that a shy elderly don who gave the impression of being almost fearful of the world outside his College would commit an action as brutal as premeditated murder, but what else was he to believe? The facts undeniably pointed in that direction.

22 The May Ball

The Sheepshanks May Ball was in full swing. There had been some discussion among the Master and Fellows after Garmoyle's death as to the propriety of holding it, but Mrs Garmoyle had specifically requested that the festivities of May Week should not be curtailed on her husband's account, so tradition had been maintained. Inspector Bunce had not altogether approved of such a sizeable gathering while the killer was still at large and clearly still hunting, but since the attempt on Smythson had occurred in a public place and as there was no means of policing the entire city of Cambridge, it seemed pointless to object to the May Ball. Moreover, Pocklington would be present, for what that was worth as a deterrent.

It was a delightful evening. The air held a caressing warmth that is seldom encountered at night in the fen country, even in high summer; the earth still rendered up some of the heat which the sun had bestowed upon it earlier in the day. The view of the river from Sheepshanks Bridge was a study in mezzotinto — a sable sky, looking as thick and palpable as velvet, served as backdrop for stars that clustered and shone like brilliants in a jeweller's shop-window. These were reflected in surrealistic mimicry by the glassy black of the dark polished water, as was the balustrade of the bridge with statues of exotic and mythical beasts perching upon it, and the shadowy trees that grew by the water's edge, and the bridges of Trinity and Clare and King's, sensed rather than seen as ebony shapes etched upon deeper ebony in receding perspective. St John's two bridges wavered and swayed and shivered in drunken repetition within the depths of this perverse mirror as though a nightmare had seized upon familiar things. Under the banks the ducks were quacking drowsily to one another and the water-reeds rustled in a light breeze. Several of the College punts were tied between the bridge and the little island beside it, so that anyone so inclined might take a turn upon the river between dances, or pole to breakfast at Grantchester when the ball ended at dawn.

Sheepshanks College takes pride in maintaining an Edwardian splendour in the matter of feasts and balls. Guinea Feast, the annual observance of an occasion upon which the Master, when carving an entrée of roast duck, found a golden guinea in its innards, still consists of eight courses and twenty side-dishes, as does Pullets Feast, the commemoration of a disreputable episode in the history of the College. During the reign of one of the Georges the younger Fellows in the absence of the Master invited several local ladies of dubious reputation to dinner; their guests appeared appropriately clad in caps and academic gowns — and nothing else. Although no one in recent history has been known to make his way through all the courses of these formidable repasts, there would none the less be a great outcry from the traditionalists if a suggestion were made to abridge the menus. At High Table snuff is still offered with the cigars after the customary toast to the Queen; and the presence of women there, even the plainest and most scholarly, is categorically frowned upon.

This insistence on retroversion extends to the preparations for the May Ball. The kitchen staff had been busy for days preparing stuffed lobster, cold salmon, crab mayonnaise, and chicken in aspic with asparagus. One boy was delegated for a full day to decorate a series of galantines for the supper-table. The *pièce de résistance* in the Hall was to be a swan in full plumage (rather tough, it must be admitted, since June is not the season for swan) which reposed regally on a magnificent platter, one of the principal treasures among the College silver. An entire table was reserved for the desserts: *gâteaux, sorbets*, trifles heaped with whipped cream, ices of various descriptions, mountains of strawberries and Devonshire cream, a veritable Everest of blancmange, and the College's own syllabub, the recipe for which was one of the most closely guarded secrets in Cambridge. It had been passed down from College butler to College butler for ten generations; not even the Master was privy to the knowledge of its ingredients.

Two dance floors had been set up, one in a mammoth white tent in Great Court and the other in a smaller pavilion in Paul's Court. The orchestra in the larger tent played waltzes with an occasional fox trot, a custom which had been retained at Sheepshanks in the teeth of a highly vocal undergraduate protest. Due to the popularity of the College's May Ball with the senior members of the University, a result of the unstinting lavishness of the preparations and the almost legendary quality of the champagne, their attack had been successfully repelled and they were placated with the tent in Paul's Court, which held a group of the most modern description. Consequently the sedate Straussian strains rising from Great Court met and clashed in mid-air in a cacophonic duel with the dissonances which emanated from Paul's.

A student of the history of dress would have found the College Fellows a mine of source-material that evening — specimens ranging from the late Victorian to beyond the mid-twentieth century were present. Fenchurch was wearing his father's evening clothes which, though a trifle greenish in cast, fitted him so well he had never bothered to purchase a replacement. Mutton's dinner jacket belonged in style to a somewhat later period; its only defect was a large spot of mildew on the collar, a fact of which he appeared supremely unaware. Lord Cavesson, who had kindly volunteered to stay in Cambridge until further notice in anticipation of a request to that effect by a nervous Bunce, was superbly turned out, though his elegant figure would have done credit to a far less notable tailor. Austrey and Professor Tempeste were respectably but unremarkably clad. Peascod wore an ancient velvet smoking-jacket with a silk hunting-stock, an outrageously incongruous costume that gave him the look of a Lawrence portrait.

Smythson had permitted himself a touch of dash on this auspicious evening and wore a waistcoat of plum-coloured Chinese brocade which Pocklington, in conventional evening dress, had commented upon admiringly. Dr Shebbeare's portly bulk was robed in decent but undistinguished black, for his figure did not lend itself to display. Grubb's ill-fitting dinner jacket stood out in this company as obviously having been rented from one of the cheaper outfitters in town. Though the

Master had asked all the Fellows to attend, he would not have done so if Rosie had not insisted. Rosie lived with her parents in one of the terrace-houses near the railway station and worked at Boots the Chemists in Sidney Street. She had barely made it through her O-levels and was uninterested in social economics, but she possessed such a plumply enticing figure that Grubb found it difficult to deny her anything she asked. So far this weakness had proved distressingly expensive and the results depressingly ineffectual. Grubb knew she was vulgar — greedy and grasping as a child and without a brain in her head — but it was her very vulgarity that attracted him.

Rosie had set her heart upon attending Sheepshanks's May Ball. Her maternal aunt was a Sheepshanks bedder, one of that grim sub-species of female who minister to the sets of rooms in College and who are notoriously chosen for their unattractiveness to undergraduates. She had a fund of stories illustrating the glories of Sheepshanks, and her descriptions of the ball to the young Rosie would cast newspaper accounts of the Queen's receptions at Buckingham Palace into the shade. They were, in fact, the only reason Rosie had paid any attention to the pimply youth who had so anxiously sought to take her to coffee after purchasing a tube of Britenezy toothpaste at her hands. As soon as he told her his College Rosie's limited but surprisingly efficient mind had begun to review her wardrobe for a possible dance-dress.

Against a background of London débutantes in elegantly *outrée* attire, girls from Girton and Newnham wearing long skirts and Indian gauze blouses, and the wives of dons and dignitaries swathed in sober muddy-hued prints which discreetly covered ageing arms and bosoms, Rosie stood out like an improbably pink artificial rose in a garden of lilies and English daisies and slightly fading hydrangeas. Her dress, of a vivid pink carnation-coloured taffeta, was festooned with clusters of sequins and swags of tulle. It billowed and rustled where the others' dresses flowed or drooped. The tulle ruffles about her low-cut bodice framed a capacious and bouncing bosom that shivered deliciously at her slightest movement like a smaller version of the vast blancmange in the Hall. Its luscious undulations attracted censorious glances from the dons' wives and drove Grubb into a frenzy of unsatisfied concupiscence. Mrs

Shebbeare, a diminutive woman in dark blue voile with a firm chin that bespoke a strong will, looked at Rosie disapprovingly as she whispered in her husband's ear. The Master directed his gaze to Rosie and his great shaggy eyebrows rose perceptibly.

Fenchurch had a pretty young girl in white, one of his many cousins, on his arm. He had a network of relations that extended over the greater part of East Anglia and was able to produce a suitable cousin for any occasion. This was her first May Ball, and while she did her best to seem worldly and blasé, it was a pose she constantly forgot. 'Oh, Cousin John,' she said now, clasping his arm in ecstasy, 'do let's dance.' At once he swept her into a waltz, his silver hair flowing in the breeze of their wake.

'I say,' remarked one of the undergraduates, poking his companion in the ribs, 'look at the Bargee; I didn't know the old boy could move so fast.' For Dr Shebbeare had enveloped his lady in a mighty Terpischorean embrace and was moving with deliberation about the dance-floor with her in his grasp, like a galleon with a dinghy in tow. As they waltzed her small bright eyes darted about, inspecting everything.

Rosie was in seventh heaven among all the nobs, though she was somewhat disappointed in the dresses of the ladies, rightly considering that there was none to compare with hers. Grubb, who hated waltzing — in his opinion it was an upper-class pursuit and therefore decadent — was none the less all too willing to take her onto the dance-floor, for it gave him an unparalleled opportunity to hold all that luxuriant femininity in his arms. So far she had proved chary of her favours, despite gifts of perfume and chocolates and a gold bracelet whose price had horrified him. Grubb's proximity did not have the same effect upon Rosie it had upon him, but she, a practical girl, fixed her eyes as they danced upon one of the undergraduates, the hero whose efforts had been chiefly responsible for making Sheepshanks Head of the River, and pretended he was guiding her about the floor in place of Grubb. She was so involved in this useful fantasy that Grubb was permitted to place a tentative hand on the curve of her generous breast, a liberty she generally rewarded with a slap when they were alone.

The dance ended. Fenchurch's little cousin looked up at him, sparkling with excitement, as he glanced about for a suitable undergraduate to introduce to her. Grubb slowly and reluctantly released Rosie from his embrace. The Master relinquished Mrs Shebbeare to Austrey, who had come up to perform his duty-dance, and moved off in conversation with Professor Tempeste. They walked out of the tent and through The Screens, the passage outside the Hall which connects the two main courts of Sheepshanks. The group playing in Paul's Court was considerably noisier than the one they had just left and they were grateful, as they passed through the cloisters under the Prye Library by means of a wrought-iron gate in the wall, for the comparative quiet by the river. By common consent they strolled past the Fellows' Garden, open for the Ball, and crossed over a little wooden bridge onto the island in the middle of the river. It was a tiny piece of land, barely large enough for an ornamental garden-house and several bushes. Later in the evening it would be a favoured spot for undergraduates to take their girls, but as the Ball had just begun the two dons had the island to themselves.

'I take it, then,' said the Master, 'that you are in agreement with me.'

'Absolutely,' replied Professor Tempeste. 'We could not make a better choice.'

'I have spoken with John and Richard, and they are in complete accord. I feel, however, that the announcement ought not to be made just yet.'

'I quite agree. Wouldn't be decent so soon, would it — stepping into dead men's shoes before they're cold and all that sort of thing. Though I hear, by the by, that there is talk of dead men's beds as well.'

Dr Shebbeare frowned. 'I make it a practice never to listen to gossip,' he said coldly. 'There may, by the way, be a problem with Smythson; he seems to feel he has a claim.'

'But that's nonsense,' protested Professor Tempeste. 'He has neither the background nor the scholarship. . .'

'There is, of course, no question of it. It would be quite unthinkable,' interrupted the Master. 'Even as Abbot's Librarian — a far less demanding post, as you know — I have found him not altogether satisfactory. And these bequests are not iron-clad, by any means; no, not at all — more what might be termed precatory; the College solicitor is in complete agreement with me on the subject. Still, Smythson too has seen a solicitor and it is possible we may have some unpleasantness over the matter.'

'It occurs to me, Master, that if he chooses to be difficult about the issue and fails, as he is bound to do, it may prove a means of ridding the College of an unsatisfactory Fellow.'

'That possibility had not escaped my notice; if so, some good would come of an unfortunate business. Though in confidence, my dear Professor, I feel that in the long run the replacement of Garmoyle will have a favourable result for the Pryevian Library. I am, of course, deeply distressed over this very painful affair, but if Garmoyle had kept on with the editing of the diaries I fear — I very much fear — that it would have had a detrimental effect upon the quality of their publication. He was failing, you know — I could see it in his work.'

'Alcohol is a curse,' said Tempeste solemnly. 'It weakens, it debilitates; it paralyses the will, it rots the intellect.'

'Not, however, in small quantities, I am happy to say,' replied the Master, who was fond of his madeira, with some asperity. 'But you are right; in Garmoyle's case the effects were beginning to show. There is no question that he had been a scholar of note, but he was slipping badly.'

'And once the disease reaches that stage, the results are nearly always irreversible.'

'You alone, my dear fellow,' Dr Shebbeare said, 'know how hopeless is the course of the alchoholic who refuses treatment . . .'

'I tried to save Garmoyle. Again and again I argued with him, begged him, pleaded with him to accept treatment, but he always refused. He actually laughed at me,' Professor Tempeste said furiously. 'The fool!'

'Quite so, and you also know how difficult it can be to remove an incompetent from a position of importance once he is installed there. So long as Garmoyle refused to resign, there was nothing I or any of us could do to replace him without causing a frightful scandal, one which would have overshadowed the College for years to come.' A cloud passed over his great moon of a face at the thought. 'And so I hope you will understand me when I say that this very sad affair may have proved a blessing in disguise — I trust I need say no more.'

'I take your meaning, Master,' the other replied as they

retraced their steps to the tent.

In the larger pavilion Peascod was enlightening Mrs Shebbeare as to the many variant versions of court-hand, and it was with some relief that she greeted the return of her husband. The dance-floor was now thronged. Little Crippen was dancing decorously, as befits a parson, with his wife, a pleasant-looking plump young woman; Smythson and Pocklington (very odd for a policeman to be a 'Varsity man — what were things coming to? thought Dr Shebbeare) were conversing with Lord Cavesson, whose punctilious courtesy would have indicated to anyone who knew him well that he was both bored and irritated with his company. Professor Tempeste noted disapprovingly that Grubb and the little shop-girl he had most inappropriately brought were slipping out of the entrance, possibly to try the music in the other tent, but more likely off for a bout in the bushes. Shouldn't wonder if she was a barmaid, he said to himself, though in that costume she looked more like a trollop than anything else; indeed, she reminded him of a girl at the Woolsack whom he had known in his less abstemious days . . . hastily he repressed this train of thought and brought his mind back to Grubb. That's what came of letting grammar-school men into the Senior Common Room; once let down the bars and there was no stopping it. Tempeste's nostrils flared in distaste as he went off in search of Mrs Tempeste, a bony, masculine woman in purple-spotted foulard who at no time in her life could have been accused of looking like a barmaid.

23 A Bout in the Bushes

'Where are you taking me, Bert? You told me we was going to have some supper in the Hall.' Angrily Rosie pulled her arm away from Grubb who, even while he winced at her shrill voice and uncertain grammar, could not tear his eyes away from the superb heavings of her indignant bosom.

'We will, Rosie, but supper won't be ready yet. I thought we might have a bit of fresh air first.' Damn, he thought to himself, she must have hollow legs. I could have sworn she'd had enough champagne to loosen her up a bit — she didn't seem to mind my hands while we were dancing.

'Fresh air!' she mocked him. 'I can get fresh air any time I like. I want to dance and see all the posh people, not wander about in the damp with beetles and things — ugh!' And though with that she brushed a flying insect off her arm, she left no doubt in Grubb's mind that she classified him among the beetles. But he was too far gone with drink and desire to care. Inflamed by the unaccustomed champagne and proximity to her full-blown charms, Grubb yet retained a low cunning. 'I was taking you to the tea-house on the island. They've a bar set up in it and all the débutantes and their escorts go out there — sometimes there's Royalty,' he said, hastily improvising and despising himself as he did so. But his blood was up and he found that at the moment he could not care less about ethics. Rosie's perfume (Boots best quality) combined with the musky smell of her skin and the fumes of the wine to make Grubb quite dizzy with lust. If he could just get her to the island where they would be alone, then surely, surely, she would be nice to him. And if she wasn't, murmured a voice in his wine-fuddled brain, if she wasn't — well, no one would hear her out there, would they? Serve her right, leading him on — she'd got to, she'd *got to* be nice to him. Surely she wouldn't have worn a dress like that if she hadn't meant him to —. He reached out and placed a trembling greedy hand on one of the gleaming hillocks that rose so enticingly out of the pink ruffles at her neckline.

'Just what do you think you're doing?' demanded Rosie indignantly, turning to face him. They had traversed the bridge to the little island and had reached the entrance to the tea-house, which had been built in the shape of a Greek temple. Its façade shone white in the moonlight, the marble of which it was constructed reflecting the moon's rays so faithfully that the building appeared to be luminous. It was obvious, however, that no lamp was lit within and that the aristocratic revellers promised by Grubb were nowhere nearby. 'Ow!' cried Rosie, emitting a screech of pure animal outrage, for Grubb had seized her clumsily about the waist and was attempting to kiss her. In the process the hand that fumbled with her breast had become frenzied and in trying to thrust it deeper into that pneumatic ripeness he had torn the stuff of her bodice. 'Aeiow!' Had Grubb possessed any remnant of academic detachment at that moment he might have reflected that her vowels would have done credit to an Eliza Doolittle, but he was beyond reasoning of any sort. Rosie pushed him away from her with a strength born of fury.

'Look what you've done, Bert Grubb,' she sobbed, holding the split silk together with one hand and fending him off with the other. 'It's ruined! I shall never be able to wear it again. I hate you!' She backed into the entrance of the tea-house with Grubb in pursuit; the push she had given him had merely made him more determined, and his glimpse of the delectably pink-tipped mound which burst forth from her torn bodice aroused him further. Rosie, becoming frightened, backed onto a rustic seat at the rear of the structure. 'Now don't be silly, Bert,' she said, striving for firmness, but her voice quavered slightly. Grubb paid no attention to her remonstrance. He fell upon her, burying his face in her bosom and forcing her into a reclining position. Rosie screamed, a startling sound in the quiet night where the only other noises were the muted pulse-beat of the dance-bands and the distant hum of traffic. It shocked Grubb out of his drunken libidinous trance into a realization of his position. 'Shut up!' he said savagely.

'But Bert, there's someone here!' Rosie was wedged against a figure in evening dress which was sprawled face downward at the far end of the seat. The shadows in the interior of the tea-house and the preoccupation of the other two occupants accounted for their not having noticed him before. Grubb, now thoroughly sobered, thought: my God! I only hope he's drunk enough not to have heard anything.

'Come on,' he said roughly, grasping her by the hand, 'we'd better get out of here.'

But Rosie, who had been sufficiently frightened to be grateful for any potential protector, no matter how far gone in liquor, refused to budge. 'You go,' she said, pulling away from him; 'I'm staying here.' She might as well go home anyway, she thought ruefully to herself; it was no use showing up at the Ball with her dress in this condition. Grubb's lubricious tendencies had by now been totally effaced, and the possible consequences of his actions presented themselves to him in lurid colours. But he was not going to leave Rosie there alone. Suppose the sleeper awoke and she poured her story of attempted outrage and assault into his ears! He wondered who it was. The back of the head with its thatch of hair silvered by the moonlight looked familiar but he could not quite place it. Funny how the shadows made it seem as if part of the slumberer's hair was dark, almost as if he was piebald. Grubb seized Rosie's hand once more and pulled her away from the bench.

'We'd best get away from here,' he repeated. At her look he dropped her hand as if it burned him and said, 'I won't touch you again, I promise. I-I'm sorry for what I did. I must have been drunk — I didn't mean to. I'll pay for your dress. Please — just please don't tell anyone. . .'

But Rosie was no longer listening to him. When he had seized her hand she had steadied herself on the shoulder of the sleeping figure with the other, and now she was staring wordlessly down at it. On her palm, showing with a dreadful clarity in the shaft of moonlight that entered through the doorway of the tea-house, was a smear of blood.

24 Dead as Mutton

Gingerly Grubb took the man by the arm and shook him. 'Are you all right?' he asked idiotically. There was no answer, but the figure fell silently back onto the garden-seat, revealing as it did so the dead face of Mutton. They saw that he must have been struck on the head by some heavy object, for the dark patch on his hair was sticky with blood, some of which had dripped down onto the shoulder of his coat — it was this upon which Rosie had laid her hand. 'My Gawd!' said Grubb, horrified, 'old Mutton's snuffed it!' Rosie, who had stood transfixed, staring down at her bloody hand, uttered a piercing shriek. 'Shut up!' Grubb said angrily; he felt queer, as if he were going to be sick. Though some of the more revolutionary social theories to which he subscribed were decidedly sanguinary, he had never seen a dead man before. 'We've got to decide what to do.' He stood lost in thought for a moment, gazing down at Mutton's body. 'We'll have to tell someone,' he said finally. 'If we don't and they find out we were here, it would look odd. Can you do something about your dress — pin a rose over it or something?' There was no answer. 'Please, Rosie — I swear I'll make it up to you if you won't tell —' He looked up pleadingly. Rosie was gone.

Grubb ran through the entrance of the little temple to look outside, but no one was there. He thought he caught sight of a glimpse of skirt beyond the bridge on the avenue which ran through the meadows of The Backs to Queen's Road, but he could not be certain and he decided to let her go. It was probably too late to catch her up anyway, and upon thinking it over he was relieved: it would save embarrassing explanations. For all his suspicion of the capitalist economic system and the world of aristocratic privilege, Grubb was in some ways a remarkably innocent young man: it did not occur to him that he might need an alibi for Mutton's murder.

He ran panting up the path from the island to the avenue on the College side of the bridge. Couples strolling in the Fellows' Garden and in the cloisters of Paul's Court were mildly surprised to see a dishevelled figure lope past — it was still early in the evening for that sort of thing. Without looking to left or right Grubb ran up to the tent in Great Court and entered, pushing his way through the dancers until he found the Master, who was just fetching himself a glass of champagne from a bar in the corner.

'Really, Grubb,' said Dr Shebbeare tartly, visibly displeased at the sight of the junior Fellow apparently tipsy, for Grubb's dinner-jacket, at best unprepossessing, was a mass of wrinkles and his tie had gone askew during the combat with Rosie. 'Really, Grubb,' the Master repeated, always a sign that he felt strongly about something, 'we cannot have this — most disgraceful. One must set an example, you know. You had better go to your rooms.' He set down his glass, preparatory to leading Grubb away. But Grubb quickly disabused the Master of his misconception by blurting out, 'Murder! Mutton!' At Dr Shebbeare's look of disbelief he said again, more quietly, 'Mutton — murdered. In the tea-house.'

The Master's famous calm stood him in good stead. After an instant of stupefaction he recovered himself and said, 'This is not the place to discuss it. Come with me to the Lodge.' Raising his head, he caught sight of Pocklington and beckoned to him. When the policeman came over, looking gratified by the Master's notice, Dr Shebbeare said urgently in a low voice, 'There has been a fresh disaster. Mr Grubb informs me that Mr Mutton — one of our Fellows, as you know — has been murdered in the ornamental garden-house on the island in the river. What ought we to do?'

Pocklington looked rather bewildered at this unexpected event, but recovered himself and said fussily, 'The first thing we must do is to see that nothing is disturbed until the local police arrive. Have you a man you can send to the island to stand guard?'

'I should think one of the waiters would do — there, that

man. He is on our kitchen staff and thoroughly trustworthy.' The Master called to a man who was slipping unobtrusively through the crowd, collecting empty glasses from tables and substituting clean ashtrays for dirty ones. 'Gillin? A word with you, if you please.' He told Gillin what needed to be done and the man melted swiftly out of the tent.

'Now,' said Pocklington, 'I must ring up the police station, and then I had better follow your man to the tea-house.'

'Once he's measured, we can move him,' said Bunce, who had been routed out of bed. Pocklington would have preferred to handle the matter himself, but the sergeant on duty had notified Bunce of the murder when Pocklington telephoned the station for men and floodlights.

The festivities attendant on the May Ball had been suspended at the arrival of the police, and a sergeant sat in the larger of the two tents taking the names of everyone present. The Great Gate had been locked, as had the other gates into the College, including the wrought-iron entrance to Queen's Road from The Backs; and a constable was stationed on the bridge which spanned the river in case someone still in the gardens or on The Backs should decide to remove himself by way of the water. All these precautions were standard and necessary, but as Bunce remarked, it was doubtful they would do any good. If the murderer had wished to leave the premises, he had had ample time to do so before the arrival of the police; and as the killer was almost certainly one of the College Fellows, it was unlikely that he would have bothered to attempt to leave the College grounds.

All the members of the Senior Common Room had attended the Ball that evening. The Master had especially requested their collective presence in the light of Garmoyle's death: since the College had chosen to hold the Ball despite the murder he felt that the absence of any of the Fellows might be misconstrued.

Bright lights had been set up in the little temple and about the nearby grounds, throwing the columns with their capitals of acanthus leaves into sharp relief against the dark shrubbery. The wooden bridge to the island cast inky shadows into the dancing water. In the angle formed between the bridge to the island and the stone bridge across the river lay several punts which gently nudged the bank as the water lapped the shore.

Mutton's body had been left as it was until the police photographer was finished and measurements were made. This had been done and they were now preparing to move him. It was easy to see that the weapon, whatever it might be, was not in the tea-house — the raking light of the police lamps left no corner in darkness. 'He must have been killed somewhere else and brought here,' Bunce said to Pocklington as they went over the ground outside the little temple. 'See those marks on the side of the path? It looks as if something has been dragged along there, the way the pebbles are scattered.'

'Yes,' agreed his colleague. 'And there's no sign of a weapon, though of course the killer could have carried it away with him.'

Bunce was quartering the grass beside the path like a questing hound. They had reached the small wooden bridge which joined the island to the shore and Bunce inspected it carefully as they passed over it, but could find no untoward signs. As he played his electric torch over the riverbank, however, he could see in its beam that some of the blades of grass were flattened down as if a heavy object had been dragged over them. The policemen followed the route indicated by the flattened grass until they came to the College punts moored by the bank. Bunce stopped short and whistled significantly. The canvas cushions on one of the seats of the nearest punt were disarranged and there was a dark stain on the upper one. 'I shouldn't be surprised if this was the place,' he said.

Pocklington pursed his lips. It irritated him to agree with his associate, even when Bunce stated the obvious. 'It would certainly appear so, but why would not the killer simply push the body into the water if he wished to conceal it?'

'He may have been afraid it would float. Also, the river is quite shallow in this stretch, only a couple of feet deep in places. He couldn't be certain no one would see Mutton's body unless he waded in and hid it under the bridge, in which case he would have got himself pretty thoroughly wet. My guess is that he wasn't worried about hiding it indefinitely — he simply wanted to make certain no one would see it and give the alarm until he was safely back at the dance. There was no one about at the time, so he bunged the body into the tea-house.'

As he spoke Bunce was examining the punt-pole which lay in

the bottom of the boat. It was an old-fashioned pole about twelve feet long, made of wood, not aluminium, and quite heavy. He had taken a handkerchief from his pocket and with this to mask his fingers was turning the pole about to see if there were any marks on it. His eye was caught by a small dark smudge near the tapered top corresponding to the stain on the cushion. Peering more closely at the punt-pole, he saw that several white hairs were caught in a splinter which projected slightly from the body of the pole near the smudge. 'Reckon he must have used this for the job. A damned awkward sort of weapon, if you ask me. On the other hand, he could have snatched it up and fetched Mutton a crack without being within reach, which would be handy.' He gave a grunt as he lifted the pole, still with the handkerchief wrapped about his hand, and hefted it. 'You could give someone quite a knock on the loaf with that, provided you were strong enough to swing it properly.' He examined the forked metal prong which was fastened to the bottom end of the pole. 'Nothing there,' Bunce said, disappointed. 'I had just hoped the killer might have caught himself or his clothes on that and given us a clue. Not a chance that he could have left prints on that wood — it's too rough — but we'll have to check for 'em anyway. Maybe the metal will show some.' Carefully he replaced the pole in the bottom of the punt and they went to inform the photographer and fingerprint-man that there was more work for them outside.

25 A Talk with the Master

The Master and Fellows of Sheepshanks were all sequestered in the Combination Room except Grubb, who had been cut out from the flock to undergo a little private grilling. They were very subdued for a time and at first there was little conversation, though gradually low-voiced discussions sprang up among them. Professor Tempeste, one of the first to regain his customary aplomb, demanded that the police afford some protection to the remaining members of the Sheepshanks Senior Common Room. 'This is an outrage,' he proclaimed angrily. 'Two murders in less than a week, both perpetrated upon members of the College — upon *Fellows* of the College — and so far as I can see, nothing has been achieved in the way of uncovering the murderer. I demand that something be done about it at once. I shall speak to the Chancellor of the University: he ought to be able to see that capable men are assigned to the case.' He glared at Pocklington — Bunce, he felt, could not be held to blame for the situation. He was, after all, only a country policeman, but the Yard man ought to have cleared matters up at once.

Bunce listened meekly to his rebukes, thankful at least that Tempeste had not been informed of the attempt on Smythson. Most likely that knowledge would have enraged him still further. Pocklington swelled up like an irate turkey-cock, but he did not dare to reply in kind. It was Fenchurch who eased the situation. 'Now, Algernon,' he said placatingly, 'you mustn't expect the police to move too quickly — they might convict the wrong man, don't you know. Just suppose they arrested you by mistake: you wouldn't at all care to be carted off in a Black Maria, would you now, eh?' This suggestion put Tempeste into such a paroxysm of temper that he was unable to speak for some time, which had possibly been Fenchurch's intention.

Bunce hastily interposed. 'Gentlemen,' he said, 'it will be necessary to interview each of you in turn as to where you were during the time Mr Mutton could have been killed and what possible motives you might have for his death. If you would be so kind as to go to your rooms until you are called, we shall endeavour not to keep you up longer than necessary. I need not remind you that the College entrances have all been locked except the Great Gate, which is guarded by a constable. It will thus be impossible for anyone to leave without permission, as we have already confiscated from all of you the keys which unfasten the other entrances. Dr Shebbeare, if you wouldn't mind remaining behind...'

'Not at all,' replied the Master.

The Fellows filed silently out of the Combination Room while Dr Shebbeare stayed with Bunce, Pocklington, and a detective-sergeant who was busy taking notes of the proceedings. Pocklington began by telling the Master about Smythson's claim that he had been pushed at the Bumps, and initiated the questioning by saying, 'Master, did you see Mr Mutton leave the tent at any time?'

'I cannot say that I did,' Dr Shebbeare answered, after pondering the question for a moment. 'At the opening of the Ball all the Fellows were in the larger of the two tents which had been set up for dancing. The senior Fellows generally stay in the larger tent,' he added, 'as the music in the other is a trifle — hem — unrestrained. But from time to time they may wander in the gardens or along The Backs if it is a fine evening, and when supper is served there is a general exodus to the Hall.'

'But it was not yet time for supper when Mr Mutton's body was discovered,' said Inspector Bunce.

'No, the Ball begins at ten o'clock, so naturally supper is not served until half-past twelve.'

'And it was — let me see — 11.52 when Grubb informed you of finding the body. No one seems to recall seeing Mr Mutton in the tent much after a quarter to eleven.'

'I do not understand why Mutton would have gone down to the river and got into one of the punts,' Dr Shebbeare said. 'He had a distinct aversion to punts. The killer must have lured him there somehow.'

'Perhaps,' said Bunce. 'The times involved are too vague to pin anything down. We don't know exactly when Mutton left the tent, and although all the Fellows have partial alibis for the hour after he was last seen, there is no proof that any one of the Fellows was in the tent during the entire period indicated. You, sir, for instance, have a joint alibi with Professor Tempeste for the time you were on the island — roughly 11.25 to 11.35. Neither of you looked in the garden-house, so we don't know whether the body was already there. As for the rest of the period in question, you were with your wife for a part but not all of it. She danced with other people and so did you. It isn't possible to prove that you couldn't have slipped out for a few moments without being noticed — while there are a great many people who can swear to seeing you most of the time, there is no one who can vouch for you during *all* of it.'

Dr Shebbeare's customary placidity fled. 'Are you suggesting. . . ?' he exclaimed wrathfully.

'I am suggesting nothing — the same holds true for all of the suspects in Mr Mutton's murder. If we could prove that any of you were definitely out of the tent alone during that hour, we might have something to go on. Equally, if we could prove that any of you stayed in the tent the whole time, it would help us. I understand that the Fellows were acting in part as hosts. For that reason many of the guests saw them at some time or other during the evening, but there is no way to prove who remained in the tent and who did not. Dr Shebbeare, have you any idea who might have had a motive for killing Mr Mutton? I'm asking you very seriously. I realize that you all held back certain information from us after Mr Garmoyle was murdered. . .' The Master bridled.

Bunce went on. 'There's no use denying it, sir. I daresay by your lights you all had good reason. But there's no gentleman's code among killers, and it's a matter of life and death now for everyone to tell the truth. It's no longer a case simply of shielding one among you who has done wrong; it's a question of preventing more killing. Who knows how many more the killer may think he has to silence? Now we have one likely lead as to motive in Mutton's case — he was down in the Combination Room the afternoon of the day Mr Garmoyle was killed. Maybe he saw the killer then and neglected telling us out of consideration for one of his colleagues — he was damn' foolish if he did. But that's a slender possibility, and we must ferret out any other motive we can find. To begin with, what sort of man was Mutton?'

'Rather an odd man even by our standards, which I expect you find odd to begin with,' said Dr Shebbeare. 'He was made a Fellow under the Sheepshanks charter, but he was an outstanding scholar as a young man and would certainly have been offered a Fellowship in any case — no question of that.'

'I don't follow,' Bunce said. 'What do you mean by the Sheepshanks charter?'

'When Sir Oliver refounded the College,' answered the Master, 'he inserted a provision that a Fellowship was to be awarded to one of his relations. In other words if a Sheepshanks descendant, direct or collateral, should express his desire for a Fellowship, he is to be given the preference provided no other descendant already holds a Fellowship at Sheepshanks. It is not an uncommon type of bequest to Cambridge Colleges; indeed, there are several others at Sheepshanks which have been drafted along roughly similar lines. I suppose one might term it a form of academic nepotism. Fortunately, it is a privilege rarely invoked nowadays. But, as I say, where Mutton was concerned it was purely a formality. He would without question have been elected even without the family connexion.'

'You say he was first-rate as a young man,' said Pocklington. 'Do you feel he had changed?'

'Quite definitely,' replied the Master. 'The death of his sister — drowned, poor girl — a tragic affair. . .'

He doesn't mind talking about it now, thought Bunce sourly to himself, when there's no longer a chance it might implicate Mutton in Garmoyle's murder.

'. . . affected him greatly. He was never the same afterward. And then the matter of his book — I expect you have heard of that? — finished what her death had begun.'

'I have heard something about it,' said Bunce cautiously.

'It was his *magnum opus* — he threw himself into it after his sister died. We scarcely saw him until it was finished. It was a biography of Catherine the Great; modern Russian history is his subject. At the time he completed it both University presses were full up, and as it happened, a trade publisher got to hear of the book through some channel or other and offered to publish it. Mutton was an unworldly sort of man and so he accepted the offer without, apparently, going over the contract carefully. You know how these things are — it sat gathering dust on the publisher's shelf until one of the bright young men there remembered that the lady in question had possessed rather a — hem — lurid reputation amongst her contemporaries. Though Mutton's work consisted largely of an analysis of the Empress's political manoeuvres, the bright young man was able, by judicious editing coupled with a suggestive title (it was *Strange Bedfellows*, as I recall) and an equally suggestive dust-jacket, to make it what is known in those circles, I believe, as a *best-seller*.' He pronounced the phrase as though it were a faintly indecent word in a foreign language. 'Most inappropriate for an academic. Mutton was rich overnight. But he was a broken man after that, and one can hardly blame him. Of course it was impossible in the circumstances to take his book seriously, but even Tempeste, who has a caustic tongue when he chooses, felt that *The Times Literary Supplement* reviewer was unnecessarily unkind in describing it as an excursion into the trivial.'

'But I thought you said the book was properly researched,' said Pocklington.

'Oh, yes, nothing wrong with it along those lines; in fact, it was quite a creditable piece of work from the historian's standpoint. A trifle dull, perhaps, but that doesn't matter here — if anything, it is apt to be an asset. Brilliance is always slightly suspect in scholarship, you see. As a quality it is unstable.'

'Then why was Mutton's book poorly reviewed?' Bunce enquired.

'My dear fellow,' the Master explained patiently, 'the one thing that simply is not countenanced in academic circles is *popular success* — the vulgarization of principle. Of course the man had to be punished. Wealth and fame (that is to say, non-academic fame) mean nothing in Cambridge, and its inhabitants must be discouraged from seeking them. There is no question but that poor Mutton had to be made an example of, though it is true that he very properly sought to expiate his offence by refusing to appropriate to his own use the moneys thus accrued.'

'What will happen to his money now? Had Mr Mutton any family?' asked Pocklington.

'He had only the sister I mentioned, who died unmarried years ago. He is distantly related to the Cavessons, though.'

'Have you any idea,' Bunce asked, 'how he has left his money?'

'You will have to ascertain that from his solicitor. The income at present is given to a charity of some sort. At one time he considered leaving his money to Sheepshanks — I do not know, however, whether he had made the arrangements for such a bequest before his death.'

'Then possible motives for Mutton's murder boil down to these,' said Bunce. 'First, he might have seen Garmoyle's killer doctoring the port when he went down to the Combination Room to leave a message for the butler — that's the most likely motive, but it leaves us with an open field of suspects. There is also the possibility that he was murdered for his money. Unless he had made arrangements to leave it to Sheepshanks or to the charity which is presently the recipient of the income, the odds are that it would go to the Cavessons — that is, to Lord Cavesson as head of the family. It's rather queer that the earl has been present on both occasions a murder was committed, and that he was at the Bumps during the attempt on Mr Smythson as well.'

'Surely you don't believe Lord Cavesson would commit murder,' said Pocklington, scandalized. Dr Shebbeare looked bland and said nothing; he may have felt some sense of relief at the prospect of suspicion falling upon someone who was not a member of the Senior Common Room.

'We mustn't overlook any possibilities, however improbable they may appear,' Bunce answered. 'I admit one doesn't expect peers of the Realm to go about killing people wholesale. None the less, it isn't unknown for a member of the House of Lords to be a murderer — look at Lord Ferrers. Look, moreover, at half the nobility of the country and what they did when there was nobody to stop 'em. I daresay they would have been astonished if anyone had told them it wasn't nice to knock off an enemy or a rival. What about royalty, for that matter?' he added, waxing eloquent. 'Most of the executions in this country were nothing more or less than legalized murder. Don't forget that the Cavessons come of very old stock — I'll wager you'd find a dozen or so of high-handed noble killers in the direct line of his descent without half looking. It used to be that the least scrupulous and most efficient when it came to killing was the family that went the farthest. That sort of trait gets bred in the bone and once it's in, it's difficult to breed it out again. Ask any kennel-man. *And I hear the family aren't too well off these days* — there was a heavy batch of death-duties when the old earl died. Reason enough for murder, perhaps, if it meant getting hold of Mr Mutton's money.'

'But there's no motive for Garmoyle's death if Lord Cavesson is the killer,' objected Pocklington.

'Ah, but isn't there? What of the Shakespeare manuscript? We've lost sight of it in all the excitement. Dr Shebbeare, what precisely is the standing of the manuscript at Sheepshanks, and why, since Lord Cavesson is hard up for money, is there any question of his not selling the manuscript if he does own it?'

'The history of the Cavesson Collection in the Abbot's Library is remarkably straightforward, as these matters go,' began the Master. 'The tenth Lord Cavesson had a scapegrace heir who went off to fight in the Peninsular War. He returned in 1812 with a Spanish wife who, some said, had been a camp-follower, and the old earl was furious. Upon his son's refusal to repudiate his wife — to add fuel to the flames, she of course was Roman Catholic and Lord Cavesson had become a rabid Pope-hater due to his French wife — he was disinherited of everything that was not entailed. The old lord died shortly afterward, some thought of a fit brought on by his son's conduct, and his personal library with the other unentailed property went to two daughters and a younger son.'

'How is it then that the present Lord Cavesson is part-owner of the manuscript?' inquired Pocklington. 'Did the title eventually descend to a cadet branch?'

'No,' replied the Master, 'the fifteenth earl is descended from both sides of the family. They have a tendency to inbreed. Where was I? — none of the younger children were particularly bookish, so they agreed to send the library on permanent loan to Sheepshanks, their father's College, as a memorial. The books, you see, were not known at the time to be especially valuable.'

'Wasn't Mutton one of the cousins of Lord Cavesson who own a part-share in the book?' Pocklington asked.

'He was, but he had removed himself from any decision-making on the subject. He told both Lord Cavesson and myself that it was up to the rest of the Cavesson family and the other Fellows to come to a decision, that he considered he had a conflict of interests.'

'What of the other Fellows?' said Bunce. 'Garmoyle, for instance. Was he for keeping the manuscript at Sheepshanks?'

'I am sorry to say that he was,' replied Dr Shebbeare. 'I too initially felt it would be appropriate, but upon giving the matter proper consideration I saw that it would be selfish to do so — the College does not have the resources to keep it here. It is, you realise, a unique object — Shakespeare's first poem and the only manuscript extant written in his holograph — and we have neither the time nor the space to provide for the scholars who naturally will wish to consult it. I feel that the British Museum or even the University Library would prove a far more suitable location. There is, of course, the Folger Library in America, but I should be most distressed to see it leave the country. I have conferred — in the strictest of confidence, you understand — with the Keeper of Manuscripts and the Director of the British Museum, who have assured me that they will do all they can to raise the funds necessary to keep the manuscript in England. I expect Mr Austrey will edit it, whether it reposes here or in London.'

'Was Mr Garmoyle very much opposed to having the *Cupid and Psyche* leave Sheepshanks?' persisted Inspector Bunce.

'I fear that he was,' the Master conceded with a sigh. 'He was a stubborn man, and he felt the glory of Sheepshanks would be somehow diminished if the Shakespeare manuscript were not to remain here. It was a foolish attitude to take when one considers that a few months ago no one knew it existed; still, he threatened to be difficult about it. I suppose he had adopted a proprietary attitude toward the manuscript on account of having found it. We need, you see, full agreement of the Fellows in order to release the manuscript. It could be done without his permission or that of Smythson, who is also against a sale, but it would take a very long time and involve legal proceedings, which would be undesirable.'

'Therefore it would be very much in Lord Cavesson's interest to have both Garmoyle and Smythson out of the way,' Pocklington said excitedly. 'And Lord Cavesson would have a larger share when the manuscript is sold if Mutton died, with the likelihood of inheriting his very large estate as well.'

'This is most upsetting,' declared Dr Shebbeare. 'Two Fellows murdered, and the life of another attempted. Where will it end? And now that poor Mutton is dead, I suppose the appointment of the new Pryevian Librarian will have to be postponed until another member of the Governing Body has been elected, as we had not yet made our decision official.'

'The Governing Body,' Bunce enquired. 'What is that?'

'The Governing Body of Sheepshanks consists of the Master and three of the senior Fellows: to wit, Mutton, Fenchurch, Professor Tempeste and myself. It is we who choose the Prye Librarian and the Abbot's Librarian and decide other important matters pertaining to the welfare of the College. We had virtually come to an agreement as to our candidate, but we felt it would be more appropriate to wait until Garmoyle's murderer had been found and the College had settled down a bit before we announced our decision. Now with Mutton dead we shall have to wait until his successor is appointed.' He sighed heavily. 'I must say, this is all making it very disagreeable for Sheepshanks. It is most awkward. I hope you will be able to apprehend the killer soon. I am grieved to think Lord Cavesson may be your man — one of the oldest families in England, you know, and connected with Sheepshanks as well. Still. . .' His voice trailed off tactfully but his face brightened. It was clear to Bunce that the Master would gladly fling Lord Cavesson to the lions if in that fashion Sheepshanks could escape the opprobrium of having housed a killer. None the less it was time to have a talk with Lord Cavesson.

26 Mrs Garmoyle

> 'And, like another Helen,
> fir'd another Troy.'
> John Dryden, *Alexander's Feast*

On Sunday morning Bunce, after only a few hours of sleep, was back in his office. Pocklington had not yet made an appearance, a favour for which his colleague was grateful. They had interrogated Lord Cavesson and all the Fellows the night before, a process which had lasted until three o'clock in the morning, but no fresh facts had emerged. Any of the men involved could have killed Mutton, since none of them had a solid alibi for the pertinent period. Grubb, as the one who had been first on the scene, had come in for some sharp questioning and for a short while it had seemed to the two inspectors that they might have found their man, for he presented all the classic signs of guilty knowledge. He had sweated heavily under questioning and the sour smell of fear had pervaded the Combination Room. But at length, in terror of his imminent arrest for murder, he had broken down and confessed that he had not been alone during the discovery of Mutton's body, and the police had corroborated his story by interviewing an affronted Rosie, swathed in a draggled satin wrapper. So that was that.

While it was true that a possible motive for Lord Cavesson had materialized, there was no other indication that he had killed Garmoyle or Mutton. His questioning had exposed no further indications of opportunity, and both inspectors were agreed in deciding to tread very lightly in that direction unless they had definite proof. Tempting though the Cavesson theory was, Bunce inclined toward one of the Fellows as killer, at least until they had some corroboration in the form of a large legacy in Mutton's will. From the little he had seen of Lord Cavesson, Bunce had contracted a great respect for his abilities: he was without doubt a man of intellect and decision. The Inspector would not put murder past him; if he felt it to be necessary he might murder and do it well, but Bunce did not like to think Lord Cavesson would kill solely for gain. Moreover, Bunce was willing to bet that he would not do so in a place where he was the only outsider and thus clearly an extraneous element, one apt to be carefully scrutinized if he should prove to have any sort of motive. No, the Inspector felt instinctively that the criminal was not the Earl of Cavesson. He believed the solution was closer to home. The Colleges were funny places, almost what you might expect a convent or monastery to be like, though Bunce's solid low-churchmanship did not permit him to envisage those strongholds of popery very distinctly. With so many persons of high temperament virtually living in one another's pockets — even the married Fellows seemed to spend a good deal of their time in College — one would expect them to get on each other's nerves. All were very ambitious men in their way, determined men, men who would not hesitate to demolish a reputation for the sake of a theory: perhaps one of them had reached a point where he was not averse to destroying a life as well.

Having come to a temporary pause in his thoughts, Bunce got out the letter he had received the day before and studied it. He vaguely recalled having noticed something odd about it upon its arrival, but Pocklington's interruption had caused the irregularity to go clean out of his head at the time. Now he wanted another look to see if he might determine what it could be. He read the letter over, examining it carefully for any unusual features which might provide a clue to the sender. 'ASK MUTTON WHY HIS SISTER KILLED HERSELF WHEN GARMOYLE REFUSED TO HONOR THEIR ENGAGEMENT.' 'Ask Mutton . . .' Not 'Mr Mutton' or 'Richard Mutton' — one of the Fellows was perhaps the writer. But he didn't think that was what had puzzled him at the first reading. '. . . Garmoyle refused to honor their engagement.' Honor . . . honor? That was it! Of course! what a fool he'd been. He was ashamed to think he hadn't got onto it right away. Unless — could it be a trick to try to implicate her? It was so obvious. She must have lived here for years — surely it was a slip she would be particularly careful not to make. Still, it was a starting-point. Whether or not it was she who had tried to cast suspicion on Mutton, she was an important factor if someone had bothered to point a finger at her in the attempt.

Bunce left his office and walked out to the car-park. The weather, apparently regretting its prodigality of the past few days, had turned grey and cool. As he swung past Parker's Piece mist clung to the grass, obscuring the façade of the University Arms Hotel which faces onto the open ground and thickening as he neared the streets leading to the river. He threaded his way down Mill Lane to the bridge by means of which Silver Street spans the Cam, past Darwin College, past Newnham's displeasing raw red brick and the unrelieved modernity of the Sidgwick Site to Cranmer Road. He had considered telephoning Mrs Garmoyle to see if she was at home, but upon second thoughts had decided it would be preferable to take her by surprise. A green Austin Princess — an expensive car for an academic, Bunce noted — was drawn up in front of the house. The Inspector rang the bell and the door was answered by Helen Garmoyle. Though the hour was still early, she was dressed to go out — for church, Bunce guessed. She wore grey, possibly as a half-way concession to widow's weeds, but it was a very becoming grey, a suede suit with a pearl-grey silk shirt which was hardly penitential in effect. Her blondeness was not now so pale: her cheeks were attractively flushed and her eyes were bright, perhaps with expectation, for they clouded instantly at the sight of him. 'Oh, Inspector Bunce, good morning. Do come in,' she said, however, and led him to the sitting-room. When they were seated she asked, 'Have you discovered who killed my husband?'

'Not yet, Mrs Garmoyle,' replied Bunce, 'though we've had some would-be helpers here and there. This is from one of them.' He handed her the anonymous letter. She took it from him, read it through with composure, and handed it back to him.

'Have you discussed this with Mr Mutton?' she asked.

'I'm afraid that will be impossible, under the circumstances,' Bunce answered. 'Mr Mutton was killed last night while the Sheepshanks May Ball was in progress.'

She gasped. 'Oh! but that makes everything worse!' She stopped as she saw his eyes on her. 'I mean, how dreadful — poor Richard. But couldn't it have been suicide? If this letter is true, then he may have been overcome with remorse and killed himself when he realized what he had done. Poor man. I do remember hearing something about his sister. It hit him very hard, I believe.'

Bunce stared at her until her eyes fell before his. He said then, 'Mrs Garmoyle, I'm quite certain you sent me this letter. Not only that, but I have proof which I believe would stand up in a court of law.'

'But I wore gloves—' she began, then stopped. All the colour left her face and she sat still as a hare that has sighted a hunter, her great eyes gazing at him.

Bunce was very pleased with himself. It had seemed too easy, a piece of cake, in fact. He really had no proof it was she. He still could not understand why she had made such a foolish slip in writing the letter.

'Why did you do it?' he asked. 'We have never at any time suspected you. It would have been impossible for you to poison the decanter without being seen by someone.' She sat mute, her lips firmly closed. 'I see,' he went on, suddenly enlightened. 'You weren't protecting yourself. You did it for someone else, for Mr Austrey.'

'He didn't do it!' she burst out. 'He would never do such a thing. But I was afraid you would think he had a reason. I know it was wicked of me. I am — was — fond of Richard Mutton. I felt sorry for him. I didn't mean to harm him — I was certain he wouldn't be convicted if he was innocent. But I was so afraid you would just assume it must be Robert, that you wouldn't even bother to see if anyone else had a serious motive. Richard Mutton's was the only one I knew about, but I was sure there were others — I knew there must be others.' She gave a shiver.

'Was living with him that bad?' Bunce asked, startled.

'I knew about Penelope Mutton because Ernest told me. He thought he was very clever to have got out of it, particularly, he said, as she had proved to be mentally unstable. I wasn't so lucky — I did have money, and he could be charming when he chose, you see. Poor girl; Ernest could be a wall of ice. When one knew him, there was nothing there but hardness and cruelty. No tenderness, no affection. And his drinking made it worse. How did you know I had written the letter?'

'You misspelt a word,' said Bunce. He pointed to a line on the sheet of paper.

'But that's perfectly correct — oh!' Her hand went to her mouth.

'I didn't know at first whether someone else had spelt *honour* American-style on purpose to make it seem you had sent the letter, or whether you had forgotten to spell it in the English fashion.'

'I forgot,' she said, staring down at the paper. 'How could I have been so stupid? I was so careful, I thought . . . but you don't suspect him?' she pleaded, turning to Bunce. 'I swear he had nothing to do with it. He had no motive — I was going to file for a divorce, so there was no reason at all for Robert to . . . kill my husband.'

'I was given to understand that Mr Garmoyle was against divorce, that he was a Roman Catholic,' said the Inspector, watching her closely.

'He was, but . . .' she faltered, 'he couldn't stop me. I told him that if he didn't agree, I was going home, to the States, to get one there. He only wanted to hold onto me because of the money. We were hoping he would change his mind, it would have made it easier for Robert here, but if he hadn't I was going to get one anyway. So you see, it didn't make any difference.'

'But what about Mr Austrey's work?' Bunce countered shrewdly. 'Cambridge is a conservative place — especially the University. It might have made a difference at Sheepshanks.'

'No, I'm certain it wouldn't, and Robert said he could always go to Yale or Har —' Too late she realized that she had said too much.

Bunce rose to go. Mrs Garmoyle looked terrified. She knew that she had managed to make matters far worse for Austrey, but she held her head up bravely and said, 'I promise you, it was not Robert. Please believe me.'

'And I promise you,' answered Bunce, 'that if Mr Austrey isn't the murderer, nothing will happen to him — I'll see to that.' But he reflected to himself that the fact they had got as far as wanting a divorce was a bad sign, with Garmoyle as set against it as he was. If it had just been an affair, now, with no longings for permanence . . . but the other was dangerous. He was almost at the door to the hall when the telephone rang.

'Excuse me,' said Mrs Garmoyle. She went to answer it and held the receiver out to Bunce. It was the police station for him;

he had told them where he could be found.

'Glad to have caught you, sir,' said Sergeant Ely. 'We've just had a lad here, name of William Pardon. He says he works at Sheepshanks College.'

'What about him?' replied Bunce. He remembered William, a spotty youth who toiled in the kitchens.

'He came in with a story about overhearing something Mr Mutton said at the Bumps yesterday. He had wormed his way up to the front of the crowd and was standing next to the group of Fellows from Sheepshanks, when he claims Mutton said to Mr Fenchurch, "It's got to be Austrey, I'm certain it's Austrey," or words to that effect. Young William got the idea Mutton was talking about Garmoyle's killer, and now that Mr Mutton has been murdered, he's certain of it. He's in here shaking like a leaf — wouldn't have come to us except his Mum made him. She told him it was his duty and if Mr Fenchurch was the next victim he'd never be able to forgive himself. Just thought you ought to know soonest.'

'Ta,' said Bunce. He looked very grave as he rang off. It was beginning to look black for Austrey.

27 Is It Austrey?

Bunce was informed by the Sheepshanks porter that Mr Fenchurch was sure to be at matins in the Chapel as he never missed a Sunday, but that he should be available in fifteen minutes or so. The Inspector amused himself until the service ended by traversing the College courts, carefully keeping to the paths, for it is to the Fellows and their guests alone that the privilege of treading upon the cherished turf of the College lawns is reserved. The morning was still grey and chill, and the geraniums and fuchsia which adorned the cloisters of Great Court looked somehow forlorn despite the brightness of their colours. Drops of moisture trickled down the ancient stones of the Chapel, which soared above the buildings surrounding it. From its interior rose a sound of unearthly sexlessness and purity, like the songs of angels — the boys' choir singing a Bach anthem. The Inspector passed through The Screens to Paul's Court, where he stood for a moment looking up at the windows of the Pryevian Library. He was still wondering about the Shakespeare manuscript.

At length he turned back into Great Court just in time to see the massive doors of the Chapel swing open and release the worshippers in their academic gowns. Behind them scampered a group of small boys in diminutive gowns and high silk hats. One of these had just shoved a smaller child, who was snivelling into his sleeve, and two others were squaring off for a bout of fisticuffs in the shadow of the Chapel porch. The owners of the angel-voices, Bunce decided, in person more closely resembled imps than cherubim.

He waited until Fenchurch emerged from the Chapel a little

behind the others, for he had paused to admire one of his favourite stone carvings in the chancel. Fenchurch was mildly surprised to see the Inspector; he had not really thought about it but had always vaguely imagined that the police, like most other people, took Sundays off, impractical though the results might be. He greeted Bunce courteously and took him to his rooms where they could be private. 'Now,' said Fenchurch, 'what was it you wished to see me about?'

Bunce had come to find out more if he could about Austrey, and he felt that Fenchurch was the man to ask. 'Matters look rather bad for Mr Austrey,' he answered, and told Fenchurch about Mrs Garmoyle, the projected divorce, and the letter. Fenchurch looked grave as he listened. 'Frankly,' said Bunce when he had finished, 'I find it difficult to believe that Mr Austrey is the murderer. I like and admire him. As for this rigamarole with the letter, Mrs Garmoyle swears that he didn't put her up to it. But there is one more piece of evidence which at present seems almost damning and which apparently is within your power to explain. Someone overheard Mr Mutton discussing Mr Austrey with you at the Bumps yesterday, and I understand he said to you, "It must be Austrey; it's certain to be Austrey." Is that so, and was he referring to Garmoyle's murderer?' Fenchurch began to speak, and Bunce interrupted him. 'I know you feel a loyalty to Mr Austrey, sir, but please to remember that this is a matter of life and death. Mr Mutton was killed within a few hours of confiding in you, and it is entirely possible if Austrey is the murderer that you may be the next victim. Also, if he realizes that one of the kitchen-lads overheard your conversation with Mr Mutton, the boy will be in danger as well. I do beg you not to protect Mr Austrey at your own peril and that of other innocent people.'

In reply Fenchurch laughed, a sound of genuine amusement. Inspector Bunce looked at him disapprovingly; he did not find murder a laughing matter. 'You mustn't think me unfeeling, Inspector,' said Fenchurch when he was able to speak. 'It is simply that you are entirely off the track. As it happens, my conversation with Mutton was of a completely innocent nature. It had nothing to do with Garmoyle's murder, or rather, only incidentally. We both are — were,' he amended, 'on the Governing Body of the College, and Mutton was merely stating the obvious: the fact that Austrey is undeniably the man for the job of Prye Librarian now that the post is vacant. So you see there is nothing in your theory.'

'Nothing in it?' Bunce said explosively. 'Nothing in it? What a dunce I was not to think of it before. With Garmoyle dead, the way is clear for Austrey to have not only his wife but his job as well. Are all the members of your Governing Body agreed on Austrey for the position? I think the Master said something about that.'

'Yes; but see here, Inspector, this is ridiculous. I assure you Austrey is not the man to do such a thing. Furthermore, can't you see that he would be a fool if he did? His motive is *too* obvious — he'd be the first person you would suspect once you knew about the incentives. It would be putting his own head into a noose. Not only that, but Garmoyle was losing his grip; it was only a matter of time before the Master would have persuaded him to resign as Prye Librarian, and then the way would have been open for Austrey.'

'If murderers were as clever as you make them out to be, there'd be very few murders committed,' answered Bunce. 'You're not taking into account the fact that Austrey knew Garmoyle had fought at one time or another with nearly everyone at Sheepshanks. It may have seemed to him that there were plenty of other motives lying about to distract the police. And it's common knowledge that Garmoyle was completely set against a divorce. That alone would be a sufficient reason, and with the Prye Librarianship as an additional motive I'm sorry to say it looks as though Austrey may well be our man. He probably thought Mr Smythson had seen him doctoring the port before dinner, and as for Mutton — he must have overheard and misunderstood your conversation with Mutton at the Bumps and thought Mutton was talking about Garmoyle's murderer. I should be very careful not to be alone with him if I were you, Mr Fenchurch. You must watch yourself until we get enough evidence to take him in charge.'

'But see here,' expostulated Fenchurch. 'I know Robert Austrey well, and I tell you he is not capable of such a base and wicked action.'

With Bunce's reluctant conviction that Austrey was almost certainly the killer, a hardening had come in the policeman's feelings toward him. Bunce found that he resented Austrey for having made him like and trust him; he felt a sense of betrayal that made him harsher toward the man. 'If Mrs Garmoyle had managed to obtain a divorce — an American one, say — in spite of Garmoyle's refusal and had married Austrey, what then?' he demanded. 'Would Austrey still have been next in line for Garmoyle's job if Garmoyle resigned as Prye Librarian? Would the Master and Fellows have approved or disapproved?'

Fenchurch looked disturbed. 'I cannot say that there would have been approval, precisely. Scandal of any sort is frowned upon here. But. . .'

'But what? I don't think you're being frank with me, Mr Fenchurch. Garmoyle had made it clear that he wouldn't let his wife go without a struggle. Everyone in College seems to have known about, or least to have suspected, the affair. Surely you can't expect me to believe that the reaction to the wife of one Fellow of the College obtaining a divorce in order to marry another Fellow of the same College would be anything other than disapproving.'

'It is not a usual occurrence,' admitted Fenchurch, 'if only because the wives of dons are not generally of a type to rouse the stronger passions; but I daresay it would all have blown over in the end. It is ludicrous,' though he did not look amused, 'to assume that Austrey would be in any way tempted to use murder as a means of avoiding such a situation.'

'Yet Mrs Garmoyle told me that Austrey was prepared to leave this country and go to one of the American universities, if necessary.' Bunce saw that he had disconcerted Fenchurch.

'Helen Garmoyle must have misunderstood. I tell you the situation would not have called for such drastic measures.'

'I admire your loyalty,' Bunce replied, rising, 'but I'm afraid I can't believe you. I wish for Mr Austrey's sake that I could.' As Bunce was at the door Fenchurch said suddenly, 'Inspector, there is one small thing I happened to notice in the Combination Room the afternoon of the day Garmoyle died. I did not mention it because it is so very minor; in fact, I had completely forgotten it at the time, but now I wonder if it might not be of some importance. It is undoubtedly of no consequence, but upon reflection it strikes me as rather curious.'

'Yes?' said the Inspector, poised for flight.

'There was a damp spot on the carpet to the left of the fireplace, in the medallion next the border. I paid little attention to it as the Combination Room is subject to damp. Patches of it frequently crop up. But I have been thinking it over, and while the carpet by the window overlooking Paul's Court is almost always moist to the touch — the east wind comes off the fens in that direction, and I fear the stonework beneath the window is not what it was in the Abbot's day — the carpet by the fireplace has never, to my knowledge, suffered from damp before. It is, after all, in a position peculiarly suited to keep it dry, and we had had a fire at lunch as it was just before the weather turned warm.'

'Indeed?' said Bunce. 'Thank you, sir. It may have nothing to do with Mr Garmoyle's death, but it's as well for me to know about it.'

On his way out he stopped at the Master's Lodge. The cadaverous butler who opened the door informed him reluctantly that Dr Shebbeare was at home; he did not approve of all these goings-on and considered policemen an improper adjunct to a gentleman's house. The Master was more cordial, though still greatly upset over Mutton's death. He invited Bunce into his library where a small but cheerful fire burned in the grate, and when they were seated said abruptly, 'Well? Have you come to a decision yet? Is it Cavesson?'

'There is no real proof yet as to the identity of the murderer,' replied the Inspector cautiously. 'I wanted to talk to you about Mr Garmoyle's position as Prye Librarian. I understand from Mr Fenchurch that Mr Austrey is in line for the job, so to speak.'

'There is no doubt of that,' answered the Master. 'He is unquestionably the man for it. But this is all in due course, you realize. It would be unseemly under the circumstances to replace Garmoyle at once.'

'Hasn't it occurred to you,' Bunce inquired, 'that the Prye Librarianship may have provided a motive for Garmoyle's murder?'

'What?' Dr Shebbeare stared at him. 'Nonsense, man,' he said testily. 'Piffle, utter piffle, I tell you! Austrey would not think of such a thing. In any case, he was bound to be Prye Librarian in the end. I can tell you — in confidence, of course — that Garmoyle's drinking had arrived at a stage where sooner or later it would have become necessary to replace him, despite the unpleasantness for the College.'

'Ah, yes; sooner or later,' Bunce pounced. 'But perhaps Mr Austrey couldn't afford to wait. There were, as I feel certain you know, other circumstances involved.'

The Master quelled him with a look. 'I do not listen to idle gossip,' he said icily. 'Austrey knew he had only to wait and he would inevitably have become Prye Librarian.'

'So it was an assured thing that Austrey would follow Garmoyle? Were there no other possible candidates?'

'None,' said Dr Shebbeare, 'except an American scholar at Harvard; and as his work is no more distinguished than Austrey's, we should naturally prefer the home-grown product. Smythson has been making a bit of a fuss: apparently he has acquired delusions of grandeur, but there is no question that we would choose *him*. I suspect he has entered himself in the lists chiefly to cause unpleasantness in the College — he is a contentious man and that sort of thing amuses him. But that is beside the point. The Governing Body are unanimously agreed that Austrey is our man. He is unquestionably the finest Shakespearean scholar of our time, and if he were not available we would bring someone of the proper calibre from outside the College. I told Smythson all this to make it clear that he has not got a chance, but he is pigheaded and persists in annoying me.'

'I don't think you realize, Dr Shebbeare, what an incentive Mr Austrey has had to murder. He was in an emotionally explosive situation, and the removal of Garmoyle would simultaneously have provided him with the two things he most covets.'

'My good man, it is far too obvious a set of motives,' the Master protested.

'To us, yes. But don't you see, his emotions may have warped his judgement — he may not see that what is obvious to him is equally obvious to everyone else.'

'No, no; I am certain you are mistaken. I should not like to think it of Lord Cavesson, but it must be he,' the Master declared. 'I know Robert Austrey well. He is not only a gentleman but a gentle man; he is incapable of such a deed. And to kill Mutton also, in order to protect himself from exposure? Never; it is impossible.' Dr Shebbeare showed far greater perturbation than was normal for him. The decorum of the College had been hopelessly upset, and this fact disturbed him greatly. Aside from his desire that the Senior Common Room of Sheepshanks should be found collectively innocent, he was unable to believe that a scholar of high quality could be capable of so injudicious a crime as murder.

'Thank you for your help, sir,' said Bunce, getting up from his chair. 'Oh, before I go, might I trouble you for another look at the Combination Room?'

'Of course,' the Master said, happy to drop a distressing subject. 'I shall take you myself; as you know, the doors are locked at this time of day, and only the Fellows and Bottom have keys. Poor old fellow, he is still very much under the weather, but improving daily, I am told,' he added as they walked across Great Court and entered a stone passageway off which a door led into the Combination Room. This was the outside entrance. Another door opened directly from the Combination Room to the Hall and the dais of High Table. No one was there when they entered. It was a comfortable room, made rather dark by the very handsome linenfold panelling which was pierced by narrow windows of mullioned stone set deep into the walls and by a commodious fireplace. At intervals portraits of deceased Fellows punctuated the walls; their fashions ran from ruffs to bands to neckcloths, enlivened by an occasional bishop in scarlet with lawn sleeves. Well-fed Victorian clergymen in muttonchop whiskers hung cheek by jowl with austere Jacobean divines. Among this comparatively sober company the portrait of Sir Oliver Sheepshanks over the mantelpiece struck a gorgeously incongruous note. It was a more informal study than the full-length portrait of Sir Oliver seated on the tiger-throne of Sultan Nawhar Allum which hangs in Hall, but in his parrot-coloured silks and gold-fringed turban with the fabulous Burridgehatty Emerald as clasp, he was a sufficiently exotic figure among the parsons.

Bunce went over to the Persian carpet which was spread in front of the now-extinct fire and examined it. It was perfectly dry. The pattern of the carpet was worked in wools of a deep rich claret-colour, almost a maroon; and though he peered carefully at the pile, he was unable to find any signs of a stain. He sniffed at the medallion which Fenchurch had indicated: was there an odour of some kind? It was difficult to tell. The wool smelt of sheep and wood-smoke and tobacco and the mustiness of years — he could not be certain of anything else. Before he left Bunce had a look at the carpet under the window which faced onto Paul's Court. Fenchurch was right. Unlike the other, it had an unpleasantly dank feel and smell. There was nothing else for him to see, so he thanked the Master and trudged across the court on the way to his car as Dr Shebbeare stood gazing after him with a troubled look in his eyes.

28 Wolf in Sheep's Clothing

Dinner in College on Sunday evening proved an uncomfortable occasion. Though one murder seemingly had not upset the College routine, a brace of homicides had proved too much even for that superbly greased and balanced machine. Bottom was still on sick-leave and William, overcome by his new responsibility of waiting upon High Table, had performed his duties clumsily, twice forgetting to offer a dish first to the Master, and dropping a soup-plate when he inadvertently caught Austrey's eye. He was certain that if Austrey heard he had gone to the police, he would be next on his list of corpses.

The unexpected and permanent removal of two of their number had discomposed the Fellows. There was little of the usual conversation at dinner, which went rather more quickly as a result, the cook's magnificent *tournedos Henri Quatre* notwithstanding; and at dessert it was noticeable, though the port decanter made its accustomed rounds, that its level was untouched. During coffee in the Combination Room, however, there was a slight easing of tension. Fenchurch and Crippen, who had sat next each other at table, continued a desultory conversation about the Chapel as they strolled in slightly behind the others. Most of Crippen's affections were taken up by his wonderful organ, but as befits a generous man he had praise to spare for the building which housed it. At dinner Fenchurch had described to him one of the roof gargoyles which he thought might be a self-portrait of the master-mason who had superintended the construction of the Chapel; earlier that day he had taken measurements of it. Now he slapped his pockets vigorously.

'Is something the matter?' asked Crippen.

'It is only that I seem to have left my expanding rule somewhere,' Fenchurch replied, looking vexed. 'It is a very good tape-measure made of steel, and I cannot think what I may have done with it — I'm certain it is not in my rooms.' He turned the long closed hanging sleeves of his gown inside out, with no result. The Chaplain appeared puzzled. 'These are a convenient place for tucking small objects. I was wearing my gown when I went up to the roof,' Fenchurch explained. Indeed, the gown was shabby enough for one to suppose that he used it to dust the gargoyles. Suddenly he brightened. 'I believe I know where it is,' he exclaimed. 'I last used it on the roof this afternoon — I must have left it out on the leads. I had better bring it in this evening. If it doesn't rain there will be a heavy dew, and the tape-measure may rust.'

'I expect to go to the Chapel for a bit after dinner — I thought that after writing part of my next week's sermon I might treat myself to a little Bach. Perhaps I could get it for you,' offered Crippen nobly after a moment's hesitation, for he was mortally afraid of heights, though he tried to hide it. Even the trip to the organ-loft was for him a journey of secret peril.

'Thank you,' Fenchurch replied as they reached the coffee-table, 'but I think I shall fetch it myself. There is a measurement which I should like to check again. One of the parapet-stones is distinctly larger than the others, according to my notes — I wonder if I could have set down the figures correctly. And I must confess,' he added, nodding to Smythson, Grubb and Austrey, who had poured their coffee and were in various stages of diluting it with cream and sugar, 'I am always glad of an excuse to look at the town from the Chapel roof, particularly in the evening light, which is so very beautiful. It mellows and gilds the landscape. I often think that if Vermeer had painted landscapes instead of interiors, he might have been able to do justice to those limpid subtleties of tone — certainly no one else has done so.'

'Vermeer! Nonsense, my dear fellow,' Professor Tempeste interrupted, coffee-cup in hand as he provided himself with a second libation. 'Constable's your man, or Turner. They're quite good enough for the portrayal of honest English countryside. There's no need to turn to a foreigner.'

'Such a pity, I always think, that Loggan's engraving of the Chapel did not turn out nearly so well as the one of King's,' said Peascod inconsequently.

'That, my dear man,' snapped Tempeste, 'has nothing to do with the conversation in hand. We are presently concerned with painting in oils, not the engraver's burin.'

Peascod was not abashed, as he had a convenient form of deafness which enabled him to hear only what he chose. This useful disability had greatly provoked Garmoyle, for it had generally prevented him from disturbing his colleague's customary serenity. Peascod continued now as though no one had spoken. 'Yes, Loggan's engraving of King's Chapel is remarkably fine, and so is the one of Trinity, you know. One cannot help feeling that he gave Sheepshanks short shrift, very short shrift indeed.' He nodded his head solemnly several times, then added unexpectedly in a low but curiously penetrating voice which extended to the far reaches of the Combination Room. 'Someone gave Mutton short shrift, poor fellow, and Garmoyle too.'

There was a silence, then a muted clatter of coffee-cups hastily set down, and a general dispersal began. It was a subject no one there cared to pursue. The Fellows drifted out into Great Court in twos and threes, thence to their rooms or their cars, and one or two of the younger Fellows, it must be confessed, to the Woolsack. Before going to the Chapel to retrieve his missing tape-measure, Fenchurch went first to his rooms to leave his gown and to fetch the notebook with the erroneous measurement of the parapet-stone and an electric torch. As he had surmised, the steel rule was not there. It must almost certainly be up on the roof. His next stop was at the Porter's Lodge, where the key to the Chapel was kept. Hobbs, who was on evening duty, lifted it from the board for him, saying lugubriously, 'These are wicked times we find ourselves in, Mr Fenchurch, sir. I never thought to see the day when murder would be done at Sheepshanks. Why, Mrs 'Obbs wouldn't 'ardly let me come to work today, she was that feared for me — I 'ad to tear meself from out 'er harms. But I says to her, "Sarah," I says, "It is my Dooty, and my Dooty I must do, whatever the cost." ' He paused impressively.

'Quite right, Hobbs; we rely on you,' said Fenchurch as he

took the proffered key.

The Chapel seemed even more vast in twilight than in the daytime. Its huge buttresses carried the soaring stone up to the deepening sky, providing an illusion of lightness that was belied by the size of the stones of which it was composed. Fenchurch stood in the fading light, his fond eye tracing the linear purity of the whole and the grace-notes of carving and ornament by means of which the sight of such grandeur, the fruit of so much labour and determination and, it would seem, blind faith — for who could be certain the fan-vaulted ceiling, that airy tracery wrought of tons of stone, would stay in place? — was made bearable. The birds were calling sleepily to one another as they settled for the night in the trees by the river. The onset of twilight made the colours of the flowers bordering Great Court seem preternaturally vivid. As Fenchurch watched, lamps blossomed in the windows of the rooms about the court.

Inside, the last light of day filtered greenly through the glass of the windows, making it appear that they floated upon the gloom. It was so dark within that Fenchurch had difficulty discerning the large mass of the rood-screen which separated the choir from the ante-chapel. It was as though he walked in some great petrified forest. The grey stone columns carved in the form of tree-trunks reared themselves to the roof eighty feet above where they spread in the bough-tracery of the vaulted ceiling, in this light sensed rather than seen. Though Fenchurch did not stop to turn on the lights, he moved briskly through the Chapel. Its proportions and the placing of its furniture were ingrained in him, and moving about in all parts of it second nature, so despite the rapidly failing light he walked with a sure step and without the aid of his torch to the small iron-bound door which guarded the mouth of the spiral staircase. Once there, he switched on the electric torch in order to find the keyhole. As there was no lighting in the staircase, only narrow slits in the outside wall, Fenchurch was forced to rely entirely on the illumination he had brought with him while he climbed the dangerously narrow steps to the roof. Once there, he refreshed himself with the sight of a Cambridge emerging half-veiled from an opalescent mist like Aphrodite from her sea-foam. Below, Sheepshanks Great Court was wrapped in a constantly changing smoke of cobweb and pearl. Entranced, he stood until the light faded and then repaired to the spot on the roof where he thought he had left his favourite tape-measure. But when he checked the coping where he expected to find it, it was not there. Fenchurch uttered an exclamation of annoyance. Perhaps when he had checked the depth of one of the roof-beams in the loft earlier that day. . .

As he re-entered the stone passage which led both to loft and to staircase, he thought he heard a faint rustle. Not rats, he hoped — perhaps a bat. They were not unknown in the loft, and there were owls nesting in the small deep-set windows below the parapet. Fenchurch dismissed the noise from his mind as he entered the loft; here he was able to switch on the electric light which had been installed on one of the massive oak cross-beams near the entrance. There were no lights in the centre of the loft or at the far end, so the faint illumination provided had to be supplemented by his torch. Care was required to stay on the central spine of the ceiling in order to avoid the thin portions of the stone. One false step could plunge the unwary to destruction on the patterned marble floor eighty feet below. The stone backbone of the great vault was broad enough to walk upon, but footing in the half-light was made uncertain by the reversed stone scalloping at the sides which formed the fans of the ceiling and narrowed the central spine in places, though the path to be traversed was never too narrow to cross in safety if one could see where to step.

Fenchurch walked cautiously to the midpoint of the loft where one of the wider sections stood beneath a huge beam. A flash on the stone caught his eye. There it was! A ray from the torch had reflected off the polished steel case of the lost tape-measure. Rather annoying, that, he thought. If he had known it was under cover he could have waited until the next day to retrieve it. He bent down to pick it up and as he put it in his pocket, swish! where his head had been only a second before, something flew with vicious precision.

Instinctively Fenchurch dropped onto his stomach and looked in the direction from which the object seemed to have come. In the gloom some feet away he could discern a figure muffled in the uniform of Fenchurch's calling, an academic gown. The shape appeared to have no head, but in the blackness he could see slits through which eyes peered. They gave it an ominous and evilly exotic aspect, like a wicked djinn in an Eastern fairy-tale. In its hand was a long sturdy pole that Fenchurch recognized as one which usually stood by the door to the loft, one he used for taking large measurements; he had cut notches along its side. Apparently his assailant had attempted to knock him off the backbone of the ceiling in the hope that he would fall through one of the thin sections of the vaulting.

While Fenchurch was thus observing his attacker, he crawled slowly backward toward the choir-end of the loft. As he did so his enemy followed, but also slowly, as there was need for caution in the uncertain light. Now that the prostrate don presented a less inviting target to knock off the central spine, his attacker used the pole in an irritating though relatively ineffectual poking motion which did not, for the moment, bid to dislodge his intended victim from the slender area of safety. But respite, Fenchurch knew, was only temporary, for he was a comparatively slight man, his fit condition notwithstanding; and though he could not precisely judge the size of his opponent, he was certain that his attacker was the larger. As long as Fenchurch could keep out of reach he was safe, but as soon as the distance between them closed he knew he was done for, and it was inevitable that the killer would follow him until he was cornered at the far end of the loft.

The thicker blocks of stone at intervals along the sides of the ceiling were spaced too far apart for him to escape by jumping from one to the other — there was ultimately only one direction in which he could go. And his enemy had all the time he needed — there was no chance of interruption. Few souls ventured up to the loft besides his classes — only an occasional sightseer whose legs were as hardy as his curiosity, and even these came only in the daytime.

Suddenly the figure menacing him stumbled and cursed in a low monotone. If he had brought a torch with him, as surely he must have to negotiate the stairs, Fenchurch thought, he must have left it at the end of the loft in order to wield the pole which he had found so conveniently to hand. The only light near them was cast by the torch in Fenchurch's hand, and as that provided little illumination in the vast gloom, presumably his adversary had stumbled on an unseen projection in his path. Fenchurch took advantage of this brief interval to inch himself about so that his head faced toward the choir-end of the loft. He reckoned thus to give himself a double advantage, for he would be able to crawl faster along the ledge of stone now that he faced in the direction he was aiming for, and in facing away from his attacker he would be depriving him of the light of the torch.

This was a decided impediment to the forward motion of the masked figure — with no light directly in front of him, he was forced to proceed very slowly and gingerly for fear of stepping off onto a weak part of the ceiling. In spite of this improvement in Fenchurch's position, however, he found himself gradually being forced, by various proddings with the pole about his person, toward the far end of the loft, where like some small animal at bay, he would meet his end. Frantically as they inched their way forward he tried to think of some means to circumvent this certainty; but his scholar's brain, finely honed through decades of study, was unable to find any escape-hatch — not even the faint hope of one.

Slowly the black figure, looking like a huge bird of prey against the single feeble light-bulb at the entrance, moved forward; slowly Fenchurch, goaded by the pole, crept on. The only sounds were the rasp of shoe on stone, the rustle of cloth scraping along the blocks which formed the ceiling's spine, and an occasional grunt from Fenchurch when the questing pole encountered a portion of his anatomy. An observer privileged to witness the singular scene might have been reminded of Charon ferrying the dead across the Styx (had the infernal boatman's taste run to punts) with Fenchurch as his unfortunate cargo. The flickering light, the gradual but constant movement of both figures, the darkness which lapped about them, making it seem that they floated on a moonless sea, lent credence to this imagery.

Even as panic began to take hold of Fenchurch's mind, he found himself counting automatically as he crossed over each transverse arch of the great vaulted ceiling . . . eight . . . nine . . . ten . . . now they had left the antechapel and were directly over the carved wooden choir-screen. For the moment he had gained slightly on his adversary, who had stumbled once more on a hidden protuberance, and so he was temporarily out of reach of the pole. As he passed over the next arch a small circle of light piercing the stone caught his eye. At first, blind to everything but his immediate peril, he paid no heed to it; then he realized it was one of the holes concealed in the ornamental leaf-shaped bosses which formed the centre of each fan-vault. In every boss was an opening several inches in diameter through which a rope supporting a kind of boatswain's chair could be threaded in order to clean the stone ceiling. He paused involuntarily. None of the other openings over which he had passed had shown a light, and he had not turned on the lights when he entered the Chapel. If the person stalking him had done so, then surely they would have been visible while he was crawling along the ceiling.

The atavistic terror which had gripped him weakened its hold for an instant and he remembered — Crippen! A wave of relief swept over him. Crippen had mentioned something about practising on the organ this evening; he must just have entered the Chapel. But how to attract his notice from eighty feet above, with tons of stone between them? he asked himself despondently. Crippen might as well be in London for all the good it would do him. Fenchurch cast a swift look over his shoulder. The man in black had recovered his balance and was closing in, though he had not yet regained enough ground to be within striking distance with the pole.

Just then, remote but very clear, Fenchurch heard the single note of an organ filter up through the openings in the ceiling. His opponent heard it too and stopped uncertainly. What if. . . ? Fenchurch groped in his pocket for the metal-cased steel rule which had brought him up to the loft. His hand closed over it and quickly, before his attacker could divine what he was about and attempt to prevent him, he thrust it through the hole and waited, his heart beating rapidly. The black-swathed figure was almost upon him as he put his mouth to the aperture. 'Help, help!' he shouted.

Though his cries seemed lost in the vastness of the great ceiling, far below he could hear a distant but satisfying crash which echoed upward, followed by far-off footsteps which ran, it seemed, down wooden steps and along the marble floor. 'Thank God!' Fenchurch cried aloud in his relief. 'Crippen has heard!' For several seconds his antagonist halted indecisively, then made up his mind to flee. Tossing the pole aside with a clatter, he began a desperate flight to the passage at the opposite end of the loft. Though Fenchurch's torch was now behind him, he was moving toward the electric light, and fear led the black-clad figure to take risks with the treacherous ceiling beneath his feet which moments ago he would not have dared.

'Hoy!' said Fenchurch. 'Stop! Stop, I say,' but the man in front of him paid no attention. Panting, he reached safe ground just before Fenchurch and with a single gesture scooped up his torch from where he had left it, switched it on and ran down the passageway. Fenchurch followed as swiftly as he could, but even so was some steps behind on the winding staircase. The figure in front of him seemed not to take the uneven steps one by one, but rather to slide down them in a single fluid motion. After his narrow escape from death Fenchurch was in no mood to find himself at the bottom of the stairs with a broken leg, so he was forced to pursue at a more sedate pace. As he neared the doorway of the staircase he heard a commotion in the Chapel, and upon emerging into the nave he encountered Crippen in a state of some agitation.

'I say, Fenchurch, what on earth is going on?' he began without preamble. 'First that ruddy tape-measure you told me you'd left on the roof came crashing down from the ceiling — it just missed the organ and damn' near got me — and then as I reached the staircase to see what was the matter, though how I would have got up those stairs without a light I haven't a notion, someone dashed past me and out of the Chapel.'

Fenchurch, who had been short of breath upon reaching the foot of the stairs, now had his second wind. 'Come on, let's try to catch him. I'll explain later,' he called, running to the Chapel entrance. Crippen obediently followed him out to Great Court, but when they arrived there, their bird had flown. No one was abroad in the court; the cloisters and paths were deserted. The only trace of Fenchurch's late assailant was a crumpled black stocking with two holes cut in it which had been hastily tossed into an angle of the Chapel porch.

Crippen went to the front gate to question the Porter while Fenchurch made an unsuccessful survey of the other College courts before his return. Their quarry had evidently gone to earth — once in his rooms he was safe from detection.

'I suppose the stocking is a sort of clue,' said Crippen hopefully, giving it a dubious look as he dangled it between thumb and forefinger. 'After all, men don't go about buying ladies' stockings very often, do they?'

'I shouldn't think a busy shop assistant would be likely to notice a man buying stockings for his wife,' Fenchurch replied. 'Half the time they don't notice what one is buying, anyway — they only look at the price.'

'Oh,' said Crippen, rather scandalized. He could not imagine a man bold enough to buy his wife's underclothes.

'I must report this incident to Inspector Bunce,' Fenchurch said. 'It is clearly the work of the murderer, though I cannot imagine why he should wish to attack me.' The nearest telephone was in the Porter's Lodge where Hobbs listened avidly as Fenchurch recounted the details of the assault to the police sergeant on duty. Neither Bunce nor Pocklington was at the station, but the information would be relayed to them as soon as they could be reached, and in the meantime a constable would be sent at once. Upon this promise Fenchurch rang off. 'Until the police arrive, I think we must take measures of our own,' he said firmly. 'Hobbs, see that the other entrances to the College are locked, and please request that no one leave the premises. If anyone enters by the main gate, make a note of his name. Do so for everyone, but it is especially urgent that you should take note of the Fellows.' Hobbs, visibly gratified by the importance of his task, declared that no one would pass by him unseen.

'For though I say it as shouldn't,' he announced, 'I 'ave a Heagle Heye. Them lads may try their tricks, as many a time they 'ave,' he added in a confidential aside, 'but fool me they cannot — I sees 'em every time. *And* reports 'em — no bribes for hold 'Obbs, though some 'as been known to try,' he finished virtuously.

'Yes, yes. We all know you are a thoroughly dependable man,' said Fenchurch hastily, hoping to stem the flow of his loquacity. Hobbs found the comparatively quiet evening watch a sore trial and sought to alleviate it by a continuous flow of speech whenever the opportunity arose: it was rare for his victims to escape in less than a quarter of an hour. Now he opened his mouth to speak again, but Fenchurch forestalled him by saying, 'Mr Crippen and I will await the police in the Combination Room. When they arrive, please be so good as to direct them there,' and the two Fellows crossed the court.

29 *Investigation*

Once more Bunce had been routed from Balmoral Cottage, but at least this time he was not supperless and was, therefore, in a reasonably cheerful mood though he had been untimely torn from his Tennyson. Indeed he was secretly a little relieved, for he had begun to read *Locksley Hall* and so far was making heavy weather of it. In a way the Inspector was glad to hear of the attempt upon Fenchurch's life, for it would seem to indicate that Fenchurch was innocent of the murders of Garmoyle and Mutton.

It occurred to Bunce briefly to wonder if Fenchurch's attacker might be the M.A. Rapist on account of the similarity of his dress, but he rapidly dropped that theory as untenable. It was true that both men wore gowns, but what disguise could be more natural to a Fellow of Sheepshanks on his way from dinner in College? All he would need to complete it was a mask of some kind and if, having removed the mask, he was seen near the scene of his crime in that garment by another member of the College, what could be more natural and unsuspicious? Add to that the fact that it was extremely unlikely the rapist had recognized Fenchurch during his rescue of Dame Hermione, and the near-impossibility of his knowing that Fenchurch planned to go up to the Chapel roof at night, and that took care of that. No, it was not a crime likely to be perpetrated by someone like the rapist. It was the crime of one who knew Sheepshanks and its routine intimately, of one who knew that Fenchurch was going up to the roof after dinner because he had heard him say so — one of the Fellows, in fact.

Upon the Inspector's arrival at the Porter's Lodge he found

the constable with Hobbs, who was full of the attempt on Fenchurch and his own rôle in shutting up the College to prevent the murderer's getaway. Surely a futile measure, Bunce thought wearily, since the killer was so patently a member of the Senior Common Room; and anyway, the murderer had probably had enough time to leave if he wished. He elicited from the constable the fact that Fenchurch and Crippen were in the Combination Room, and went to join them. As he walked across the deserted court Bunce thought how easy it would be to pass unnoticed through this quiet place. Lamplight shone through cracks in the curtains of some of the sets of rooms around the court, but there was little illumination in Great Court itself. It would be simple to flit in and out unseen among the columns of the cloisters, where fantastic carvings cast fantastic shadows among which it was virtually impossible to tell whether anything moved.

In the Combination Room Fenchurch, aided by Crippen, gave him a concise account of the events in the Chapel. 'Who was at dinner this evening? Who might have heard your plans to go up to the roof?' asked Bunce. 'And — equally important, I should think — who could and who could not have heard Mr Crippen say that he was going to the Chapel later to practise? While it undoubtedly would have been possible for the killer to enter and leave the Chapel without Mr Crippen hearing or seeing him, particularly if the organ was being played at the time, surely the murderer would not have chosen to make his attempt with someone else there. It's true he could have waited behind the staircase door until he heard the organ and then crept out under cover of the music, but I hardly think he would have planned matters that way. No, I think that if he had overheard Mr Crippen's plans for the evening as well as yours, he would have waited for another opportunity. So it is vital to find out who could have heard what both of you said after dinner.'

Both men thought. 'All the Fellows were present at dinner, as was Lord Cavesson,' Fenchurch answered after a moment. 'Crippen and I began our conversation at the dinner-table, but I believe that I did not mention my design of going up to the Chapel roof until we were on our way to the Combination Room for coffee.' He meditated. 'Yes, that is correct, because it was not until then that I missed my tape-measure. We were the last to go in to coffee, were we not, Crippen? and it was as we did so that you said you might practise this evening, because you kindly offered to fetch it for me. It is possible that no one overheard you as the others, I recollect, had preceded us.'

'What of your decision to go up to the roof of the Chapel? Someone must have overheard that.'

'I know I mentioned it in the hearing of several of the Fellows. Don't you remember, Crippen? Tempeste and I entered into an argument on art-criticism as a result.'

'And Peascod — if you will recall, he joined in the discussion,' chimed in Crippen.

'Let me think who else was nearby at the time: Smythson, I believe. Yes, because I remember asking him for the use of the cream jug when he had finished with it.'

'And Austrey,' the Chaplain added. 'I had not realized he was directly behind me and I accidentally trod on his toe when I stepped back from the table after pouring my coffee. I felt very badly about it, though he kindly assured me no damage had been done.'

'And Grubb, I think, was standing beside Austrey. Several others were in the room, but I don't recall whether they were close enough to hear us.'

'That would be the Master and Lord Cavesson, then, who are the only ones who might be in the clear. We'll have to see what the others say concerning their whereabouts,' said Inspector Bunce. 'Had you mentioned your plan of practising to anyone before dinner, Mr Crippen?'

'No; in point of fact, I had only just decided during dinner to rehearse. I had planned to attend a meeting of the Purcell Society, you see, which was cancelled unexpectedly. I am quite certain that the only person I discussed it with was Mr Fenchurch — no one who had not overheard me speaking to him could have known I would be in the Chapel tonight.'

'That doesn't help us much, then,' said the Inspector. 'As far as we can tell, no one knew that Mr Crippen would be in the Chapel after dinner, whereas everyone but the Master and Lord Cavesson seems to have known that Mr Fenchurch was going there. And there's no absolute guarantee that Dr Shebbeare and Lord Cavesson mightn't have heard or been told Mr Fenchurch's plans too. We'd best have them all in and find out what we can.

Do any of the other Fellows know of the incident yet?'

'Only the Master,' replied Crippen. 'We thought we ought to tell him when we ordered that the College gates be shut.'

'Then the next step is to find out which of the Fellows are in their rooms and request them to stay there until notified. We can have them down here one at a time and hear what they have to say. Is there anyone you could send around to summon them? My sergeant was detained at headquarters, and I should prefer that the constable should stay on guard at the gate. Perhaps the Porter could go.'

'Bottom can send someone,' Fenchurch said. 'He has just recovered and insisted on returning to us after dinner tonight, though Dr Shebbeare urged him to go home and rest.' He rang a bell and the butler appeared, still drawn from his recent bout with fever. 'Ah, Bottom, would you be so kind as to send a boy from the kitchens on an errand, if someone is still there? You mustn't go yourself, you know, as you are so recently recovered and the night air might have an adverse effect.'

'Thank you, sir,' said Bottom, bobbing his head in acknowledgement of Fenchurch's thoughtfulness. 'There's William — he's a sensible enough lad. I'll fetch him from the kitchens.'

'I'll come with you,' offered Bunce. 'It will take less time.'

William, having duly received his instructions, made his way around the courts of Sheepshanks with his message. He had been instructed to employ brevity and restraint in carrying out his errand; and indeed, had been given only the most necessary information by Inspector Bunce. The latter, however, had reckoned without the highly efficient and lurid underground telegraph of the College servants. Hobbs's assistant in securing the gates, upon the completion of his task, had immediately gone round to the kitchens where clearing-up was still in progress. There he had been given a warm reception while he recounted the murder attempt as gleaned from Hobbs with sundry florid (and some wholly imaginary) embellishments. Thus the bare narrative entrusted to William by the Inspector sprouted, in the telling, a wealth of detail which was positively baroque in its variety; and by the time William had worked his way halfway around Great Court to Smythson's rooms his story had assumed all the formalism of an epic. As Smythson opened the door to his knock the boy began.

'Please, sir, Mr Fenchurch 'as been knocked on the 'ead and pushed through the roof of the Chapel,' he related with relish, 'and the perlice is 'ere and nobody is to leave his rooms, and everyone is to come and be hinterviewed but not until they sends for you, but Mr Smythson is to come now. 'E was chased up the stairs and over the roof by a man in black seven foot high what had a pitchfork and. . .'

Pocklington, who had been standing by the fireplace, came up behind Smythson. 'Good God, they will want me!' he said. 'I must go at once. Where are the police, my boy?'

William, irritated at this interruption of his tale, persisted, 'And then 'e fell through the ceiling and broke a 'ole in the stone. . .'

'That's quite enough of that,' said Pocklington. 'Where is Inspector Bunce? I must join him.'

'The Inspector said as no one was to come until called for,' William insisted stubbornly. He took up his tale once more. 'And all 'is bones is broke to pieces —'

'You stupid boy, I am a policeman — don't you recognize me? Tell me at once where Inspector Bunce is to be found.'

But William was not certain. He had last seen the Inspector in the kitchens but he had no idea where his headquarters, so to speak, were situated. Smythson, more accustomed to the workings of William's mental processes, said to the boy, 'Where am I to go to be interviewed? Surely Inspector Bunce must have told you.'

'He said to go to the Combination Room, sir,' replied William. He prepared to launch once more into his description of the horrors which had befallen Mr Fenchurch, but was balked of his object when Pocklington paid no more attention to him, saying to Smythson, 'I shall come with you, Alan.' The boy followed them out the door, consoling himself with the thought that others still waited to be told the news, and they parted company at the foot of the staircase.

30 Bunce Makes an Arrest

'I should be much obliged, Mr Smythson, if you would give me an accounting of how you have spent your time since dinner.' Inspector Bunce's tone approached the brusque; so many murders and near-murders understandably were making him nervy.

'Certainly, Inspector, I shall be happy to do so. Upon leaving the Combination Room I went directly to my own rooms — Inspector Pocklington can vouch for me, as we met in Great Court. He was on his way to see me.'

'Yes, that is so.' Pocklington's voice squeaked slightly and he coughed to clear his throat. 'I had walked over from the Woolsack after dinner to visit Mr Smythson.'

The room was becoming stuffy; Bunce noticed that the London Inspector was perspiring a little though Bunce himself did not feel especially warm. 'What time was that?' the local policeman queried.

'It was just half-eight,' Pocklington answered. 'I am certain because I looked at my watch when I arrived in Great Court — I thought the Fellows might still be at dinner, and if so I planned to take a stroll by the river until they had finished.'

'That adds up. Mr Fenchurch tells me dinner was over early tonight and that no one lingered afterward in the Combination Room. And has Mr Smythson been with you ever since?'

'We went directly to his rooms and were still there when the boy came to fetch him.'

'You're in the clear then, Mr Smythson. Lucky for you that you have a habit of consorting with the police in their off-hours.' Bunce cast a darkling look at Pocklington. As Smythson left, he leaned back to await the next Fellow with a sigh. The case was getting beyond him and he was desperately worried, afraid that more people might be killed before it was over and powerless to prevent it. Austrey must be the man responsible for the crimes, but there was not enough proof against him to stand up in a court of law. The chain of coincidence connecting him to the murders, however, was sufficiently strong since Fenchurch was the man to whom Mutton had mentioned Austrey's name at the river-bank. Austrey must be getting panicky. Apparently he thought Mutton had had some proof of his guilt which he had confided to Fenchurch, and therefore had determined to get rid of both men.

As conjecture this story was very pretty; as probability it was almost certainly what must have happened; but he needed proof. His sergeant was supervising a search of the loft, but it was a thousand to one against anything useful turning up.

Though nothing conclusive against Austrey emerged from the questioning, several of the other Fellows were definitely cleared. By Pocklington's testimony Smythson could not have conducted the attack on Fenchurch; nor, according to Fenchurch himself, could Crippen, who was playing the Chapel organ in the nave while the killer was up in the loft. Dr Shebbeare had gone directly to his study after dinner to work and might conceivably have slipped out through the french doors unknown to his wife or the butler, but Fenchurch was positive that his attacker was not as heavy a man as the Master, who had a readily distinguishable figure. Austrey had gone to his rooms alone, and had no way of proving he had not been the masked figure; the same was true of Lord Cavesson. Grubb had gone to the Woolsack for a quick drink, but as he had left the Combination Room before the others, he could have returned in time to attack Fenchurch — the barmaid was not certain how long he had been there. In spite of Rosie's testimony Grubb was not entirely in the clear in the matter of Mutton's death, for there had been an interval of some minutes at the May Ball during the period in question when she had gone to adjust her make-up, leaving Grubb alone.

Professor Tempeste had (he said) gone directly home after dinner, but as his wife had been at a Temperance Meeting she could not corroborate his statement. Peascod had gone over to the University Library to work on a manuscript he was deciphering but had not arrived there until after nine o'clock, according to the desk-porter. That could be accounted for by his customary vagueness — he said he had allowed himself the luxury of a potter along The Backs on the way — or it could bear a more sinister interpretation.

While they waited for word that the men had finished the search in the loft, Fenchurch was summoned to sign his statement. As he recapped his fountain-pen he remarked to Bunce, 'I suppose you were unable to discover anything about the damp spot on the Combination Room carpet.'

'I had a look at it but I couldn't make anything of it, I'm afraid.'

'A pity,' observed Fenchurch. 'The odds were against it meaning anything, of course, but I did think there was just a chance it might have been connected with the cupboard.'

'The cupboard? What cupboard?' asked Bunce, completely mystified.

'The cupboard next to the fireplace, naturally; what other would I mean?'

The Inspector stared at him. Fenchurch had appeared remarkably composed after the attempt on his life, but evidently he was not as calm as he seemed. The balance of his mind must in fact have become temporarily tilted under the strain of recent events, for no cupboard was to be seen in the room.

Fenchurch correctly interpreted the wild eye which Bunce cast at the fireplace. 'Has no one told you about it?' he inquired. 'Dear me, how very remiss; though it doubtless has no bearing upon Garmoyle's murder. I would have mentioned it, but I simply assumed that someone else must have done — it is such common knowledge that I expect no one thought to remark upon it.'

He rose from his chair and crossed to the left-hand side of the stone fireplace. Running his fingers over the linenfold panelling, he felt about for a moment. Then they heard a click and a small section of the wood panelling swung forward. 'It was built,' said Fenchurch, assuming the pedant's rôle, 'for the use of the Master — a Roman Catholic — in Elizabeth's reign. It has been ingeniously concealed, don't you think? No one uses it now; it is small and so shaped as to be of little use. He kept his breviary, candlesticks and crucifix with a receptacle for holy water there. Years ago Palinode (one of our senior Fellows, now retired) stored Hebrew scrolls in it — my word!'

The door had swung open and in the depths of the cupboard were to be seen the shattered remains of a decanter.

'Bless me — how very odd,' said Fenchurch. 'One can only suppose that the murderer must have dropped the decanter, but if so, where did he find another?'

'Where indeed?' the policeman replied grimly. 'I was told there were none missing from the kitchens.'

Bottom, who despite his enfeebled condition had refused to leave until the Combination Room was closed for the night and no longer needed his ministrations, was sent for and tottered in, supported by a minion. Both were unshakeable in declaring that the roster of College decanters was complete.

'But how can it be? Here's another,' Bunce said in exasperation, waving one of the pieces so recently disclosed by the secret cupboard.

'Don't see 'ow that could be, sir,' Bottom replied stolidly. 'Ours is a special pattern — never seen no others like 'em, myself.'

'Your count must be off, then — there must originally have been nineteen,' Pocklington insisted. Bottom drew himself up to his fullest height and spoke in outraged accents.

'My count is correct. If you don't believe me ask the Bursar, Mr Fenchurch. It's true, isn't it, sir?' he appealed to the Fellow.

'We keep careful track of them,' Fenchurch agreed. 'If one of the decanters were to be broken, I should be informed. I may say that no such incident has occurred since I have been Bursar: to my knowledge we have always had eighteen.'

'But there's something fishy going on. This is the same design as the others, isn't it?' Bunce asked Fenchurch. Bottom brought in one of the decanters from the sideboard in the Hall, and together they compared it with the fragments. There were pieces large enough to show that the broken decanter was of the identical pattern as those belonging to the College.

Bunce decided to leave this new mystery until the morning. He and Pocklington sent the others off to bed while they waited for notice that the search of the loft was completed. As Bunce was putting the statements obtained from the Fellows in his briefcase, there was a knock at the door and his sergeant stepped in. From his beaming face it was evident that he was the bearer of good news. 'We found something, sir, by the door to the loft. Just what the doctor ordered, it is,' he said jubilantly. Suddenly abashed as he recalled Pocklington's presence, he silently laid a small object on the table which they had been using as a desk. Bunce, who was nearest to it, picked it up to examine it. It was a silver cigarette lighter; on the bottom of its case was engraved in the facsimile of a small and markedly feminine hand: 'Darling R all love H.'

Austrey, unconscious of the damning evidence discovered against him, had planned to spend Monday morning in his customary scholarly pursuits. There was a spelling in the *Cupid and Psyche* manuscript which he wished to verify as one used in the First Folio of Shakespeare's plays; and in order to do so he found it necessary to repair to the Anderson Room, the University Library's repository for rare books. As he walked across Sheepshanks Bridge on the way to Burrell's Walk and his destination, he caught a glimpse through the trees of the Library's tower, that notoriously phallic symbol of Cambridge.

The rare books room of the University Library at Cambridge forms a hideous contrast to its equivalent in Oxford's Bodley. The scholar who consults a volume in one of the bays of Duke Humphrey, the rare book reading-room of the Bodleian, performs his researches in surroundings permeated with an atmosphere of medieval peace. The day stretches before him in infinite leisure, as though hours might as easily be years or centuries: a sense of timelessness pervades the studies of one who performs his labours in umber twilight at a desk where once clerks pored over chained volumes written in a crotchety Gothic hand.

It is regrettable that Cambridge's chief library possesses no antique nook, no venerable cranny where the learned may contemplate the erudition of past ages in a setting suitably archaic. Instead, the graceless brick edifice which so brazenly rears its obscene tower to dominate the Cambridge skyline provides for the purpose a room more fit for the filing of forms by drab and faceless minor civil servants than the faun-filled researches of classicists or the gilded and jewelled imaginings of medieval scholars. The Anderson Room, an uninspiring oblong, is furnished with sturdy, utilitarian and unlovely tables and chairs constructed of yellow oak. Raising one's eyes from (for example) the elegantly spare type-face with which Nicolas Jenson printed his edition of Pliny, one is abruptly and rudely recalled to the present rather than gradually acclimatized, as one is at Bodley: indeed, a scholar in the Anderson Room is apt to incur a case of the aesthetic and intellectual bends.

Austrey chose a table near a window and spread out his notes while an attendant went to fetch his books. But contrary to his usual custom, he found it difficult to immerse himself in the work before him. Fleshly thoughts raced unbidden through his mind, and he could not (or would not) expel them. Austrey was very happy that morning. The fruition of all his hopes and desires was at hand; and if he had occasional twinges of guilt, they did not disturb him unduly. It was the thought of Helen Garmoyle that most occupied him, but the Prye Librarianship was also dear to his heart, and he anticipated its possession with pleasure. In the past week Austrey's world had been turned topsy-turvy, most agreeably so as it now appeared, and he looked forward to the enjoyment of the two much-coveted prizes.

When his book was brought to him he sat absently turning the pages as his thoughts continued to wander. The present tendency of his mind to picture Mrs Garmoyle in various stages of enticing undress and amorous poses combined with other, more tangible distractions — the noise of elderly dons tottering along the pathway outside, heard through the open window; the stertorous breathing of ancient scholars exhausted by the effort of turning folio pages — to make concentration impossible. Austrey had just decided to give the whole thing up and return to his rooms at Sheepshanks when one of the library attendants sidled up to him. A sallow, bony young man with lank hair and rimless spectacles, he was plainly rattled. 'There is a policeman to see you downstairs at the desk, sir,' he whispered hoarsely. 'He requests that you will come at once — the matter, he says, is urgent.' There is a peculiarly carrying quality about a whisper, and Austrey found himself subjected to a barrage of glares from the other occupants of his table, who clearly resented the interruption. In deference to them he gathered up his papers as quietly as possible, then handed the book he had been working with to the attendant. 'I shan't be needing this again today,' he said.

When he arrived at the desk in the entrance hall, he found Bunce, with his sergeant in attendance, gazing irritably up at the portrait of the Cambridge bookseller 'Maps' Nicholson in cocked hat and periwig. The Inspector was both annoyed and indignant, for he had been refused admittance to the Anderson Room; refused entry, indeed, even to the first floor of the University Library. In vain had he stated the nature and urgency of his business, in vain invoked the majesty and omnipotence of the Law— the desk-porter had remained firm. It was the rule of the University that no unauthorized persons were allowed beyond the ground-floor entrance without the permission either of the Librarian or of the Under-Librarian in charge of issuing readers' tickets; and as neither gentleman was then in the building, it was as much as his job was worth, he intimated, to permit the police to go up. Finding him immovable, Bunce had at last reluctantly consented to the sending of an emissary.

'Good morning, Inspector,' said Austrey cordially when he had descended the stairs. He liked Bunce, and in his present mood he was disposed to be amiable to all the world. 'What can I do for you?'

Bunce did not respond to his greeting. 'I'm sorry to have to tell you, sir, that you are under arrest for the murders of Ernest Garmoyle and Richard Mutton, and the attempted murders of Alan Smythson and John Fenchurch,' he replied. 'Come along with me, if you please.'

Austrey stood very still. His golden reveries in the Anderson Room had vanished like soap-bubbles and a terrifying reality had taken their place. 'There— there must be some mistake,' he stammered.

'There's no mistake,' said Bunce stonily. 'We found this in the Chapel loft where Mr Fenchurch was attacked. It's yours, isn't it? Don't bother to deny it; we've found others to identify it.' He held out the silver lighter.

Austrey stared at it. 'My God, yes; it's mine, all right. But I wasn't in the loft, I tell you. Someone must have taken it and left it there to implicate me — I missed it several days ago.'

'That's what they all say. I did think you'd be able to think up a better story, Mr Austrey, you being a don,' Bunce remarked in a disappointed tone as he and the sergeant walked Austrey between them down the Library steps to a waiting police car.

31 Fenchurch's Hypothesis

'You must be feeling cock-a-hoop, my boy,' said Jenkins jovially, poking his broad countryman's face through the doorway of Bunce's office. 'Nobbled the College Killer at last, I hear.'

'Yes,' Bunce answered with a glum expression. 'He hasn't confessed to it yet, but there's no doubt that he's the man.'

'Then what's the matter with you? You should be on top of the world and instead you look as if you were going to a funeral. Tell you what — it's nearly eleven. Come round the corner and I'll stake you to a pint — that'll buck you up.'

Bunce shook his head. 'No, thanks, Peter,' he said.

Jenkins regarded his friend with exasperation. 'He was one of your pets, wasn't he — he and Fenchurch. I suppose that's why you're moping about. Snap out of it, Alf. It's not your fault he did 'em in. Look on the bright side — at least he and Fenchurch weren't in collusion on the job. If you think you've got troubles, what about me? In spite of that fancy newspaper story we cooked up, there hasn't been a sniff of the rapist. I'm as far from catching him as ever I was.'

'I've been meaning to talk to you about that,' Bunce said, rousing himself with an effort from his depression. 'Something rum happened the night Mutton was killed. I was too busy then with the murder to think of connecting it with anything else, but I've begun to wonder since.' He told Jenkins of Grubb's finding of the body with Rosie and how she had run away. 'At the time I thought only that the girl must have been afraid of getting mixed up with the police — people of that class often are — but one of our constables, Sennett, knows her. He lives in the same street, and his sister saw the girl at the cleaner's — she was taking the evening frock she had worn to the Ball to see if it could be mended. Sennett's sister told him the front was badly torn — Rosie said she caught it on a twig but it looked as though it must have been done in a brawl of some kind. You might have a talk with the girl. She was badly frightened on Saturday night, and I'm beginning to wonder if it was Grubb, not the body, that scared her. Why did he take her to such an isolated spot? She let slip he'd told her there was a bar for drinks set up in the tea-house but the College staff say they've never had one there, and I got the impression that anyone who goes out to the island is generally after a bit of you-know-what.'

'My God,' Jenkins said slowly, 'to think you may have had the rapist under your nose all the time. It could be him — it could very well be him; but it's not his usual *modus operandi*,' he continued with more caution. 'And it would be a terrible risk to take. The girl would have been almost certain to tell someone.'

'My guess is that he's been afraid to commit another assault in his usual get-up,' Bunce said. 'He may think, after seeing Figgins's newspaper account, that it would help us somehow to catch him. Now if that's so and Grubb is the rapist, he has undoubtedly been feeling thwarted lately. It's probable that the more he is prevented from attempting rape, the more he needs to attack a woman. He may have been driven to try something at the May Ball he hadn't intended simply because he hasn't his usual outlet. And from what I've seen of his Rosie, she's the sort would drive a man to rape even if he hadn't got it on his mind to begin with.'

'It's farfetched,' said Jenkins slowly, 'but you may have something. He's tall, he has ready access to an M.A. gown — not that it isn't easy enough to get hold of one — but the main thing is, he's got a tendency that way, if what you say about the girl is so. Give me her address, will you, and I'll have a word with her.'

On the morning after the most shattering day seen at Sheepshanks since an afternoon several centuries earlier when the Master and seven Fellows were arrested as Jacobite sympathizers, Fenchurch walked in the Fellows' Garden after breakfast in order to soothe his mind. The Fellows' Garden is a relic of a more pious age: though most of it is bedded out in flowers, a monastic herb-garden, looking much as it must have done in the Abbé Dieudonné's time, is tucked into one corner. Huge ancient elms that have happily and unaccountably escaped the ravages of the Netherlandish pox shade the walks, which in June are heavy with the scent of roses and stock and the murmur of bees.

Fenchurch paced along one of the paths in great perturbation of mind. His heart was heavy, both for the sake of his College and his friend. His friend, it must be confessed, came first; though no doubt Dr Shebbeare would have disapproved of his priorities. Sheepshanks had weathered many storms in the centuries since its foundation and was likely to surmount even greater crises in the future. Grubb's arrest for rape was unquestionably a shocking affair, but scarcely without precedent in the College annals: Fenchurch, well-versed in Sheepshankian lore, recollected a certain Fellow of Agnus Dei who had carried off an heiress and, in the words of the indictment subsequently drawn up against him, *'eam defloruit.'* It was Austrey's plight which upset Fenchurch. It was considerably easier for him to believe that Grubb might perpetrate a rape than it was for him to credit his old friend and associate with committing murder.

The well-kept flower-beds contended in vain for his eye as he passed by them; he cogitated with his gaze bent on the ground. As a result he was brought up short beside a peony clump, having just missed bumping into Smythson, who was so absorbed in a letter he was reading as also to be totally oblivious of company in the garden. The two men apologized to each other and Fenchurch, finding his solitude broken in upon, left the garden to wander down by the river. This was not a satisfactory alternative, as the weather was fine and the banks were lined with undergraduates, but to Fenchurch it was preferable to a garden with only one other man in it, if that man was Smythson. Encountering him even in his engrossed state had been disagreeable: Fenchurch was a charitable man but he consorted no more with the Abbot's Librarian than was absolutely necessary.

However the human mind, even the most highly trained mind, is a curiously erratic organ, subject to more vagaries of conduct than even psychologists care to think; and the sight of

Smythson coupled with his desire to exonerate Austrey produced a new train of thought. There were many reasons for Fenchurch's dislike of Smythson, and now one of them gave him an idea. The more he thought, the more plausible it seemed; and to substitute Smythson for Austrey in the prison cell would be far from displeasing. He deliberated for a bit, and having decided it could do no harm to try, turned his steps towards Parker's Piece and the police station. There he was fortunate enough to find Inspector Bunce alone in his cubicle of an office; Pocklington at that moment was at the Woolsack, giving the details of Austrey's arrest to a reporter from the London *Sentinel* and intimating that he was chiefly responsible for his apprehension.

Fenchurch tapped lightly on Bunce's door. 'Might I have a word with you, Inspector?'

Bunce looked up from his desk in surprise. He had not before encountered Fenchurch away from his natural setting and found it a disconcerting experience. This quintessential don seemed out of place amid the strip-lighting, frosted glass partitions and other appurtenances of modern bureaucracy; he was a distinct anachronism among the chrome-edged desks (the metal already peeling) and plastic padded swivel-chairs.

Bunce drew up a quasi-Scandinavian armchair and waited until his guest had settled into it. 'What can I do for you?' he asked uncomfortably. He knew very well that Fenchurch had come to protest Austrey's arrest, and he did not wish to discuss the matter.

'Inspector,' said Fenchurch earnestly, leaning forward in his chair to emphasize what he was about to say, 'you cannot believe that Robert Austrey is the man responsible for the murders which have been plaguing Sheepshanks.'

Bunce rose and walked to the other end of his office, then turned to face his questioner. 'Mr Fenchurch, I can see no point in discussing Mr Austrey's arrest with you — it would only upset the both of us. I don't mind telling you that I had hoped Mr Austrey wasn't the criminal, but he's the one with the strongest motive and we have a piece of proof there's no getting around. I've no doubt at all he's the man we want; and as I don't wish to quarrel with you, we had both best keep our tongues between our teeth.'

'But I don't think Austrey is tall enough to have been my assailant.'

'Come now, Mr Fenchurch,' said Bunce, losing patience with this inept attempt to clear Austrey, 'you know you said you couldn't be certain of the man's size. Austrey may have looked taller because of the lighting.'

'You must listen to me, Inspector. I'm certain it wasn't Austrey — I think it may have been Smythson.'

'Mr Smythson? No, it couldn't have been; you're dead wrong there.'

'But there is a reason, I tell you, why Smythson might have had a lady's stocking in his possession. At first I thought anyone might have gone in and bought one to use as a disguise, but I have since changed my mind. Why would the killer have bought a mask to have in readiness when he had no way of knowing in advance that I would be alone up on the roof of the Chapel? No one could have known about it until after dinner that evening — I did not myself know that I would be going.'

Bunce, who had been attempting to break in on Fenchurch's speech, said slowly, 'I hadn't thought of that. But,' as the indisputable fact reasserted itself in his mind, 'he must have bought it and then held it in reserve in case of need. It must have been Austrey — he's the one with the motive. And besides, it couldn't possibly have been Smythson. He has an alibi.'

'An alibi?' Fenchurch was crestfallen. 'You're absolutely certain? Because Smythson has a motive too, and what's more, I tell you, he might have had a stocking in his rooms without any previous plan to disguise himself.'

'Look,' said Bunce. 'To be frank, I'd like it to be Smythson. I wish it were Smythson as much as you do, but it's impossible. Just because he's got a lady-friend who leaves her stockings in his rooms doesn't mean he's the murderer — he can't be, because he couldn't have followed you up to the loft.'

'It wasn't a lady-friend,' replied Fenchurch morosely. 'You're certain he couldn't have attacked me?' But he sounded defeated.

Despite his better judgement Bunce was becoming interested. 'Half a moment — if it wasn't a lady-friend, who was it?'

'That makes no difference if Smythson could not have been my attacker, does it?' Fenchurch countered. 'I see no point in smirching a man's reputation if it hasn't a bearing on the crimes you are investigating.'

'It's true he has an alibi, but what you say makes me think it could be a funny sort of alibi,' answered Bunce slowly. 'If you care what happens to Mr Austrey, if you really believe he is innocent, it might not be a bad idea to tell me what you know about Smythson.'

'You understand that I can prove nothing,' began Fenchurch reluctantly. He felt a strong distaste for meddling in the private lives of his associates. 'But years ago, as an undergraduate, Smythson had a certain — reputation. One assumed he had outgrown it, as is often the case; but on the other hand it is possible that he has not.'

'You're speaking in riddles, Mr Fenchurch. You'll have to be a lot clearer before I'm sure of what you're getting at.'

The donnish mind is apt to prefer obliquity as a means of expression, perhaps because it is most easy thus to identify minds of the same bent and temper. With Bunce, however, it was necessary to be direct. Fenchurch saw his error and apologized. 'As an undergraduate Smythson was taken up by Edgar Welkin — you may have heard of him, the Wagstaff scholar who had a circle similar to Forster's at King's — and became a member of the St Jude's set.'

The light began to break more strongly on Bunce, but he sat silent and waited for the rest.

'It was a pastime of which I have never partaken and therefore I did not keep abreast of their — amusements, but I do recall hearing some talk of *dressing-up*.' He pronounced the final words as though they pained him to utter. 'So you see, if he has not entirely cast off these early influences, it is possible that he might already have had such an article of clothing in his possession.'

'D'you mean to say,' asked Bunce incredulously, 'that your precious College objects to adultery on the premises but doesn't mind a ponce or so in residence?'

'Smythson's behaviour as an undergraduate would have no bearing on his present position at Sheepshanks. Good God, if every man were to be hounded for his youthful indiscretions half the posts in Cambridge would be empty!'

'I wasn't speaking of youthful indiscretions — I meant present ones. It was you who suggested he might still be indulging in these pastimes — have you any grounds for such a statement?'

Fenchurch hesitated. 'You will doubtless think this very unfair of me,' he said at last, 'but it is — only a feeling. At Sheepshanks, after all, one's privacy is respected. There has been no scandal associated with Smythson since he came here as Abbot's Librarian — no open scandal, though he has had some rather odd young men in his train; I see them occasionally on their way to his rooms. He has remained friends with Welkin, but they do not see a great deal of each other. Still, there is nothing definite in that: Welkin has always preferred them young and dewy. They would no doubt be rivals now in that respect. All that I really have to go on are his past predilections and an air of — how can I describe it? — of sly furtiveness which he sometimes assumes.'

Bunce sat wrapped in thought for several moments. 'That might put quite another light on the situation,' he said at last.

'How?' Fenchurch demanded. 'Since Smythson has an alibi it can't be of any use, unless you know of someone who knew he had the stocking and stole it from his rooms to use in the loft.'

'Not so fast; not so fast. I'm beginning to wonder if his alibi is as watertight as it seems. What if I told you that I suspect the man who provided it of having similar inclinations? It makes me think they might be in collusion.'

'But why do you suppose they would conspire together to commit the murders?'

'I didn't mean that — a spot of blackmail was what I had in mind.' Bunce thought. 'I ought not to take any notice of what you've just told me,' he said finally. 'It's too indefinite; there's almost certainly nothing in it. On the other hand — it's strange that he's become so matey with Pocklington.'

'With Inspector Pocklington? Why do you find that odd?'

'Because he's a queer too, or my name's not Alfred Bunce. That was damn' stupid of me — I thought they had got friendly simply because Pocklington is the same class as Smythson and I'm not. It's he who gave Smythson his alibi; and now I think back, he seemed a bit nervous at the time, I couldn't think why. It never occurred to me. . . What if they had been up to some hanky-panky together and Smythson threatened to expose Pocklington? Maybe a man could survive that sort of scandal at

Sheepshanks, but not in the police, he couldn't. Pocklington has friends who can shield him in the normal course of events: so long as he's discreet about his little diversions nothing will be done, but if once they get in the open he'll be out on his ear, no two ways about it. The Prime Minister himself couldn't cover for him, and he knows it. And if Pocklington lied about Smythson's alibi in order to protect himself, then Smythson could have been your attacker. He has no alibi for either of the murders, and as for his falling into the river, he could have faked it to divert suspicion from himself. You say you know of a motive for Smythson — do you mean a new motive, or the one we already knew about: anger at Garmoyle because he took the Shakespeare manuscript out of the Abbot's Library?'

'Inspector, we were fools not to see it before — or rather, I was; you could scarcely be expected to understand all the ins and outs of the personalities here in so short a time. But the fact of the matter is that I have been reprehensibly blind: *Smythson has the same motive as Austrey.*'

'You're not making sense,' objected Bunce. 'First you tell me the man's a homosexual, and then in the next breath you say he's Austrey's rival for Helen Garmoyle.'

'Not that motive — the other one, the Prye Librarianship. We none of us took him seriously, but I see now that he must have been very serious indeed.' Raising his hand to fend off Bunce's incipient protests, Fenchurch continued. 'Hear me out before you reject Smythson as the killer. He is ambitious, but so far he has not been successful. He rowed as an undergraduate but was not in the first boat. He did not take a first at Cambridge though he had hoped for one — I suspect that Welkin spoiled him and made him think he was more promising than in fact he was. He was a good-looking young man, so after going down from University he went to London to try acting as a profession. Upon finding he was second-rate at that as well he went over to the BBC, where they are sometimes impressed by Cambridge credentials, and became a writer-announcer. There for a time he enjoyed a modest success with semi-scholarly interviews — you know the sort of thing: "Was Prince Albert a Secret Drinker?", with several learned professors to take the *pro* and *con*. He interviewed Welkin at this time (I believe the subject was "Wagstaff — A Poet for All Passions") and they renewed their acquaintance. It was Welkin who proposed Smythson to the Master when the post of Abbot's Librarian became vacant — Dr Shebbeare is perhaps excessively impressed by Welkin's reputation and inclined to accept his advice on academic matters a little too uncritically. The Master prides himself on his standards of academic excellence but he is, in my opinion, over-ready to take men such as Welkin at their own valuation. He regrets his choice now, I think, and would be happy if another man were Abbot's Librarian. But I am certain that Smythson, in his self-conceit, does not see this. If he did, he would never have had the effrontery to put himself up for the Prye Librarianship. We did not take him seriously; we were wrong.'

'But Dr Shebbeare has told him he will not be considered for the post,' interjected Bunce.

'Yes; but upon thinking the matter over, I am sure he simply does not believe it. The man has an actor's vanity, and other elements are involved which might make him feel assured of success. The Master has told me that Smythson tried to bargain with him by saying he would agree to the selling of the Shakespeare manuscript if he were made Prye Librarian. Also, Welkin may well be prepared to go to bat for him again; and like Sir Oliver Sheepshanks, Paul Prye made a stipulation in his will which was intended to control the College's choice of the recipient of his benefaction. In Prye's case he indicated that the preference for the librarianship should go to one who, like himself, had "earned his living in Towne [that is to say, London] by his witts and his pen," or failing a suitable candidate along those lines, to anyone who at one time had taken up acting as his means of livelihood. This request, I may say, has not been observed for many years but Smythson, because of his background in the theatre and the writing he did for the BBC, threatens to sue if necessary to obtain the post.'

'I thought Fellows of the Colleges had to be clergymen back in those days,' objected Bunce, who recalled once reading something of the sort in a newspaper article about the University. 'Wouldn't it have been impossible to find a candidate for Prye Librarian then who had made his living as an actor?'

'Distinctly unusual, certainly, but not impossible. At the time of his divorce and the recalcitrant Master's removal, Henry

VIII revised the statutes of Agnus Dei at the suggestion of Thomas Cranmer, who had been a Fellow of Jesus and who was influenced by Bishop Stanley's example at his old College. As a result both Master and Fellows were given an unusual amount of freedom — only one of the latter being required to take Holy Orders. So you see, if the College were to stick to the letter of the law in filling the post, Smythson would definitely fit Prye's requirements.'

Bunce took several moments to digest this antiquarian titbit. At length he said, 'It seems funny, doesn't it, that something done in Henry VIII's time should be capable of inciting a man to murder in this day and age. So you really think Smythson is the murderer?'

'I do, Inspector. When one considers the crimes from that angle, everything falls into place. Garmoyle was killed because Smythson wanted his job. I expect that Austrey, who was by Smythson's reckoning his only possible rival for the post, was meant to be the chief suspect from the beginning. The incident at the Bumps was intended to remove any possible suspicion from Smythson himself. Mutton's murder and the attempt on me can be explained very simply — Smythson was afraid we might have seen something incriminating since we both went into the Combination Room whilst he was poisoning the decanter, and he was not taking any chances. As for the evidence of Austrey's lighter, it's a bit too obvious, isn't it? Nothing could have been easier than for Smythson to pick it up in the Combination Room when Austrey wasn't looking, with the idea of using it to point suspicion at its owner.'

'Then why didn't he leave it with Mutton's body?' Bunce objected.

'Perhaps he hadn't taken it then; or perhaps he killed Mutton on the spur of the moment and hadn't got the lighter on him at the time. I should assume that he must have gone to his rooms to get the stocking-mask before the assault on me, when he could have picked up the lighter as well,' Fenchurch pointed out.

'I don't know,' Bunce said. 'It fits together very neatly, the way you've got it figured, but there's still Smythson's alibi. It's only a guess on my part that Pocklington may be shielding him, and I don't know how to break him down. To be frank with you,

I'm not in a position to put any pressure on him. Technically he's my superior on the case, and I'd find myself out of a job if I suggested he might be a party to faking a murder alibi.' He wore a worried frown.

'I sympathize, Inspector,' answered Fenchurch, 'but I am convinced that Austrey is innocent, and I suspect that you would not be averse to finding Smythson was the criminal. I do not ask you to go against your duty and your conscience; but I do beg that you keep an open mind and that you explore every possible avenue that might lead to the murderer even though you have Austrey in custody. See if you cannot break Smythson's alibi in some way— I am certain the truth lies in that direction.'

As he walked out of the police station to Parker's Piece and the sunlight, Fenchurch felt suddenly old. He knew his friend was innocent, but there was nothing more he could do to persuade the police of the fact. Bunce, left alone in his office, was in a state of equal dejection. The theory Fenchurch had presented was certainly plausible and Bunce had an instinctive presentiment that Pocklington was lying, but he did not see that there was anything he could do about it.

32 Positively the Rapist's Last Appearance

Beyond that section of The Backs which appertains to Sheepshanks and over Queen's Road lies the College's Cricket Ground. This impossibly green stretch of lawn serves at certain seasons as a backdrop for the leisurely movements of young men clad in white flannels of an equally improbable refulgence. The scene is Arcadian: from the avian sanctuary abutting the Cricket Ground on the far side birdsong of countless varieties fills the air and harmonizes with the melody of a small brook, an offshoot of the Cam, which meanders along the perimeter of the cricket oval. Clumps of daisies, white and red-tipped, embroider the luxuriant grass; and the spectators so essential to the game are provided with strategic areas of shade by vast elms which act as a permanent stage-set for this summer ritual.

Once more the unpredictable weather had turned warm, and the idyllic setting supplied for this most English of sports was peopled by an audience of undergraduates of both sexes and a sprinkling of dons, as well as several local workmen who had been cleaning the drains in the New Court of John's. Outdoorsmen by nature and feeling the need of a little fresh air after their effluvious labours, they had brought their lunch to the edge of the Cricket Ground to combine nourishment with a spot of rustic entertainment. It was a peaceful and soporific scene they gazed upon as they munched their bread and cheese, for the match was proving a torpid one. Slow bowling was the order of the day: the path of the red-leather-cased ball was a study in arrested motion, the batsman leaned languidly on his bat while waiting for the sluggish projectile to approach, the umpire gave a barely suppressed yawn. As this lethargic contest neared its apogee many of those on the sidelines were openly napping under the spreading branches of the elms.

The workmen, too, who had avoided the shade, were in an advanced state of lethargy, a result of the injudicious but pleasing combination of beer and sun. In the distance the muted cries of punters and puntees drifted from the water along The Backs, now and then punctuated by a faint splash as yet another punter, emboldened by admiring feminine glances or parental approbation, overreached himself and toppled in. Two of the workmen were beginning to nod and one had actually emitted a muffled snore when a commotion in Bede Close, a small cluster of houses on the other side of the road bordering the Sheepshanks Cricket Ground, aroused them. Piercing shrieks in a powerful female voice rang through the silken air and the three men jumped to their feet. The rest of the onlookers, who were farther away from Madingley Road, appeared not to have heard. They slept on while the cricketers, also unaffected by the sounds, continued their somnambulant motion.

'Wot was that, Mick?' asked the snorer, rubbing at his eyes as he turned to his mate.

"Aven't a clue, but it sounds as if we'd best take a look,' the man thus addressed responded. He was a tall strapping fellow with a shock of fair hair, wide shoulders, and the face of a choirboy. All three ran at once to the mouth of the close: the screams, which were still issuing from that direction, came from one of the houses in the little cul-de-sac. As they did so a police constable on a motorcycle darted past them out of the close on his way to Northampton Street, and though they shouted and gesticulated in an effort to make him understand that his services were urgently required, he continued unheeding on his way.

"Ere!' said Mick. 'That's rum. Why didn't t'bloke stop when we 'ailed 'im?' They pounded after the motorcycle, shouting at its rider to stop, but their demands were ignored and the cyclist, who had too much of a head start for them to catch him, was soon lost in the heavy traffic on Northampton Street. As they returned to Bede Close to find out what had occasioned the screams, they met a woman running up the street toward them.

'Have you seen a motorcycle go past?' she asked. She was a beefy woman in her middle thirties, wearing an apron which was somewhat askew, and with a bruise on her cheekbone.

'A copper come out of the lane on one,' said Mick. 'We tried to stop 'im when we heard screaming, to get 'elp, loike, but 'e didn't 'ear and we couldn't catch 'im up — 'e were goin' too fast. Wot's up, then?'

'That was no policeman,' she replied angrily. 'I thought it was when he came over from Churchill College way, but I soon found out my mistake. I was hanging up my laundry in the back garden when I first saw him. He stopped for a moment over by those trees,' she pointed to a spinney of beeches on a corner of the Cricket Ground out of sight of the players and spectators, 'and the next thing I knew, there he was at me. I couldn't see his face with that stocking over it, but when he got close I could see his uniform wasn't right — it was kind of stagey-looking — and he was wearing lavender satin shoes. I ask you! He tried — well, I won't tell you what he tried,' she said grimly. 'There's things it isn't decent to talk about. But he didn't get away with it, the pervert! It was lucky I had a full watering-can standing by — I warrant he'll have a black eye that'll last him for a bit.'

The workmen were properly outraged by this attempted insult to British womanhood by one disguised as the chiefest of her appointed protectors. Mick was prepared to scour the streets of Cambridge singlehanded in search of the miscreant, but his companions persuaded him that it was a job better left to the efforts of the police, who would presumably treat an impostor with the rigour he deserved. He assuaged his feelings, however, by directing the formation of a cordon of his comrades in front of the house on Bede Close to protect the rapist's intended victim while she rang the police station.

33 The Hunt is Up

'I say, Smythson, whatever happened to your eye?' asked Weldon of Corpus. He was usually a tactful man and not in the habit of mentioning physical peculiarities to the faces of their possessors, but the luridness of Smythson's black eye had elicited a response from him before he realized it was out. And indeed, Smythson's black eye was one before which other lesser black eyes paled by contrast: it was impossible to imagine an eye more swollen or more variegated in colour. Its iridescence was positively prismatic, embracing every hue in the spectrum. No one shade predominated in this polychromatic gorgeousness, and over all lay the unhealthy sheen of an oil-slick. The closest one might come to an accurate description was to label it *gorge de pigeon*, or possibly to liken it to a fire-opal. Smythson's attempt to minimize his injury by daubing it with talcum powder had only served to accentuate its garishness.

'Too stupid of me — I tripped over a chair in my rooms this morning and came a cropper,' said Smythson with an embarrassed cough at his clumsiness. They were standing within the iron-picketed enclosure in front of the Senate House, waiting for the doors to open to admit them for the congregation of the Regent House and the bestowing of degrees. Those unacquainted with the ways of universities would have found it a surprisingly brilliant assembly that awaited entry. The undergraduates upon whom the baccalaureate was about to be conferred were comparatively crow-like, it is true, in their black gowns whose hoods were lined in yellowed rabbit-fur that had seen better days; and the Masters of Arts were no less sombre, if rather nattier, with their hoods of white silk — but the Doctors, ah, the Doctors! Strutting about in scarlet robes, even the mousiest academic felt a peacock for the day; and then the robes themselves were only part of it. Each Doctor, instead of the modest square (except the Doctors of Divinity, whose caps were of velvet) wore a black velvet Tudor bonnet embellished with gilt tassels. In addition, each scarlet robe had hanging sleeves lined (as were the hood and facings) with variously coloured silks — dove-shot for Divinity, pink for Law, cerise for Medicine, a lighter scarlet for Letters. The exceptions to this rule were the Doctors of Music, whose robes of cream damasked silk were edged with crimson. Though most of them would indignantly have denied it, these normally sober gentlemen quite enjoyed promenading in such splendid attire within the view of townspeople and tourists.

Far off, two straggling groups of marchers were seen to approach from opposite directions. 'What is that?' Weldon asked in surprise, his attention diverted from Smythson's mishap. As the marchers drew closer they could see that the group on Trinity Street was entirely composed of young men who, as they came near, were seen to be very precious young men. Most were neatly, not to say exquisitely dressed, though the prevailing taste might be considered a trifle flashy by the average Cantabrigian, and a voluptuous wave of scent preceded them. The foremost man, who sported a gold ring in one ear and a rose satin shirt unbuttoned to the waist, carried a banner announcing in florid letters: 'CAMBRIDGE QUEENS — RIGHTS FOR HOMOSEXUALS.'

The contingent arriving from the direction of Trumpington Street consisted, on the other hand, of young women — an extraordinarily dowdy lot, even for Cambridge. Some wheeled prams containing small children, others carried papoose-like bundles of babies on their backs. In the van the most Amazonian of these females hoisted high a placard on which was inscribed the legend 'KIDDIE CRÉCHES — FREE WOMEN FROM THE HOME.'

'Good God,' murmured Weldon, watching them in horrid fascination, 'what will happen when they meet?'

As the demonstrators made their several ways toward the Senate House, it was clear that a confrontation was imminent. Southey of St Jude's, who much to the disgust of his more conservative colleagues was wearing beneath his gown a jacket in tan and orange plaid with an openwork magenta tie, was seen to confer with one of the Esquire Bedells. Now he spoke to Weldon. 'It seems the Vice-Chancellor had heard rumours of a demonstration of some kind,' he said, 'but he thought it wouldn't come off. No one knows precisely what they are up to, but it is thought they may attempt to storm the Senate House in order to disrupt the presentation of degrees.'

'But what on earth do they want?' asked Weldon.

'Cambridge Queens are demanding a faculty and lectures for what they term Homosexual History, the posts to be filled by a Professor and lecturers of the same — er — persuasion. They want a compulsory survey course of lectures for first-year undergraduates, to begin with the Greeks and Romans. Eventually they wish to expand this course of study with departments in Homosexual Literature, Art History, and Music.'

'What about the women?' demanded Weldon. 'Surely they are not in sympathy with the others.'

'I understand they are students' wives who want full-time baby crêches where they can leave their children, with the option of taking them home for the weekend if they wish. The more militant are also demanding crêches for fathers where their husbands can be dropped off, so they will be totally freed from the drudgery of housework.'

A cluster of worried dons had gathered about him. 'And are they supporting each other in their endeavours?' inquired Fenchurch.

'No, no, not at all; quite the contrary. They have often been in disagreement. The Vice-Chancellor is distressed. He fears a bloodbath if they clash.'

By now the two groups had met in front of the serene Palladian façade of the Senate House and were glaring at one another. *'Canaille,'* hissed the Regius Professor of Astronomy as he swept past them to join the procession, which was still forming.

There was growing agitation in the academic ranks. 'Why has not the Vice-Chancellor alerted the police?' demanded Woodhouse of King's. 'It is remiss of him, very remiss.'

'He told me that the rumour was indefinite — there was no mention of where or when the demonstration might take place.

In any case, I am not at all certain that having the police here mightn't make matters worse.'

An ominous muttering arose from the Kiddie Crêches group as a member of the Cambridge Queens contingent hurled the epithet 'brood-mare' at one of the Valkyries opposite. 'Fancy-boy,' she retorted with a sneer, and for a moment it seemed as though a confrontation was inevitable. A temporary truce ensued, however, while their leaders went into conference. The bulldogs, those stalwart constables whose function it is in top-hat and morning dress to accompany the Proctor on his rounds as he apprehends unruly undergraduates, drew protectively closer to the Vice-Chancellor, and one of the Esquire Bedells grasped his silver mace like a truncheon. Weldon, who had recently given up smoking, nervously fingered a well-worn cigarette which he kept in his pocket as a placebo. Dropping it, he uttered a stifled exclamation and stooped to retrieve it from the ground. As he did so his eyes travelled carelessly over the trouser-legs of those near him. Suddenly he froze. 'Smythson,' he gabbled, 'Smythson — my dear fellow, whatever are you wearing?'

Smythson looked down at his feet: upon them, only partly concealed by the folds of his trousers, was a pair of ladies' lilac brocade bedroom slippers with tulle pompoms on the toes. Those nearby, who had glanced down when Weldon spoke, instinctively averted their gaze — while they were not unused to private eccentricities, the public spectacle of a colleague in women's shoes was too appalling for comment.

'My God,' said Smythson, aghast. 'My God, I forgot.' Before his neighbours could grasp the import of his unexpected footwear and move to stop him, he had bolted. Tucking up the skirts of his gown, he pushed his way through the astonished crowd to the gate and fled in the direction of the warren of lanes and colleges off Trinity Street.

'Hi! stop him!' cried Weldon, who by this time had made a correct assessment of the situation.

'Stop him! Stop him, I say!' Southey and the others immediately about him took up the cry. They made an attempt to follow Smythson, but it was slow progress moving through the packed mass of academics and students. Smythson had made a swift exit, taking those about him by surprise and pushing quickly past them, but his flight and the subsequent chase headed by Weldon and Southey had startled the others present and as a result there was an agitated milling about which was detrimental to pursuit.

'Quick — we must stop him,' called Weldon; and his cry reached the ears of some of the undergraduates who were lined up at the back of the dons.

'Right, sir; not to worry. We'll get him,' an undergraduate near the gate called cheerfully. 'Come on, Smith, Brown, Jones.' He and his friends gave tongue and galloped off in pursuit trailed by the others, gowns billowing behind them and hoods bobbing in unison as they ran. Youthful high spirits and limber muscles produced a spurt of speed which gave those in the lead a glimpse of their quarry. 'Tally-ho,' squeaked one overwrought Sheepshankian (known for overriding the hounds in the hunting-field) as he caught sight of a flutter of black ahead. He was answered by another budding Nimrod, who shouted 'Yoicks — yoicks,' and waved his cap in an effort to urge on the pursuers.

Some of the senior members of the University stayed where they were, feeling no doubt that it was beneath their dignity to go skittering about the byways of the town. Others, more sporting, kilted up their gowns and gave chase behind the students. The demonstrators stood about uncertainly for a moment, then followed at the rear, still carrying their standards. There was some inimical jostling between the two groups, but in the main they stayed well apart and avoided contact with each other. At first Smythson, with his long legs and early start, kept well ahead of his pursuers despite the unorthodox footgear he was wearing. He dodged through Senate House Passage up Trinity Lane, through Trinity College and out to the street. At length, with the hue and cry behind him sounding closer, he found himself at the entrance to the little path that bisects All Saints Passage off St John's Street. With a grunt of relief (since he was beginning to tire) he made for it as a fox to his earth, for by that means he could cut across to Sidney Street; and as none of the hunters was yet in sight he would have a good chance of shaking them off. They would not, upon their arrival at John's Street, know whether he had gone north to Bridge Street, west through St John's College or

Sheepshanks to Queen's Road, east through the passage to Jesus Lane, or over to Sidney Street where he might lose himself in the shops.

Without a pause he ran along the path until he reached the fork, then halted in horror, for streaming into the passage from John's Street he saw the members of Cambridge Queens. They had been left in the rear by the other hunters and so had gone off on their own scent. Now they stood all along the passage, blocking any hope of escape. None of the young men had any idea why Smythson was being pursued — the only people with that information were Weldon and those near him — but it was clearly a waste of time to demonstrate without an audience, so for lack of anything better to do the Cambridge Queens had joined the field. Now the fox stood at bay before them, his eyes darting from side to side as he calculated his chances of forcing a way out. But it was impossible: they were solidly packed along the narrow stone-paved footpath and their leader, a youth named Quiver, stood before him.

'Here's a piece of luck,' said Quiver to one of his neighbours. 'We've got the bloke — I wonder what they want him for.' His glance travelled thoughtfully down the dust-stained figure until it reached the feet: Smythson had not discarded the ladies' slippers he was wearing during his precipitate flight, reckoning that he would make worse time over the uneven stones if he went barefoot. He had, as a matter of fact, grown quite used to wearing women's shoes. It had been his custom to slip a pair on when he was alone in his rooms as well as on the occasions when he and his friends indulged in what Fenchurch scornfully referred to as 'dressing up' for he rather liked the dainty look they gave to his feet, which fortunately were small so his wife's shoes fitted him.

As Quiver took notice of the lilac slippers protruding from beneath Smythson's trousers, his face gradually changed. 'What d'you know, lads — he's one of us!' He pursed his lips in a soundless whistle. 'So that's why they were after him — a clear case of persecution.' He stepped up to Smythson. 'I want to shake your hand, sir. You are the first gay don who has ever held to his convictions and maintained his right to wear what he pleases in public. Well done, sir.' Vigorously in his enthusiasm he pumped Smythson's unresisting hand up and down. 'This will issue in a new era for those of us who are gay. We shall wear whatever we choose whenever we wish — corsets to classes, earrings to tutorial, lingerie to lectures, nylons to rowing-practice — the possibilities are infinite. And you will show us the way; you will be our mentor. Forster, Keynes, Welkin — none of the gay dons have had the courage to do as you have done. What do you say?' he asked, turning to his followers.

Smythson stood paralysed as a mighty 'hear, hear' rent the air and a multitude of eager hands reached forward to lift him to the shoulders of two of the burlier demonstrators. Feebly he protested, but it was no use; the fervour of the Cambridge Queens was not to be withstood. Though he looked wildly about for an escape route, there was none. At his rear he could hear the faint cries of the hounds, temporarily checked, and to right and left the way was blocked by the demonstrators. Meekly Smythson submitted to his elevation, philosophically reflecting that desperate as was his position, had the exponents of Kiddie Crêches been the first to take him, he might have been torn limb from limb by shrieking Maenads. His two bearers triumphantly carried him out to Trinity Street, followed by the rank and file. There erstwhile members of the commencement procession who had been scouring the colleges in search of the fugitive emerged from gates and doorways and hurried over as they caught sight of him. The game was up.

34 Tying Up Loose Ends

It had been an unusually busy day for the Cambridge police. First the report on the rapist's latest attempt had come in: a Mrs Ted Chick had been attacked in the garden of her house in Bede Close and the criminal, wearing a constable's uniform, lavender satin shoes and a black eye, had escaped from the vicinity on a motorcycle.

The costume reportedly worn by the culprit posed a problem in giving chase. No matter how stagy-looking (as Mrs Chick had described it) the uniform worn by the rapist might be at close quarters, at a distance it had fooled his prospective victim; and his would-be captors were forced, at sight of another member of the police, to perform a curious sort of dance in which each blue-clad form edged cautiously closer to the other until at last they were *vis-à-vis*, and recognition of a comrade-in-arms was possible. This procedure frayed even the strongest nerves, and there was heartfelt gratitude when word went out that the rapist had been captured.

Grubb, who was released with apologies, took his detention in very ill part, grumbling against what he termed the Gestapo tactics of the Establishment. He refused to shake Inspector Jenkins's hand, saying sulkily that his treatment was no more than what might be expected from an élitist arm of the State but he did not see why he should pretend to countenance it

The other members of Sheepshanks's Combination Room heaved a collective sigh of relief for Smythson was charged, not only with rape, but with the College murders as well. Upon his arrest (after a memorable scuffle, for the members of Cambridge Queens persisted in the belief that he was being persecuted for transvestism, and defended him to a man), Inspector Pocklington had broken down and confessed what Bunce had suspected — that he had lied to provide Smythson with an alibi for the attack upon Fenchurch. They had become lovers during Pocklington's stay in Cambridge, and Smythson had threatened to expose the policeman's homosexual activities to the authorities at Scotland Yard unless he backed him up. Under this pressure the London Inspector had agreed to say that he had arrived at Smythson's rooms some fifteen minutes earlier on the Sunday evening than in fact he had; but he swore that in doing so he had had no idea of Smythson's guilt. Pocklington declared he had genuinely believed in the attack upon Smythson at the Bumps and, he claimed, had simply thought the man was tired of being badgered by the police.

Pocklington persisted in this lame excuse even after it was reluctantly elicited from him that on his way to Smythson's rooms that evening he had encountered their owner not far from the Chapel and obviously in a hurry — this at a time which coincided with the flight of Fenchurch's attacker from the Chapel loft. Despite Pocklington's assertion of ignorance it was plain that he must have had a strong suspicion that Smythson might be involved in the murders; and even without certainty it was of course inexcusable for a police officer to lie in a matter of the sort. Even his powerful friends could not save him now. He was discharged in disgrace from the C.I.D. and charged as an accessory after the fact in the assault on Fenchurch.

Still the Fellows of Sheepshanks were not, in the circumstances, unhappy over the outcome. The terrible sense of strain and suspicion was dispelled at last and they were not disposed to quarrel with the manner of its removal. Preferable though it might have been to find that the killer was not a member of the College, from the first that had been an unlikely solution. They were glad, at least, that it was a man whom none of them had much liked; indeed, the Master was scarcely able to conceal his elation at the departure of the Abbot's Librarian and wrote a stiff letter that very day to Welkin of St Jude's, who had originally recommended him for the post.

The day after Smythson's arrest Inspector Bunce and Inspector Jenkins were invited to Mr Fenchurch's rooms to discuss the ramifications of their cases. Sherry glasses and a decanter were set out in the dining-room, and upon the arrival of the policemen Fenchurch poured them a celebratory libation. He himself was drinking beer, he explained, as he was still in training for the walk in aid of Dr Barnardo's Homes, but he was certain they would prefer sherry; Sheepshanks's sherry was a byword among the fanciers of that wine. Both policemen eyed his glass longingly as they assured him that sherry was just what they wanted.

'We were all wrong, you know, as to motive,' said Bunce, settling into the leather sofa by the fire. 'Not about the motive for Garmoyle's murder — you were dead right about that, Mr Fenchurch — but about Smythson's reason for killing Mutton and the attempt on yourself.'

'I gathered from Inspector Jenkins that Smythson recognized me at the bathing-pool with Dame Hermione and thought, when the newspaper article came out, that I had recognized him in some way.'

'That's right,' put in Jenkins, visibly embarrassed. 'We feel right bad about that, after telling you there would be no risk.'

'Don't worry, Inspector; how could you have known? It was a chance in a thousand, and worth taking in the circumstances. If Smythson thought I knew he was the rapist, why did he suppose I had not reported it to the police?'

'He believed you were holding off to protect the College's reputation, but that your telling us you recognized something about him meant you were likely to disclose his identity soon, and so he tried to kill you before you did so. He coshed Mr Mutton at the May Ball in mistake for you. He saw him from the back, sitting in the punt, you see; and you both are — were — much the same height and build with white hair,' said Bunce.

'Then he did not lure Mutton into the punt?'

'No,' Bunce replied. 'I had had rather an upsetting interview with Mr Mutton earlier that day concerning his dead sister, and we think it may have set him to thinking about punts and the river. Apparently he went down there of his own accord.'

'So Austrey and I were correct in our doubts of the validity of Smythson's accident at the Bumps. He contrived it to divert suspicion from himself.'

'Not quite,' Jenkins explained. 'Actually it was an attempt on you. He planned to push you in at the instant the boats went past. I understand that you don't swim.'

'No, I am afraid of the water. It is rather a joke in College.'

'Just so. He knew that you don't swim and that you would probably get a crack on the head to boot — as he did. But you stepped back just as he made his move, and so Smythson nearly drowned in your place. Afterwards he decided to make the most of his mistake by letting it seem that he was the intended victim of the assault.'

'After his two failures to kill you, at the races and the May Ball, he was getting desperate,' Bunce chimed in. 'He had no way of knowing, as he thought, how long you would keep quiet about his rôle as rapist; and once that came out he was ruined, with a stiff jail-sentence thrown in for good measure. So when he heard you say on Sunday night that you were going up to the Chapel roof after dinner that evening, he followed you up. He was expecting Pocklington in his rooms that evening, but thought he wouldn't appear until nine. That was the time Pocklington was invited for, but he was so excited by the prospect of some more carrying-on with Smythson —' Bunce's voice shook with disgust, 'that he arrived a little beforehand.'

'Smythson thought, you see,' added Jenkins, 'that you would be alone in the Chapel and he knew you would have to go through the loft on your way to and from the roof. He planned to push you to your death through the Chapel ceiling, having planted Mr Austrey's cigarette-lighter by the door to the loft so we should believe he was the murderer. You were quite right in thinking Smythson killed Garmoyle in order to obtain the post of Prye Librarian. He thought he was on to a sure thing because of the clause in Paul Prye's will, but just in case he intended to make certain that Mr Austrey would be blamed for the murder.'

'That way,' Bunce said, 'he could get rid of his closest rival for the post and at the same time provide the police with a tailor-made killer so they wouldn't suspect him.'

'But why did he bother to wear a mask when he attacked me, since he intended to kill me?' asked Fenchurch.

'He told us he was afraid someone might see him going into or out of the Chapel as Pocklington so nearly did, but if he was wearing the stocking-mask they couldn't be certain he wasn't Austrey.'

'He had the idea from the mask he wore during the rape attempts,' interjected Jenkins.

'Pocklington saw him as he was leaving the Chapel — he was actually discarding the stocking on the Chapel porch as Pocklington approached. When the lad William was sent round to Smythson's set of rooms with a message that he was to be interviewed by the police, Smythson knew that he had to keep Pocklington from telling us what he had seen. So on their way to see me he threatened to expose him as a homosexual — I understand they had had a bout together on Saturday evening before the May Ball. Smythson told Pocklington that if he were arrested for murder he would have nothing to lose by telling the police all about their little romp, which I gather was a particularly nasty one of its kind,' he added with distaste. 'That, Smythson said, would finish Pocklington's career, and the only way he could avoid it was by keeping his mouth shut about the incident. Smythson sweetened it with assurances that he had only planned a little joke on Fenchurch which had turned sour and said he was afraid it would be taken the wrong way if we found out about it, but of course Pocklington knew perfectly well, no matter what he says now, that there was something wrong going on. He broke down and told us all about it after Smythson was brought in for the rapes. He was afraid it would make matters even worse in the end if he didn't, as he thought it was all bound to come out eventually.'

'But one thing I do not understand,' said Fenchurch, who was in some matters unworldly. 'Since Smythson's proclivities admittedly lie in the other direction, how can he be the rapist? Surely the two are incompatible.'

'You'd think so, wouldn't you?' Jenkins answered. 'But they sent a psychiatric big-wig down from London who says it all fits in. You see, Smythson's wife —'

'His wife?' Fenchurch exclaimed. 'But he hasn't a wife. I believe he was married once, but he obtained a divorce. The lady in question was a most unsuitable person to be a don's wife, the Master told me.'

'Smythson lied about the divorce,' said Bunce. 'Apparently he married early on while he was working as an actor in London. He was AC–DC for a while and who knows, poor chap — he may have hoped marriage would steady him. His wife was a minor actress — never hit the big-time though she was from an old stage family — Roxana Bracegirdle, her name is. She discovered pretty quickly that he had his rum side and left him, but you know what actors are — they're apt to be casual about the proprieties, so she never got round to divorcing him though there was plenty of evidence at the time. Now, after all these years she is thinking of retiring from the stage to marry — a rich grocer from Brighton, I hear he is. She says he saw her play *Trelawney of the Wells*, and it was love at first sight.'

'He's very respectable,' Jenkins interpolated, 'one of the pillars of a certain echelon of Brighton society, and she's not taking any chances on losing him. I gather he would take a homosexual husband in his stride but not any aspersions on his fiancée's purity, so she didn't want to give Smythson a chance to file first, using any little irregularities she might have committed as due cause. I had a chat with the lady yesterday. She's still on tour and by a lucky chance her company is playing in Peterborough. She hadn't seen her husband in years but she didn't trust what she remembered, so instead of approaching him about a divorce she hired a Cambridge detective agency to see what they could dig up.'

'Do you mean to say a private detective has been pursuing his enquiries in Sheepshanks?' demanded Fenchurch. 'Disgraceful!'

'That's right. It didn't take him long, since Smythson's rooms are on the ground floor in Great Court, to earn his keep by finding out that he was carrying on an affair with one of his students. As soon as Mrs Smythson was in possession of this evidence she informed him that she was suing for divorce, citing a male co-respondent. This information threw Smythson into a state, as you can imagine. He had been toying with the idea of killing Garmoyle so that the post which he felt was his by right would be available to him, and now he came to the conclusion that murder was imperative. The divorce proceedings, with his wife as the injured party, would stir up a scandal which would surely rob him of any chance of being made Prye Librarian *unless* he was appointed before the news broke. As has been noted in Mr Garmoyle's case, once a man is in a post it is very difficult to remove him, no matter what his conduct.'

'That *is* very true,' Fenchurch replied. 'I have often observed the phenomenon, particularly at Sheepshanks, where Dr Shebbeare is especially reluctant to draw attention to any frailties of the members. Had it been otherwise, he would undoubtedly have attempted to replace Garmoyle as Prye Librarian some time ago. As matters stood, however, much as the Master disapproved of Garmoyle's behaviour, I think he would have hesitated almost indefinitely before attempting to remove him from the position.'

'Yet you told me Austrey had no reason to kill Garmoyle because it was likely to happen at any moment,' Bunce said reproachfully.

Fenchurch had the grace to look embarrassed. 'I am certain it was bound to come soon,' he protested, 'but the Master tried every other expedient first, such as asking Garmoyle to accept a co-editor for the diaries. I was not intentionally attempting to mislead you, Inspector.'

'I didn't think you were,' Bunce answered, his good-nature restored. 'But I did think for a while you might be allowing your feelings to get the better of your head. So,' he continued with his narrative, 'Smythson cast about him for some way to get rid of Garmoyle. He couldn't wait him out, you see, because of the impending divorce suit, but he reckoned that once in the saddle as Prye Librarian, he would be unlikely to be unseated even if there was a scandal. So the problem as he saw it was Garmoyle. He decided to kill him. First he made certain Garmoyle found out about the affair between his wife and Austrey by telling him about it — he hoped by that means to exacerbate Garmoyle's drinking, which was crucial to his plan.'

'I see,' Fenchurch said thoughtfully. 'In that way he meant to make it possible to poison Garmoyle with the second decanter of port.'

'Yes — your feeling that there was something odd about the damp spot on the Combination Room carpet was absolutely correct. Smythson concealed the extra decanter in the little cupboard beside the fireplace — I'll tell you more about that later — and on the days Garmoyle dined in College he would switch it with the second port decanter when there weren't enough guests to warrant using the back-up port in the normal course of events. He had to switch the decanters back again afterwards, of course, because otherwise the poisoned port might have got mixed up with the decanter the other Fellows drank from and killed off the lot.

'On the day Garmoyle was murdered the decanter containing

the arsenic — which, by the way, had a chip out of the bottom so he was able to identify it — slipped from Smythson's hand as he was taking it out of the cupboard. Hastily he mopped up the mess, hid the pieces in the cupboard, and took one of the decanters from the sideboard up to his rooms where he doctored it with a spare vial of the arsenic which he had secreted with the extra decanter.'

'I thought something of the sort must have happened,' Fenchurch answered. 'But I could make nothing, I confess, of the enigma of the nineteenth decanter — unless our records are in error — that must be it. There is no other possible explanation. But I cannot understand how the mistake in accounting could have been carried on for so many years without being discovered.'

'No, you're out there,' said Bunce. 'What really happened is one of those coincidences that make life pure hell for a policeman — begging your pardon, sir. Several weeks ago Smythson went up to London for a meeting with his wife and her solicitor. During his stay in Town he saw a decanter identical to those in the set the College owns in an antique shop window. He already had the idea of killing Garmoyle in the back of his mind, and seeing the decanter gave him a plan of how to accomplish his purpose.'

'But,' Fenchurch objected, 'if he was homicidally inclined, why not kill his wife, who was causing all the trouble? Surely that would be the simpler method.'

'That's what I said,' Jenkins broke in, 'but you see, by the time he knew about her plan to divorce him she had already obtained legal advice, so if she had been killed it was known that he had a made-to-order motive.'

'I can see that would have complicated matters,' said Fenchurch. 'Moreover, with this plan to murder Garmoyle he could rid himself of the Prye Librarian and his rival for the post at one stroke; that is, if he succeeded in his rather elaborate scheme. Do you know, in a way Smythson was cleverer than he knew — as his chance to be appointed Pryevian Librarian was so slender, no one considered he had sufficient motive to kill Garmoyle, whereas Austrey clearly had.'

'Smythson didn't dare to kill his wife,' Jenkins went on, 'but he was in a rage at her for what she was doing to him. His fury was so intense that it broke out periodically as a hatred for all women — and he had a previous tendency in that direction anyway, remember, with his homosexual leanings — so as a vent for his anger at her, whenever his rage built up to a certain point he would rape any woman he came across. Rape for him was not a release of sexual desire but an outlet for violence — it helped him to let off steam, you might say. That's Sir Marmaduke Hussey's opinion, anyway — he's the specialist Scotland Yard sent us.'

'And it all ties in,' added Bunce. 'On Tuesday, before Smythson made the assault on Mrs Chick, he had a letter from his wife's solicitor informing him that the case was about to appear on the court-calendar; that, apparently, was what set him off. And his wearing of women's bedroom slippers when he committed the rapes fits in with his homosexual activities — it's an expression of his half-repressed wish to be female, don't you see. The ones he wore, by the way, had belonged to his wife — he kept them for his own use when they parted. He stored them along with the motorcycle and his other props in a disused shed on the Sheepshanks Rugby Ground.'

'Where,' asked Fenchurch curiously, 'did he find the policeman's uniform he was wearing when he was caught?'

'He told us he borrowed it from the wardrobe department of the Amateur Dramatic Club — the A.D.C., I think you call it. Smythson sometimes acted as an adviser to the club, because of his theatrical connexions. I understand he considered it a likely place to meet undergraduates who might be of his — hem — persuasion. As for the motorcycle, it turned out to be one of the lot that was reported stolen from outside pubs. He found it with the key in it the evening of the first rape, fancied the idea of some quick transport, and drove it off. Later he changed a couple of the numbers on the licence plate with some dark-coloured tape so it couldn't be readily identified.'

Fenchurch, who considered rape a vulgar crime and thus scarcely worth discussion, reverted again to the murders. 'It was very foolish of Smythson to remove the Shakespeare manuscript just as he was expecting to poison Garmoyle,' he mused. 'One would have thought he would take great pains not to draw attention to himself at such a time.'

'He told us he wasn't absolutely certain Garmoyle would

drink the poison. He was playing a sort of Russian Roulette with Garmoyle: in fact he has succeeded in persuading himself that he didn't kill Garmoyle at all, that it was simply God's will that he started on the second decanter. The way Smythson did it, he had no way of knowing when or even *if* it would happen, though he did everything to ensure it short of pouring the stuff down Garmoyle's throat through a funnel. Of course once the Prye Librarian drank the poisoned port, Smythson couldn't put the manuscript back in the Prye Library without the risk of being caught at it by the police who were searching the Library for clues to Garmoyle's murderer. And even if it had been less dangerous, I'm not certain he would have put it back — it was just too good an opportunity to show up Austrey.'

'He won't admit it even now, but we're fairly sure it was he who told Lord Merlin about the existence of the manuscript out of spite when it was removed from the Abbot's Library.'

'I suppose,' said Fenchurch, 'that Smythson must have waited in the Combination Room until he knew Bottom had gone down to the wine-cellar.'

'He told us he went down at 6.15 to switch the decanters, thinking no one was likely to be about then,' Bunce replied. 'The butler wasn't there, so he took the poisoned decanter from its hiding-place, planning to conceal it under his gown; he had come from a supervisory session with one of his students so he was still wearing it. When he dropped the decanter, he hid the pieces (as you know) in the cupboard and took away the spare from the sideboard to doctor it. All this he did before 6.30; by the time Bottom came in he had gone. Upon his return to the Combination Room, he waited to replace the decanter in the sideboard until he heard Bottom leave the Hall. He told us he put a bit of Sellotape on the bottom so he would know which was which and peeled it off as the decanter was passed about. We checked the sideboard door for fingerprints after the murder as a matter of course, but he had used the closed sleeves of his gown as mittens so we found none of his prints. I don't mind telling you,' he added, growing expansive, 'that I'm very glad it's over. It's a case that was distressing to my feelings, especially when it came to arresting such a pleasant gentleman as Mr Austrey.'

'It's a shocking thing — murder in a place like Sheepshanks,'

Jenkins remarked, shaking his head. 'Like finding a corpse in a church.'

'Where you very nearly did find mine,' said Fenchurch. 'I agree that a College is an unexpected place for murder to crop up, though interestingly enough, only yesterday I came across a precedent in my reading: in 1755 one of the Fellows of this College was brought to trial for the murder of a colleague who had refused to return a volume he had borrowed from the defendant. Eventually the charge was reduced to manslaughter — a jury of his peers agreed that the provocation to violence had been irresistible — and he claimed benefit of clergy. But I am very happy that Austrey has been cleared. I cannot imagine a more suitable candidate for Prye Librarian — a pity, had he been the killer.'

'I expect he and Mrs Garmoyle will be getting married as soon as it's decent. She's a very agreeable lady, for an American,' Bunce observed.

The two inspectors finished their sherry and departed despite Fenchurch's hospitable offer to refill their glasses; for each, unknown to the other, intended to suggest a stop at the Woolsack for a pint and a chat with the buxom barmaid.

Once more the port was passed along High Table — a less populous High Table than it had been a week before; once more the decanters glowed ruby and amber; once more the last rays of the setting sun penetrated the windows of the Great Hall. Sir Oliver on his gilded throne gazed with benign arrogance out of a frame upon which was carved the Sheepshanks motto, *Revenons à nos moutons*, and the Sheepshanks arms. High Table had an unusually festive air that evening, chiefly due to relief at the resolution of the crisis; but it must be confessed that the permanent removal of Garmoyle and Smythson contributed not a little to the conviviality. Austrey was quietly and unashamedly dreaming of domestic delights and (to a lesser degree) the more austere pleasures of the Prye Library. The Master was enjoying the prospect of presiding over a College free (for the moment, at least) of those twin demons Drunkenness and Discord. Once more the Fellows felt safe in their cloister; the aura of fear and mistrust which had invaded Sheepshanks during the past week was gone and an atmosphere of undisturbed peace drifted down upon them like dust immemorial.

Peascod, in one of his disconcerting ventures into frankness, spoke for them all when he said (during the fish course), 'I shall not need to lock my door tonight. Thank God there is no longer any fear of being murdered in our beds. If I were you, Master, I should order a Thanksgiving Service for our deliverance in the Chapel. And,' he added with senescent glee, 'I may use the Abbot's Library whenever I choose now. Smythson would not give me a key because he said I mis-shelved the books.'

An embarrassed silence followed this indecently bald statement, though others were reflecting along the same lines. Fenchurch was calculating the chances of a protégé of his for the post of Abbot's Librarian; Grubb was meditating upon the far superior accommodation in Great Court lately belonging to Smythson, which might soon be his; Professor Tempeste, to whom pederasty was a vice second only to insobriety, was silently rejoicing that the cankers were out.

As the Fellows retired to the Combination Room for coffee it was Peascod who, garrulous from a glass more of madeira than was his habit, voiced Smythson's epitaph. 'I always knew it must be Smythson,' he said brightly to no one in particular as he reached for his coffee-cup, absentmindedly trailing the hanging sleeve of his gown in the cream-jug as he did so. There was a dumbfounded silence after this pronouncement, which Peascod chose to regard as amazement at his acuity. 'Yes,' he said smugly, basking in the unaccustomed sun of his colleagues' rapt attention. 'It was obvious from the first that it must be Smythson — who was, after all, not in the top flight of scholars. His mind, I fear, was commonplace, and I knew at once that only a second-rate brain would fix upon such a crude solution as murder. But the police did not consult *me*.'

AUTHORS GUILD BACKINPRINT.COM EDITIONS are fiction and nonfiction works that were originally brought to the reading public by established United States publishers but have fallen out of print. The economics of traditional publishing methods force tens of thousands of works out of print each year, eventually claiming many, if not most, award-winning and one-time best-selling titles. With improvements in print-on-demand technology, authors and their estates, in cooperation with the Authors Guild, are making some of these works available again to readers in quality paperback editions. Authors Guild Backinprint.com Editions may be found at nearly all online bookstores and are also available from traditional booksellers. For further information or to purchase any Backinprint.com title please visit www.backinprint.com.

Except as noted on their copyright pages, Authors Guild Backinprint.com Editions are presented in their original form. Some authors have chosen to revise or update their works with new information. The Authors Guild is not the editor or publisher of these works and is not responsible for any of the content of these editions.

THE AUTHORS GUILD is the nation's largest society of published book authors. Since 1912 it has been the leading writers' advocate for fair compensation, effective copyright protection, and free expression. Further information is available at www.authorsguild.org.

Please direct inquiries about the Authors Guild and Backinprint.com Editions to the Authors Guild offices in New York City, or e-mail staff@backinprint.com.

0-595-20923-8

Printed in the United Kingdom
by Lightning Source UK Ltd.
101218UKS00001B/382